I0778875

For Billy,

The light during my own dark solstice

THE DARK SOLSTICE
AN EMPYRIAN ODYSSEY:
BOOK I

N. L. WILLCOME

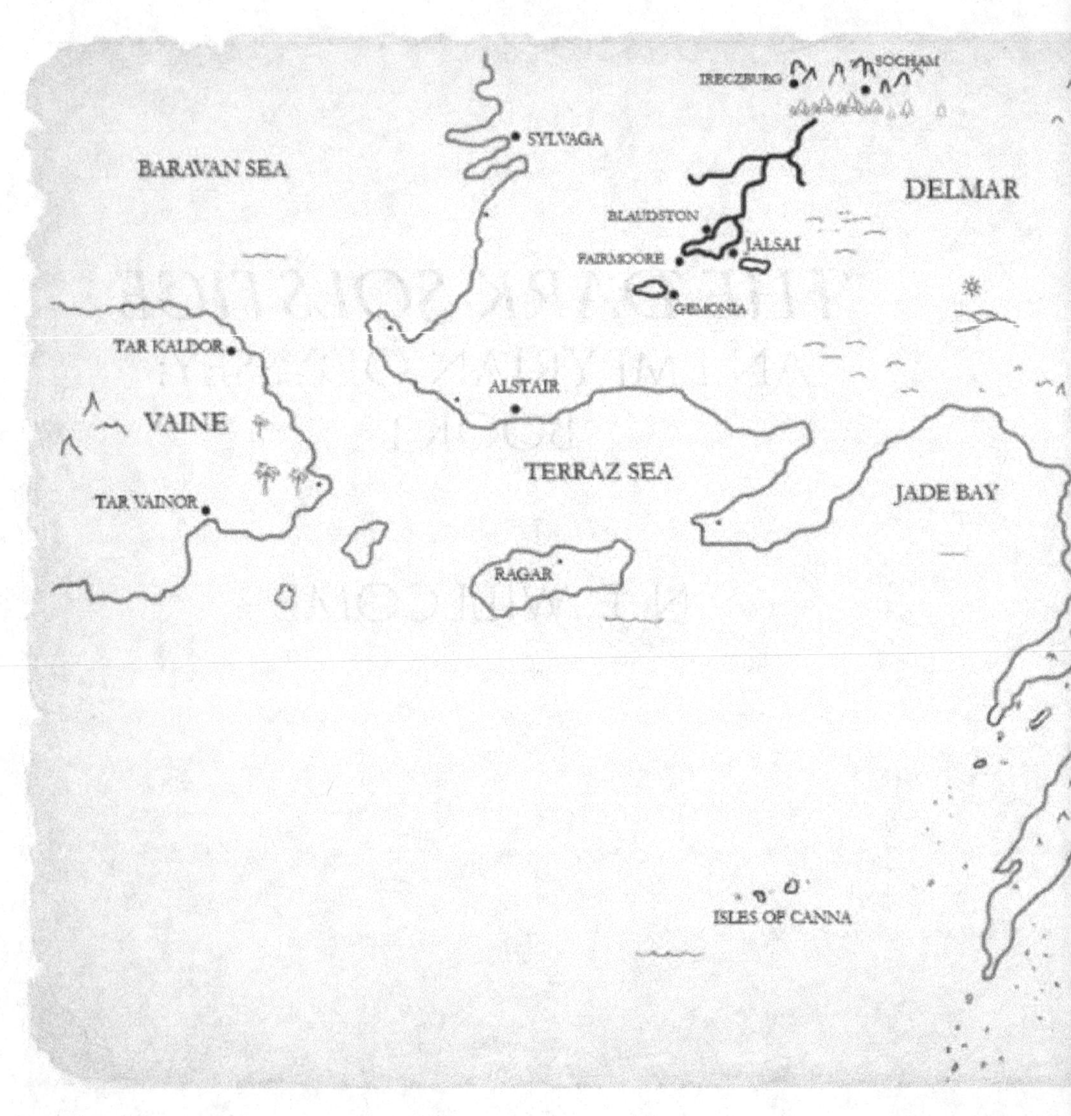

BARAVAN SEA
SYLVAGA
IRECZBURG
SOCHAM
DELMAR
BLAUDSTON
JALSAI
FAIRMOORE
GEMONIA
TAR KALDOR
VAINE
ALSTAIR
TAR VAINOR
TERRAZ SEA
JADE BAY
RAGAR
ISLES OF CANNA

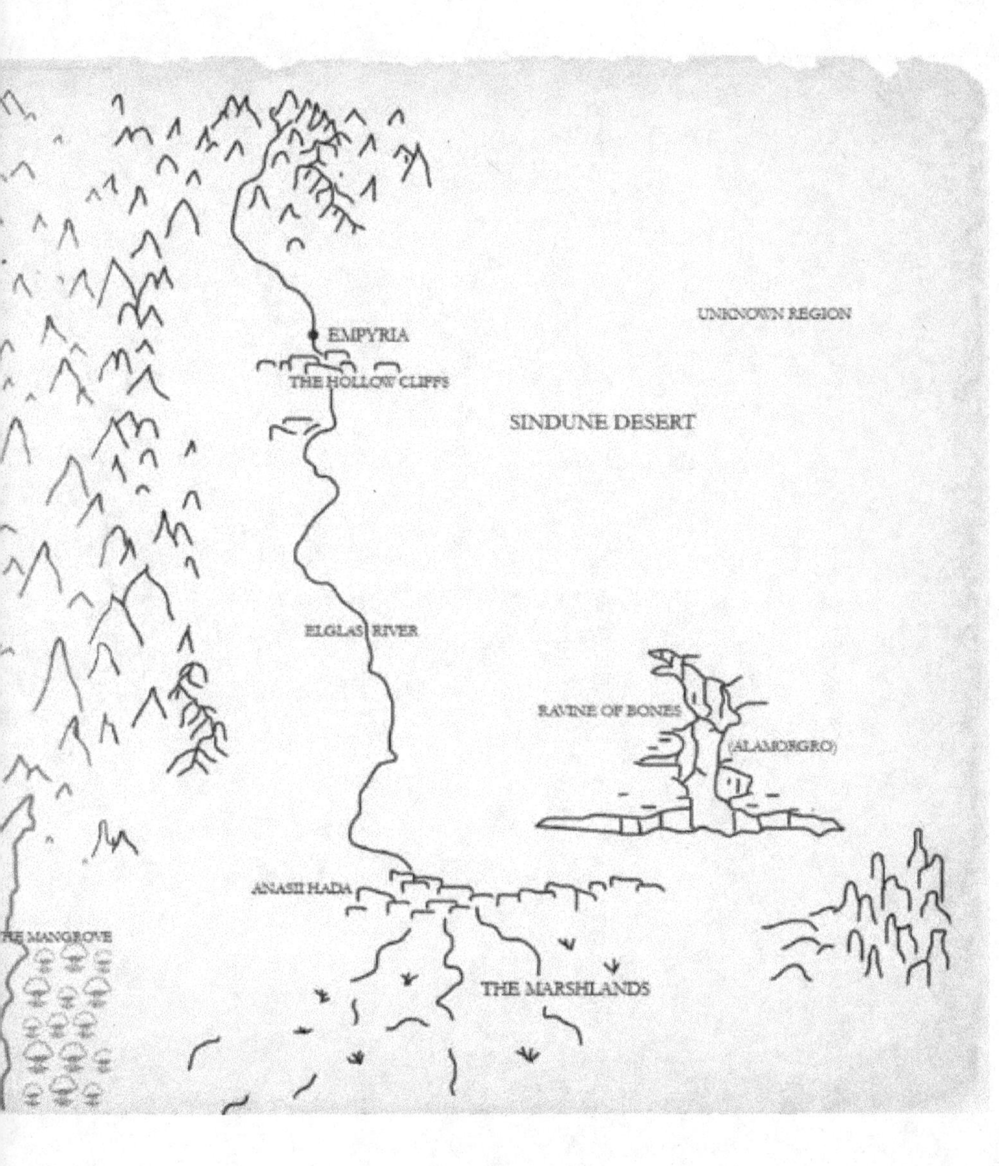

EMPYRIA
THE HOLLOW CLIFFS
UNKNOWN REGION
SINDUNE DESERT
ELGLAS RIVER
RAVINE OF BONES
(ALAMORGRO)
ANASII HADA
THE MANGROVE
THE MARSHLANDS

Scan this QR code with your smartphone camera for access to the
Spotify Reading Playlist for "The Dark Solstice."

(Must have a Spotify account and be logged in to access.)

Scan this QR code for access to the official YouTube Ambience Playlist
for "The Dark Solstice."

Copyright © 2025 Hardcover Edition
Printed by IngramSpark

Cover design by N. L. Willcome

ISBN: 979-8-9933194-0-7

A MA'DIIN LULLABY

Fear the dark and the murky deep
When waters still
And lions sleep.

Listen not to the demon's wail
Or fallen breath
In wind's last sail.

Watch for eyes in the silver lake
But mind the stare
Of fury's wake.

Seek the light and the halo's rise
Through clouded veil
Of shadowed skies.

When dawn awakes and battles cease
Let gods return
With endless peace.

PROLOGUE

It was a strange, eerie feeling, he thought, waking up in the morning and knowing he was going to die that day. He had felt it coming. It had been building up like the crescendo of a symphony, the waves of pressure steadily increasing with each beat of his heart. He had sent the servants away days ago and closed the gates. He wanted to be alone; just him and the knowledge of his impending end. It surrounded him like a fog now, closing in on him, creeping all around and brushing his cheeks with cold lips and the promise of ceaseless night. And it was all because of the Ma'diin and a choice he had made many years ago.

The Ma'diin. He had managed not to think about them for many years. But now with the coming of Lord Urbane, one of the most highly respected men in Delmar and the western cities and once his friend, the Ma'diin were all he could think about. The "Marsh People" was what they used to call them, when Empyria was just a city on the eastern edge of the world. He had travelled south with a group of eager explorers, like himself, that were ready to discover what resources lay beyond the vast desert they lived in and had ended up stumbling upon an entirely new world, one already inhabited. They had found the Ma'diin by accident; they had gotten lost in the marshes and had been found by the Ma'diin and taken to one of their villages. The Ma'diin were wary at first, as could be expected, and it took many days of careful communication and patient learning before the Ma'diin would even let them out of the huts they detained them in, but soon the Ma'diin started to trust them and even began showing them how to fish and build mud flats. It was a bountiful region, an oasis in the middle of the desert. They were poised to begin a prosperous relationship.

He ran his hand through his graying hair and swirled the murky liquid in his glass with the other. He could almost feel age setting upon him as each memory from that time resurfaced with disturbing clarity. He had struggled for sixteen years to keep these memories buried and now it seemed they were coming back with a force that even his usually sharp mind couldn't keep at bay. He remembered the months after several of the Ma'diin had agreed to come back with them: he had fallen in love with one of them. The only problem was that the woman he had loved had already claimed another. But what came after…

He emptied his glass and shoved it away, disgusted with his own weakness. A wonderful encounter with another culture had been poisoned by his own dark jealousy. Feelings of guilt rolled through him, forming a painful knot in his chest. He looked down at the letter he had just finished to Lord Urbane. It had taken him half a bottle of Arak to work up the courage to write the letter and the other half to finish it. It explained everything. He deserved to know.

He shoved his chair back and stumbled to the veranda that overlooked the Elglas River, bracing himself on one of the stone pillars. The setting sun threw out red daggers of light from behind him across the water, cutting thin slices out of the shadows cast by the buildings. He wanted to hide from the light, escape from the shadows, but he was trapped in a past that would not let go. It clawed its way out of his memory now and forced him to remember. He could see her face, her devastatingly beautiful blue eyes. She smiled at him. He reached for her. If only he could touch her one more time maybe she would love him back. He could tell her how much he loved her and how sorry he was. He tried to shake the wind-blown sand out of his eyes, making his vision blur. She stopped smiling. Her face contorted into a silent scream. The shimmering fabric around her head blew back, revealing empty eye sockets. Her face began to disintegrate until the mirage was replaced by the swirling water.

He turned away from the sight, his fists clenched against the sides of his head. His feet started moving, but he didn't know where he was going until he was in front of the mahogany chest in his room. Breathing heavily, he unfastened the iron latch just below where her name was inscribed in the wood. It was hers, but he had kept it and it was his second greatest secret. He lifted the lid with shaking hands. Her veil lay on top of the inner contents, the black one she used to wear with the little gold jewels that dangled across her cheeks, but he dared not look beyond that. Instead, he took out the velvet pouch that was tied to the inside of the lid. He didn't know why he had kept it here, in this sacred coffer with the rest of her things. The only reason he could give was that they came from the same world. The pouch was the size of his hand, soft and easy to bear, but the object inside was another burden entirely. He had not looked upon it in weeks. At first, he had felt freed of a great chain, as if he could finally breathe again after being trapped in a sandstorm, but then the past began to creep up behind him and the guilt settled on his shoulders like a cold wind.

Without opening it, he took the pouch and took it back to the veranda. He raised his arm and with a throat-tearing howl he threw it into the river below.

He fell to his knees, sobbing. The harsh truth of what he had done was too great to endure. The guilt overwhelmed him now, multiplying the pain in his chest. He sank to the floor, feeling the emotion crush him. He let it. It would be over soon. His past wouldn't haunt him anymore. The world would go on, Empyria would go on, and he would be free. His eyes fluttered and he let out a ragged sigh as his last tears streamed down his cheeks.

CHAPTER ONE

Every year on the eve of her birthday, Tamsin Urbane would remember the strange woman that came to see her when she had turned nine. Strange, Tamsin called her, because she was blue. Tamsin couldn't recall the gifts she had received, the smell of sweets floating through the kitchens, or even who the other guests were, but she did know that the strange woman had not been on the guest list. Tamsin had been taken to bed early that evening, exhausted by the day's excitement, though the adults still continued to dance in the great hall. But she had woken suddenly to find a dark figure crouched over her, one hand extended as if to touch her cheek. The woman froze when she saw Tamsin was awake. She wore a cloak that blended into the late hour, like it was sewn from the night sky, and her hood covered most of her face, though Tamsin remembered the shadow around her face glittered like sapphire dust. And her hand, lingering in the space between them, looked as if it had been painted with the neck feathers of a peacock.

Tamsin remembered being afraid, but the woman's smile was warm, friendly, and when she spoke her voice sounded like violin strings, raw and hypnotic. She had said, *"An epic tale is filled with extraordinary people who don't know they're in one."* She smiled again, curiously, as if she had been speaking to no one in particular, but letting the statement echo around them until the words faded and were forgotten. But Tamsin did not forget. Despite her fear, she hung onto every word and remembered them every year after.

Even when her friends said she had only been visited by a dream fairie and her parents eventually put it off to a child's imagination, she could not forget the strange blue woman or what she had said.

That night, her day maid, Sherene, had come to check on her and Tamsin could still remember the startled look on her face when she came in. The strange woman moved to the window as silently as a whisper and disappeared as if she had never been there at all. Sherene had screamed, causing the rest of the household to congregate in Tamsin's room to see what was going on. After getting accounts of what they had seen (or thought they had seen), Tamsin's father, Lord Eleazar Urbane, took action and over the next two weeks searches throughout the city were made and Tamsin was under strict watch from the house guards.

She had, more than once, confronted Sherene about what she had seen, but Sherene had convinced herself that all she had seen was a shadow, a trick of the moonlight played on old eyes and a young mind. "People are *not* blue," she would say.

The strange woman was never found, nor did Tamsin ever see her again, but even after all the drama of it had died down and the incident became yesterday's gossip, Tamsin was no longer allowed the care-free attitude of a young child. She had wanted nothing more when she was young than to be in one of the adventures she had heard her father tell of his days as an explorer and would re-enact the tales, often ending with a scraped knee or two and a scolding from Sherene. She even set the drawing room's drapes on fire once, though to this day she couldn't explain how it happened. But ever since that night, her mother dragged her out of her imagination and to luncheons and cotillions, her innocent childhood fantasies were soon pushed to the side to make room for more appropriate, and less flammable, activities. It always seemed, however, that no matter how hard she tried to conform to her mother's proper expectations, there was something fundamentally different about her that made it hard to fit in. Her mother told her once that there was a little southern blood in her from the Frig Islands on her father's side, which accounted for some of the traits that differed from her other pale, blonde relatives like her olive skin and dark, unruly hair, but her mother said the mixture of mainland and island blood had been quite scandalous at the time so it was best not to bring it up. Nor did Tamsin bring up the blue woman again, though that night seemed to have marked her in a way that distinguished her from her peers.

Tamsin's differences from the other girls of lording society only grew as she became older and she was soon aware that it wasn't just her distant heritage that separated her, but the realization that she *could* never be like them. No matter how many luncheons or functions her mother took her to, she was never the social flower that was interested in the latest Jalsaian fashions or the men that admired them for it.

Her mother blamed her father for it, for filling her head with wild stories, but Tamsin secretly loved him all the more for it and when she turned fifteen he started bringing her with on his ambassadorial trips to the outlying cities of Delmar. Though these were never like her father's stories, she did not partake in any of the actual negotiations (tedious doldrums of conversation her father once called them) between the lords and diplomats, which gave her the freedom to experience everything Jalsai couldn't give her. Her mother had more than one stern conversation with her father about the matter, because how was Tamsin ever supposed to find a husband if she was always running off? Her mother fit the job perfectly; she didn't bat an eyelash when she had to dismiss a servant, but the house may as well come crashing down if there was a candle out of place. Tamsin knew her affinity for wandering around Delmar with her father irked her mother to no end, but Tamsin abhorred the idea of managing a household. She would rather sit in a roomful of cigar smoke with the notoriously bad-tempered Lords of Sylvaga than pick out lace patterns for their next tea luncheon.

So when her father announced they were moving to Empyria, Delmar's easternmost outpost city across the Ardent Mountains and the very place he had lived eighteen years ago, just before she was born, Tamsin was ecstatic. He told them that the Lords' Council had decided to send him to Empyria as Lord Wohlrick's replacement. Lord Wohlrick was old and the pressures placed upon him would soon be too much for him, her father explained. He tried to assuage their shock by telling them how advanced and civilized the city had become since his days there. Well, her mother's shock. Tamsin herself was excited; all of her childhood adventures came creeping back from her memory and she wondered if this would be the start of her own real adventure. And she thought of the blue woman. Her mother, however, went on the attack. Tamsin had never seen her mother get so angry and oppose her father so vehemently before. Though Lavinia Urbane was a delicate beauty with hair like fine gold and a face that brightened any room like a bouquet of flowers, she was not a quiet woman and she took her responsibilities as a proper lady very seriously. It was more than simple surprise at the news; Lavinia outright refused the notion altogether. She demanded to know why they had chosen *him* and at one point even accused him of volunteering.

"Aren't there other lords in Empyria?" she had asked. "Surely, Empyrian affairs can't be that difficult that they can't handle on their own."

Her father did his best to placate her concerns, reminding her that each region's capital had to have at least three governing lords, but when she showed no signs of backing down he looked at Tamsin and then at the door and Tamsin quietly excused herself, knowing that the arguing had only just begun. She listened at the door for only a moment, but their voices had gone too low for her to hear anymore and with a pitying shake of her head for her father she headed for the library to see what else she could learn about Empyria. Her mother put up an opposition that lasted for days, one any military commander would have been impressed with, but in the end her father's decision was final and the preparations for their departure began.

There wasn't much written about the desert city, and Tamsin could almost understand why after they left the Cities and crossed the Ardent Mountain range. Ever since leaving the safety of the mountains all there was to be seen for leagues in either direction was sand. The Sindune Desert was the largest this side of the Terraz Sea, though Tamsin was unprepared for just how expansive it was and she couldn't imagine anyone building a city amidst the ever-changing dunes. There was one road that connected the mountains to the city, though it was often buried in sand and they had to send riders out to find where it picked up again. It made travelling tediously slow, but they had been warned by the mountain folk, with whom they had spent several days replenishing their supplies and waiting for their escort from Empyria to arrive, that getting lost in the Sindune meant almost certain death.

They had been on the desert road for over a week now and everyone's nerves were starting to unravel. Conversation between the women in the wheelhouse had all but vanished and the only sound was the swishing of fans as they tried to stave off the heat. Tamsin noticed the increased edginess in the riders' faces and had heard quiet comments about the pace of the caravan and their depleting water reserves. Hearing this only increased her own nerves.

She took out the book she had transcribed from the library and started reading, hoping to calm her restlessness. It was not very thick, and the section about Empyria didn't even fill up one chapter, but she re-read the pages again anyways. Empyria had been settled almost three hundred years ago after the Golden War and the fall of the Ottarkin Empire. The Council of Lords, which replaced the defeated Ottarkins, gave amnesty to those that renounced their ties with the old order and their beliefs and pledged themselves to the new Council. But there were still those that refused to give up the old religion, which the Golden War was fought over, and they decided to leave the Cities to escape persecution. They crossed the Ardent Mountain range, which made up the easternmost border of the Cities at that time, and countless leagues of desert until they came across what is now known as the Elglas River. Empyria was built on the Elglas, which in the common tongue meant *savior*, and the Ottarkin exiles and their descendants lived there, untouched and unknown, for a hundred years. Then, an expedition from the Cities came across the desert city and after many years of negotiations and subsequent expeditions Empyria became an official colony of the Cities.

There wasn't much after that, though her father was able to fill in some of the holes. He said that Empyria was too valuable as an outpost to the eastern frontier to leave control to a group of zealots whose ancestors had been savage butchers so the Cities continued to send more and more people to Empyria. He said that to ensure the peace, religion was not banned completely as it was in the Cities, and those who still worshipped the old gods could do so. This part made Tamsin nervous; she had learned about the old religion from her tutors, but had never met someone who actually practiced it, since it was in fact forbidden. Her father reassured her though that it was usually only the elders who still worshipped, and only in private, and when he had lived there the two cultures had become so blended you couldn't tell who still clung to the old faith and who did not.

The wheelhouse lurched to a stop, causing the book to fall from her lap. The sound of galloping hooves could be heard and Tamsin pushed back the canvas flap that covered the wheelhouse window to see some of the riders racing ahead, sending up plumes of dust in their wake.

"Fathri, what's going on?" she called out to her father.

Lord Urbane brought his horse around next to the wheelhouse (the closer they had gotten to Empyria the more he had insisted on riding outside with the others) and pointed to where the riders were fast disappearing. "Look Tamsin! We made it." He sat up a little straighter in his saddle and Tamsin could almost imagine him as a younger explorer reaching Empyria for the first time. Though age had granted him a fuller beard and a few more creases around his eyes, it did not cover up the young adventurer completely. He spurred his horse to catch up with the others.

When the dust settled, Tamsin could see shapes in the distance, but they looked oddly rigid in this soft landscape. At first she thought they were cliffs at the edge of a small mountain range, but there was something strange about them, something that didn't quite fit in with the natural landscape. It looked like a conglomerate of alternating flat and jutting plateaus, but as they moved closer she could start to make out the defining features of the city wall. The wall, supposedly, encircled the entire city, a fact Tamsin very much wanted to see if it was true. The round, stone turrets spaced along its length were tall, protruding out from the wall as if they had grown up through the stone like oak trees, the likes of which she had only seen in the cold castles of the northern cities of Ireczburg. Hills of sand crept up the sides of the wall like frozen waves and formed large slopes on either side of the main entrance, which stuck out from the wall like the snout of a giant animal. They passed through a large gate that had gargoyles carved into the stone archway on either side of the opening. One had its mouth open and claws outstretched as if it was going to grab them and pull them inside. The other appeared to be climbing the arch, its wings fanned out behind it and its tail wrapped around the column. It gazed, almost longingly, upward towards the sky, like it was waiting for the day when it would break free of its stone chains. They were unlike any gargoyles she had seen in the Cities, which looked like little horned humans, hunched over on the roofs of buildings watching the people below. These ones reminded her more of lizards or birds. She wondered if they were from the original architecture when the city was built.

Tamsin couldn't help the shiver of anticipation as they passed the stone creatures and emerged into the city. There was a large courtyard just inside the gates with a contingent of soldiers already lined along the edges to greet them. The foot soldiers wore common brown leather and stood behind the more decorated officers who were festooned in silver armor with royal blue banners and helmet plumes. These men had to be the Empyrian High Guard. The banners had golden birds embroidered on them so it looked like they were flying as the fabric waved back and forth in the wind. In all of her travels with her father she had never seen such a large military presence to welcome them before.

As soon as the wheelhouse came to a halt she swung the door open and jumped out, unable to contain her curiosity about the city to the cramped confines of their traveling home any longer. She did a slow turn, taking in the scope of the courtyard and the buildings around her. The bright colors of the soldiers' uniforms stood out starkly against the sandstone that formed the core of the buildings behind them. There were two stories of open hallways surrounding the courtyard with simple arches and columns to support the weight. Adorning these arches were tall, potted trees with trunks like stacked rings and leaves that sprouted from the top like exotic headdresses. She noticed others moving about the archways; some had stopped to watch the newcomers, others were hanging long, blue drapes down the columns. As her gaze turned to the center of the courtyard she saw a large statue of a man surrounded by a circular pool…or what would have been a man, but the upper half had been destroyed.

One of the foot soldiers stepped forward to take her father's horse and no sooner had he dismounted than a barking laugh escaped him. He walked over to Tamsin, a bright smile on his face. "I didn't realize at first. We must have arrived just in time."

"Just in time for what?" she inquired.

"The winter solstice." He pointed to the long, blue banners. "It was quite the production when I was here last." He put his hands on his hips and breathed deeply, taking in the courtyard and the memories that no doubt came with it.

Tamsin was aware of the dryness in her mouth. It was hotter than the warmest day in the Cities and this was the start of their winter season?

One of the Empyrian High Guards stepped forward. "I apologize for the unorthodox welcoming committee my Lord," he said, his accent slightly less lofted and a little more earthy than their own. He had close-cropped white hair and tanned wrinkles around his eyes. "The Lords are indisposed at the moment."

"That's quite alright Commander," her father reassured him, unfazed by the news. They shook hands and it was a few more minutes as they arranged for the escort to take them to their new home before Tamsin could ask him about it.

"Why would they celebrate it being this hot?" she asked him quietly as she stepped back into the wheelhouse.

He chuckled. "The winter solstice marks the beginning of the rainy season here," he said. "It will rain for a week, give or take a few days. And out here, water is more precious than gold." He tapped her forehead affectionately. "Remember that." Then his forehead furrowed a little and he turned back to look around the courtyard. "Though they seem to have made some…additions since I've been gone.

Tamsin followed his eyes up and down the trees, then settled on the pool around the half statue.

"The statue, Fathri. Who was it?"

"The lord who found Empyria and brought it back under Delmarian rule. You can see how the Ottarkins took to him. But don't you worry; that unrest was settled long ago. Let's go see our new home."

The new Urbane residence was nothing like Tamsin had been accustomed to. It didn't have a black iron fence separating it from the neighbors, glass windows, or a garden in the backyard. It didn't even have a yard to speak of. The "mountains" she thought she had seen from the caravan were actually huge ziggurats, towering over the rest of the city as if they had been built for gods, not people, and one of them was to be their home. They passed through a half-wall surrounding the ziggurat, with more arches perched atop it, creating the appearance of a compound, for Tamsin could think of no other word to describe it. The ziggurat itself was a stony fortress, towering five stories high. There was a large stairway leading up to the third level, bypassing the lower levels that they learned were primarily used by the servants. Men in light blue tunics were there as they stepped out of the wheelhouse, ready with cream-colored parasols to protect them from the sun and ladles of water should they be thirsty. The tier above the third level split into two separate towers. Her mother said they looked like giant ant hills.

The third level was one large, open space, divided only by stone pillars and gauzy white fabric that could be pulled closed. The outer rim of the level was completely open to the outside with a wide, shaded veranda encircling it. There was a half-wall surrounding it, save for the stairs that connected it to the next levels. Below, she could see the tops of the lower levels, laden with lines for hanging laundry and trellises for small plants, and from somewhere within she heard singing.

The rest of the new servants waited at the top of the stairs that divided on either side to stairs that wrapped up and around the verandas to the next levels. They were dressed in the same pale blue as the others. The men wore wide pants and vests with backs that ended just behind their knees, though they wore no tunics underneath, revealing their cinnamon skin. The women were less exposed with simple dresses that twisted around their waists and crossed over their shoulders, leaving their arms and shoulders bare. Their clothing was nothing like the current fashions in the Cities with full-length skirts, sleeves made of gauzy organza, and necklines that only left the breastbone and neck bare. Her mother looked them up and down as if she were sizing up the enemy and made a quiet comment about living in a brothel. Only two of their servants from the Cities actually made the trip with them: Tamsin's personal maid, Sherene, who had been with her since she was a baby, and one of her father's stable hands, who Tamsin had heard had no living family in the Cities and came only to make sure they didn't lose any horses during the trek through the desert. None of her mother's maids had chosen to come with them.

Her parents' rooms were on the next level in one of the "ant hills" and while they were being shown around Tamsin was taken to the other, which was to be her living quarters. The outer veranda was open to the outside, like the last, but the interior was walled off into several, more private rooms that were lit by hanging lanterns and torches. The only room she recognized was in the very center and had steps leading down into a giant, square bath, otherwise the other rooms were very dark and small with few furnishings. There wasn't a clear receiving room, study or even a drawing room. There were no bookshelves, potted plants, paintings, or other items that she was accustomed to back home. It was like she had stepped into a sandcastle.

She climbed the last set of stairs to the very top level, gripping the edge of the stone half wall tightly as the wind picked up momentum this high up. She found her room there; some of her things had already been brought up. Stone pillars supported the ceiling in various spots throughout the room and the concave walls met on the other side of the room where a small archway revealed a balcony overlooking the eastern horizon. From there she had a clear view of the river and the rest of the city beyond it. It was breathtaking, borderline exhilarating, to see the maze of streets and buildings from this height.

"What do you think?"

Tamsin turned away from the view and saw her father standing in the doorway by the stairs. He always had a polished, authoritative air about him, but here in Empyria's harsh landscape his rugged build seemed quite in tune with his surroundings. "Honestly, it's a bit overwhelming," she said.

"I know the feeling," he said with a sigh, joining her on the balcony. "I remember the first time I came here, looking out over the city as you are now."

"You're not going to start reminiscing about the old glory days are you?" she asked, smiling with both her lips and eyes.

"It had its share of hardships," he replied quietly, turning to look out across the city.

Tamsin frowned. Her father had been so excited this whole time to come back to Empyria. Why the sudden dismal turn? Perhaps he was just as tired from the long journey as she was. "Well, you have Mathri and me this time. I think we'll turn out to be much better company than soldiers and horses."

"I'm glad that you are here with me Tamsin. I want nothing more than for you to feel at home here. Your mother will come around eventually. I hope."

Tamsin grimaced. She had already endured months of her mother's venomous mood and was looking forward to its end.

Her father put his arm around her shoulders. "Come on. I'll take you on a tour."

"Why is the bathing room on the fourth level?" Tamsin asked as they descended the stairs. "It doesn't seem very practical."

Her father chuckled. "Not to us, no, or the servants I imagine, but they weren't used for bathing when the Ottarkins originally built them."

"What were they for then?"

Her father pursed his lips a moment. "Let me just say that the old religion included animal sacrifice."

Before Tamsin could even wrinkle her nose at the implication a member of the Empyrian Guard stepped in their way.

The guard nodded respectively to Lord Urbane. "I'm here to inform you that your presence has been requested at the Armillary," he said.

"What's the Armillary?" Tamsin asked.

The guard gave her a patronizing look. "Immediately," he added, not answering her question.

"For what purpose?" her father asked. "Surely any business can wait until my family and I have settled."

The guard looked tired. "I was told to escort you as soon as you arrived," he said. "There has been an incident."

"What kind of an incident?"

The guard looked at Tamsin again with a flash of his eyes. One Tamsin had often seen before on certain diplomatic trips with her father when her presence, a woman's presence, was unexpected.

Her father turned towards her. "Tell your mother I'll try and be back before dinner. We'll go on a tour tomorrow, I promise."

The guard led him away and Tamsin did as she was told and delivered the news to her mother. She went up to her room after, to avoid the frantic movements of the servants as they tried to accommodate her mother's orders.

She took a deep breath at the top of the stairs, letting it sink in that this is where she would live now; this was her home.

Looking in, she couldn't help but think how strange the room was. She felt, rather, hoped that no animals had been sacrificed in here. It was almost a perfect circle with a ring of pillars to support the ceiling near the center where a metal, free-standing fireplace stood. There looked to be a painting that ran the entire length of the walls, broken up only on the opposite end where it opened into the balcony. She walked around, trying to figure out what the painting was supposed to be, but it was like trying to put a puzzle together without all of the pieces, for it was chipped and faded in some spots. She could see though, that whoever had painted it had put a great deal of time into it; the detail in some areas was exquisite. It was a pity more care had not gone to preserve it.

There was a vanity and a writing desk on either side of the bed and across from them on the other side of the room was an armoire and a changing partition. There was a small table next to the partition with a ceramic bowl of water set on it. She found a towel in the armoire and dipped it in the water. She wiped her face and the back of her neck first and then sat down on the stool behind the partition. She took her shoes off and started rubbing off the layers of dirt that had accumulated from their trip. As she scrubbed, she realized it wasn't the room that seemed strange to her, but rather the furniture in it. The simplicity pleased her, but they still seemed out of place, as if they decorated the room of stone too much. The faded mural was the only thing that felt natural and she wondered what the room had been used for previously.

Behind the partition, the painting transformed into a woman whose nose had chipped away until half of her face had blended into the sandstone. She held a golden rope in one hand and held her other arm away from her body so her fingers were pointing straight up. Where her palm was though, there was a dark line running up and down the wall. It looked almost like a crack in the wall, but the line was too straight to be random. She furrowed her brow, wondering why the artist would have painted a straight line on the wall. She brushed her fingers over it and her eyes widened as she felt the faintest current of cold air coming from it.

She jumped when a loud thud sounded behind her. She came out from behind the partition just as a servant was leaving from depositing a large trunk on the floor. A moment later, her personal maid, Sherene, came in.

Upon seeing the towel in Tamsin's hand and her bare feet, she made a *tut tut* noise and set down the small case she was carrying. "You should have called for me, Miss Tamsin," she said, brushing some invisible sand off her skirt. Her round cheeks were flushed and some stray strands of hair threatened to escape from underneath her hair wrap. Tamsin had always envied Sherene's hair. Where Sherene's (and most girls back home) was thick and golden and molded perfectly into large buns and curls, hers was limp and refused to keep any sort of shape other than mildly straight. She often wore it down, when she wasn't obligated to go anywhere, because it softened the narrow angles of her face more so than when it was pinned up. And it was nearly longer than her waist now, something she was secretly proud of. Sherene was a hand taller than Tamsin as well, and had a fuller figure, but she was always busy and full of energy. At one point in her childhood, Tamsin had been certain that her maid had a twin because she always seemed to be everywhere at once.

"I can do things on my own, you know," Tamsin said. "I'll be eighteen soon. I don't need someone holding my hand every minute of the day."

Sherene snorted, amused. "You'll be glad for the help when you're as old as I am."

Tamsin rolled her eyes. "When I'm as old as you are, you'll still be scolding me for one thing or another." If her mother had been at all lax in her upbringing, Sherene had surely made up for it.

Sherene smiled and wagged a finger at her. "You're right about that Miss Tamsin!" She chuckled to herself and started unlatching the trunk.

Another servant appeared at the top of the stairs and deposited another case next to the others. He bowed briefly to

Tamsin, wiped his forehead with his sleeve, and left without a word.

Sherene shook her head. "I don't understand why they had to put your room at the top of a mountain. A few more trips and I'll be as skinny as a sapling!" She started pulling out dresses and hanging them in the armoire.

Tamsin studied the carvings on one of the pillars. "I never asked you," she said.

"Asked me what?"

"If you wanted to come here. I guess I just assumed that you would," she said, feeling guilty for not thinking of it before.

Sherene paused from her work. "This place is strange to be sure, but I have looked after you your whole life and I couldn't let you run off having adventures without me," she said with a smile. Then under her breath, "Lords know you've been going on too many without me already."

Tamsin smiled too. Even with her preference for solitude over social gatherings, Tamsin had many shadows in the Cities, but Sherene was her favorite. Though she shared similar opinions with Lavinia, she never asked Tamsin to be someone she was not. And Tamsin liked to think it was because they had grown to be friends, not because she was technically Sherene's superior. She was grateful that Sherene had come, but she also knew Sherene would be spending a lot more time with her mother until she found a new personal maid.

The thought dampened her mood slightly, but she looked forward to exploring the city with her father, the only other person whose company she was extremely fond of. She looked out the archway to the balcony overlooking the city and thought about the wall that encircled it. The city may as well have been an island; the hundreds of leagues of desert that surrounded them would keep them in the walls as sure as any sea. But why build the wall at all? Surely people didn't just go wandering off into the desert.

"What do you think is out there?" she asked. "Beyond the desert, I mean."

"For all I know it goes on forever," Sherene said and then she peered at Tamsin with suspicious eyes. "I know that look Miss Tamsin. You put a stop to whatever curiosities that brain of yours is conjuring. It's no good wondering about what's out there when you have a whole city at your fingertips."

Tamsin frowned, but she knew Sherene was right. "I know," she said. "I'm just getting caught up with all of it. It's exciting living at the edge of the known world, don't you think?"

"Aye, Miss Tamsin, it is. But this is as far as I want to go, so I better not catch you trying to sneak off out there. It's wild country beyond those walls. Nothing like the Cities."

Tamsin agreed, but in the back of her mind she made a note to ask her father if anyone went outside the walls, and if they did would she ever be allowed to go.

They managed to get all of her things unpacked just before dinner was called. Sherene helped her change and then she met her mother on the third level. A table had been set up near one corner on the west side, laden with candles. The setting sun was an incredible sight from this height and bathed everything in view in a warm orange light.

Her mother was already seated at the head of the long table, sitting tall and poised as always and she waited until Tamsin had taken her seat before she motioned for the servants to bring the first course.

"Fathri isn't back yet?" Tamsin asked.

Her mother didn't reply, but started eating her food, letting the empty chair across from her speak for her.

They ate in silence for a while, until Tamsin could take no more. She knew her mother was not happy, but it was no reason to behave like a pouting child. Her mother had told her, on more than one occasion, that a woman's duty was to her father or her husband and his house and that she should always strive to be obedient and helpful. Her mother was always the perfect picture of poise and a prime example of the values she wanted to install in her daughter. Tamsin couldn't help but wonder why this move aggravated her mother so much and what about this place could make her forgo her natural character and oppose her father.

"I think we should try and like this place," Tamsin said after several long minutes, "for Fathri."

Her mother put down her fork and rubbed her temples. "I'm tired. I'm going to bed." She pushed back her chair and got up. "Finish your meal and do the same." She didn't even wait for Tamsin to respond before she turned and left, leaving Tamsin alone in the waning light.

Tamsin slowly opened her eyes as the sound of voices penetrated her sleep-ridden mind. She had fallen asleep in one of the chairs on the veranda waiting for her father to return. She rubbed her neck and turned around in the chair. Her father was standing nearby with a bedraggled servant who looked as if he had been plucked right from his bed chamber.

"There was a chest with these letters carved into it," her father was saying. He had a strange, almost desperate tone to his voice. "Where is it?"

"Fathri?" Tamsin got up and both her father and the poor servant jumped at the sound of her voice.

"Tamsin? What are you doing up?" her father asked, quickly dismissing the servant and coming over to her.

"I was waiting for you," she yawned. "Is everything alright?"

"It's nothing to worry about. Come on, let's get you to bed," and he escorted her up to her room.

But she persisted, fighting back more yawns. "Did some of the luggage get misplaced?" she asked.

He shook his head. "No. Don't concern yourself with it." He smiled, but it did not reach his eyes. "Go to sleep Tamsin." He kissed her on the forehead and the last thing she saw before her eyes closed was a piece of parchment clutched in his hand with a seal of an S pressed in red wax.

CHAPTER TWO

The next day, several of the other Lording Ladies came to welcome them. Lavinia was panicky at first; the compound was still in disarray from the move. She ordered some cakes to be made (as quickly as possible) so she wouldn't have to serve tea alone. She apologized for the state of things, but the other Ladies said they understood and waved it off with smiles. If there was one thing her mother prided herself on it was being a good hostess.

The servants sectioned off a corner of the veranda with partitions of soft, white gauze that rippled in the breeze and drew the canopy over for shade. The Ladies took their seats and introduced themselves as Lady Mary Regoran, her daughter Emilia, Lady Fiona Wohlrick, Lady Cerena Allard, and Madame Belinda Corinthia, the commander's new wife.

"We apologize that our husbands are not here," Lady Wohlrick said. She was elderly; her soft blue eyes almost hidden under great folds of wrinkles and her hands shook slightly as she grasped her cane, but she still had an aura of authority around her. Her grey hair was piled neatly on top of her head and her tone was as clear as a bird's. "But they are far too busy these days, even now that the ceremony is over."

"Ceremony?" Lavinia inquired.

"Lord Saveen's funeral was the day before yesterday," she replied. "Of course they are still investigating, but the word is that he drank himself to death."

"He was prone to bouts of overindulgence," Lady Regoran said. She was a plain looking woman and Tamsin got the sense she was quite practical and was not someone who would overindulge in anything.

"I am terribly sorry to hear that," Lavinia said. "I will send our condolences to Lady Saveen."

"No need to bother," Lady Regoran spoke up. She had tight lines around her eyes and mouth and looked as if she had been scowling for the last forty years. "Lady Saveen does not exist. Rickard is survived by his nephew, Cornelius, who is Captain of the High Guard. It is a pity that the social affairs of Empyria are not public knowledge in the Cities, especially to the other Lording families."

Lavinia noticeably blushed, clearly displeased at Lady Regoran's insinuating comment that they were uneducated to Empyrian affairs, and Tamsin was more than willing to testify for her mother's social prowess and the lack of any information on Empyria, but Lavinia pursed her lips and remained quiet.

"News is always slow to travel over the mountains," Lady Allard said, giving Lavinia a friendly smile. She was tall and thin and her blond hair was braided and wrapped delicately at the base of her neck. "The social atmosphere here is a smaller pool than in the west, so I think we'll be able to get you caught up in no time."

"Is the celebration for the winter solstice still going on?" Tamsin asked. She had overheard two of the servants whispering about it the previous night.

Lady Regoran scoffed. "The celebration is for the easterlies. It's a nuisance and unnecessary disruption if you ask me."

"Nobody asked you mother," Emilia said, speaking up for the first time. She inspected her nails as if she were bored. She shared her mother's scowl and looked even less thrilled to be here. Lady Allard had no children, Lady Wohlrick's eldest was recently married and moved to the Cities, and Madame Corinthia was not much older than Tamsin and Emilia and held her hands conspicuously over her only slightly round belly. It seemed the lording class of Empyria was devoid of anyone Emilia's age. She was roughly the same height as Tamsin, which was shorter than most people she knew, and had the same dark hair, though hers was neatly swept up on top of her head with just the right amount of perfect ringlets cascading down to frame her cheeks.

"Don't be spiteful Emilia. It is beneath you," Lady Regoran said, sounding just as bored. "The Lord's Ball is just over a month away and much more appropriate."

"Where we see the same people who talk about the same things year after year. Would you excuse me for a moment?" Emilia got up and walked towards the front veranda before anyone could blink twice.

Everyone was silent for a few moments and then Lady Allard asked what news they had brought with them from the Cities.

Tamsin caught her mother's pointed look and politely excused herself to check on Emilia. She looked on the front veranda first and when she didn't find her there asked one of the servants if they had seen her. He pointed to the stairs and motioned upwards. She frowned, but followed his directions anyway and headed straight to her room.

Emilia was sitting on her bed glancing around the room when Tamsin got up there. She rolled her eyes in annoyance when she spotted Tamsin. "Don't tell me my mother sent you to fetch me."

Tamsin paused in the doorway, unsure how to take the girl's behavior and seeming lack of boundaries. "I came on my own," she said.

Emilia looked at her for a moment, trying to figure her out as Tamsin did the same. Finally, she pulled up the side of her skirt and took out a small flask hidden in her stocking and took a drink.

"What is that?"

Emilia gave a short laugh. "Something to help my nerves." She replaced the flask and smoothed her skirts over it. She hopped off the bed and started walking around. "Is this your room?"

Tamsin nodded, taking a couple steps in.

"Hmm," she said. "I remember when I first came here. Lords it was awful. It felt like there was a noose around my neck, squeezing tighter and tighter every day."

Tamsin bit her lip, thinking that the girl obviously didn't want to be here or in Empyria at all for that matter, and that image of the wall when they first arrived flashed into her thoughts. She wondered if she would ever see it from the outside again. "When did things change?"

"Change? Things don't change around here. When I figured that out, that's when I realized I had to make my own rules. You follow your mother to all her little luncheons and tea parties and you'll realize the same thing."

"I actually prefer to be out with my father. He's a diplomat. He travels—."

"Oh yes," Emilia interrupted. "I know all about your father," she said with a sharp laugh. Then she was quiet for a moment. "You know, the solstice celebration is tonight. It's the biggest event of the year."

"But I thought your mother said the ball isn't for another month?"

"That's right. But this isn't the Lord's Ball. This one's a secret."

"Why is it a secret?"

Emilia sighed, as if she were explaining something to a child. "My mother would never let me go if she knew where I was going."

"Why not, if it's the biggest event of the year? My mother is always trying to get me to socialize more. I'm sure she could talk your mother into letting us go."

"I highly doubt that," she scoffed.

"Why?"

"Because it's on the east side. That's where the religious sect holds out. The solstices were originally observed by the Ottarkins, until the Lords spun it into a secular, seasonal thing with no real meaning."

"Are you—do you…associate with them?" Tamsin asked. She had never met someone who was religious. She didn't know what to expect.

"Do I practice the old religion, you mean?" Emilia grinned. "No, but they put on a great party." She opened up the armoire and pulled out Tamsin's most expensive dress: a deep bronze ball gown with a swirling gold pattern overlay around the bodice and skirt with sleeves of gold satin. "This," she said, "is what you are wearing tonight. It's gorgeous."

Tamsin knew her mother would probably ship her right back to the Cities if she knew she was planning on wearing her best dress to a function she wouldn't approve of. "You don't think it's too formal?"

"Of course not. You should see what I have picked out. It almost puts this to shame."

"Well, if you think—."

"It's perfect. Everyone dresses their best for this, trust me. They don't do any virgin sacrifices…anymore," Emilia said with a wicked gleam in her eyes.

One of the maids knocked then and announced the Ladies were leaving.

"Meet us by the front gate of the city at eleven. You remember how to get there?"

"Yes, but I can't just go waltzing out of the house in that dress at that hour," Tamsin whispered tersely.

"Fine," Emilia said indifferently. "We will pick you up here. Be ready," and she walked out.

The maid, still standing in the doorway, raised her eyebrows at Tamsin before she disappeared after Emilia.

Tamsin let out a breath. She wondered if it was worth all the trouble to go to some silly party, but Tamsin was itching to see a little Empyrian culture. She went downstairs to see the Ladies out with her mother and then spent the rest of the afternoon contemplating what she would do. She couldn't deny her curiosity; seeing a religious celebration was something she couldn't even imagine. Her mother might not approve, but her father would want her to experience Empyria to the fullest. She barely ate at supper, too nervous to do anything but move the food around her plate. Luckily, her mother seemed too preoccupied to notice, telling her father all about the luncheon with the other Ladies. It was funny, how one afternoon had changed her mother's whole demeanor. She was back in her element again, which was one thing to be grateful for at least.

Tamsin thought it was a good time to bring up her conversation with Emilia and briefly mentioned she would be coming over tonight. An initiation of sorts, Tamsin said as she spooned a hearty mouthful of soup into her mouth, to welcome her.

Lavinia was so besotted with the idea that Tamsin was making friends so quickly that she hardly asked any questions about it and went on to explain how good it was to have Tamsin finally settled in one place and not roving across the countryside. Her father would smile and pat her hand affectionately, but remained rather silent throughout, and Tamsin knew he was afraid if he argued it would break the spell his wife seemed to be under as Tamsin knew if she took up this familiar battle it would only lead to questions about tonight. So she took her secret victory and ate her soup.

Emilia was waiting for her at the designated time outside the compound walls. She handed Tamsin a lantern and the two of them made their way through the empty alleys and outdoor halls down to the river where there was a small boat and three others waiting for them. Emilia introduced them as the son and daughters of some of the officers as they rowed across. It was the only way to get to the east side unless one wanted to go across the portcullis bridges or through the Armillary, all of which were guarded at all times she explained.

Tamsin tugged at the laces of the dress Emilia had picked out, trying to loosen the too-tight corset that dug uncomfortably into her ribs. She gave up when she saw the others glancing at her. She couldn't see what they were wearing for they were all covered in cloaks, something Tamsin had left behind thinking that her travelling cloak would not be required going to the party.

It did not take as long to cross the river as she thought it would, and all of her self-consciousness over her attire abruptly ceased as she got her first close-up view of the Armillary halfway across. As the bend in the river edged away, Tamsin was able to get a full view of it. A dome was the only word that came to mind, but it was much more than that. Two bridges reached out to it from either side of the river; the one from the west side had a curved ceiling running its length with open air arches on the sides. These bridges met at the outer ring of the Armillary, which appeared to be a veranda that encircled the main body of the building and was outlined by the flickering light of torches. She could not see much of the main part of the building, which was hidden by the veranda and other open-air hallways that wrapped around it, but she could see the rounded ceiling because it glowed in a stunning mosaic of blue, emerald, amber, and gold. But it was not the reflection of the stars on metal; the domed ceiling was made of *glass* and the light was coming from within. It was like an altar to the stars, collecting all the beautiful colors of nature in one sphere to pay homage to the night sky. There were also two towers that flanked the stunning dome, a taller one on the northwest side and a shorter one on the southeast, both with pointed roofs that looked too sharp even for the birds to land on. She did not know how a building that large and made of stone could support itself in the water, but upon further inspection she saw that the bulk of it was actually built on a shallow island in the middle of the river, while the rest of the outer veranda and walkways were held up by massive columns.

It was a pity that they had to bypass the great structure in a rowboat. She could only imagine that the inside was as magnificent as the outside. She was less concerned about not knowing anything about the east side, let alone the west side, now that her mind was occupied with the sight of the great building. And the others seemed to know where they were going.

Emilia whispered something to one of the girls, Penelope, (Tamsin recalled her name), a sturdy girl with simple beauty, as they climbed out of the boat onto the stone docks and then made an announcement that they were taking a small detour. Penelope's eyes widened in the moonlight and she opened her mouth to speak, but Emilia grabbed her hand and pulled her along the dock up to the bank. Tamsin followed them between buildings and under arches, and even though the construction was nowhere near the grandeur of the west side, her mind was alight with adventure now. The buildings here seemed to overlap each other in no particular order and wooden shop stands crowded the already narrow streets, though they were all closed for the night.

They went down a short flight of stairs to an underground alcove. Emilia knocked on a wooden door and a minute later it was opened by a bent old woman, taller than Tamsin still, with wiry black hair tipped with grey. Her gnarled hands gripped the door like talons and her weathered skin stretched taut over her bones. The skin under her eyes was so thin it revealed blue veins underneath and her lips were almost completely white. Had her eyes not been as direct as arrows and filled with suspicion Tamsin would have thought a corpse had answered the door.

"What do you want?" the old woman asked.

Emilia swung her small purse in front of her, jingling the coins inside and the old woman opened the door so they could enter. The only light in the room came from the few candles strewn throughout. There was a slight haze to the air and there were logs in the hearth, but it was dark. There were cupboards and tables filling up the corners, piled high with bottles and decanters. Parchment was strewn about the floor haphazardly, some buried beneath thick layers of dust, and there was a formidable sized pile of sand pushed up against one of the walls.

The old woman disappeared behind a cabinet and Tamsin leaned in closer to Emilia. "Who is she?" she whispered.

"That's Miss Mora," she replied with a devilish grin. "She's as old as the hills and an absolute walnut, but she keeps the good stuff."

Mora reappeared and handed Emilia a bottle and a small package. She gave the others bottles as well, but when she looked at Tamsin her eyes flickered in surprise and she stared for an uncomfortably long time.

Emilia looked back and forth between the two. "Mora, this is Tamsin Urbane," she said, as if she were speaking to a small child. "She's new."

Mora continued to stare. "So he has returned," she said quietly.

"I have an idea!" Emilia said dramatically. "Tamsin wants a taste of the old religion. Perhaps you want to read her palm Mora?"

"She's a fortune teller?" Tamsin asked.

"I'm not a cheap peddler of fortune and tricks," Mora said sharply. "I'm the last remaining seer of the family Veerain of Alamorgro. I am the only one who can tell you your true fate."

"Thank you, Mora," Emilia said, overly sweetly, and then to Tamsin, "We'll be waiting right outside." She turned and left with a barely concealed smirk on her face and the others followed suit before Tamsin could even object.

Mora closed the door behind them and faced Tamsin, her inquisitive eyes burning right through the last of her wonder.

"I—I think I should go with th—," Tamsin started, but was immediately interrupted.

"Is your soul open to the will of the gods and the light of the truth?" Mora asked.

Tamsin had never met someone who believed in the old gods before and she was not sure how to respond or even if she should. Mora definitely did have a *mad* sort of appearance and Tamsin had no desire to provoke anything that would turn it from mere appearance to actual temperament. "People don't have souls," Tamsin said, trying to sound confident, "and the gods don't exist."

"One of the soulless," Mora said, but she didn't say it disapprovingly, rather she said it with pity. "Then open yourself to the truth and welcome it when it stands before you." She then instructed Tamsin to choose one of the vials.

Tamsin didn't recall hearing about Alamorgro in her history lessons and had no idea what kind of tricks this woman used, but if playing along would get her out of here sooner then she would. There were so many vials Tamsin didn't even know how to begin to choose. She wandered through the maze of them for a moment and then, uncomfortable with the old woman watching her, snatched one off the nearest table. It was barely the size of her palm, but it was heavy and she wondered how something so small could weigh so much. She couldn't tell what was inside it because the vial itself was black as onyx. There was a single silver thread tied around the neck and there was some kind of engraving etched into the glass itself, but she didn't recognize the mark. She handed it to the seer.

"That way," Mora said, pointing to a stairway in the back of the room. Tamsin glanced wistfully back towards the door where the others had disappeared, sighed resignedly, and preceded Mora down a few more stairs and into the appointed room. Unlike the first, this room was strangely bare save for two pedestals in the center of the room and a lantern with green glass shutters hanging on the wall that cast the room in an unearthly light. The pedestal on the left held a translucent glass bowl filled halfway with water and the one on the right held an irregularly shaped brown bowl that looked like petrified wood. It contained a layer of light grey pebbles and had shallow ring-like cracks encircling it.

Mora stepped around to the other side of the pedestals and removed the cork from the vial Tamsin had chosen. "Place your hands in the bowls," she said, her voice slipping into a soft monotone whose words had the hum of having been repeated many times.

Tamsin reached up and first dipped her left hand in the water then put her second on the small pile of pebbles. Mora poured a few drops in the water from the vial, mumbling a few words that Tamsin didn't know. The bowl started to swirl with color as if a storm cloud as dark as plum had formed in it. Then she poured some over the pebbles, which hissed like hot water being poured over a bed of coals, but they remained cool to the touch.

Mora placed the tips of her fingers on the surface of the water, causing tiny ripples, and then her others on the pebbles near Tamsin's. She squeezed her eyes shut and her forehead furrowed as she concentrated. She hunched over slightly and then moaned as if she was in pain.

Concerned, Tamsin moved to help the old woman, but with a howl Mora grabbed her wrists and, with more force than Tamsin thought she possessed, held her hands where they were. Tamsin tried to pull free, sloshing water over the edge of the bowl on the left, but the Mora's grip was unyielding. "Let me go!" she cried, afraid, but the seer ignored her.

The old woman's eyes were wide as she stared into the bowl of water, as if she saw something horrific there, and started speaking quickly. "Befriended or betrayed? It has already begun! Drowned in a sea of darkness, risen by the twin stars, cursed by the moon, one will fall, the other hidden. The fire will grow and illuminate the dark! But lies run deep and traitors emerge into the light. It has begun. Trust leads to trickery leads to loss and the grey space between where nothing and everything exists. Look for him there. Betrayed by the guiltless one before the exodus…" She looked over then at the other bowl. The cracks around the outside had started to change color; from light brown they had turned to bright green, then blue and purple almost as if the bowl was made of amethyst and tourmaline and the petrified wood was only a thin disguise. "Wear the veil and see clearly for the first time the path in the water," Mora continued. "The path that leads to the place where the dark and light collide. You will see nightmares unleashed onto earth and see the face of madness as has not been seen for thousands of years! He has awoken! It has begun!"

With great effort, Tamsin ripped her arms out of the bowls, the woman's fingernails tearing through her skin, and stumbled backwards. Mora slumped forward over the pedestals, looking up to stare at Tamsin with deliberate intent.

"You are not who you think you are," she said softly. "Blood binds us tighter than oaths."

Tamsin staggered up the stairs as fast as she could, but Mora made no move to follow, only stared and let Tamsin's blood drip from her fingers. Tamsin reached the vial room, but tripped and fell into one of the tables, knocking over a dozen bottles and sending glass shards scattering across the floor. She regained her footing and fled out of the old woman's dwelling and into the street where she nearly collided with another person.

"Whoa! Easy there luv," the man said, catching her before she fell to the ground. He was easily three times her size and smelled strongly of ale. He looked her up and down with bleary eyes. "Well you're awf'lly pretty. Where'd you come from?"

Then another one stepped over. "Looks like you caught yerself a classy one, Reynold."

Tamsin stumbled away from them and searched frantically around for Emilia and the others, but she didn't see them anywhere. Where had they gone?

"You look a little lost hun," the second man said, but the smile on his face made her think he had no intention of helping her.

It took every ounce of willpower she had not to break into a run and flee. She was close to crossing the line beyond just mortification and into a more tangible fear. "I'm q-quite capable of finding my way," she said, turning and walking hastily away. But the footsteps she heard behind her informed her that these two weren't finished with her yet.

She had just made it to the first cross street when three more figures stepped into her path. She stopped suddenly and one of the men behind her bumped into her, almost knocking her down, but before he could get a hold of her, two of the three figures in front of her intervened and shoved the man back. The third hooked an arm through Tamsin's to steady her and hung back while the other two, a boy and a girl, stood between them and the drunkards. The boy held a torch in one hand and held it out in front of him as if challenging them to come any closer. He was tall and thin, but his wide shoulders gave him an imposing presence.

The girl was tall as well, though everyone seemed tall to Tamsin, and shouted out angrily to the two men. "Go on now, get out of here!"

"Aww, c'mon Gia. We found her first," the one called Reynold replied.

"Go back to the party and fill your cups," the girl said, flipping something shiny at them.

Despite his inebriation, Reynold caught it easily and pocketed the coin. He tipped the brim of an invisible hat towards her and smiled. "Always a pleasure, Gia," he said and then the two of them staggered on their way, the last few minutes already forgotten in search of their next drink.

The boy and the girl came back to where Tamsin was still being supported by the third and only then did Tamsin realize that the person holding her arm was Penelope. Tamsin looked around, but Emilia and the rest of them were still nowhere to be seen.

"Are you okay?" Gia asked. The torchlight illuminated her wavy blonde hair and strong features. Where Penelope was soft and amiable-looking, Gia was striking, with a long straight nose and high-cheekbones. Had her dress not been two inches too short and her feet not bare Tamsin would easily have guessed her to be noble-born.

Tamsin hadn't even realized she was still trembling until she took a moment to collect herself, but she nodded.

"I'm sorry about those guys. They're harmless really. Morons, but harmless," the tall boy said, holding out his hand. "I'm Enrik."

Tamsin held out her hand to shake his and thank them, but Penelope grasped it and turned the back of her hand up. "What happened to your hands?" she gasped. "Oh my, Tamsin, I'm so sorry, we never should have left you there!"

Gia's light eyes flashed. "Did they do this to you?"

Tamsin looked at the back of her hands where Mora's fingernails had carved long, dark lines into them. Only now did she start to feel the sting and she winced. "No, no it wasn't them."

"Enrik, do you have anything in your bag to wrap these with?" Penelope asked.

Enrik searched in the satchel he was carrying for a moment and then pulled out a white roll of gauze.

Tamsin started to protest, saying it really wasn't that bad, but Gia took the gauze and started wrapping her hands anyway. "You must be new around here. Did you come in with the latest caravan?" she asked.

"How did you know?"

"Because you wouldn't have left cuts like these untended. Believe me, the first time you get sand somewhere it shouldn't you'll understand why." Her eyes twinkled then. "Penny told us on the way over," she confessed. "I'm Georgiana, by the way."

"I'm Tamsin. Thank you for helping me. And I'm truly alright Penelope," she added, trying to assuage the guilt from Penelope's face.

Georgiana tied the gauze into knots on the tops of her hands. "There, all set. We can get you back to the Armillary if you like?"

"No!" Penelope cried. "Tamsin you must come with us! Please let me make it up to you!"

"I know it wasn't your fault," Tamsin said, but the look of guilt was still so strong on Penelope's face that she couldn't say no and with Enrik and Gia's support, she agreed. And she needed to rid herself of Mora's disturbing actions.

The three of them then led her down a couple streets and came to a smaller version of the square that she had seen when they first arrived. There were birds and pigs being roasted over fires, barrels full of wine and ale being dipped into by eager mugs, and boisterous, bearded men with girls on their laps whose clothes hung loosely around their shoulders. Some people smiled at them and waved and Tamsin could see the curiosity in the glances thrown her way, but nobody stopped their celebrating to bother them.

"Is this the solstice celebration?" Tamsin asked. It was nothing like she had imagined and much less formal than what Emilia had led her to believe. The fact that it was outside was shocking enough. One of the fires caught her attention and on the other side of it, with a glass halfway to her lips, stood Emilia in a circle of people, laughing and smiling.

Tamsin stared at her for a moment, a surge of hurt and betrayal at Emilia's duplicity flowing through her, and then she turned to the others. "I don't really feel much like celebrating after all. Perhaps you could take me back yet?"

Georgiana frowned. "We don't get many reasons to celebrate out here, so we make the most of it when we do. But the three of us won't be staying either, so we can take you back if you want."

Tamsin hesitated. She had already been abandoned once; the last thing she wanted was to run off with a bunch of strangers in a city she was even less familiar with. But suddenly the words of the blue woman came back to her. *Epic tales are filled with extraordinary people who don't know they're in one…*

"We're going to the wall to see the Hollow Cliffs," Georgiana said, sensing her question.

"It's a tradition of ours. You have to come," Penelope said invitingly.

Tamsin's own adventure was off to a rocky start, but if she tagged along, she thought looking at each of their faces, then maybe she could be a part of someone else's. And that might not be so bad.

And the thought of going to see the wall was too enticing to give up. She smiled and nodded. "I'd love to."

CHAPTER THREE

"Shouldn't there be guards up here?" Tamsin asked as they climbed the stairs up to the allure, the walkway above the wall. The stairs were narrow and cleverly concealed within the wall itself; the doorway had only been what seemed to be an alcove for a statue of a soldier twice her size holding a spear and shield, but when you stepped inside, the right wall of the alcove disappeared and gave way to a dark stairwell.

Georgiana grinned. "This is Reynold's section to watch tonight." Reynold. One of the men in the street. Probably passed out by now, Tamsin thought.

The allure was wide enough for two horses to walk side by side comfortably and a good three stories above the ground level, though there was a barrier wall on each side, like at the compounds, which eased any fear of falling off of it. The stonework was quite precise and Tamsin couldn't think of anyone who wouldn't be impressed just by the sheer enormity of the structure.

Tamsin went over to the outer barrier wall and looked out over the eastern expanse of the world, her breath taken away even in the darkness. All that sand and untouched land, stretching out to touch the star-studded horizon, thousands of years old and yet made new again from being beheld by new eyes. She had nothing but the desert around her for weeks, but somehow seeing it from this height, and only separated by a few feet of stone, made its power only more tangible. The desert was the authority here.

Enrik placed his torch in one of the metal brackets placed in regular intervals along the wall and Tamsin tore herself away from the view and followed them as they made their way south. It wasn't too long before they came to an archway with a large canopy over a section of the wall. It was the part that bridged the east and west sides over the river, the southern portcullis bridge. There was a steady thrum from the churning water underneath, but Enrik assured her the structure was sound and the echo off the ceiling made it sound worse than it was.

Then he hopped up onto the barrier wall in one of the windows carved into the side of the canopy and held out his hand. Penelope skipped over to him, a smile on her face, and let him help her up next to him. Then she took a step off and disappeared as easily as if she had turned a corner.

Tamsin's mouth hung open in horror, though any exclamations of shock escaped her.

Georgiana squeezed her arm comfortingly. "Penny's fine. Come on, I'll show you." They walked over to the window together. Georgiana lifted her skirt with one hand and let Enrik help her up on the ledge. "There's a step, just here," she pointed below her on the outside. She stepped down and seemed to be floating just on the other side, but then she took another step to the side and disappeared just as Penelope had done.

Tamsin swallowed and gathered the layers of her ball gown. She took Enrik's outstretched hand and stepped up onto the ledge, simultaneous feelings of dread and excitement rising in her throat. Enrik steadied her though and she stepped out into the darkness, relaxing a little when her feet hit hard stone. She looked to her right and saw how Georgiana and Penelope had vanished. A series of protruding blocks acted as stairs to the roof of the bridge's canopy. Tamsin heard the girls calling her from above, encouraging her to come up.

"I'll be right behind you," Enrik said reassuringly.

Gripping the folds of her skirt in one hand and placing the other on the wall next to her, Tamsin took one step up, then another, then another, refusing to look at the rushing water below until she had no more steps. Panting slightly, she looked around and saw Penelope and Georgiana's beaming faces. Enrik came up a second later, grinning as well, and the four of them took a minute to look around them at the lights of the city, the sparkling river snaking its way through, the mosaic beacon of the Armillary at the epicenter, and the dark glow of the desert surrounding it all.

"It never gets old does it," Georgiana said to no one in particular and the others nodded in content agreement. Not everyone was as jaded by the desert and the heat like Emilia. Tamsin found herself nodding as well, though she was too struck by wonder to care that the others had seen this numerous times and this was only her first. This view of Empyria and the feeling of shared awe was what she had been hoping for.

During the next two hours they took turns looking through the spyglass that Enrik had brought with him in his bag. It was mostly just sand and rocks beyond the wall, but they showed Tamsin the Hollow Cliffs that lay further to the south. The Hollow Cliffs were thus named for the many caverns they contained from when the Ottarkins had mined them to build Empyria. What was left was a series of caves and tunnels that stood about three leagues away from the city. From their vantage point above the wall it looked like a jagged rectangle blotting out some of the stars in the distance, but through the spyglass Tamsin could see even darker shapes littered throughout that she imagined were the aforementioned caves.

Tamsin sat a few feet from the edge next to Georgiana, not quite as comfortable as Enrik was who sat on the edge tapping his dangling heels on the wall. Penelope lay on her back, staring up at the stars. Georgiana and Enrik had been passing the spyglass back and forth between them for the last half hour. Though it was interesting, there wasn't much that could be seen through the spyglass in the dark and Tamsin had given up her turn for the broader view her own eyes allowed.

Penelope sighed. "It's late. I don't think they're going to show."

"Who?" Tamsin asked, wondering who else was coming.

"Just a few more minutes," Georgiana said, the spyglass transfixed on the Hollow Cliffs.

Penelope sighed again. "We don't really know *who*. Not for sure anyway." She propped herself up on her elbows. "But they come to the Cliffs every year on this night."

"People from the city?" Tamsin asked. She didn't think people were allowed outside the wall.

"No," Enrik said. "Our best guess is that they are nomads who wander the desert and the cliffs are a regular stop on their route."

"Do they ever visit the city?" Tamsin asked.

"No, nobody comes through the gates unless they're from the Cities or mountain villages," he replied.

"They can't be nomads, Enrik," Penelope said. "Nobody could survive out there."

"That's not true," Georgiana said, her eye still glued on the Cliffs.

"Oh here we go," Enrik said, giving her an exasperated look, as if they've had this argument before. "Georgiana believes that if you follow the river far enough you'll get to the "marshlands" and there's people that actually live there."

"It's true!" Georgiana said. "My father has proof!"

"Has anyone else ever seen them? No," Enrik said, answering his own question. "They're only a myth."

"They're more than that. They're real," Georgiana said, and Tamsin knew she believed every word.

"Have you ever gone out there?" Tamsin asked, intrigued by the idea that there could be people living out there beyond the wall, nomads or otherwise.

Enrik nodded. "The first year we saw them we snuck out there, but we never found anything. They were long gone by the time we made it out there. It was a hard climb, but you have a great view of the city from up there. You can see for leagues and leagues."

"Yeah, but you left out the part where you got lost in the caves and me and Gia had to rescue you," Penelope said, trying to contain her laughter.

Enrik's face flushed even in the darkness and this sent the girls into a fit of giggles.

"Look, there they are!" Georgiana suddenly shouted and all laughter abruptly ceased. She handed Tamsin the spyglass and pointed her in the right direction.

Tamsin put her eye to the glass and directed it to the top of the cliff. It took her a minute, but then she saw them: two tall, dark figures standing there. They were too far away to make out any distinguishing features, but the shapes on the top of the ledge were dark enough against the cobalt sky to stand out and were undeniably human.

"Maybe they're ghosts," Penelope mused, looking out at the ridge. "Cursed lovers doomed to haunt the cliffs every year on this night."

Georgiana and Enrik both rolled their eyes and Tamsin smiled, amused by her imagination, though she couldn't help the chill of renewed excitement that made her arms tingle. There were *actual* people out there. Even if there were only two of them; they weren't alone out here. She handed the spyglass to Penelope.

"I wish they would do something," Penelope said after a minute. "They just stand there like statues."

"Maybe they are statues and they only appear by the light of the solstice moon," Enrik said dramatically.

Penelope shoved the spyglass at him. "Now you're just teasing," she said. She stood up and stretched. "It's late Enrik. You should take me home."

He looked at her incredulously. "But they've just appeared!"

Penelope raised an eyebrow at him and his shoulders slumped. "Lead the way your ladyship," he said. Penelope swatted at him and he grinned. "Gia? Tamsin?"

"I should make sure my father got home alright," Georgiana said.

Tamsin was not quite ready to go back just yet. She wanted to linger in the wonder and feeling of adventure a little longer. "I think I'd like to stay a little while yet," she said. "If you need to go don't stay on my account," she added, not wanting to be an encumbrance.

"Go check on your father Gia," Enrik said. "I'll come back and take Tamsin home too when she's ready."

"You just want to come back to watch the 'nomads'," Penelope said, and Enrik shrugged.

Georgiana was still hesitant to leave Tamsin by herself, but Tamsin assured her she would be fine until Enrik returned and

Georgiana's sense of duty to her father eventually convinced her to go. Tamsin hugged her and Penelope, thanking them for coming back for her and for bringing her here, though the ordeal with the seer and Mora's words were all but forgotten already. Enrik gave her the spyglass and then they said their goodbyes with Enrik's promise to return.

Once they had gone, Tamsin took a few deep breaths of the night air, feeling quite small in the world, but for the first time like she had a place in this strange environment. *Friends have that effect,* she thought, happy to realize that she did have friends here. The future was as wide open as the desert around them. There would still be social engagements and her studies to attend to, but there would also be midnight rendezvous on rooftops and countless other adventures just waiting to be had. A mischievous voice that sounded a lot like her childhood self whispered to her, reminding her of long-forgotten adventures she used to dream about. Compelled by this feeling of reclaiming something she had thought as lost, she moved to the edge of the canopy and crouched down, looking down at the river below, though she could hear more of it than she could see. She pushed away the prick of fear in her stomach and let the feeling of adventure dominate that space instead. It took her a minute to get her skirt situated due to its fullness, but she managed to swing her legs over the edge.

She sat up a little straighter, letting the feeling of sitting on the edge of civilization rush over her. Though she was not on its exact edge, she remembered. She picked up the spyglass and looked toward the cliff again. After a moment she was able to find where the two figures still stood.

She lowered the spyglass a moment, her brow furrowing, thinking that her eyes were playing tricks on her. But she looked through it again and there was no mistaking what she saw: three people, not two.

She frowned. Hadn't Penelope thought they were lovers? How could that be if there were more than two?

She kept watching. Then another appeared on their left.

Then another.

And another.

Her heart pounded wildly inside her chest and turned her excitement into alarm as easily as if it were churning milk. Something didn't feel right. Two people one night out of the year was innocent. It was a passing curiosity. But—she counted seven total—*seven* was different. Seven was a group. Seven could turn to ten or twenty or more. It could be a prelude to something else, something big.

She quarreled with herself for the briefest of moments before deciding she needed to tell somebody. She set the spyglass down and backed away from the edge, gathering her skirt so she could stand. She didn't care if she got in trouble for being out this late and without telling anyone. Someone had to know. Her *father* had to know. She went over to where the hidden steps were and carefully stepped down onto the first, placing her hand against the wall so she would not lose her balance. But then she remembered Enrik. What would he think if he came back and she was gone? She could leave the spyglass on the windowsill...

The spyglass! She had forgotten it on the roof.

She spun around without thinking and her foot slipped off the step. Her hands flew out to catch herself and her fingers latched onto the edge of the roof. A cry jumped out of her throat as she dangled in the darkness and her chest heaved as panic swelled inside of her. The laces of her corset were suddenly too tight as she struggled to hang on, her breath starting to come in ragged gasps. She tried to swing her leg back up onto the step, but the weight of her skirt made it impossible. Darkness started creeping around the edge of her vision and she cried out again, a pitiful peep of a sob.

Then her fingers slipped off the edge, but the darkness had already closed in by the time she hit the water.

CHAPTER FOUR

A pair of glowing eyes looked out over the desert, mirroring the stars that lingered in the grey sky. The first bands of sunlight were starting to appear so Haven pulled his hood up and reattached the n'qab that covered his eyes and forehead. He stood alone on the ridge now, breathing in the last of the night's coolness before it succumbed to the heat of the day. The world was peaceful up here, the air less polluted with the cares and troubles of the lives below, but he had brought his up with him, contemplating them most of the night. It was unusual for him to be so pensive, but their task was only a day away now and they had already run into a complication. The time for preparation was over. The time for action had begun.

He made his way down from the ridge and was surprised to see the Kazsera, Ysallah, waiting at the bottom. His oath-brother Kellan was with her and stood quietly to the side, but Ysallah paced back and forth, her deep red cloak billowing out behind her. She looked up at Haven's approach and stopped her pacing, the weeks of hard travelling showing on her face.

"Is the girl still asleep?" Haven asked her.

That was the complication. During the night Kellan had gone down to the river to collect some fish when he had seen something much bigger among the rocks on the bank. He had carried her back to their camp on the south side of the cliffs. She was soaked and had a few cuts, but she was alive. Even though her clothing was strange, he could tell it was not meant for desert living. She had to have come from the city, though they had scouted the surrounding area around the city the day and night before and had seen no activity outside the massive wall. So how did she end up here?

"Yes," Ysallah answered him. "Bregan and Karnak are watching her."

The two sha'diin, tribesmen, she mentioned were the fastest of her village, but did not have the night-sight like Haven and his oath-brothers. It had slowed them down considerably, since they were forced to travel at night due to the dangerously hot temperatures of the desert during the day, but Bregan and Karnak were resilient and had adjusted to the rigorous schedule as best they could.

Two of their members were missing though. "And Oman and Samih?"

"They are at the river," Kellan spoke up.

Haven nodded and the three of them headed in that direction. Their rations had run out a week ago and now they were forced to rely solely on the river for nourishment. Since leaving the marshlands there had not been many opportunities to hunt. The river offered not nearly the bountiful assortment of fish that their homeland did, but the desert was even worse, keeping its inhabitants well hidden. The creatures they had managed to catch were small and ill-suited to feed their band of seven and every Ma'diin learned how to fish at an early age so it was in their best interest to stay near the river. And since it was a constant source of water, it lessened the amount they had to carry.

Haven glanced at the Kazsera, noticing her stiff posture. Her hair was pulled back into a thick braid, sharpening the edges of her narrow face and long nose and revealing the tight lines around her eyes. She was a generation older than Haven, had been friends with his mother, and was more than capable of this mission ahead.

She was one of the more decisive clan leaders of the Ma'diin, her mind as sharp as the red-handled knife she carried, and would be the one negotiating with the northerners, though Haven would be the one translating for her. The clan his father belonged to had hosted the foreigners many years ago when he was only a small child and his father had learned their language and passed it on to his son. He hadn't spoken it in years, but he had still been chosen for this venture mainly for that reason. The fact that he was a Watcher was just an added asset.

Oman greeted them when they reached the river and Samih climbed up the bank with a net of fish, the bottoms of his rolled-up pants soaked with water.

"Samih, put your cloak on," Kellan barked.

His cloak was like a second skin to Haven, but Samih had joined their clan only a few months ago and was still adjusting to their way of life. Haven knew little of Samih before his transition. He had been just another member of the Ysallah'diin, young, a good fisherman, and loyal to his Kazsera, though unluckier than most.

Haven had been younger than Samih when he transitioned, but he had welcomed the danger and the prestige that came with being a Watcher. A life of fishing and reed-weaving was not what his life was intended for. He had made the sacrifice for his people, had embraced the night, knowing that one day it would cost him his life, but that day was not today. He had been raised for this life, like Oman and some of his oath-brothers, but Samih had not prepared for this; it had chosen him without warning or invitation. Samih's transition had been a tragic accident, one Haven was responsible for. Samih had survived, but had not spoken a word to Haven since. Ysallah had thought it a good idea to bring Samih with them, arguing that it would do him good to get away from the hunt and have some time to come to terms with his new life, though Haven knew that she hoped they would start mending the feelings of bitterness and guilt between them. Haven was not surprised at Samih's behavior though; kind sentiments towards the Watchers from the sha'diin had always been a tenuous thing.

Samih scowled, but put on his cloak anyways. He dumped the fish at Oman's feet and went back to the river with his net.

Oman shook his head and began cleaning the fish. "He should sulk less and be a little more grateful that Haven didn't let him die that night," he said. Oman was the eldest among them, older than all the Watchers even in the marshlands. He was a brilliant fighter, his age was a testament to that and he had trained many of the Watchers, Haven included, but his usually unyielding patience had begun to wear thin as of late.

"You shouldn't be so harsh on him," Haven said evenly.

"Like the way you've been harsh on yourself?" He hmphed. "This is his life now. He needs to come to terms with that."

"It's not that simple." Haven's jaw clenched and his hands balled into fists almost on their own accord.

Another life had been lost the night he failed Samih. He could remember Samih before his transition only because he had been a part of Ysallah's tribe and Haven had been a frequent visitor to one of the Ysallah'diin: Lu'sa. She had not lived to see the next sunrise.

"Why don't we discuss more urgent issues?" Kellan said, sensing his brother's rising tension. "Like what are we going to do about the girl?"

Oman sighed. "We wouldn't have to discuss this if you hadn't brought her to us."

Kellan's lip curled up. "I couldn't just leave her there. She would've froze, or worse." Kellan was in his early twenties, the same as Haven, and often acted on emotion rather than logic. He was compassionate, easy to anger, quick with a blade and his words, and had garnered much attention from the ladies of his tribe before becoming a Watcher. But even through his impulsiveness and hot-headed arguments his loyalty to his oath-brothers was unshakeable.

"What will happen when others come looking for her?" Oman asked. He was like Ysallah that way, practical, always thinking ten steps ahead.

"We have to meet them eventually," Kellan replied. "That is why we came after all."

Haven felt the ghosts of his past subsiding as he tried to focus on their current situation, grateful, though a little irked, that Kellan was able to read him so easily. He had gone through scenario after scenario in his head about how they would make contact when they finally reached the foreign city, but none of them had begun like this. "If she wakes up before anyone comes, then we will take her back to the city ourselves. You can stay here, Ysallah, in case anything is misunderstood and something should go wrong."

The Kazsera nodded.

"Shouldn't we keep her as leverage then?" Kellan asked. "For the negotiations?"

Ysallah threw him a reproachful look. "She is one of them, not one of us. We cannot steal her, otherwise we risk open war and we won't get the chance to negotiate."

Haven was realizing how unprepared they were for this. They had not discussed how they were to actually interact with the foreigners. It all depended on how they were received he had always thought. But now the weight of their mission was settling upon him.

"But she is not our kind. If we used her—," Kellan started.

Oman looked up, his look alone enough to interrupt him. "You will heed the Kazsera's words."

Kellan's eyes narrowed, focusing solely on Oman. "She is not *my* Kazsera."

Haven knew Oman's words would be taken the way he had meant them: a warning, but Kellan was right. He didn't owe his allegiance to this Kazsera, or any. The Watchers were beyond the direct control of the Ma'diin leaders, though the Kazserii's position was still one that demanded submission by all others. So far Kellan had stayed true to that, but Haven knew his character well enough to know that out here, away from home, Kellan would push the limits.

"We are here for one purpose," Oman reminded him. "Remember that."

"And you remember who you are talking to, *brother*. You are not my superior."

Oman may as well have been. It was rare for a Watcher to live past his thirties in their line of work and Oman had nearly doubled that. He had more experience than Haven, Kellan, and Samih combined and if the Watchers were to have any leader it would be him. "If she becomes a distraction for you, you will be sent home, for you will no longer be useful here. I need you focused, Kellan. Don't forget what we are fighting for." Oman resumed cleaning the fish, ending the conversation.

Kellan turned to Haven and mouthed *distraction?* at him, but Haven shook his head, willing him to let it go. Haven didn't judge him. Everyone's nerves were starting to fray. They were made for killing, not this. Haven's muscles burned from the absence of their familiar movements. His mind seemed to be scorched as well. He worried about the task ahead, but every night he seemed to worry more and more about how they were faring back in the marshlands. There were not enough of them to protect everyone as it was, but with the four of them gone…it was not something he liked to dwell on.

Samih came back with a couple more fish in his net, but paused before he gave them to Oman. He pointed past the others and they all turned.

Haven had his fingers already wrapped around his weapons, but there was no need to pull them out. Running towards them was Bregan, his figure outlined by the sharp orange streaks of the sun as it broke over the horizon, shouting at them with urgency. The girl was gone.

CHAPTER FIVE

When Tamsin awoke, it wasn't to her warm, soft bed, Sherene throwing open the drapes to let the morning light in, and the honeyed smell of breakfast wafting up from the kitchens below, but to the hollow sound of the wind and a lingering chill deep in her bones. Her eyelids felt like they weighed a hundred pounds as she tried to open them. All she could see through her bleary eyes was sand, bathed in the burnt orange of a sunrise. Her mind tried to catch up to what her senses were slow to tell her. She wasn't in her bed. She wasn't even in Delmar anymore. She remembered going to the wall with Georgiana and Enrik and Penelope and seeing the Cliffs and the seven and then falling…so how did she end up here? And where was here? She couldn't remember anything after the water had swallowed her.

She rubbed her eyes and saw she was underneath some kind of burlap tent and its unfamiliarity confused her. It reminded her a little of the makeshift tents that the soldiers that accompanied them to Empyria had used, but the material was different, more natural, and it was completely open on one side, like half of a cocoon. She noticed that there were several others of these tent-like structures forming a loose circle around a pile of flat stones where the remains of what used to be fish lay.

But it wasn't the fish bones that sent ice through her veins: it was the figures underneath the other tents.

She froze, her senses screaming at her that she was not where she was supposed to be. The surprise of it stifled her limbs for what seemed an eternity and all she found herself capable of doing was holding her breath. She watched them for several minutes, but the figures lay motionless. There were only two of them, but there were five other tents that were empty. Life started to return to her and her instincts were telling her to leave. She crawled out from underneath the tent and got to her feet as quietly as she could. She willed her heart to stay inside of her chest as it beat against her ribs like a hammer, but the two men in unfamiliar garb still did not move. They were bare-chested and had curved knives attached to belts at their waists. She felt no need to investigate any further. The circular camp was at the base of a cliff so she tip-toed away outside the ring of tents so she could get her bearings…and saw a woman standing in the desert.

But it wasn't just a woman. It was the blue woman, Tamsin was sure. She was a hundred yards away, but the cerulean shimmer was unmistakable.

It did not occur to her that it was odd to see the blue woman from her childhood here, but rather Tamsin felt a certain connection to her, a draw that pulled her feet forward. It was as if the blue woman was trying to guide her away from the camp, from the unfamiliar to familiar. Was she here to protect her? Tamsin had not been in any danger the first time the blue woman appeared, so why show up now?

One of the sleeping men stirred behind her and it was enough to jolt her senses. So she ran. She ran until the tents fell away from view into the sand and her lungs burned for air, but the blue woman didn't get any closer. A sinking feeling formed in her stomach and only then did she stop. She rested her hands on her knees for a moment, letting her breath catch back up. When she looked up again the blue woman was gone. She looked and looked, but she had disappeared. Only then did she realize that she had no idea where she was or where she was going. She had irrationally fled, possibly from the only shelter for miles and she was wandering around completely lost.

Seeing the blue woman again had overridden her better judgment. Those men could have been mere fishermen, which would explain the fish bones and the fact that she was alive right now instead of at the bottom of the river. But there had been seven tents. Last night she had seen seven figures on top of the ridge. She had assumed that they had camped at the bottom of the cliff they had seen last night. So logically if she went away from the cliff, then she would reach Empyria, which was just north. But so far she hadn't seen any sign of the city and by now she should have. She needed to find the river, *now*. If she could do that, then she had a good chance of finding her way back home. She shielded her eyes as she looked around to see the position of the sun, but then she realized that it was coming from the wrong direction. The sun was rising on her left, not her right. She looked back. The cliffs were there, but they looked different; they weren't the same as the ones she had looked upon last night. And she could see more ridges outlined in the other direction, far in the distance.

She had only one choice left to her and that was to keep walking and hope she headed the right way.

"Haven, you can't go after her."

Haven tightened the straps that held a knife to the side of his boot as if he had not heard Ysallah. But even though he did not owe her his allegiance, he had no wish to insult her. "With respect, Kazsera, you cannot stop me."

"But I can," Oman's deep voice cut through the wind as he crossed his arms over his chest.

Haven stood up to face him, unintimidated by the warning, but questioning why Oman was siding with Ysallah. They both knew the only way he could stop Haven from going would be to fight him. Kellan had been right earlier: Oman was not their superior, just like Ysallah was not their Kazsera. They had other bonds that they were bound to, but allegiance to one man or woman was not one of them. And it wasn't like Oman to waste time like this. So Haven was left to wonder at Oman's show of superiority.

Bregan jumped in, immediately acting as peacekeeper between the two, but then took a deliberate step back as he realized the tension-filled space between them was not the safest place for him to be. He put his hands up, still hoping to broker peace. "C'mon, she couldn't have gotten far, Oman. We could still go after her."

"You're just trying to make up for the fact that she disappeared on your watch," Kellan spoke from where he was leaning against a boulder watching the sides unfold.

"Karnak was supposed to watch her too!" he tried defending himself.

Ysallah growled in irritation at him, silencing him. "I take responsibility for my sha'diin's carelessness."

Haven turned away and grabbed his water skin from underneath his *buurda* and tied the strings to his belt. Then he started walking away from camp.

"This is just the kind of distraction I wanted to avoid," Oman said, following him.

"She is not a distraction," Haven countered. "She is a *life*." He kept walking as Oman stopped behind him.

"We cannot split up this close to the foreign city!" Ysallah shouted after him.

Haven ignored her. He should've grabbed some food, but he didn't want to lose any more time. He would start at the river first, thinking that was where she may have headed. It would give him the chance to fill his water skin as well.

Before he could take his next step, a flash of light shimmered brightly on the spinning silver blade that shot just in front of his hood. It landed several yards away from him, its hilt sticking out of the sand.

Haven paused and turned back, staring at Oman's empty hand with a salty stare. Bristling, he marched back, grabbing one of his own knives from his belt. If Oman wanted a fight, then he would give him one.

"Think this through," Oman said deliberately, drawing another blade from within his cloak. "Going after this girl won't bring Lu'sa back."

Hearing her name stopped Haven's advance as swiftly as if the sand had turned into a frozen river around his feet.

Kellan sprang up from his perch against the boulder, immediately sensing the betrayal coursing through Haven's blood. He put himself between the two before the ice could thaw around Haven's feet, giving Oman a reproachful grimace. Even if it was Haven's motivation, Oman should have known better, especially with Ysallah here. He glanced at the Kazsera, but her face was a stony mask.

"Move," Haven told Kellan, his tone dangerously low.

Kellan shook his head. "As much as I would love to see you rip Oman's tongue out for that," he threw another disappointed glance toward Oman, "he's not wrong."

Haven took a step forward and Kellan put his hands up, urging Haven to keep his anger in check.

"You're not wrong either," Kellan said. "What if, *what if*," he emphasized as Haven tried to step around him, "I go check the cliffs and you go check the river. If we haven't found her by midday we'll assume she went back to the city and we meet back here."

"We'll only lose half a day," Kellan continued, turning to Oman and Ysallah. "You can strategize while we're gone."

Haven could feel his anger slowly starting to let go of the hold it had on him as Kellan continued to argue with them. But he wouldn't change his mind.

Samih stood up suddenly. "Just let them go," he said, the annoyance clear in his voice.

His statement took everyone by surprise. Every so often Samih displayed an appropriate amount of youthful defiance, usually in the form of sulking quietly alone, but this was different, this was direct. And it seemed to be enough to jar Oman out of his stubbornness.

Oman lowered his blade with a disapproving shake of his head, but said, "Midday. No longer." He looked over at Ysallah, his bright, silvery eyes ending any more debate.

She looked like she still had some venom left in her, but conceded with a nod. "I will complete this mission, with or without your Watchers," she said before stalking back to the camp.

Oman pressed his lips together, but didn't say anything. He gave a look to Kellan and Haven and then pulled his hood further over his face as he turned to follow Ysallah.

Kellan scrunched his eyebrows up in a look that asked if Haven was good, and Haven nodded. If he couldn't find the girl, it would at least give him a few hours to clear out the anger from his veins and the nightmares of the past that clung to his mind like cobwebs.

Kellan seemed unconvinced, but squeezed Haven's shoulder briefly, trusting his brother, before turning and walking towards the cliffs.

Haven watched him and the others go for a moment then turned and walked towards the spot where Oman's blade was still embedded in the sand. When he reached it, he bent down, about to pull it from the ground, but noticed something. He knelt down, grabbed the hilt and slowly slid it out of the footprint barely etched in the sand. He brushed his gloved hand over the fine grains, noticing how some of them seemed to have a blue shimmer to them. He looked up and saw more of them faintly pressed into the sand leading into the desert. The wind was starting to pick up and he knew he only had a little time before the desert reclaimed them, and her.

CHAPTER SIX

Hours passed and the desert only seemed to grow around her. The ground had changed from a crumbling, rocky terrain to soft, shifting sand. It was a burnt gold color with streaks of red and copper running through it in wavy lines. The sun hadn't even reached its peak and the heat was already at an unbearable level. There was a wind coming from her left, but it only seemed to blow hot air around. There was no camp, no river, no nothing. The cliffs she had seen seemed no closer, nor no further. The air shimmered around her like a translucent curtain, making her dizzy. She had lost her shoes in the river and her bare feet burned and ached from walking in the unstable sand. Her throat felt swollen. Her father would be so disappointed to see her like this, but she didn't know what to do so she sank to the ground, letting the despair she had been trying to swallow overcome her. She would have cried, but the sun had dried up any moisture and energy she had left.

She didn't know how long she laid like that, too weak to do anything but exist. Then a shadow fell across her. At first she thought it was a cloud, bringing miracle shade to the damning heat, but then she felt something lift her up and touch her lips and a cool liquid poured down her throat. It was a struggle, but she forced herself to drink, hoping to ease the pain in her dehydrated body. She heard someone say *slow, slow* and she took smaller sips, though she felt she could consume the entire river, which, ironically, she almost did last night.

The shadow above her transformed into a man and she blinked hard, wondering if the heat had made her delirious. He was covered head to toe in a dark cloak and the upper half of his face was hidden by some kind of veil inside his hood. His movements were gentle and sure, but hasty. He wanted to help her she felt.

He took off part of his cloak, leaving his hood in place, and covered her with it. He lifted her off the ground as if she weighed nothing and carried her away. Though she couldn't see anything, she was grateful to be out of the sun and the cloak was surprisingly cool against her skin, so she did not object. He fell into a quick rhythm and she would have dozed off had the wind not picked up suddenly. The fabric of his cloak blew in and out around her and she squirmed uncomfortably as it pressed in against her face. The force of the wind soon slowed the man's pace considerably and he finally had to stop so he could brace himself in the sand. He set her down and she untangled herself from the cloak, getting a face full of sand in the process. Everywhere around them the sand lifted from the ground and flew past them as if it were fleeing from some terrible danger.

"What's happening?" she yelled over the howling wind, shielding her face with her hands and arms, though she doubted he heard her for she could not even hear herself.

They turned to look and what was behind them was something Tamsin could never have imagined in her wildest dreams. The ridge she thought she had seen earlier was rolling towards them with devastating certainty. The ridge was actually a massive cloud and loomed not so far away, tumbling over the ground, consuming the land and the sky in its path. It stretched out in either direction as far as she could see and billowed out towards them like a tawny sail. It grew and expanded, seemingly slowly, but the speed of the wind warned her otherwise. It would be upon them within an hour's half.

The man yelled back something that sounded like *haboon*; she didn't know what it meant but she could hardly hear above the wind anyways. The man pointed towards the left edge of the cloud far in the distance and Tamsin thought she could make out the outline of the cliffs. But even if they ran they wouldn't make it and they both knew it. She looked around almost frantically for something, for anything they could hide behind, but there were only dunes around them. She pointed to one of the dunes that ran parallel to the storm's edge, thinking that they could at least protect themselves from some of the wind on the leeward side. They ran to it as quickly as they could, stumbling through the sand and staggering against the wind, but when they reached it the man motioned to climb to the top. Tamsin inwardly balked at the idea, afraid that they would be blown right off, but she let him help her up and by the time they reached the crest of the dune the storm was nearly upon them.

The man ripped off part of his sleeve and tied it around her nose and mouth so she could still breathe but her face would be protected. He pulled her to her knees and then knelt in front of her with his back to the wind. For the first time she was able to see into his hood. There was a veil that covered the upper half of his face, but she could see his mouth and chin and he mouthed the words to her: *no fear.* There was no time to be afraid, no time to dwell on the mistakes that had brought her here, no time to wonder what might've been, and even though her mind was dumbstruck by the force of nature they were about to face her body quivered from its own set of instincts to run. She nodded, though she felt anything but brave. The muscles in his jaw twitched and he threw the cloak around her again and wrapped his arms around her like a vice, holding her in place.

In any other circumstance, she would have felt uncomfortable being in such an intimate proximity to a man, but as the winds buffeted them and whipped the world around them, she was grateful for him. Right now, it didn't matter who he was or where he had come from. He was her anchor and her shield. She clung to him and buried her head against his chest.

There was a small, triangular tear in the cloak around her and through it she watched as the giant sand cloud enveloped them. Within minutes it completely blocked out the sun and all light as easily as if it had snuffed out a candle.

"What in the seven hells of old were you thinking?"

Lord Urbane couldn't keep from pacing as Lord Regoran scolded his daughter Emilia. She had just finished telling them what had happened last night. Lord Urbane had left early to go to the Armillary that morning, hoping to catch up on the paperwork that had piled up after Lord Saveen's passing. A courier arrived around noon with a message from his wife asking if he had taken Tamsin with him to see the Armillary. He asked the courier to explain, confused and a little irritated as to why Lavinia would think so and interrupt his work, but the courier only knew that Tamsin had apparently missed breakfast and could not be found anywhere in the compound. He asked if his wife was having another luncheon with the lording ladies, remembering how Tamsin used to hide when she was younger whenever her mother's friends came over for tea, but the courier did not know. Lord Urbane told him to tell his wife that Tamsin was probably just exploring and to be a little more patient. He felt guilty because he had promised her a tour of the city and due to the amount of work that had been waiting for him he had been unable to do so yet, but she should have told someone where she was going and taken an escort. Later, he received another message from his wife, this one adamant that something was wrong. One of the maids had come forward saying she had seen Tamsin leaving the compound late last night with Lord Regoran's daughter and that she had still not come home. Lord Regoran was working at the Armillary as well so Lord Urbane went to explain that Tamsin was missing and if his daughter knew where she was. Lord Regoran summoned Emilia to the Armillary and questioned her. At first she denied knowing anything and said the maid must've been mistaken, but Lord Regoran was not a man to have the wool pulled over his eyes so easily and revealed that he knew she had snuck out to the solstice celebration last night. The look on her face was all he needed to confirm it and she soon confessed what had transpired the evening before. Now she stood before them and a handful of others, including Captain Cornelius Saveen, who had already sent some of his men into the streets to look for Tamsin.

"You might be able to hide your actions from your mother, but not from me. I apologize, Eleazar, for my daughter's behavior." Lord Regoran turned his attention back to his daughter, whose cheeks were flushed, but stood as straight as a board and held her father's angry stare. "If you insist on partaking in such vulgar behavior, then fine, be my guest, but don't drag someone else into it!"

Emilia's nostrils flared and her cheeks darkened an even deeper shade. "We were only drinking father! If you and mother would ever let me do *anything* I wouldn't have to go behind your backs!"

"Do not start with me Emilia. You're in enough trouble already."

Lord Urbane put a hand on Lord Regoran's shoulder, trying to calm him. They would never get to the bottom of this if it turned into a shouting match. "What happened Emilia? I have a hard time believing Tamsin would partake in such an event."

"You're right. I could tell she didn't think it was appropriate."

"She was right," Lord Regoran said.

Emilia glared at her father.

"So did you let her go?" Cornelius asked. "Did she get lost on her way back perhaps?"

Emilia shook her head, angry tears starting to well in her eyes. "Maybe, but not right away. We took her to see Mora and—we left her there. It was only supposed to be a joke!"

"Wait a moment. You took her to see the seer?" Cornelius asked incredulously.

"It was just a joke," she said quietly, tears running down her face. "When we didn't see her at the festival we thought she went back on her own."

Cornelius motioned to one of his men. "Go to the seer's dwelling. If Tamsin isn't there, then bring the woman here."

The guard nodded, taking a few more men with him.

"I'll take you home, Emilia," Lord Regoran said, his tone controlled. "I'll be back as soon as I can, Eleazar. Don't worry, we'll find her."

Lord Urbane nodded and continued pacing, which was perhaps the only thing he could control right now. Not knowing where his daughter was or if she was safe had planted a black seed in his heart and it grew with every minute that passed. Time went by agonizingly slow as they waited for the guards to return, but his thoughts were racing with fear. His heart nearly stopped when he heard footsteps, but it was only Lord Regoran returning as he had promised. He and Cornelius Saveen conversed in hushed tones, but Lord Urbane did not hear anything that was said, trying to remain stoic as he struggled to put one foot in front of the other. Waiting like this was a woman's game. He should be out there looking for her.

Just as he decided that he had waited long enough, shouts were heard coming down the hallway. He knew that voice, but it was not the one he had hoped for.

The guards half dragged, half carried the old woman in, who spat at them and hurled curses at them. Two of them had to hold her arms as they brought her before the lords.

Lord Urbane's resolve wavered just a little as the old woman's gaze locked onto his. She looked just as she had over a decade ago.

She smiled at him. "You remember me, don't you? Good. Distance and time cannot change destiny. Do you remember what I told you?"

"I remember."

"Then you realized that I spoke the truth."

Lord Urbane glared at her. "You have said many things, but the truth is rarely one of them. You prey upon the weakness of others and spread only fear and lies."

"Lies? *Lies?!*" She let out a cackling laugh that echoed throughout the chamber and made a few of the guards flinch. "It is not *I* who is the liar among us, is it Eleazar?"

"Enough of your games woman! You saw my daughter last night. Where is she?"

Her eyes squinted. "She is on the chessboard now. The gods have had their eyes on her since before she was born and now they have made their first move. You cannot stop it. It has begun."

Cornelius stepped forward. "You realize madam that if you know the whereabouts of Lady Tamsin and refuse to tell us you will be interrogated…and it will not be pleasant."

The woman turned her gaze to Cornelius and gave him a sour look. "You think I fear your wolves? Ha! Let them snap at my heels! Let them gnaw on my bones and see what fate the gods choose for them!"

"You will tell us or I will cut off your head and toss it in the river," Cornelius said, a little too harshly.

Lord Regoran held up his hand in a restraining gesture. "It doesn't need to get that far if you just tell us where she is."

She licked her cracked lips. "Arak. Give me some Arak and I will tell you where she went."

"This is not a negotiation," Cornelius said.

"Arak," she repeated. "As payment for the bottles she broke."

Lord Urbane reached inside his coat pocket, the old woman watching him as still as a cat, and withdrew a flask. It wasn't Arak; the volatile drink from across the Terraz Sea was banned in most of the Cities for its hallucinogenic effects. "It's from the Cities. Try it," he said as the woman wrinkled her nose disgust. "You'll like it."

She scowled, but took a sip anyways. Her eyes closed in contentment. "The soulless ones make a strong drink."

"Now tell us where she is," Cornelius said.

Her eyes opened to narrow, contemptuous slits. "She did not want to hear the truth so she ran."

"Ran? Where did she go?"

"Into the spider's web. She will try to escape, but she will not succeed." She took another swig from the flask.

"Riddles and more riddles," Cornelius said. "She won't tell us anything."

"If any harm befalls her, I swear I will hold you accountable," Lord Urbane said, pointing his finger at the old woman.

"To say she will face danger on her path would be a harsh understatement. Responsibility and danger go hand in hand; they are always connected. She is caught in the web along with the rest of us. There is nowhere to run. It has begun."

"Lock her up," Cornelius said to the guards. "Keep her there until Lady Tamsin is found."

The woman hissed at them and clutched the flask to her chest as they led her away. "You cannot shield her from this Eleazar!" her shouts echoed down the hall.

"This isn't the first time she's been brought in," Cornelius said. "She's a drunken, superstitious fool."

"She may be, but I know her and she believes what she says. If she thinks Tamsin is in danger then we need to find her. *Now.*"

Cornelius nodded in agreement. "My men are already scouring the east side. The easterlies were out in droves last night so someone was sure to see her."

Lord Urbane rubbed a hand over his face. Two days. He had barely been back two days and things were already starting to unravel. He didn't like second guessing his decisions, but what he hated even more was admitting that Lavinia may have been right, that coming here had been a mistake.

He noticed Lord Regoran watching him, a question in his gaze.

"What is it?" Lord Urbane asked sharply.

"I wasn't aware you knew the seer."

"I had the misfortune of meeting her during my first visit here."

"What did she tell you?"

Lord Urbane scowled. Seeing the old woman again had brought back a whole slew of memories, none of which he wanted to relive or discuss. He turned to Cornelius. "Just find her."

Lord Urbane went back to his study. He tried to focus on some of the papers in front of him, but it was no use. He could not concentrate on anything. He wrote a letter and sent a courier back to his wife, letting her know what was going on and reassuring her that they would find Tamsin soon. The more he thought about it the more he was certain that someone else was involved. Tamsin was a smart girl; if she had gotten lost after she visited the seer, she would have found help, but maybe she had found the wrong person. So that meant someone had her and was keeping her from getting back. But it was strange because they had received no ransom note of any kind and he refused to believe she was dead. She was worth more alive to someone who had the audacity to kidnap a Lord's daughter.

He unrolled a map of the city across his desk. So far they had searched the compound, the Armillary, and three of the five sections on the east side of the city. One of the last ones was the sector bordering the southern gate. It looked to be made up mostly of dwellings, a blacksmith shop, and a stable. From what he had heard, the solstice celebration had taken place on the opposite side of the city. He pressed his finger on the remaining one. It was the fishing district next to the river. If Tamsin had tried to come home, she would've had to come through this district to get to the Armillary. But he just had the horrible feeling that she would be found in neither of those places. He slid his finger over the parchment to the double lines representing the Elglas that ran through the city, under the Armillary and disappeared off the bottom of the page.

There was a knock on the door and Cornelius entered. "The southern district came up empty, but my men are searching the last one now."

"What about the west side? Has anybody searched this side of the river?"

"We've informed all the guards at the compounds to notify us immediately if they hear or see anything." Cornelius stood tall, both hands clasped behind his back. He was the spitting image of his uncle, only twenty years younger. His hair was sandy blonde, casually brushed to the side, and his beard freshly shaved. His nose was long and pointed, but his light blue eyes were wide and sharp as whips.

Lord Urbane shook his head, turning his attention back to the map. "They won't find anything."

Cornelius frowned. "You shouldn't give up. I'll have my men search again."

"I'm not giving up!" Lord Urbane snapped. "I'm saying they won't find her because she's not in the city anymore."

Cornelius's eyes narrowed as he tried to follow Lord Urbane's words. "What do you mean?" he asked.

Lord Urbane motioned for him to look at the map. "Is the portcullis still in place where the walls meet at the river?"

"Of course, but it remains open, otherwise dead fish overwhelm the banks this time of year—you think Tamsin got out through the river?"

Lord Urbane dragged his finger to where the map ended just outside the wall. "She's not in the city anymore Cornelius, I can feel it."

Cornelius stared at the map, stunned. He called for one of the guards and ordered him to alert the Commander that they should expand their search outside the city, to focus around the riverbanks, and to get him another map, one that showed the desert past the southern wall. When it was brought, he laid it on top of the first, holding down the edges. There was nothing much to it; the Elglas snaked back and forth across the page, cutting the map in half. On either side lay desert.

Footsteps could be heard coming down the hall and they looked up to see the Commander and a few guards walk in.

"What is it?" Cornelius asked.

Lord Urbane stood up straighter. There could only be one reason why they weren't searching…

"We've encountered a problem," the Commander said. He was perhaps in his sixties with close-cropped white hair. Lord Urbane remembered him from before, though he could not recall his name.

"What kind of problem?" Lord Urbane asked, coming around from behind the desk.

"There's a sandstorm coming, my Lord," he said. "By the time my men start searching outside the walls the storm will already be upon us."

"But my daughter is out there!" Lord Urbane bellowed. "I'll be damned if I let a little storm delay us any longer!"

Cornelius put a hand on his shoulder, but he shrugged him off, beyond irate.

"How bad, Commander?" Cornelius asked.

He didn't reply, but with the grim look on his face he didn't have to.

"Sound the horns," Cornelius said to the guards, "and make sure the compounds are sealed. We'll wait out the storm here."

"I won't leave Tamsin out there!" Lord Urbane cried. "We need to—."

"What we *need* to do is stay put and wait until the storm passes," Cornelius barked. "Have you ever been in a true sandstorm Lord Urbane? It's darker than night, you can't see anything and you can't breathe because the wind sucks the air right out of your lungs. The sand feels like it's ripping you to shreds. You're more likely to wander into the river and drown if you try to find your way through it than actually make it out. If we send men out there now there's a very good chance we won't see them again."

On a rational level, Lord Urbane understood. He had never experienced a storm of this magnitude before, but his parental instincts were clouding his judgment and all Cornelius's speech had done was reaffirm those instincts.

The Commander gave him a sympathetic look. "We don't know for sure if she's out there my Lord," he said, "but if she is, her best chance would be here." He pointed to a spot on the map that depicted a ridge just south of the city. "These cliffs aren't too far away and they're filled with caves. If she was anywhere nearby, that's where she would've gone. And it is possible to survive a sandstorm," he added. "Captain Saveen is living proof of that."

Cornelius shot him a look.

"However," the Commander continued, nodding respectively to Cornelius, "I must agree with him. This one is going to be trying for all of us and it's not worth risking more lives on a hunch. I'm sorry my Lord."

Lord Urbane was nearly shaking in anger at the absurdity of it all, but they were right. There was nothing more they could do right now. They were as helpless as lambs being led to a slaughter. "As soon as the storm passes I want a contingent out to those cliffs," he said, his voice gruff with emotion.

The Commander gave him a curt nod and he and his men left without another delay to make the final preparations before the storm reached them.

Lord Urbane sank into a chair, leaned back with his face in his hands, and thought if gods really did exist, then they had a cruel sense of humor, as if they had waited for him to return to this place before they sought retribution for his sins of the past. Tamsin was out there, he could feel it, but even if she somehow survived the storm she could still suffer from asphyxiation, blindness, or worse. She didn't deserve this. *Just hang on*, he thought, foolishly hoping that she would hear.

Outside the stone halls and glass dome, beyond the high wall and watchtowers, the storm cloud stalked across the desert like a rabid beast, foam spewing from its mouth, its eyes fixed on the city, unwavering in its intent.

CHAPTER SEVEN

He could do nothing to ease her fear, nor did he know how much longer he could endure the battering winds. Every breath was a battle, every muscle begged to be released from the strain. If he lost focus for even a moment the wind found a foothold and threatened to send them reeling with the wind. Twice, he almost lost his balance and he was forced to dig deeper into the sand even though he could already feel it creeping up his legs. Being on top of the dune saved them both from being buried under the sand, but if it kept up for much longer then it wouldn't matter. His body was slowly betraying him, though he refused to let go. The girl still held onto him as tightly as she had hours ago when the storm began and as long as she wasn't giving up neither was he.

And then the wind current changed. Like two mice under the shadow of a bird of prey swooping down to crush them, they crouched down together, the moment they had been desperately fighting to hold off finally and inescapably upon them, but the killing blow never came. Instead of being uprooted by its talons, the shadow suddenly lifted and as quickly as the storm had caught them it was gone.

Haven scarcely dared to open his eyes, but when he did the darkness was gone and the sun had returned to the sky. The storm continued to roll on its path, but they were no longer in it. He stretched his stiff muscles and took the cloak off the girl, shaking off the loose sand. She blinked a few times and looked around them with small, wide set eyes, like she didn't quite believe that it was over. Flakes of sand fell of her eyelashes, revealing the glimmering blue beneath them. She pulled his sleeve down from her face and took a deep breath and then erupted into a fit of coughs. He reached out to help, but she waved him away and when she was finished she looked up at him with the biggest smile he had ever seen. Her face, hair, and clothes were all the same shade of dusty brown, but her smile glowed like the moon. There were tear streaks through the layers of dust on her cheeks, but there was no more fear in her eyes. He felt a strange sense of pride over her for being so brave, for not giving up.

It took them a few minutes to dig themselves out; the sand had completely covered their legs and had started to climb up his back and when they were finally free it took them both a few tries before they were able to stand up completely. There was no time to waste though, the sun would be setting soon and the temperature would be dropping and they were without food and shelter until they got back to camp. He was sure he would be fine, but the girl had been through a trifecta of survival situations within a very short period of time. He was amazed that she was still able to walk, something which he himself was struggling with. Protecting them from the storm had tested his strength like nothing ever had before and his body was protesting the continued movement. His whole body shook uncontrollably, frustratingly, and he was forced back to the ground when his legs could not support him any longer.

The girl could have run and left him there to pursue her own path as she had originally intended that morning and he wouldn't have been able to stop her. The cliffs were within sight and she would be able to find her way back to the city if that was her destination. But she didn't. Instead, she knelt down next to him, concern and understanding flickering across her face.

He hated to show weakness in front of anyone, but he had no other choice until he regained some of his strength. And she looked exhausted as well. He took out his water skin; there was still half left and he gave it to her. She sighed after she had taken a few slow swallows and her eyes cleared a little, which was a good sign, but he knew it would not be enough.

"I'm Tamsin," the girl said. "What's your name?"

Haven furrowed his brow, trying to remember the foreign words his father had taught him many years ago. It was like encountering a familiar scent from the past and trying to recall what it was. He could only shake his head.

She spoke slowly, seeming to understand his lack of understanding. "My name is Tamsin," she said, tapping her chest with her hand.

He understood now. "Haven," he said, resting his hand on his own.

The corners of her mouth turned up in a fleeting smile. "Thank you for finding me."

He nodded, trying not to think of what would have befallen her had he listened to the others.

"Are you from Empyria?" she asked. "Were you sent to find me?"

"Empeeriia?" he repeated, the simple word sticking to his tongue. He realized he could understand her better than he could speak it himself. He drew a circle in the sand, then pointed to the north. "Viillage...iin...rock?" She nodded. "No," he said.

Her eyes narrowed in thought. "That was your camp back there, wasn't it? By the cliff?"

He pondered her words for a moment then nodded.

"You were on the cliff last night. You were one of the ones I saw." She studied him now, as if it were the first time she was really seeing him. "Who are you?"

I am a killer. The thought escaped before he could stop it, but he did not say it out loud. Usually he had better control than that. The stress his body was under must be affecting him more than he realized. As if on cue, his hands started to shake, though he wondered briefly if it was exhaustion or his errant thought that made him tremble. He clenched them into fists, but she had noticed.

She smiled empathetically at him, any suspicious curiosity gone, and handed the water skin back. "Here, you need some too."

Her kindness moved him. A Kazsera would never drink from the same skin as a Watcher. He had to remind himself that she was from the northern city; that she was not a Kazsera, though if he were to judge by her clothing alone, which was exquisitely detailed despite being torn and dusty from the elements, he would say she could be the equivalent of a Kazsera where she was from. Maybe she could help them. Maybe their answer had fallen right into their laps. He took the water skin and took a sip. "We be Ma'diin," he said, answering her previous question.

She tried repeating the word. "And where do the…Ma*deen* come from?"

He took another drink, allowing himself time to find the words. Each time she spoke more started to come back, but it was like pulling one's feet out of the mud. "Down of river. Water land."

Her mouth puckered in what might have been amusement. "It must be far from here."

He nodded.

She bit her lip before asking her next question. "What are you doing here? I mean, why did you come?"

"We go to village iin rock—Empeeria," he said, trying out her word for the city again.

There was that flickering smile again, probably at his pronunciation, but he didn't mind. He tried to choose his words carefully. "We...speak with Kazsera."

"Who is Kazsera?" she asked.

"Kazsera be most important," he said. "Kazsera be first spear of many spears."

She pressed her lips together and tilted her head slightly to the side, working out what he said. "I think you mean the lords...? I'm sure they would speak with you in exchange for bringing me back safely."

He could see her watching his reaction on the last word. Though he had come back for her despite the storm, she was now wondering what he intended for her now. "Then we go," he said.

She nodded and it was agreed. They both got to their feet and started out again. He allowed her to cling to his shirt to keep from swaying and she allowed him to lean on her, though only a little for she was much smaller than he. The terrain became much firmer by the time they reached the face of the cliffs, though they had come up a little farther along than where their camp was. They were both shaking their heads trying to stay awake when Haven saw several dark figures running alongside the cliff face towards them. He sank to the ground, relief flooding him, and Tamsin did the same, too weary to support him. The poor girl could barely keep her eyes open. She tugged on his arm though. "Come on, Haven. It's only a little further..." But she made no move to get back up. She leaned against him and closed her eyes.

"Help is coming," he said in Ma'diinese.

CHAPTER EIGHT

Ysallah was the first to spot them and she ran out to meet them, Bregan and Karnak following close behind. "Haven, what happened?" she cried.

"We got trapped in the storm," Haven replied. Bregan supported him with one arm under his shoulders as they lumbered back into camp. Karnak carried Tamsin's sleeping form over to the fire and laid her down. "Wake her up. She needs food and water," Haven told them.

"You're exhausted," Ysallah said, though Haven could see she was not pleased with him.

"Where are the others?" he asked as Bregan helped him to sit. Oman, Kellan and Samih were nowhere in sight.

A cloud passed over her eyes. "I don't know. When you went to look for the girl, we waited, but we saw the storm approaching and you still hadn't returned so they went to look for you."

He cursed under his breath. He didn't just have Tamsin to worry about, but the other three as well. "They should not have left you," he said, rising to his feet.

"You should not have left," she bristled. "You're the only one who can speak to the northerners Haven. If we lost you—."

"You would've found another way," he said. He and Tamsin had barely survived the storm. If his brothers had been caught in it as well...

"What are you doing?" she asked, suddenly realizing he was on his feet again.

He took a deep breath. Here he was cursing his brothers for acting foolishly and yet he had done the same thing and was contemplating doing it again. No doubt it was wiser to stay here and wait for their possible return, but it was his fault they were out there. He could not abandon them.

Ysallah seemed to read his mind and put a firm hand on his shoulder. "You're not going after them Haven." The pressure on his shoulder was enough to make him sway and Ysallah put her other hand on his arm so he didn't fall. "See? You're in no shape to go anywhere."

Ysallah's countenance softened a little. "Rest Haven. We won't abandon them, but you need to rest first."

Haven wanted to protest, but his body could not fight any more. He sat back down and leaned against the cliff face. Karnak brought him a bowl of something warm to eat and he managed to eat a little, but the last thing he remembered was Ysallah taking the bowl from him just before it slipped from his hands as he dozed off.

Dusk had come and gone when he awoke again and the fire burned brightly in the dark, forming an orange glow against the rock wall. Tamsin was sleeping under one of the buurdas and Ysallah sat across from her, watching her with an unreadable expression. Bregan and Karnak were sitting nearby, talking quietly together.

Ysallah turned to look at him as Haven stirred and then back to Tamsin. "I bet her eyes are blue," she murmured.

Haven rubbed his hand over his face, trying to rid himself of the lingering drowsiness. "What?"

"She reminds me of someone I knew," Ysallah said. "Her eyes were blue."

"Have the others returned?" Haven asked her, unsure where Ysallah was going with this and concerned that she was delaying a difficult conversation.

"Oman is down by the river…with Kellan and Samih."

Haven rose to his feet, wincing at his stiff muscles with a twitch of his lip. "They're back? When? Are they alright?"

"They're fine. They returned about half an hour ago. They're washing the sand off their clothes, I think. Something you might consider," she said, raising an eyebrow at his appearance. But she was smiling.

Haven felt like smiling too, but Karnak started shouting suddenly. They both turned to look and saw at least a dozen lights charging at them down the side of the ridge with more emerging from some tunnel a little ways away. With his night sight, Haven could see men, riding some kind of four-legged animals and at the rate they were charging they had spotted them. Some were holding sticks with fire blazing from the ends and others held weapons similar to their own, shiny and pointed. Bregan and Karnak started frantically trying to gather their supplies and weapons, but Haven grabbed Bregan, startling him.

"Leave them!" Haven bellowed. "Get the Kazsera to safety. Take her to the caves! Karnak, go alert the others!"

"Haven?" Tamsin had woken up and was staring out at the fast-approaching hoard.

He rushed over to her. "Come! Hurry!" There was no time to translate.

But she planted her feet. "I think those are my people Haven! They've come for me!"

He understood the look of hope in her eyes more than her actual words, but he knew an attack when he saw one and was not about to let her take that chance. Just then something slammed into him, sending them both crashing into the buurda she had been sleeping under. He regained his feet and withdrew his blades just as the man whipped his beast around to make another pass at him. He had reached them quicker than the others, but this time Haven was ready for him as he charged again, his weapon a large, round shield. Haven launched himself at the man and used his weight to drag him to the ground.

"Haven, no!" Tamsin screamed, just as he was about to deliver the killing strike.

He snarled, flipped his blade around and knocked the man unconscious with the handle. He should have slit his throat for attacking them, but he didn't have time to think about it. Two more of the men had caught up to them and were racing after Ysallah and Bregan. Haven sprinted after them and yelled out a warning. Ysallah stumbled and fell onto the ground just as one of the men swung his flaming stick in the place she had been. Bregan was fighting off the other with his knives, but the animal kept dancing just beyond his reach. Haven immediately felt the flames' presence and extinguished them with just the thought, giving him the advantage of complete darkness. The first one tried to swing his now flameless stick at him, but Haven grabbed hold of it and used it to unbalance the man and yank him down. This one was a brute though, covered in a second metal skin and he used his weight to propel himself and the two of them wrestled back and forth on the ground, each trying to gain the upper hand. Finally, Haven was able to bring his knee up and when his back was on the ground he used his foot to shove the man backwards. He jumped up and, using the man's own momentum, slammed him against the rock wall. The man slumped to the ground in a clanging heap.

Haven helped bring the second man down so Bregan was able to take Ysallah and run into the nearest tunnel. He looked back and saw the other men had caught up and slowed their charge and now surrounded Tamsin. She spoke frantically to the men, but he could not understand what she was saying and then one of them grabbed her and lifted her in front of him onto the beast. He started barking orders and then the group split, some going back the way they had come and others staying behind.

He heard a *psshh* and saw Bregan waving him over from the tunnel they had ducked into.

He shook his head decisively and pointed back in the tunnel, giving his own silent orders to the sha'diin. Karnak had successfully gotten away and the other Watchers would be here very soon, but Haven could not wait that long. He snuck along the wall, intent on wreaking havoc among the ones that stayed behind. They were cautiously surveying the scene, their flameless sticks lying useless in the sand, and helping their injured comrades back onto their animals. Bregan had actually managed to rough up the second man rather well, Haven noticed proudly. He crept along the wall in the darkness; the closest one was only an arm's length away, oblivious to the impending danger. One of the animals snorted and stamped nervously at the ground with a long, hoofed foot, its eyes staring directly at Haven. He tightened his grip on his blade, ready to strike. Fighting men was not like fighting the beasts back home, but he would make short work of them nonetheless. He raised his blade an inch and then an idea struck him. He only paused a moment and he knew what he was going to do. He waited and let the men climb atop their beasts. They moved quickly back along the ridge wall, but not as quickly as the others for they were now without their flaming sticks to guide them. Haven sheathed his blades and silently followed them. Their animals were aware of him; they tossed their heads and flicked their tails in agitation, but the men were as blind as headless snakes without their lights. He kept enough distance between them so the animals would not give him away, but he kept a steady pace, relying mostly on the adrenaline pumping through his veins and when they reached the village of rock it was almost too easy to slip in behind them unnoticed.

The city had weathered the storm, but the streets were a wasteland. Crates and debris littered the alleys, flags hung to their poles by shreds, and people moved about in slow motion, just starting to emerge from their dwellings to survey the damage. It was hard to believe that just the night before people had been celebrating, laughing, and dancing in these very streets. Nature had flipped a coin it seemed and instead of life in the form of rain, she had bestowed upon them a very different kind of storm, as if to remind them that they weren't impenetrable behind their high walls. Though despite her fury, the city remained intact.

Tamsin should have felt relief when they passed through the gates and into the protective confines of the city walls, but she had to clench her fists around the horse's mane to keep them from shaking. Things felt reversed somehow; she should've felt safe with the Empyrians, but they seemed more like abductors than her rescuers. The way it all happened, so quick and violent, left her more anxious than ever. She was worried, not for herself because she knew her father wouldn't let anything severe happen to her if she was to be punished for leaving the city, but for Haven and his companions. She doubted if she would ever see him again and after everything he had done to protect her he deserved more than to be attacked like a criminal.

Instead of going to the compound, they passed through a smaller version of the outer gate and dismounted in a small courtyard, just big enough to contain all the horses comfortably. The walls that contained the courtyard were not as tall as the ones that encircled the city, but there were stairs on each side that led up to the parapets that crossed over the gate and disappeared into a tunnel behind the opposite wall that led into the Armillary itself. Tamsin saw someone come running out of the tunnel and down the stairs as one of the lieutenants helped her off the horse.

"Tell Captain Saveen that we have the girl," the lieutenant said to the man, who took off back the way he had just come.

"Aren't you going to tell him about the others that were out there?" one of the guards asked him as they led Tamsin up the stairs. She stumbled on the first step, barely able to put one foot in front of the other without trembling.

The lieutenant deftly scooped her up in his arms, his metal armor not nearly as comfortable as Haven's arms had been, and continued up the stairs and over the walkway. "Of course," he said, "but that's something you should tell in person, not through a messenger." They disappeared into the tunnel and it was completely dark, save for the moonlight that shone through the archways on either side. "Why aren't these torches lit?" the lieutenant asked as they passed several unlit torches anchored to the walls.

"They must have forgotten to relight them after the storm went through," the guard said.

"No matter," the lieutenant replied. The tunnel was short enough and they passed into a perpendicular hallway that Tamsin had seen from a distance that encircled the Armillary. The outer edge was rimmed with tall arches, leaving the view of the river almost unobstructed while the inner wall was decorated with columns and wide double doors every dozen feet. Soldiers opened one of these doors and the messenger from before emerged and the lieutenant inquired as to Captain Saveen's whereabouts.

"He is getting Lord Urbane," the messenger said, ushering them into the room.

Her father was here! Tamsin thought, a lump forming in her throat. Someone she knew, someone she loved more than anything in the world. He was on his way which meant her ordeal was over. It made the dryness in her throat and the throbbing in her limbs not as merciless, though she still couldn't see straight and felt as if someone had used her as a human torch.

Then she felt the lieutenant's body stiffen and heard his sharp intake of breath.

And then she heard that voice, that exotic smoothness of a spring rain now growling like a tiger. "Let her *go.*"

Haven.

No one moved for a long moment and then Tamsin slowly slid out of the lieutenant's arms and turned around to see Haven standing behind him with a long dagger pressed against his neck.

Taken by surprise, the Empyrians were slow to react. Some reached for their weapons, but none dared to take any steps forward, lest they be responsible for their superior's death.

"Tamsin good?" Haven asked her.

"Yes, Haven, I'm alright," though she kept a tight grip on the lieutenant's arm to keep upright. How had he gotten here and past the guards? But more importantly, why? He didn't owe her anything, especially after he had saved her life. Was he here for revenge then, for being attacked at the cliffs? "They're just trying to protect me. They won't hurt us." But the threatening stances of the Empyrian guards made her doubt that. And she could see that Haven wasn't buying it either, though she didn't know how he expected to get out of this one.

Haven's blade remained where it was.

"You're outnumbered," one of the guards said. "You'll never get out of here alive."

Panic rose in her throat. She didn't want to see anybody die here. She gently placed her hand on Haven's arm. "Please don't do this, Haven." After everything he had done for her she didn't want him to throw it all away.

"I ask Tamsin one thing," he said. "Then I go."

"Anything," she said.

"Bring Kazsera to cliffs. Tomorrow," Haven said.

"Step away from him, my lady," the guard said.

Haven's jaw clenched. "If come tomorrow," he said loud enough for the guards to hear, "and attack again, I kill."

Tamsin had been shocked when the fighting broke out at the cliffs and she knew that she had only just stopped Haven from killing that man. His threat was not empty.

One of the guards lunged forward and the next moment the room was thrown into darkness. The fire from the torches vanished as quickly as if they were candles on a cake. There were startled shouts and the clang of metal, and Tamsin's hand tightened reflexively on Haven's arm. There was shadowed movement all around her and then suddenly she was moving too. She gasped as someone's arm wrapped around her waist and lifted her off the ground. She was set down behind a pillar, out of the melee, and then he was gone. She pulled her knees to her chest and covered her ears, trying to drown out the sound of clashing swords and painful cries.

And as quickly as it had started it was over. With a spark, the flames of the torches and candles were alight once again, illuminating the aftermath of the chaos, which had lasted only seconds. Most of the soldiers were on the floor, dazed and disoriented, while a few others were turning in circles, waving their swords at the empty air. Tamsin exhaled shakily.

Haven was gone.

The sound of voices and boots clacking against polished floor could be heard coming and a moment later more soldiers appeared around the curve.

"What happened here?" A uniformed young man strode to the center and the soldiers who weren't lying on the floor yet saluted him.

"There was a man, Captain Saveen," the lieutenant who had carried her said, climbing slowly back to his feet.

"A man? I thought you found the girl?"

"We did, sir. They had her at the cliffs. One of them must have followed us here."

"They? Who?"

The poor lieutenant stumbled on his words and he looked helplessly at his fellows, but nobody seemed to know what had just occurred.

Then another figure spoke up, "Where is my daughter?"

Tamsin choked back a sob as her father stepped into view.

They turned to look at the sound, but she couldn't see their expressions as tears blurred her vision. She tried to stand and used the pillar for support, but any strength she had left seemed to forsake her. Hands were around her in an instant, pulling her up and into a tight embrace. She hugged her father as if he was her lifeline and he let her stay like that, not caring that the others were watching.

"She was with them, my lord, at the cliffs" the lieutenant came over.

Lord Urbane slowly pried her to arm's length. "Is this true?"

She wiped the unwelcome tears out of her eyes and nodded.

"One of them followed us back and threatened to kill us," another soldier said.

"Did anyone see where he went?" Captain Saveen asked.

"No, sir. The lights—everything went dark. We couldn't see anything."

"Find him. I want the wall patrol doubled and nobody goes in or out of here without my say so."

Her father was eyeing her appearance carefully, not just her torn, sand-caked clothing or her dirt-smeared face, but her reaction to all of this. "Did they hurt you?" he asked.

She tried to muster the composure that her class dictated, to try and regain some control of what was going on, but she found herself drained of all poise or care, so she merely shook her head. She glanced at her feet, painfully aware that her current state of dishevelment had been caused by her own irresponsible behavior. "They didn't hurt me. He—Haven helped me." She tried to explain what he had done for her, but her frayed mind couldn't seem to form any coherent thoughts and the words fell from her lips in tangled knots. And it didn't help that she couldn't stand on her own without shaking. She clenched her fists in frustration.

"Tamsin, honey, it's alright. You're safe now. We won't let anything happen to you." He cradled her head against his chest. "Cornelius, can you spare a few men?"

"I don't want anyone leaving until I know it is secure," the young captain replied.

"He won't have gone far," her father said. "What did he look like Tamsin?"

"I never saw his face. It was always covered. Please don't hurt him," she pleaded. "He saved my life. All he wants to do is talk."

"He said something about a meeting at the cliffs," the lieutenant said, "but I couldn't understand with who. His dialect is not from around here."

"He told me he was from the water lands," Tamsin said.

Her father suddenly grew very still and the look in his eyes confused her. It was almost like he was afraid. "Who is he meeting with?" he asked her.

"He wants to meet with the lords. The Kazseera I think he called them. Tomorrow." His expression worried her. All the color had drained from his face. "Fathri, do you know these people?"

The others looked at him expectantly, but he did not answer. Instead, he said, "Is Lord Regoran still here?"

"Yes," Cornelius replied.

"Good. Gather the others as well. We need to talk, immediately. Is there a healer in the Armillary?"

Cornelius looked at her and then nodded. "Come with me." He then led them down the open hallway a little ways and then through a set of doors to a small chamber.

"Tell your men to stay close…and to keep away from the shadows," her father said, helping Tamsin into a chair near the round fireplace in the center of the room.

"What do you *know*?" Cornelius asked.

"I need to tend to my daughter. I will be with you in a moment." He started throwing logs into the empty pit.

Cornelius stiffened, said he would get the healer, and left the room, closing the door behind him.

Tamsin watched her father anxiously as he grabbed a torch from the wall, lit the wood, and stoked it, until it was much larger than was necessary for the size of the room. The smoke wafted up into the dark shaft high up in the ceiling. He went to a small table and poured her a glass of water, which she drank greedily, though every swallow was painful. He offered her a piece of bread as well, but she waved it away, feeling her stomach turn at the thought of it.

"You can tell me the truth Tamsin," he said after she had finished. "You're safe here. Did they hurt you?"

"I told you: he saved me, more than once. This is all my fault, not his. He was trying to get me back, but we got caught in the storm. He could've left me, but he didn't. He stayed and I owe him my life. Please don't let them hurt him."

The healer came in then, an older woman dressed in heavy, cream-colored robes with a black sash tied around her waist and from it hung several small pouches and looping strings of light-catching beads. She crouched down next to Tamsin and quickly examined her. "Heat exhaustion," she said, her voice sounding as leathery as her hands felt when she touched Tamsin's forehead. She glanced at the fire. "That won't be necessary."

"Believe me, it is," Lord Urbane said. "I'll be back as soon as I can."

"You're leaving?" Tamsin asked.

He smiled at her, like a father would comforting a small child, but the lines in his forehead betrayed his concern. "Don't be afraid. Stay by the fire and don't leave until the guards come to take you home." He kissed her forehead, made a comment to the guards to keep the fire lit, and left before she could say another word.

Haven looked down at the gathering of men from where he sat, perched on a ledge that extended around the room high up near the ceiling. Stone pillars protruded from the walls and ran vertical up the length of the walls, giving the illusion of a giant birdcage, and converged around the smoke hole in the ceiling where Haven had climbed into the room. The fire they had constructed in a lowered ring in the floor allowed for ample shadows among the high pillars, hiding Haven easily enough from any eyes that might wander up.

The man that had embraced Tamsin earlier (a member of her tribe Haven guessed) walked into the room and instantly the others there began barraging him with questions. He was a robust man and carried the weight of authority on his shoulders, though his shoulder length hair had the grey color of the elders starting to emerge. He waved his hands downwards and the others gradually took their seats around the fire, still grumbling to themselves.

A younger man, the one Haven had heard called Captain Saveen, remained standing. "Will you tell us now what you know?" he asked.

Tamsin's tribesman nodded. "I trust you have brought them up to speed on what's been going on?"

"There's been an intruder?" another man spoke up. He wore heavy purple robes and leaned forward on a golden cane embedded with deep green jewels that glittered in the firelight. "And there are more outside the wall?"

"They are not from Empyria or the Cities," Captain Saveen said.

"Who are they?" another asked.

"They claim to be from the south, from the marshlands," Tamsin's tribesman said. "I am certain it is the Ma'diin."

A murmur spread around the room as hushed exclamations of surprise and confusion were voiced.

"Where is the intruder?" the purple-robed man inquired and all eyes turned to Captain Saveen.

"Those who aren't on damage control from the storm or guarding the wall are searching for him now," he replied.

Haven couldn't help the smile that spread across his lips.

"You're sure that it's the Ma'diin, Eleazar?" another asked. He wore a stiff, beige tunic and furnished a thick beard. "They haven't been seen or heard from since…"

"Since I was here last," Tamsin's tribesman said. "I am certain it is them. If your uncle was still alive, Captain, he would say the same."

Captain Saveen folded his arms across his chest, his expression unreadable. "My uncle spoke little about the Ma'diin. What he did say was not very encouraging. A primitive culture, full of gods-fearing savages and assassins in the dark."

"Assassins?" the bearded one said in concern. "Is that why they are here?"

"My daughter and Lieutenant Riggs have said they want to meet with us. Tomorrow," Tamsin's tribesman said.

Haven focused on the man a little more closely now. So this man was not just Tamsin's tribesman, but her father, and from his role of importance within the group, he assumed one of the lords she spoke of. One of the kazserii. And from the sound of it he seemed to know about the Ma'diin from a previous encounter.

"A group of assassins want to talk to us?" another said incredulously. He had a large waist that was almost too large for the chair he was sitting in and big, unruly eyebrows. "What could they possibly want to talk about?"

"It's a trap," the man in the purple robe said. "They'll kill us as soon as they are close enough. The one almost killed your men, Cornelius, and then he escaped before anyone knew what had happened."

Captain Saveen bristled.

Tamsin's father sighed. "They're not assassins, they're more like hunters. They won't kill anyone unless their lives are at stake."

"How do you know?" the bearded one asked.

"Because if they wanted to kill us, then we'd be dead already."

Silence. Haven agreed with his assessment.

"But you found Tamsin," the bearded one again. He seemed genuinely concerned. "And she is safe?"

Tamsin's father nodded.

"Lieutenant Riggs said they had taken her hostage," Captain Saveen said.

"Tamsin assured me that this was not the case," her father said.

"How did she end up with them in the first place?" the purple-robed one asked. "And how did she get outside the wall?"

Haven saw Tamsin's father and the bearded one exchange glances. "That is not important right now," her father said.

"You should have her sent for. See if she can give us any more information."

"It's out of the question, Lord Wohlrick," her father said. "I don't want her involved in this any more than she already has been."

"But she could have vital information," the purple-robed one, Wohlrick, argued.

"I'm sure my men will find him before its necessary to question her," Captain Saveen said.

Haven highly doubted that.

"And what about the others still at the cliffs? Are your men searching for them?" the bushy-eyebrowed one asked.

"Those cliffs are filled with caves and tunnels," another spoke up. Until now he had been silent and Haven couldn't clearly see him because his back was turned to him. All he could see was the top of his cloud-white hair, closely cropped to his head. "If our men go searching for them out there, in the dark, they could be walking into an ambush. Better to wait until morning."

"So what do we do?" Wohlrick asked.

Several of them started arguing and he couldn't make out what they were saying. The white-haired one leaned over to Tamsin's father and whispered something into his ear. Tamsin's father shook his head.

Captain Saveen withdrew something from inside his shirt and poured it over the fire. The flames leapt up suddenly, snapping angrily at the air.

Haven flattened himself against the wall. He hadn't dimmed the fire earlier because Tamsin's father seemed to know something about their abilities with fire and he didn't want to give his presence away.

The others all stopped their arguing at once, distracted by the burst of the flames, and they all looked at Captain Saveen with different levels of annoyance.

"To prevent any other kidnappings and threats, true or otherwise," he said, "the only choice we have is to meet with them tomorrow."

"Captain Saveen is right," the white-haired man said. "We can find out what they want tomorrow, but until then we should use our time in a more productive fashion."

"How are we supposed to do that when we don't know why they're here?" the bushy-eyebrowed one asked.

There was a murmur of agreement around the room.

"Maybe we do." Tamsin's father stared at the fire, but his hand was fiddling with something in his pocket. "Your Uncle wrote to the Lords Council several months ago. He was building something, something that would 'change Empyria forever,' I believe he put it."

"What was he building?" the bushy-eyebrowed one asked.

"A dam," the bearded one said, covering his mouth loosely with his hands as if he had just now figured it out.

Haven was not familiar with this word, but he still listened closely.

"You knew?" Tamsin's father asked.

"I found papers in his study with plans and drawing," the bearded one said, "but I had no idea he actually intended to go through with it."

"What were you doing in his study, Lord Regoran?" Captain Saveen questioned him.

The bearded one, Regoran, narrowed his eyes, but Wohlrick dismissed it with a wave. "Never mind that. Obviously he could not be trusted. Why would he do this without consulting us?" Wohlrick asked.

"Why is not important right now," Tamsin's father said, "but the fact is that if the Ma'diin are here, then it means that it has been built, or at least has already been started. Why do you think I came back here?"

"You were going to negotiate with them," Captain Saveen said, realization dawning on him.

"That was my intention, yes. If we reached out first, then maybe we could have avoided this surprise visit."

They could only be talking about the wall that Haven's people had found in the river, he decided, keeping a mental tally of which ones knew about it and which did not. Tamsin's father and the bearded one seemed to be the only ones in the know, but only by association of Captain Saveen's kin, though Haven had no idea who this man was or why he wasn't with them now.

"Your uncle had been petitioning the Cities for years for more men and supplies," Tamsin's father said, "under the guise of using it for Empyrian construction. After his letter though, I became suspicious."

"So here we are, cleaning up another one of Saveen's messes," the bushy-eyebrowed one said, dabbing his forehead with a small cloth. "If he wasn't already dead, I'd kill him myself!"

Captain Saveen looked like he was ready to jump across the fire and stick the bushy-eyebrowed one with his sword. He was the only one in the room who had a weapon besides the guards posted at the door and the white-haired man, who was concealing a small knife whose handle was protruding slightly from his right boot.

"But Eleazar said they wouldn't hurt anyone, so there's no point in getting so worked up Lord Allard," Regoran said, standing up and holding his hands out as if to prevent any violence between the bushy-eyebrowed one and Captain Saveen.

Haven admired his restraint. A threat to another tribe's man was as good as declaring war back home.

"Well now that we have an idea of why they are here, is there anything about them that we should know?" the white-haired one asked.

"Yes," Tamsin's father responded, sounding wearied. "They have their own religion, politics, social customs. It's all very intricate."

"That's right. You lived with them for a time didn't you?" Captain Saveen asked.

Haven's spine stiffened and he eyed Tamsin's father more carefully.

"How do you know about that?" Tamsin's father asked.

"My uncle may have kept some things hidden, but others he discussed quite openly, if you gave him the proper motivation of course." He waved the little bottle he had used to spark the fire. "Like how you were married to one of the Ma'diin."

Haven's eyes narrowed. His remembrance of the language was improving by the minute, but what he heard couldn't be right. *It wasn't possible…*

"That has nothing to do with this," her father snapped. "I'll tell you anything you want to know, but I will not discuss that."

The other men then started asking him all kinds of questions about the Ma'diin, about the different tribes and who was in charge, about their numbers and what kind of weapons they used, and to his credit Tamsin's father answered them well, but Haven suspected he was withholding a lot. He spoke no more about the Watchers or their abilities. Haven knew he had heard enough when he realized Tamsin's father would not speak any more about the Ma'diin woman he had been married to. He needed to get this information back to Ysallah and the others. He momentarily subdued the fire until everything beyond the circle of men below was cast in darkness and he climbed back up the smoke hole and disappeared into the night as if he had never been there at all.

Captain Cornelius Saveen glanced around the room suspiciously. There was no one else in the room besides the others and yet he felt as if he were being watched. *'When did it get so dark?'* he wondered and motioned for one of the guards to bring more wood. After the fire had been properly stoked he quietly inquired if there was any news about the intruder's whereabouts, but the guard just shook his head. He dismissed him and turned his attention back to the conversation.

"Remember gentlemen," Lord Urbane was saying, "In Ma'diin society, women are revered almost as much as the gods. If one of them decides they want to start a war with the others, then her tribe will drop everything and go to battle, no questions asked."

"It sounds so…primitive," Lord Wohlrick commented, adjusting the collar underneath his purple robes.

"It's loyalty," the Commander said. "Something every man, or woman, in power requires if they expect to keep that power."

Cornelius understood. He expected no less from those under his command.

"Which is an important thing to keep in mind," Lord Urbane replied. "If you address their Kazsera directly tomorrow, it would be wise to treat her with respect. The others will defend her honor with their lives, or yours."

"But she is a woman," Lord Allard said, folding his hands over the peak of his round belly.

"She is their commander-in-chief," Lord Urbane said firmly. "Speak to her as you would the rest of us."

Lord Regoran let out a sharp laugh. "That probably isn't a good idea," he said. "I would suggest that Lord Allard have as little interaction with them as possible, with all due respect of course." He nodded towards Lord Allard.

"I will go meet them tomorrow," Lord Urbane said, before Lord Allard could reply to Lord Regoran's jab.

"I will go too," Cornelius volunteered. He had a feeling that Lord Urbane knew a lot more than could be covered in one night and would rather be out there and at risk than waiting inside the walls to hear what transpired second-hand. The Ma'diin's existence was not commonly known even among the Empyrians and the few that did almost never spoke of them. His late uncle had been part of an expedition that encountered them over a decade ago, but he was always loathe to talk about them. His uncle had masked it well, playing it like the Ma'diin were so insignificant that it was a bore to speak of them, but after always finding an empty bottle of Arak after these conversations Cornelius suspected something different. Other than the few secrets he was able to discern he was as much in the dark as the other lords. Cornelius didn't like that. He liked being in control and knowing what was going on in his own city.

"I will join you as well," Lord Regoran said.

"Then that at least is settled," Lord Urbane said. "The rest of you should stay here in case anything should happen."

"Agreed," Lord Wohlrick said.

They talked some more until the top of the midnight hour, discussing the dam and the possible directions the negotiations could go tomorrow. Cornelius didn't go directly to his captain's quarters after they finished though. Lieutenant Riggs was waiting outside the council room for him and explained that something had arrived for his late uncle, but when Cornelius asked him what it was he couldn't answer, and he didn't know how it had gotten there or who had sent it either. No other caravans had arrived since Lord Urbane's three days ago.

So Cornelius went to his uncle's vacant compound and told Riggs to wait outside. There was a long, wooden box on his desk, of a color so dark it was nearly black. It was as cold as stone. He undid the leather ties and removed the lid. Inside was a scimitar of such a fashion as he had never seen before. Its handle was as white as bone and was etched in a way that almost resembled tree bark. The blade itself was shaped like a soft S and the design along the flat side of the blade looked like vines creeping up to the needle-thin point. It would have been a beautiful blade had it not been covered in blood.

Cornelius looked down at the gruesome thing over the bridge of his nose. The stench of death still lingered on it though the blood had already dried. The fact that nobody knew where it had come from only added to the disturbing aura around it. Its appearance and the Ma'diin showing up couldn't be a coincidence, but why would the Ma'diin send it to his uncle? They had to have known it was his uncle who gave the order to build the dam, but how? If the Ma'diin wanted to kill them they would just do it. They had proved that earlier. They wouldn't send a warning like this.

He noticed something on the inside of the lid then. Written in blood were the words:

There is nowhere to run
It has begun

Cornelius stared at it then carefully placed the lid back on the box. He slowly walked out of the study. He asked Riggs if the seer was still in her cell. Riggs confirmed it. Cornelius thought a moment. The message echoed Mora's words from earlier. Was she in league somehow with the Ma'diin?

"Keep her there until I say otherwise," Cornelius said. "And—." He almost told Riggs to toss the grisly thing in the Elglas and then he thought better of it. "Take the box to the vintage room above and have one of the servants collect my things from my quarters. I'm moving in."

Haven returned to where their camp had been and was both relieved and concerned to see the glow of a fire. He would have scolded the sha'diin for letting Ysallah out in the open again, but then he saw a dark shape coming towards him and he recognized Oman. They clapped each other on the back in greeting, both glad to see the other alive, and Oman immediately slipped an arm under Haven's when it made him stumble.

"Ysallah told us that you and the girl were caught in the storm. I knew it was a foolish thing to go after her," Oman said.

Haven was weary beyond reckoning. He had been up for two moon cycles, survived a sandstorm, and had infiltrated the northerners' village. He thought he earned a reprieve from any lectures. "It would have been worse if we hadn't."

Oman gave him a questioning look, but didn't say anything further until they had reached the others. Ysallah, Bregan, Karnak, Kellan, and Samih: they were all accounted for and for a minute there were exclamations of joy and relief as their small company was whole again. They all sat around the fire and Samih handed out warm bowls of padi. They all wanted to know what had happened at the northerners' village, but Haven wanted to hear about the others first. Kellan and Samih had been close enough to the cliffs yet to make it back when the storm hit and Oman had been lucky enough to find a small outcropping near the river to take refuge in. When they had finished recounting their stories, Ysallah could no longer hold her patience and insisted that Haven tell them what happened. He recalled what had transpired, from finding Tamsin in the desert, to following the northerners back to the village, and giving them his demands before disappearing again. He gave extra detail to the conversation he eavesdropped on among the leaders and how one of them, Tamsin's father, claimed to have been married to one of their own. This seemed to baffle them, though Ysallah's expression changed just enough for Haven to think that she knew something. Haven had only been a child when the northerners visited the Ma'diin lands last and he remembered little of it except what his father had taught him of their language, but Ysallah was old enough to remember.

"Do you know something about this Ysallah?" he asked.

"The Kazsera before me was allies with the tribe who hosted the northerners," she said. "Your father's tribe Haven." Deep lines creased her forehead. "Their Kazsera left to go back north with them. It is possible what you heard was the truth."

"That is how the Kor'diin came to be?" Kellan asked, speaking of the only tribe without a Kazsera.

She nodded.

Oman, too, recalled when the northerners arrived, though he had little contact with them. "Some of the Kazsera's sha'diin went with her, but none ever returned. Something happened, the Kazsera was killed and the sha'diin were exiled from the north and the marshlands after avenging her death."

The others were curious about what had happened to them, but Oman said they were long dead now. Ysallah seemed to withdraw into herself as he spoke a little more about the northerners, lost in her thoughts, until she finally instructed everyone to get some rest. The Watchers of course ignored this, but helped set up the buurdas and Kellan volunteered to take first watch.

Though Haven was not used to sleeping at this time of night, his body needed to rest and he was just about to let his heavy lids close when Ysallah inched closer to him and quietly asked him if there was anything else she needed to know about the northerners. He said he had told them everything, his breathing already starting to slow, the dark warmth of sleep only moments away.

"Haven, do you think they will come?" she asked.

Under normal circumstances he would have stayed up as long as she needed to feel comfortable with the situation and gone over the facts as many times as she wanted to ease her nerves, but he could no longer deny his mind and body the desperate rest it required. Even as he nodded he felt the tug of unconsciousness and he slipped into a deep sleep.

CHAPTER NINE

The horses stamped and snorted impatiently, sending little clouds of dust into the air around their hooves. They sensed their masters' apprehension. His men were starting to glance at each other and the surrounding cliffs nervously, most of them had never been outside the wall before, but Cornelius Saveen would never allow himself to show such open apprehension. "Hold steady," he commanded. He dismounted his own horse and walked over to where Lord Urbane was standing slightly ahead of the rest of the group. There was no movement from the cliffs ahead of them or farther off to the southwest. The sound of the river was a steady reminder of their geographical vulnerability. The cliffs were riddled with caves; who knew how many Ma'diin could be hiding in them and if they used the riverbank to sneak up behind them then they would be cut off from the city entirely.

"I haven't led my men into an ambush, have I?" he asked Lord Urbane.

Lord Urbane shook his head. "Last night would have gone a lot differently if they had wanted to attack us," he said, rubbing his beard. "They got into the city without a problem. They wouldn't need to lead us out here to kill us."

"Then where are they?"

Lord Urbane was silent. He didn't know any more than the rest of them. So all they could do was wait.

Cornelius glanced back at his men. The horses had stopped pacing and their ears were pointed forward. Their nostrils flared in the wind. He turned back and scanned the ridgeline. "They're here," he said.

"I don't see anything," Lord Urbane said.

"We're downwind," he said. "Look at the horses."

He didn't have to because just then four figures could be seen walking across the sand towards them, appearing through the heat like a shimmering mirage. The smallest of the four was the most noticeable, clothed in deep red fabric with tiny gems that glittered when she walked. *She,* Cornelius realized. Their Kazsera, no doubt. She had a long braid laid across the front of her shoulder and he had to blink a few times to make sure he was seeing it right: her skin was…red. But as they got closer he could see patterns of color on her face and he realized it was some kind of powder or paint. Two of the others had the same dark red powder streaked across their arms and hands. They took up flank just behind the woman on either side of her. Their chests were bare save for the straps that held their weapons in place. The fourth was taller than the others and covered head to toe in black robes. The only visible part of him was his mouth; the rest of his face was hidden under some kind of veil.

Lieutenant Riggs stepped up next to Cornelius. "That's the one, in black."

"So it is a Watcher then," Lord Urbane said quietly.

"What is that?" Lieutenant Riggs asked what Cornelius was thinking.

"He is one of the assassin—hunters I spoke of last night. They are different from the other tribes. I'm surprised one of them came this far."

Cornelius didn't like that Lord Urbane was surprised, especially since he was the one that had prepared the rest of them. "The Watchers you call them. How are they different?"

"You see the two flanking the Kazsera? They are more than likely her tribesmen. But the Watchers answer to no one. They are loners. Their kind precedes even this desert. I've never seen one in the daylight before…"

"They are cowards that creep in the night like rats," Riggs said, his pride still visibly wounded from the previous night.

"Don't do or say anything," Lord Urbane warned. "Let's see if we can get through this with all of our heads still attached."

The Ma'diin stopped several yards away and both sides took the sight of the other in for a long minute. The woman raised her voice and spoke in a strange tongue and it was the Watcher who translated for her. Cornelius looked out of the corner of his eye at Riggs, who gave the slightest nod of his head, confirming the Watcher was the intruder from last night. His voice was heavily accented and rough as sandpaper, but the words were clear enough to make out. He pointed to the Kazsera and said, "Ysallah, Kazsera of Ysallah'diin. Her give many thankings to meet here."

"We are honored to be in your presence, Ysallah," Lord Urbane replied, bowing low. "I am Lord Urbane and this is Lord Regoran," he said, motioning to his right. "We are lords of Empyria."

"Two only? No more?"

Cornelius exchanged a concerned look with Lord Regoran. How could the Watcher know there were other lords? How much could he have possibly learned from his brief stint in the city?

Lord Urbane seemed unfazed. "They await our return back in the city."

The Watcher nodded and conveyed this to the Kazsera, Ysallah.

Cornelius decided to play his hunch and asked, "And where are the rest of you?" He had hoped one of them would glance or give away where the others were, if there were indeed more, but the Watcher was too smart to take the bait and the others didn't seem to understand an ounce of the common tongue. The Watcher murmured something to Ysallah, who surprised Cornelius by stepping forward and addressing him with a smile, though her eyes were as sharp as flint.

The Watcher said, "Ysallah say her will call others. They want to repay for attack last night."

The soldiers shuffled uneasily behind them. The soldier in Cornelius wanted nothing more than to accept the challenge, having been blindsided and humiliated by the ease in which the Watcher had penetrated the city and surprised them all. His men would be working double shifts for a month to make up for their incompetence last night.

"We apologize for last night," Lord Urbane said. "We were taken a bit by surprise."

"I promise you it won't happen again," Cornelius added. He threw a deliberate look at Riggs so he knew what would happen if they were caught off guard again.

Ysallah spoke again, quickly and deliberately and the Watcher translated, "Ysallah only speak with Lords now. Ysallah want to know why people make wall in river."

Lord Regoran gave Cornelius a sidelong glance. "They get right to the point, don't they?"

"We want you to know that the building of the dam was not sanctioned by any of us. One of the lords, who is now deceased, started the project before anyone else was consulted," Lord Urbane said.

"Lords not know?" the Watcher asked.

Lord Urbane dipped his head a little guiltily. "I had my suspicions, but I did not live here at the time and could do nothing to dissuade him before he began construction of it. The others had no knowledge of it."

The Watcher seemed to accept this and relayed it to the Kazsera. She nodded and the Watcher dictated as she replied, "Her forgive Lords for not knowing. Now Lords bring wall down?"

The lords looked at each other and Cornelius knew that they had no intentions of deconstructing the dam.

"The dam won't block the water off completely," Lord Regoran said. "At times when the water flow is high we can allow more to go through to prevent flooding. I can show you how—."

The Watcher held up his hand and Lord Regoran stopped. "Lords not bring wall down? Why?"

"We believe Lord Saveen's purpose was to turn this desert into usable farmland to provide for the people that live here," Lord Urbane said. "If they had more water, they would be able to grow their own food here."

The Watcher shook his head and said something indiscernible. Ysallah responded and he took a moment before he replied. "Nothing grow here. Take many water and nothing grow. Take many water and *Ma'diin* land not grow." His words were eerily controlled.

"You don't understand," Lord Regoran said. "We can make this land fertile—."

"Lords not understand!" the Watcher growled suddenly, any guise of patience gone, and the lords took an involuntary step back. Ysallah folded her arms across her chest, as if she was perfectly fine with whatever form the Watcher's anger took. At least he still had control over his actions if not his temper. He spoke quickly in their language.

Cornelius didn't need to speak the Ma'diin's language to understand that the Watcher was frustrated and even their

Kazsera's smile had vanished. Either he didn't know how to explain what he meant or he was praying to the gods to give him patience not to kill every single one of them. He glanced at Lord Urbane, who was furrowing his brow, curiously.

Ysallah hadn't taken her eyes off them and now she stared at Lord Urbane directly. "Haven, siid has nas," she said.

Lord Urbane sighed and closed his eyes as if he had been caught doing something he shouldn't have and Cornelius realized then what the Kazsera had said. *He knows*, he thought. He noticed the beads of sweat that dotted his forehead.

The Watcher focused on him now too. "Bravii nas Ma'diin," he said. It was not a question, but an accusation.

Lord Urbane touched his fingers to his forehead and then the back of his hand. "Cree doma," he replied. "Very poorly," he said, glancing at the others who all looked slightly surprised. "I'm afraid I do not speak your language as well as you do mine."

It shouldn't have come as a surprise, Cornelius thought afterwards, that Lord Urbane knew how to speak the Ma'diin's language.

The tribesmen bristled and even Ysallah seemed piqued and said something harsh in her language, though she had been remarkably composed up until now.

"I understand how serious the situation is," Lord Urbane said, (and the Watcher translated back to her) "but if we could show you our plans, which are in the city, we will show you how it works. It would be our honor to have you."

Ysallah looked upon them as if they were vermin and was deciding what the best way to eliminate them was and Cornelius wondered how long it would be before she ordered her bodyguards to attack, though he doubted they needed much more provoking. For all his warnings about not insulting them, Lord Urbane was quickly becoming their biggest liability. She said something to one of her tribesmen, who nodded curtly, put two fingers to his mouth a let out a loud whistle.

Some of the horses threw their heads and skittered about underneath their riders. Cornelius straightened, his hand ready to pull out his sword in a moment should the man's sudden signal be a prelude to an attack.

But a minute went by and nothing happened. Ysallah's expression betrayed nothing, but Cornelius bet she was taking a small amount of pleasure in the worried looks of the Empyrians. Then Lord Regoran pointed out past the Ma'diin to where two more men in black cloaks were walking towards them. They were each dragging something across the sand and Cornelius' stomach dropped when they reached them and deposited the two scouts he had sent ahead at their feet. They were unconscious, but appeared uninjured.

Lord Urbane and Lord Regoran both looked sidelong at Cornelius who refused to look back at them. He stood by his decision to send scouts ahead, but it was humiliating to see his men, yet again, outwitted by these primitives.

"I thought you said they were loners?" Lieutenant Riggs hissed at Lord Urbane.

Lord Urbane didn't answer, but returned his attention to the Watchers, trying hard to mask his own unease.

"It doesn't matter," Cornelius said, discreetly motioning for someone to take the two unconscious scouts back. "We outnumber them."

Lord Regoran scoffed. "And how many of your men outnumbered the one last night?"

Lord Urbane said something quickly, earnestly in the Ma'diin language and Ysallah's expression slowly changed from distrust to curiosity. She asked him a question and he replied quietly, his tone pleading.

Though she was formidable and her stare alone held enough power to bend those lesser than her to her will, she was still a woman, Cornelius thought, and he would not be made to look weak in front of his men as Lord Urbane did now. "We should not be the ones begging for mercy."

Without warning Ysallah strode forward, stopping only near Lord Urbane to brush her fingers off the back of her hand, and walked past them. The Empyrian soldiers jumped back and those on horses moved them sideways away from her. Her tribesmen followed quickly behind her as she cut a path through them and towards the city.

Lord Regoran looked incredulously at Lord Urbane. "What did you say to her?"

Lord Urbane merely shook his head. "I bought us a little time. Quickly now," he said motioning for them to follow her. "We wouldn't want her getting there before us. The last thing we need is the wall guard to stop her."

"And what about them?" Lieutenant Riggs asked about the Watchers who remained standing where they were. "Are they coming?"

"Count on it," Lord Urbane said and he and Lord Regoran went hurriedly after Ysallah and her tribesmen.

"Ride ahead," Cornelius instructed Lieutenant Riggs. "Tell the Commander that we just invited the hyenas to dinner."

CHAPTER TEN

There was only one thing Tamsin had wanted to do when she got home: sleep. But her mother and Sherene had clucked over her like a couple of overprotective hens. The other maids hung back, throwing curious glances at her until Sherene had scolded them and gave them orders, just like she used to at the old household. They had bathed her, fed her, and tended to her wounds, only a few scrapes it turned out thankfully. Her father had reappeared after the tedious process and once the questions started, he immediately dismissed everyone, though Tamsin knew he couldn't stop the stories that would be flying around by morning, considering half of the city had been looking for her. He carried her up to her room and tucked her in bed, something he hadn't done since she was little.

"What happened, Eleazar?" her mother asked him, but Tamsin had fallen asleep before she could hear her father's reply.

When she awoke, it was still dark, though she felt like she had slept for days. Her mind was alert, but her body creaked and groaned from being still for so long. Sherene slept soundly in a chair next to the bed, her hands folded together across her lap. She was wearing a different outfit than the one Tamsin remembered her in and wondered if she had indeed slept through a whole day. There was a tray on the table next to her with soup and tea, but they had both gone cold. Her feet were tender, but she padded her way down to the lower levels anyway, knowing if she didn't eat something her rumbling stomach would likely wake the whole household. It took her a while to find the kitchens, but she eventually found the pantry and was able to locate a bowl of pears and a half loaf of cinnamon-crusted bread. She sat down at the empty servants' table, sadly aware that she lacked the knowledge to cook anything for herself, though it tasted just as good as any formal dinner and devoured it in minutes.

When she had finished, she intended to go back to her room, but she saw a light steadily growing outside the arched doorway. Not wanting to get caught down there, she ducked underneath the table just as the voices were loud enough to hear. She hoped they would keep on walking, but she saw two sets of boots turn and come into the kitchen from the space between the floor and the tablecloth.

"Take a fresh horse from the stable. Don't let anyone see you," one of them said. He walked over to the shelves, took a few things off, deposited them on the table, and went back for more. "I told Pak to bolster the southern wall so the east gate will be clear until morning."

"Why do *I* have to go? I just got back!" the second one replied.

"Because you got us involved in this!" the first one hissed angrily, making Tamsin jump when he banged his fist on the table. Then more calmly he added, "Because if I go Captain Saveen will get suspicious, and I need to keep him occupied. He decided to move into his uncle's compound. If he starts sniffing around—."

"You shouldn't have shown him the box! Of course he'll start poking around now."

"I had no idea it was from *him*!" the first one said, clearly trying to speak quietly, but letting his frustration get the better of him. "Obviously he had no idea that Lord Saveen passed, why else would he have sent it?"

"Because *I* had no idea that he died. A little heads up would've been nice. Instead I come back and find the whole city turned upside down. What in the seven hells happened to Saveen anyway?"

"Lord Saveen died of his own making. Didn't have the stomach for this I guess."

The two were silent for a minute as they continued to stack the things on the table and Tamsin put a hand over her mouth to hide her heavy breathing. What were these two talking about? And what did it have to do with Captain Saveen? Just then one of them dropped something on the floor with a loud clang and the jar rolled under one of the chairs and stopped when it hit Tamsin's other hand. Her eyes grew wide and her heart pounded as the chair was pulled back and a hand lifted up the edge of the tablecloth…

"Just leave it," the first one said and the hand retreated. "Hurry up. Put the rest in here."

"What are you going to do about the Ma'diin?"

"Nothing. Not until we hear from the Master. And not while Lord Urbane is here."

"What does he have to do with it?" the second one asked.

"He has history with them apparently. If he finds out what's going on, I don't trust that he won't go straight to them."

If Tamsin's hand wasn't already covering her mouth, they would have heard her gasp for sure. The fact that her father had history with the Ma'diin was not in itself surprising; she had concluded as much from his odd behavior at the Armillary. But what were these two talking about and how was her father involved?

They gathered the goods off the table and moved towards the doorway and Tamsin heard the second one ask, "What are you going to do?"

The first one paused under the archway, then replied, "I don't know yet. Just make sure the Master knows the Ma'diin are here." A moment later they were gone.

She pushed a chair out of the way and scrambled out from underneath the table as soon as she could no longer hear their boots clacking against the floor. She ran, barefoot, back through the halls and up the stairs without really seeing where she was going, but somehow she managed to make it back to her room.

Her head felt hazy, like a sunset on a hot summer night. She crawled back under the covers, but too much was going through her mind to go back to sleep. Should she tell someone? What would she tell them? That she hid underneath the servants' table while two men discussed…what exactly? She didn't even know who those men were. But they had mentioned her father and that worried her. It was none of her business, what her father had done in the past, but she couldn't get it out of her head. Her mother would tell her that it was a waste of time, muddling over something that did not concern her, so she came to the conclusion that for now it would be best to keep her eyes open and her mouth shut. She had already caused enough trouble and she didn't want to be responsible for any more. The one man sounded like he was going to do exactly what Tamsin was going to do: be watchful. What either of them were watching for she didn't know. But those men, whoever they were, were no friends to the Urbanes or the Ma'diin. Of that she was certain. But until she knew more, what warning could she give?

Even if she had wanted to, the chance to confront her father never arose. The next day she barely saw him. He left before she got up in the morning and didn't return until after sundown. She soon learned that they had met with the Ma'diin at the Hollow Cliffs the day before (the day she had slept through) and had returned to the city with them. The lords had been negotiating with them all day at the Armillary.

Cleanup after the sandstorm was progressing slower than usual for the city was abuzz with the news of the Ma'diin's arrival. For some, the Ma'diin hadn't been seen in over a decade and for others it was as if they had walked right out the pages of a mythical tale. Rumors flew as to what they were doing here and what they wanted and crowds frequented the areas in front of the gates to the Armillary, but the building was heavily guarded at all hours. Nobody entered or left the Armillary without an entourage of soldiers, which is what Tamsin encountered that afternoon.

She expected to see her father among them when they showed up at the compound, but he was not there. Captain Saveen was with them, however, and he marched right up to her where she was having tea underneath the awning on the main level veranda. She dismissed the servants, assuming that he had some urgent message for her mother about her father, but she was not at the compound she informed him. Lady Allard had wanted to show them the market districts and Lavinia had agreed to go. She told Tamsin she still needed to recuperate after her ordeal, but Tamsin had overheard her tell Sherene that she didn't want her outside the compound while the Ma'diin were anywhere in the city.

Cornelius smiled though and sat down in the chair next to her. "Actually, I came to see you," he said. "I wanted to make sure you are doing alright, and to formerly introduce myself."

She stared at the cup of tea in her hands, remembering with embarrassment how she must have seemed that night. "That's very kind of you, Captain."

"Please, call me Cornelius."

"Okay, Cornelius. Thank you for everything you did and for checking on me, but don't you have more important matters to attend to than me? Or are the Ma'diin gone?"

"No, the Ma'diin are still here," he said, his expression turning slightly sour. "The negotiations aren't going as well as we had planned."

"Are you allowed to be telling me this?" she asked, glancing at the guards standing nearby, though she secretly hoped he would divulge more.

"Well I had hoped that you would accompany me back to the Armillary," he said. "You could even sit in and listen to the proceedings if you wish."

She almost spilled tea all over her lap and she quickly set it down on the table between them. "My father would never allow it," she said hastily. "Women never sit in the Lords' Council."

"Your father already agreed," he said smoothly. "The other lords think it's a good idea too. And—," he paused and leaned in closer, "technically it's not a Lords' Council." He winked.

Tamsin felt her cheeks flush. Though her father had taken her with him to many cities for diplomatic reasons, she had never been a part of any negotiations. Was he finally reconsidering? Perhaps her initial involvement could prove useful, though she had already told him everything that had happened.

"As it turns out, the Kazsera of the Ma'diin has been inquiring about you," Cornelius said, guessing her next question. "We all think it would help smooth things out if you were present."

Her palms began to sweat as her excitement turned to confusion. "But why would she care about me?" *And why not Haven?* she thought. "I nearly got one of her men killed." What if the Kazsera was angry with her for endangering Haven? He had almost died in the storm protecting her. But then again, she did want to make sure he was okay.

"You also saved one of my men from them did you not? My lieutenant says you stopped one of them from slitting his throat at the Armillary. You've earned a place there. Don't worry, I won't let anything happen to you." He flashed a comforting, chivalrous smile and despite her reservations the chance to sit in with the other lords was too tempting and she allowed him to escort her out of the compound.

There were groups of curious onlookers when they reached the Armillary, but nobody tried to hinder them. They murmured to each other and stared, but Tamsin had not thought to grab a parasol nor did she have a hood to lower over her face. They passed through the gate and walked up an identical set of stairs like the ones she had been carried up that led to the long tunnel, which was actually more like a narrow bridge. Something nagged at the back of her mind as they walked through the tunnel and past the open arches that allowed the sun to illuminate it, making it look quite different than it had the other night. She paused at one of the arches and stared out the window at the river bank and the moving water of the Elglas, trying to figure out what it was that bothered her so.

"Is something wrong?" Cornelius's voice disrupted her musings.

She shook her head. "I don't know. I'm sorry." She couldn't shake the feeling that she was missing something; that there was something that she wasn't seeing. The sight of the tunnel had triggered something, but she couldn't put her finger on it.

"You have nothing to worry about," he said, leading her away from the window and down the hallway again. "I promise I won't let anything happen to you. You needn't be afraid." Though he mistook her hesitation, he smiled that charming smile again and she immediately forgot about whatever wisp of a thought she had been trying to remember.

They passed through a fan-shaped room and through a series of arched doorways before reaching another room that had at least a dozen guards stationed outside the doors. They pulled the doors open for them and Cornelius led her inside.

The room was a cacophony of raised voices and hands, at least on one side. The lords were arguing amongst themselves, pointing and shouting while ten other Empyrian guards stood stoically behind them. On the other side were the Ma'diin, who were watching the lords in silence. Three of them wore the same dark robes that Haven had worn and they all turned to look at them as they entered, though she couldn't tell which one was him for they each had the same strange veil under their hoods that hid their faces. Then their Kazsera stood up, her eyes fixed on Tamsin. The lords slowly became silent as they noticed the Kazsera and then Tamsin.

Tamsin's father stood up from his seat and walked over to them, clearly angry. "Captain Saveen? What is the meaning of this?" he hissed quietly.

"Lord Urbane, I invited your daughter here to join our discussions today," Cornelius said cheerfully, walking by him with Tamsin in tow.

Tamsin's mouth went dry. Her father's expression indicated he had no idea she was coming. Cornelius had lied to her.

"This is a private meeting," her father said. "I—." He came face to face with Cornelius and lowered his voice even more. "I told you the other night that I didn't want her anywhere near here." He shot a glance at Tamsin, who was now wondering why she had agreed to this. From the look on the other lords' faces they had not been expecting her either.

Cornelius smiled and lowered his voice as well. "Your daughter is already involved in this," he said. "The Ma'diin will come around to our side if she is present. I guarantee it."

"You shouldn't meddle in things that you know nothing about!"

Tamsin winced at her father's words, feeling even more mortified than she had the other night, but then she caught a glimpse out of the corner of her eye as one of the robed men took a step forward and then stopped. "Does their Kazsera really want to see me?" she asked the two of them and from her father's silence she knew that Cornelius had not lied about that.

Then the Kazsera spoke up. She spoke quickly, in a language Tamsin didn't understand, but it sounded quite serious.

Her father was the one that answered, to Tamsin's surprise. She had not known her father knew how to speak their language.

"What on earth is going on?" Lord Allard asked, his cheeks red and puffy. "Eleazar, she should not be here!"

Her father looked as if someone had just pulled a rug out from under him. He ignored Lord Allard and stammered on his next words. "Ysallah, w—with all due respect," he started and then he switched to Ma'diinese, conversing hastily with the Kazsera.

There was a touch of sad understanding in the Kazsera's eyes, but it was quickly replaced with something more resolute as she replied. Then she pointed directly at Tamsin.

Tamsin's eyes were wide as she glanced over at her father, but he offered her no inclination as to what was going on. She tried to contain her trembling, but she couldn't tell if the others noticed or not.

"What is it?" Lord Regoran asked.

Her father took a moment before answering, then said, "She has invoked sh'pav'danya. It is an exchange."

One of the bare-chested Ma'diin walked forward, stopping at the fire pit in the center of the room and took out a small knife from his belt.

The Empyrian guards jumped out of their stone-like state and drew their weapons, ready to defend their lords, but there was no need. The bare-chested Ma'diin held out his hand, palm up over the empty pit and slowly drew his knife across it so everyone could see the dark red blood that dripped from between his fingers.

The lords stood there with either their mouths open or twisted in disgust. Tamsin's breath came in quick pants and she had to steady herself on Cornelius's arm.

"Have we lost all sense of decorum?" Lord Wohlrick muttered. "Eleazar, what is happening?"

Her father seemed to be waging an internal war. His face was strained. "Sh'pav'danya," he repeated slowly. "It is a ritual used when two tribes are in disagreement with each other. It is supposed to prevent a war from happening, but can do the exact opposite in some situations."

Tamsin's heart pounded loudly in her ears. She couldn't take her eyes off the blood as it dripped into the pit.

"One person is chosen from each tribe to go to the other and must remain with that tribe until the issue is resolved," her father continued. "The chosen draw blood as a symbol of each tribe's willingness to cooperate in good faith, but if one tribe betrays the other during the negotiations, then it turns into a symbol for what could happen. The chosen's life then becomes forfeit."

"That may be the norm where they're from," Lord Regoran said. "But that's not the way it works here. She can't just demand that we hand one of our people over." He glanced at Tamsin.

It sunk in then that was what her father and the Kazsera had been arguing about. They wanted *her*. So that's why the Kazsera had wanted to see her. She had planned this, to exchange one of her men so she could exact her revenge on Tamsin for putting Haven in danger. But was getting her revenge really worth the life of one of her own?

"She can demand it," her father said, nodding his head over in the Ma'diin's direction. "She has the power to back it up."

"We can't seriously be considering letting them have Tamsin," Cornelius said. "If it must be done, why can't one of us go instead?"

"Because the Kazsera cannot be chosen," he said, glaring angrily at Cornelius. "In our case, that is us."

Tamsin stared at the Ma'diin as her father argued with Cornelius. She looked from the one's bloody hand, to the Kazsera's proud stance, and then to the ones in the dark cloaks. One of them seemed more on edge than the others and this was where her gaze held. She could not see his face, but she could sense his eyes on her and the words she had heard in that terrifying storm came back to her: *no fear*. She remembered his arms around her, keeping her safe, protecting her, showing her courage in a storm that could have killed them both. Before she knew what she was doing, her feet were walking towards the fire pit.

Her father and Cornelius both reached out to hold her back, but it was too late by the time anyone realized what she was doing.

The Ma'diin she had been watching walked over to the pit as well and took a place by her side. She looked up at the dark hood. "Haven?" she whispered.

The Ma'diin nodded almost imperceptibly and she took a deep breath. If the Kazsera did have harmful intentions towards her she believed that Haven would protect her.

"Tamsin, you don't have to do this," her father said. "We can find another way."

"Not without insulting her," Tamsin said, indicating the Kazsera. She remembered how Haven had surprised the guards the other night and managed to escape untouched and now listening to her father speak of them like these three could undo an entire army, she knew they couldn't afford any missteps. If she could help, then she would. And despite her mortification at being an unwanted presence, she still wanted to witness the rest of the negotiations and this would ensure her that.

"Ready?" Haven asked her.

She nodded and Haven took her hand in his and held it palm up, just like the other Ma'diin had done. He took out his own knife, this one slightly larger than the other. Her pulse quickened and she held her breath as he rested the cold metal against her skin. She gasped, but the blade did not bite into her; instead Haven moved the blade over a hair and rather than cutting her hand, he cut the top of his fingers where they curled around her palm. She looked up at him, confused, but he sheathed the knife and pressed her fingers over his so when he removed his hand hers was covered in his blood.

She was too stunned at what he had done to notice when he led her over to a chair near the other Ma'diin. He ripped off a piece of cloth and tied it around her hand to keep up the illusion and so nobody would see that she really didn't have a cut there. He remained next to her, crossing his arms over his chest, as if challenging anyone who might try to take her back, and hid his fingers underneath his sleeve.

The bare-chested Ma'diin who had cut his own hand walked over to the lords, who looked more alarmed and confused than ever, and stood near them, a determined, proud grimace on his face.

The Kazsera smiled and then turned her attention back to Lord Urbane.

Her father let out a deep breath and gave her an understanding look. "We must reach an agreement. *Today*, gentlemen. There is no more time for arguing." He took his seat.

The discussions were quite tedious. Mostly her father and the Kazsera spoke together, but were often interrupted so he could dictate what was being said to the other lords. It was easy to see that they were quite put out by the whole arrangement, especially after two days of the painstaking talks, but they had no other choice. And the exchange between Tamsin and the tribesman not only seemed to keep their tempers in check, but to have sparked an idea as well.

"Perhaps we could send an envoy out there," Lord Regoran suggested.

"Yes," Captain Saveen agreed. "And we could show the Kazsera how it operates in person then."

Her father rubbed his chin, contemplating. "How long would it take to reach it Commander?"

The Commander sighed. "Judging from what the Ma'diin have told us, I would have to say a week or two, maybe more, and I would send a whole contingent, not just a few men."

"Would they agree to it?" Lord Wohlrick asked. "Our new friends don't seem to possess an excessive amount of patience."

"On the contrary, they are being extremely patient with us," her father said, and then he spoke to the Kazsera, explaining their idea. After a few minutes discussing it with her men she replied and her father smiled, the first smile Tamsin had seen on his face since it all started. "She will agree," he said, "but she has conditions."

"And what would those be?" Lord Wohlrick asked.

"We will go to the dam with her. Show her how it works in action and if she decides it is acceptable, then the dam can remain."

"And if it isn't acceptable?" Cornelius asked.

"Then they will be forced to take matters into their own hands. There will be no more negotiations, which means it would probably mean war with the Ma'diin."

The lords looked grim, but Cornelius spoke up. "It is the best option we have."

"You accept this then?" Haven asked.

Her father looked at the other lords, confirming they were all in agreement, and nodded. "We will go with you."

"When you say we, I hope you don't mean all of us." Lord Allard laughed. "Most of us haven't been outside the wall in years."

"He's right," Lord Wohlrick said, tapping his golden cane on the floor.

Her father stood up. "I will go," he said. "And as your man is in our charge, Ysallah, I will let him come too, as long as Tamsin is allowed to stay here."

Tamsin held her breath as they waited for the Kazsera's answer. She had been racked with fear of not knowing what was going to happen to her now that she was in the Ma'diin's care, but maybe her father would be able to get her out of it.

Ysallah's eyes were angry as she replied and Tamsin's hopes fell as she heard the determination in her voice, but it was Haven who interrupted her, not her father. He and the Kazsera spoke back and forth quickly, as if he were trying to convince her of something. Then, after a tense pause, she nodded.

Haven turned to the lords. "I stay. Sh'pav'danya not be broken then."

There was a murmur among the lords as they realized one of the Watchers would be remaining in their midst.

"It's truly settled then," her father said, before they could argue the point. "Commander, how soon can your men be ready?"

"They will be ready tomorrow and I will go with you Lord Urbane. Captain Saveen can manage in my absence."

Her father nodded gratefully and the Commander and Cornelius excused themselves to make their preparations. Cornelius tried to catch Tamsin's eye as he was leaving, but she refused to meet his gaze. Her father was right: people should not meddle in things that they had no understanding of.

"Ysallahkazsera, we shouldn't do this," Kellan pleaded, using her most formal title. "They can't be trusted."

"The deal has been made," Ysallah said as they were escorted to the outer courtyard where the meal was being served that night. The meeting had disbanded hours ago and the lords had invited them to dine with them now that there was a sort of truce between them. "I didn't see you come up with a better idea."

"I would just kill them and be done with it," he said.

"That's why we didn't put you in charge," Oman said.

"I still don't like it," Kellan grumbled. "And you should not have to stay here, Haven."

"Haven understands their language," Ysallah continued. "He can manage things here. Urbane can speak our tongue, so we will be able to converse with him."

"What if they are lying to us? What if the wall is permanent and cannot be moved to let water through? Haven's life is in danger here should the negotiations fail."

"Our lives are in danger no matter where we go," Haven said. "If war with the northerners comes to pass, then I will do what I can from here, but until then I will stay alert and hope it does not come to that."

They reached the courtyard, where a few of the lords and military officers were already present. A long, raised table had been set near one end of the yard, adorned with candles and bowls of strange, overly-pungent food. While the others cautiously inspected the food and the tiny weapons placed at regular intervals along the table with raised eyebrows, Ysallah pulled Haven aside, wishing to speak to him alone.

"You will have to be extra vigilant here, you know that?"

Haven studied her a moment. Ysallah knew he knew how to look after himself. But he was curious as to what she was really getting at so he simply nodded.

She looked around at their surroundings, focusing on the tall tridents that held lighted candles throughout the yard, but it was only to avoid Haven's gaze. "I know you're not happy with the sh'pav'danya," she said. "I had hoped for a different outcome, Haven, but it is well that you are staying. Thank you."

"You do not have to defend your decision to me, Ysallah." It made sense to have someone who knew the other's language on each side. But it was not like her to feel guilty, or to show gratitude to cover up that guilt. "What do you need?"

Her chin lifted slightly. She liked being easily read as much as Haven did, but he was in no mood to play games, especially from someone he had been travelling with for weeks. "While you are here I want you to keep watch over her," she said. She was about to say something more, but then stopped.

He knew who she was talking about and had already made the unconscious decision to keep his eyes on the girl. Tamsin seemed to have an uncanny ability of getting into trouble and he had no desire to see any more harm befall her, which was why he had spared cutting her hand. She had been through enough and didn't need any more added from his side. But he asked Ysallah why she was so interested.

"You know the rules of the exchange Haven," she said, but her tone was slightly too high. Just a hair too dismissive. "She belongs to us now. Keep her safe."

Haven didn't question her any more, but knew he needed to observe more than just the northerners tonight. He trusted Ysallah and knew her to be a rational Kazsera, but her interest in Tamsin went beyond the sh'pav'danya and he needed to know why.

Tamsin arrived shortly after the sun fell with her father who never let her get more than an arm's length from his side. Her light skin glowed in the torchlight and she wore a long flowing dress of blue and gold that crossed around the base of her neck and fell around her body like a waterfall. He almost didn't recognize her from the girl he had found just a few days ago, clinging to him with every ounce of strength she had, fighting to stay alive. She belonged somewhere else, surrounded by green and sky and life, not contained by this dead rock. Her eyes lingered on him for a moment before her attention was directed elsewhere.

Everyone was given a place at the table, though it took several stern looks from Ysallah to get Haven and his brothers, who were used to eating on reed mats if not the ground itself, to sit with the rest of them. Even the sha'diin looked uncomfortable and did not eat anything until their Kazsera had. The Empyrians indulged in a red drink that seemed to loosen their tongues and it wasn't long before they were talking loudly, the awkwardness of the gathering eased for a time.

"Do they always wear those ghoulish things?" Lord Allard asked, indicating the Watchers' dark robes. "Why do they not show their faces?"

The n'qab inside of their hoods covered their eyes, but not their mouths, so they were still able to eat uninhibited.

"It is a symbol of their tribe," Lord Urbane said, who sat across from Haven. "Think of them like the Empyrian High Guard. They wear their armor and the Watchers wear their masks."

"I suppose it's better than the other two," Lord Allard said, pointing to Bregan and Karnak's bare chests. "Though if I was in that kind of shape, I wouldn't wear clothes either!" His laugh echoed throughout the courtyard.

The sha'diin looked to Haven for enlightenment, but he only shook his head and watched Lord Urbane, wondering why he had kept the real reason for the Watchers' n'qabs hidden from his companions when the look on his face made it clear that he knew the truth.

"You should know better than anyone why they must wear those, Urbanekazser," Ysallah said in their native tongue.

Ysallah was picking up the language quickly, Haven thought. He had said nothing about what Urbane told them.

Lord Urbane paused and then stabbed a piece of meat with the tiny three-pronged weapon. *"Why would you say that?"* he asked.

"You don't think I know who you are? You hide it well, but the more you hide from your companions the more you reveal to me."

"I hide nothing," he said. *"You may ask me anything. I will answer in truth."*

Ysallah leaned forward and her eyes flicked to Tamsin and then back. *"Does she know about your past?"*

They stared at each other for a long minute, each testing the other in the silence between them. It was Lord Urbane who looked away first and he shook his head. *"I am trying to protect her."*

"So am I."

This made him blink a few times. *"I don't understand. Why did you choose her for the sh'pav'danya then if you knew it would endanger her?"*

"If I had chosen you or any of the others, the Watchers wouldn't think twice about killing you if things go badly. But her, her they will not touch. It was the only way I could protect her and you."

Ysallah had known what she was doing when she chose Tamsin and she had been right. But why protect them?

"And him?" Lord Urbane asked, glancing at Haven.

"Haven has agreed to watch over her in our absence. He has already risked his life once to save her."

Lord Urbane nodded. *"Tamsin has told me as much."*

"I would not trust anyone else with the task."

"Then it would seem I am indebted to you both," he said. *"You have my deepest thanks."* His tone was sincere, but his eyes were still wary.

"I would rather be allies than enemies, Kazser," Ysallah said, handing him a plate of bread.

He stared at it and then slowly took a piece. *"And if the latter is our fate, will you try to take her?"*

Haven had never seen a man look so haunted, but at the same time he knew if it came to it, he would fight.

Ysallah merely smiled. *"I am not a thief, Kazser. I do not take what isn't mine."*

But she had claimed her, in front of everyone, and in her eyes, Tamsin already belonged to her.

The tops of Haven's fingers itched where he had cut them and he fiddled with the edge of the bandage as he wondered why Ysallah cared about this girl so much. He noticed Oman watching him out of the corner of his eye and quickly slipped his hand under the table, returning his attention to the others, hoping Oman would do the same.

Their serious tones had attracted Tamsin's attention and she watched her father with a worried expression from the other end of the table. The man next to her, Captain Saveen, was repeatedly trying to make conversation with her, though she barely said more than a few words to him at a time. She hardly touched the food in front of her; course after course was brought to them, but she showed little interest. Haven wondered if she was still feeling the effects from the other day or if she just thought it smelled strange and was overcooked, as he did. After the last part of the tediously long meal had been taken away and the only thing still being served was the red drink, Tamsin excused herself from the table. Before she left, she surprised everyone by asking to have a word with Haven. Everyone stared in silence, and the looks exchanged between his brothers did not go unnoticed by him. Haven got up and walked a little ways away from the table with her, feeling everyone's eyes on his back and not caring.

When it was just the two of them, she faced him. "I wanted to say I'm sorry," she said, "for putting you in danger. Running away—that was beyond foolish of me." Her tone was soft, truly earnest, though had she known he was in danger almost every day of his life she would've known an apology wasn't needed.

"Fooleesh of me too," he said, only half kidding.

That wide smile reappeared on her face, almost reaching up to her eyes, which glittered in amusement. It was the first time he had seen her relaxed all evening. Staring up at the dark hood of a Watcher was enough to set even his own people's knees trembling, but this small, innocent girl stood within his shadow without the slightest trace of fear. It reminded him of someone he used to know.

The others had risen from their seats and Tamsin's father came over, putting a protective hand on her shoulder. "Come Tamsin. Let me take you home now."

She nodded, but held up her hand for one more moment. She leaned in closer to Haven and whispered, "Why did you do that? Why did you cut your hand instead of mine?"

"Haven, are you coming?" Oman asked. They were all standing waiting for him.

She took his hand in hers as if to keep him there so he would have to answer her. The move surprised him so much he was sure she could see his shocked expression through his n'qab. Her thumb brushed over the top of the cloth he had wrapped over the cuts on his fingers. He had held this girl in his arms and carried her halfway across the desert, but something about this touch unnerved him. It was too intimate, too close. He took her hand and gently placed it back at her side then walked away to join his kin, glad that no one could see the expression on his face.

He followed them back to the room they had been given at the giant stone flat in the river, the Armillary the northerners called it, with high stone pillars and a ledge open to the night air overlooking the river. He put his arm out when Ysallah tried to go in, blocking her from entering. Her eyes flashed at his boldness, but he did not move. He extinguished the torches nearest them and dropped his hood with his other hand so she could see his face. "Tell me you will not jeopardize the mission for her," he said.

"What are you talking about?" she asked, but her feigned ignorance did not fool him.

"You have claimed her in the sh'pav'danya. If the northerners' wall is what they say, then you will lose that claim."

"You think that I would start a war with the northerners just to keep the girl?"

"Tell me I'm wrong."

She glared at him. "You are wrong. If I put the life of one in front of the lives of many I would not be Kazsera." She took a few deep breaths until her expression softened. "What you heard the other night, about Urbane's past with us. That is true, but Tamsin is ignorant of it all." She sighed. "I would not put it past these men to kill her just to break the truce. And if we lose her, we lose Urbane's support. So you can ease your fears, Watcher. I have not lost sight of the goal."

That may have been the case, but she seemed to have new goals as well. After Ysallah and the sha'diin fell asleep Haven spoke to Kellan, confiding his reservations. "Watch her Kellan. She's still hiding something." And it had something to do with Lord Urbane's past dealings with the Ma'diin.

CHAPTER ELEVEN

"Stop fidgeting, Tamsin," Lavinia said with an irritated glance. "It's unbecoming."

Tamsin held her hands behind her back, out of her mother's sight, and continued to rub the back of her hand. The marks Mora's nails had left were already turning a soft pink, but they tingled where Haven had touched her when he cut his fingers during the sh'pav'danya. She had washed his blood off afterwards, scrubbing furiously until her skin was raw, but the strange, numb sensation still lingered. It was as if her mind had tricked her into thinking that he really had cut her hand.

She watched the Ma'diin from across the courtyard where she waited with her mother and the other lords as the caravan readied themselves for their departure. They had been delayed a day due to another sandstorm that enveloped the city in a hazy cloud. Though it was not nearly as powerful as the one they had faced in the desert, Tamsin was still more than willing to wait this one out within the high walls of the compound. She didn't know where the Ma'diin had been during the storm, but they were here now, clearly eager to get on their way. There had been a slight disagreement about their mode of travel, which delayed them again. Tamsin gathered that the Ma'diin had never seen horses before as the men were quite agitated around the animals and refused to go near them when they were presented, though their Kazsera studied them with interest. In the end, her father, Ysallah, and a few of the Empyrians were the only ones in stirrups and the other horses were packed with food, tents, and supplies.

It was late in the afternoon by the time everything was settled. As the caravan departed, her father sidled his horse over to them and gave Lavinia a quick kiss on the hand. No words passed between them; only a shared look of determination as her mother silently commanded him to return to her and him promising to do just that. He gave Tamsin a cold smile and then spurred his horse into motion. The others fell in line behind him as he led them out of the courtyard. The Ma'diin formed a protective barrier around Ysallah, though they were careful to keep a little distance between them and her horse. Ysallah actually looked quite regal up there, as if she had been riding all her life. She stared openly at Tamsin as she moved by. Tamsin met her gaze, refusing to be the first one to look away. She would not let the Kazsera get away with thinking she was her property. Eventually, Ysallah looked away and continued with the rest of them out of the west gate. They turned south and soon the only thing Tamsin could see were their tracks in the sand. And a lone, cloaked figure standing just outside the decorated arch, watching them go.

The rest of the lords and onlookers began to talk amongst themselves and the flow of daily activity slowly resumed. Her mother was talking to the Commander's wife so Tamsin took advantage of her distraction and walked over to Haven, feeling a gentle pang of pity. Her father was out there, but for Haven it was everyone he knew. When she reached him, she could see the muscles in his jaw working, but his hood was up so she couldn't see the rest of his face.

She rubbed the back of her hand absentmindedly again. "I don't know who is more stubborn," she said, hoping to spark a conversation, "your Kazsera or my father."

"Ysallah," Haven said without hesitation.

She frowned. If that was true and things didn't go well at the dam, then she hoped Ysallah wouldn't try to collect on the deal she made. And she worried about how far her father would go to protect her, putting his own life at risk. Though Haven had proven that he would go to lengths to protect her as well.

"Will she be angry when she finds out what you did?"

His back stiffened slightly, but he remained silent.

They had that in common at least. Despite her father's stony farewell, she hoped his journey would soothe his anger towards her for what she did at the negotiations. She could not remember the last time he had shown so much displeasure and it left her feeling quite cut off from the one person who knew her best. It was why she would not ask Haven again why he hadn't cut her hand in the exchange. She was used to feeling alone, but never by her father, and the feeling was not one she wanted to discuss. Though knowing Haven might be experiencing the same gave her a little comfort. "Well I hope they are able to find common ground."

His hood rustled slightly in her direction. "They already have," he said in a voice that sent shivers up her arms. He turned to go back into the city, but stopped as if an invisible door had closed in front of him. His head moved up and over as he studied the arches for a moment, just as Tamsin had when they first arrived. He took a step back and said something in his own language that sounded to Tamsin either like a curse or an exclamation of awe.

Tamsin once again gazed upon the pair of lizard-like stone creatures that festooned the entrance, only this time she was closer and could see the details. They were easily fifteen feet long from nose to tail. Most of them had worn off from years of exposure to the wind and sand, but she could still see the crescent moon-shaped ridges where the stone mason had carved the scales into the creatures' hides. She could see the individual teeth of the one whose mouth was open in a snarl and her head could easily have fit in one of its outstretched claws. The details in its eyes had faded, giving it an unnerving, sightless quality. Two horns protruded from the back of its skull and curled over the beginning of its neck. "Are there animals like this where you're from?" she asked, standing on her tiptoes to see inside its mouth. The stone mason had even given it a forked tongue like that of a snake. Tamsin had always thought that lizards and other reptiles preferred the dry heat of the desert to swampy marshes, but then again she had never seen a reptile outside of a book.

"Not with wings." His voice was so low she almost didn't hear him.

Just then a group of guards came over, stopping just before their boots left the shadow of the tunnel and warily insisted on escorting Tamsin back into the courtyard so they could close the gates. She didn't know what made them more nervous, her being with a Watcher or being outside of the wall. She took a moment to look south again, catching a last glimpse of her father atop his horse then let the guards lead her back into the courtyard. "Are you com——?" she started to ask when she realized Haven wasn't following, but when she looked back Haven had disappeared.

She only had a second to wonder when she heard her name being called from across the courtyard and saw a tall, blonde girl running over to her. Georgiana crushed her in a big hug, oblivious to the startled looks around her.

"Thank the lords you're alright!" Georgiana exclaimed when she finally let go. "We heard you were found, but nobody would tell us if you were okay. I'm so sorry Tamsin!"

One of the guards went to separate them, but Tamsin waved him away. "It's alright. I'm fine." She heard a grinding sound and looked behind to see the gates closing. It was a bit unnerving how Haven was able to appear and disappear so easily, but she understood if he wanted to be alone right now. She hooked her arm through Georgiana's and led her over to a less crowded spot under one of the shaded walkways, memories of that night starting to resurface. "Why didn't anyone come looking for me?" she asked.

Georgiana's eyes fell to her feet. "Enrik said he went back for you, but you were gone. He thought you left. We didn't hear until the next day that you were missing. And then we heard the rumor that you were outside of the wall and then the storm hit…"

Georgiana was speaking so quickly Tamsin had to grasp her hands to get her to slow down. She wasn't angry with her or any of them; rather she was grateful that Georgiana even cared enough to apologize for something that wasn't even her fault. It was a trait she had seen very little of since coming here and she did not want Georgiana to blame herself and suffer because of it.

"I don't want you to give it another thought, okay?" Tamsin told her gently. "It was my fault. When I saw more than just the two on the cliff, I panicked and—." Tamsin paused, remembering something. There had been seven. Seven of the Ma'diin on the cliff that night. But at the exchange and at dinner she had only seen six. And again, just now, only five had left with the caravan.

"So it's true?" Georgiana asked, her eyes sparkling with curiosity. "The strangers came from the south? Are they the marsh people?"

Tamsin nodded, looking around the courtyard, wondering where the seventh Ma'diin had been all this time and where he was now. Maybe Haven wasn't alone after all…

"Would you like to come over for dinner sometime?" Georgiana asked. "I'd love to hear about them and I'm sure my father would too. That is, only if you want to, of course," she added, finally noticing Tamsin's preoccupation.

"Of course I would," Tamsin replied, coming back to the present. She was genuinely glad that they had plans to see each other again. Georgiana was a sweet girl and Tamsin would be happy if the only thing that came out of the difficult last few days was a friendship with her.

Just then a middle-aged woman started yelling at them from down the walkway, wearing the pale blue colors associated with the servants.

"I have to go," Georgiana said hurriedly and only then did Tamsin notice Georgiana was wearing the same clothing as the older woman. She hadn't realized she worked in one of the compounds. Georgiana said a hasty farewell and rushed over to the older woman.

Tamsin walked back over to where her mother was still talking to the Commander's wife.

"Who was that?" Lavinia inquired quietly.

"A friend," Tamsin said, even though she knew her mother disapproved of mingling with the servant class. Next to her, holding a parasol over her mother's head for shade, Sherene shared a smile with Tamsin.

Haven watched the guards take Tamsin away and then turned his attention back to the stone creatures. He slid one of his knives out and held it up to one of the winged beast's talons. He flipped it in his hand so the handle curved the same way as the talon. It came to a point at the tip that mirrored the blade on the other end. The handle was almost as long as his forearm and bone-white with a black streak running over the curved edge. Though the stone talon was a sandy beige color and chipped away in spots, the talon and the curved handle of Haven's knife were nearly exact replicas of each other.

With a flick of his wrist he returned the knife to his belt, eyeing the stone beasts with a new sense of caution, as if they would suddenly shake off the sand and rubble and leap into the sky. He didn't know when these creatures had been carved into the stone, but the carver couldn't have done it without seeing what Haven had seen. But there was one difference that made his blood run like icy thorns through his veins. He had no doubt that the creatures whose likeness were bound to the archway were long dead, but the world was a large place, much larger than the Ma'diin liked to admit, and there were still territories that remained unknown.

He stared at the large cloud of dust heading towards the cliffs to the south. He knew he would not abandon his post, especially after what the Kazsera had told him, but there were things he needed to do now, things he needed to find out. He slipped back into the shaded tunnel leading into the city just as the gates closed, sealing him inside like the finality of a tomb.

CHAPTER TWELVE

Tamsin sat under the shade of the awning on the third level veranda, watching the rise and dip of the birds as they circled over the fisherman pulling their nets up from the depths of the Elglas. She had been watching them most of the morning, and she found it was a relaxing respite from the frenetic path her thoughts had followed since her father left with the Ma'diin the day before. She thought about the men she had overheard in the kitchens, about her father's past with the Ma'diin, about Ysallah's claim on her, about the missing seventh man, and about Haven. Her thoughts always seemed to circle back to him.

Sherene walked into view, effectively ending Tamsin's peaceful morning by announcing that she had a visitor. Tamsin got up and saw the last person she was expecting when she turned around: Cornelius Saveen. She tried not to let her displeasure show as he acknowledged her, giving her a polite bow.

"Lady Tamsin. It's lovely to see you again," he greeted her in a smooth voice. "I hope I haven't inconvenienced you by showing up unannounced."

She turned around and went back to watching the birds and the city below, in no mood to entertain him, especially after their last dinner with the other lords and the Ma'diin. He had acted like nothing had happened at the Armillary, like he had not manipulated her. She sighed when she did not hear him leave. "Did you need something, Captain? Or have you come to lie to me again, in my own home?"

She hoped to offend him so he would leave, but he would not be deterred so easily. "First, I wanted to apologize for my behavior the other day at the Armillary. I was an ass, forcing you to join us like that. I don't know what I was thinking. Please accept my apology." He took a few steps closer to her, but kept a respectable distance away from her.

She did not like being angry at people, it gave her headaches and was a waste of time, so to ease the knot she could already feel forming between her eyebrows she nodded, hoping that was all and that he would now take his leave.

"Thank you," he said and continued as if his apology had erased all of his transgressions. "Second, I was hoping you could help me with something. As you know, one of the Ma'diin agreed to stay behind with us. Unfortunately, I haven't seen him since the dam company left. Do you happen to know where he is?"

She shook her head no, keeping her expression vacant. In truth, she hadn't seen Haven since then either. She had assumed he would be at the Armillary in discussions with the other lords, but finding out he was in fact not there, or anywhere since Cornelius was here looking for him, worried her.

He frowned, staring at her for a second. "Hmm, well, if you do see him will you tell him to come see me? I think it would be good for us to spend some time together. If our two peoples are going to be working together we should spend this time getting to know each other, don't you think?"

That was probably the truest thing he had said. Tamsin simply nodded.

He smiled. "Speaking of getting to know each other, how would you like to have dinner with me tonight?"

This caught her off guard and she stared at him as if he had just asked her to jump over the compound wall. "I don't think—."

Suddenly her mother came sweeping across the veranda. "She would love to, of course." She smiled, showing all of her teeth in the way Tamsin knew she usually reserved for special banquets and social functions when she was trying to impress someone.

Cornelius flashed a similar smile and kissed her mother on the cheek. "You must be Lady Urbane," he said.

"Please, call me Lavinia," she said sweetly.

Tamsin looked around to see if there was somewhere she could escape to while they exchanged pleasantries.

"Well, it's lovely to meet you Lavinia. I'm Cornelius Saveen. I'm afraid I must be going though. Tamsin, can I be expecting you tonight?"

Tamsin was about to say no, but the look her mother was giving her prompted her to nod, though she kept her lips pressed firmly in a thin line.

"Good. I'll send someone to pick you up at seven." He bowed to each of them and took his leave.

As soon as the door closed Tamsin turned to her mother. "What was *that*?"

"I don't know what you mean," she said innocently and started walking the other way, but Tamsin wasn't letting her getting away with this that easy.

"Mathri, stop. Why did you tell him I would have dinner with him? Do you even know who that was?"

"Of course I do. He's the Captain of the High Guard and heir to the Saveen estate. I think it's a good idea for you two to get to know each other a little bit. Don't argue with me. You're going to have a lovely time. Now let's go upstairs and find something for you to wear tonight."

Tamsin grudgingly followed her mother to her room and looked out towards the river while her mother rifled through her clothes. She didn't even pretend to be interested. She didn't like

Cornelius enough to waste time thinking about what would make her look the prettiest for him. But she had to admit, this was the happiest she had seen her mother in a while so she would go, eat, and tell her she had a good time when she got back.

Her mother decided that she didn't own anything exquisite enough to dine with the Captain of the High Guard, especially after ruining her other gown, which Tamsin thought she should not be punished for, and summoned the local dress maker who brought with him a trunk full of over-the-top choices. There were a few dress styles that Tamsin was familiar with, that had the corseted bodice and full skirt, but what was new here was five years outdated back in the Cities. Then she found one that the dress maker told her was the popular style worn around here by some of the natives on the east side. It was a soft, gauzy material that looked like it draped over and around the body. The dress maker had her try it on and Tamsin was surprised by how light it was. Layers of red, orange, and pink fabric, embellished with tiny jewels, wrapped around her body while the skirt fell in vertical waves around her legs. Her mother wore a disapproving look, but Tamsin would not underestimate the importance of breathing again, not after her encounter with the Elglas, so she told her mother if she couldn't wear this dress then she wasn't going.

Later, back in her rooms, with the sunset-colored dress laid out on the bed, Tamsin stared out the back entrance, past the river into the desert beyond. The landscape was darker than usual for this time in the afternoon and she could see clouds in the distance.

"Do you think another sandstorm is coming?" she asked Sherene, who had finished pinning her hair up and was now dusting a light beige powder on her face.

"Those don't look like the other sand clouds we've had lately. I sure hope there's rain in there instead. This desert sun is not good for the skin," she said, grimacing at Tamsin's darkened complexion. Her excursion in the desert before Haven had found her had turned her normally olive skin the color of honey. "The cook told me that if it is a good year, there will be a few rain storms in the next few months. We might get one tonight if we are lucky. And if we do, I want you to come home straightaway. You don't want to get caught in another storm, rain or sand."

"Maybe I should stay home then, just in case."

"Oh no," Sherene said, waving the powder brush at her. "I would rather face a hundred of those storms than your mother if you don't go."

After her face was sufficiently covered she got dressed and before she knew it there was an usher at the bottom of the stairs, waiting with a small, two-wheeled cart to take her away. The cart reminded her of the wagons the merchants used to haul flour bags and wheat, but this one had a tasseled canopy over it and was laden with plush cushions. There were no horses hitched to it, but instead it had two long handles on the end that the man used to pull the cart himself. Tamsin had been expecting to be taken to the Armillary or the military housing, but was surprised when they pulled up to another compound almost identical to her own. She stepped tentatively out of the cart and followed the torch lit stairs up to the third level. Another servant waited at the top and escorted her up to the next level on one of the "horns." Inside, she was led through a narrow hallway adorned with gold-framed paintings and folded drapes into an intimate dining room where Cornelius was waiting.

"You look lovely," he said, crossing over to her and kissing her hand. He led her over to the table and pulled a chair out for her. He took his own seat at the opposite end, but there were ample enough candles dispersed throughout the room that reflected off the glassware that she could still see him clearly.

"Thank you for inviting me," she said curtly, eyeing the strange decor. Though the compound seemed very similar on the outside, the interior was quite different. All the wood furnishings were dark walnut, heavy, and ornately carved. The brass candelabras were shaped like antlers and there was a thick rug covering the floor that Tamsin realized was some kind of animal skin. Tamsin had seen rustic villas before, but this lacked even a little bucolic charm.

"My uncle loved this house," Cornelius said, watching her inspect the room, "but I admit his taste was on the darker side. He was especially fond of his Arak collection, though I never acquired a liking for the stuff."

"I've never heard of it."

"It's a local drink, banned in the Cities, very potent. My uncle kept a pretty impressive store."

"My father has his own collection of wine," she said, "though he's not much of a drinker." She bit her lip, immediately regretting the words as she recalled what the Lording Ladies had said in regards to Lord Saveen's death.

But Cornelius didn't even flinch. "My uncle used to boast about his drinking prowess. He said your father tried, but no one could match him."

"Your uncle knew my father?"

He nodded. "Yes, I even believe they were friends once."

"What happened?" she asked, her interest piqued now. Maybe this evening wasn't a complete waste if she could learn something about her father's past here. She took a spoonful of soup.

"My uncle didn't like to talk about it much, never when he was sober at least, but they got into a feud. They both loved the same woman you see. A Ma'diin woman."

The soup went down like tar, though not because it was poorly made. Suddenly the room seemed too dark, too confining and she tried to keep her composure. She could see Cornelius watching her, trying to discern how much she knew. "What happened to her?" she asked, trying to sound indifferent to it all, though hearing about her father's past affairs from Cornelius Saveen was uncomfortable enough to unhinge her. She put her spoon down so he would not see her hand shaking.

"She died," he said bluntly. "My uncle was devastated by it. My own parents died a few years after and I moved out here, but he was not the same uncle that left the Cities when I was a boy."

Tamsin suddenly felt bad for asking about it. Cornelius had lost both of his parents, his uncle just recently, and she felt guilty for being angry at her own father for keeping secrets from her.

"And that's how the feud between them started and ended," he said. "My uncle decided to stay here and your father went back to the west."

She nodded, taking another spoonful as she tried to process the information.

"But let's leave the pasts of old men to the past. I'd much rather talk about the present." He raised his glass. "To us," he toasted.

Tamsin lifted hers, though it seemed to weigh as heavily as her thoughts. "To us," she echoed reticently and took a sip.

The topic remained light and a little contrived for the rest of the evening. They would be talking and he would suddenly throw in a compliment about her eyes or her hair. She would thank him politely and look anywhere else but his face, hoping not to encourage his charming behavior. After six courses dinner was finally over and Tamsin was relieved to finally be able to go home, but Cornelius reminded her of his uncle's Arak collection and he led her up the stairs to the top level. It was dark and obviously hadn't been used in a long time so Cornelius grabbed a small torch and showed her around. There was the collection of Arak bottles filling several shelves and Tamsin was reminded of Mora's room of bottles. There was a desk that matched the style of the dining table facing a small balcony that overlooked the western edge of the city. The sun had long since set, but there were no stars out tonight.

He led her over to the desk then where there was a long wooden box lying on top of it. He prompted her to open it and she carefully lifted the lid. Inside was an S-shaped sword about as long as her arm from handle to tip. It was hard to tell in the wavering light, but there appeared to be some kind of design etched in the silver blade. An oily, citrus smell wafted up when she had opened it as well, as if it had just been cleaned. "Is this your uncle's?" she asked.

In the torch light, Cornelius' half smile was caught somewhere between amused and grotesque. "It was a gift for my uncle," he said. "He died before he received it."

"Oh, I'm sorry. I'm sure he would have appreciated it very much. I've never seen anything like it."

"Are you sure?" he asked. "Never?"

"I'm sure," she said, furrowing her brow at his question. It was like he wanted her to have seen this before, but she knew she hadn't. Any of her father's swords she had seen had all been straight-edged; nothing curved like this.

The breeze coming through the open archway was cool and Tamsin was reminded of Sherene's words. "I should be going home," she said. "I have no desire to be caught in another storm."

"You could always stay here," Cornelius said, "in separate rooms of course," he added before she had time to be scandalized by what he was suggesting.

Tamsin's skin crawled at the thought of sleeping within these garish walls. "I'm sorry, but my mother would never allow it. I don't know how courting is here, but in the Cities—" as soon as the words left her lips she knew how Cornelius would interpret them and it was too late.

He turned to her and before she could explain herself, brought his face down and engulfed her mouth with his own. He wrapped his arm around her waist and brought her even closer.

The kiss was so sudden it took her a moment to comprehend what was happening before she pulled away. She raised her hand to slap him, but his hand caught her wrist.

Tamsin froze despite her lungs feeling like they would leap out of her chest.

Cornelius brushed his thumb against the inside of her wrist. "I like your spirit Tamsin; it intrigues me. But it's not going to be enough if you want to survive here. You're going to need an ally. A man who can take care of you." He stared at her a moment, then opened his hand, letting hers slide out.

Tamsin took a step back, questioning every charming word out of his mouth that evening. "Well, let me know when you see one," she said, hoping there was enough venom in her voice to hide her fear.

But Cornelius only walked back over to the desk, smiling. "Terrence, see to it that Lady Tamsin gets home safely."

A man stepped forward out of the shadows, making her jump. She hadn't known he was there. Cornelius handed him the torch and she saw the man was clothed in light blue, but the torchlight reflected of the metal handle of a sword hanging from his belt. He motioned towards the door and Tamsin stepped quickly through, glancing back just before to see Cornelius placing the lid back on the box, his back to her.

Tamsin could only wonder how things had ended up like they did as Terrence led her downstairs to where the man with the cart was waiting for her. Her skin tingled uncomfortably in the evening breeze as the wind picked up. They made it to the Urbane compound just as the rain started. The man retrieved a parasol from a back compartment in the cart and motioned to walk her up, but she declined and thanked him anyways. She wanted to walk alone and clear her head of the night's events. But even the time it took to walk up the stairs was not long enough to compose herself and the rain only added to her discomfort.

Tamsin nearly slipped on the slick stone as she reached the main level and saw a cloaked figure standing in front of her.

Haven.

She stared at him, all of the questions she had the last couple days, mixed with the emotions of tonight left her feeling drained. "Where have you been?" she asked over the sound of the rain hitting the stones.

Water dripped off the edge of his hood. "I make sure it safe," his voice rumbled low like thunder.

"Safe would have been you standing in the shadows instead of Terrence," she mumbled drily, but Haven's appearance now was slowly melting her nerves despite that they were both standing in the rain and the tight lines around his mouth and the slight hunch in his shoulders told her he was probably in need of some rest. "Come with me," she said and he followed her inside. "I'll have Sherene make you up a room." There was still a fire going in one of the center cauldrons and she offered to take his soaked cloak, but he made no move to give it to her. "It's all wet," she said. "It will dry faster by the fire."

He shook his head.

"Wait here," she told him and she went upstairs to her parents' room and grabbed a few of her father's clothes and one of his old cloaks. She was about to go back down when her mother appeared in the doorway.

"Tamsin, you're back! I thought I heard someone come in. Look at you, you're soaking wet. What are you doing with your father's clothes?"

"They're not for me," Tamsin said regretfully aware that she had forgotten all about her mother. Surely, she would not be pleased that one of the Ma'diin was downstairs.

Her mother looked at her quizzically. "Then who are they for?" Then her face lit up unexpectedly. "Did Cornelius come back here with you? How sweet of him to see you home safely." She was about to turn and head downstairs to thank him, but Tamsin grabbed her arm.

"No, Mathri. It's not Cornelius." She paused. "It's Haven."

Her mother looked at her in confusion for a moment and then yanked her arm away and went downstairs. Tamsin followed closely behind her, afraid of what she was going to say.

"Mathri, wait," she said when they reached the bottom of the stairs, knowing her mother's obliviousness to the rain was not a good sign. "I said he could stay here."

"Absolutely not," her mother said, making no effort to be quiet.

"We've housed dozens of diplomats back in the Cities" Tamsin countered, her irritation growing as she remembered it was her mother who had made her go to that awful dinner tonight. "Haven is no different."

"I will not have one of them roaming about the compound in the middle of the night!"

Haven appeared from around a pillar then, causing her mother's march to stop abruptly. "I go," he said.

"No," Tamsin said firmly. "Mathri, please. He saved my life. I owe him."

"Tamsin owe nothing. I—," Haven started to say, but Tamsin silenced him with a look.

She turned back to her mother, waiting for her answer. "If Fathri was here, he would let him stay."

"Do not presume to tell me what your father would or would not do," she said, but as she stared at them with narrow eyes Tamsin could see the lines around them start to soften. Then Lavinia sighed and said, "He can stay on the veranda until the rain stops."

Tamsin smiled. "Thank you Mathri." At least the veranda had the canvas flaps that could be put up so he wouldn't be in the rain. She motioned for him to follow her, but her mother put out a hand.

"He can go by himself. And you can go upstairs to your room Tamsin. Change out of those clothes and go to bed." She folded her arms across her chest and waited.

Tamsin looked apologetically back at Haven, but he just nodded and walked away.

Her mother pointed towards the stairs and held out her hands for the dry clothes Tamsin was still holding. Tamsin gave the clothes back and went upstairs to her room. She changed into her nightclothes, wondering about her mother's hostile behavior.

She waited until she was sure her mother had gone to sleep before she grabbed her own cloak and went downstairs to the kitchens and grabbed a few things. She went back up to the veranda and found Haven sitting with his back against a pillar, looking out at the rain, which was now driving down in sheets. He looked up at her approach.

"I didn't know what you would like," she said, offering him the plate of biscuits, cheese, and dates she had gathered.

He nodded, then touched his fingers to his head and then brushed them off the back of his hand. Then he took the plate and inspected its contents.

She stood there for a moment, debating whether or not she should stay, until Haven looked up at her and offered her a piece. She chuckled, a little awkwardly, "Oh no, I'm not hungry." Then to avoid any further embarrassment she sat down next him and listened to the sound of the rain drum against the canvas above their heads. The water poured off the edge several feet in front of them so it ran over the veranda wall like a wide curtain of a waterfall. She realized she felt more comfortable now, sitting here next to Haven than she had the last few days. She felt safe. "What did you mean earlier, about making sure it was safe?" she asked. "What are you afraid of?"

His cheek twitched. "Not afraid. Only careful."

She wondered for a moment what he could mean. "Do you think that people will try to hurt you?" As they had tried at the Hollow Cliffs. "Because you're a Ma'diin?" she asked, but he didn't answer her. Instead he just looked out into the rain.

She felt guilty for the way he had been treated thus far, by her mother especially. "Not everyone is like that," she said. "The way my mother acted isn't your fault." Then she thought: could the real reason be that her mother *knew* about her father's past with the Ma'diin?

Haven took a biscuit off the plate and held it in front of her. She took the hint with a sheepish smile and nibbled on it while she wondered just how much her mother knew. Then Haven surprised her by saying, "Mother be careful, like me. She protect Tamsin. *You*," he tried the word out. Then he said it again, more confidently this time, satisfied that he had it right. "She be right to fear me."

She noticed for the first time how young he actually seemed. Though his face remained firmly hidden beneath his hood the rough overtones in his voice were accented by something she couldn't quite put her finger on, but led her to believe he was actually younger than he seemed. Now that they had a quiet moment to just talk, she could listen to and hear the softer parts of his voice. Not just the growl of a lion, but the purr of a housecat. She smiled to herself at the image.

"But you won't hurt anyone," she said with certainty. "You won't hurt me."

His hand paused just before the biscuit touched his lips. "No, not you."

There was a weariness to his answer, and something else, when he said that. She scrunched up her nose, unsure of the right question to ask. She wanted to ask if he was alright. She had not had the chance to ask him since the storm, but she remembered how frustrated he had seemed at himself in the desert when she had had to help him. Instead she asked, "When was the last time you slept Haven?"

He shook his head, sending tiny droplets flying off his hood. "Not important," he said. "Not rains for many days."

"You only sleep when it rains?"

"No. Amon'jii not like water. They hide when it rains. I not watch for them now."

"Amon'jii," she said the strange word slowly.

"Animals," he said, as if that explained it.

It didn't sound familiar to her. All she had seen so far out here were bugs. She shuddered and then remembered the stone creatures on the archway outside the city's entrance and how Haven had studied them. "And why do you watch for them?"

"We hunt them."

"You hunt them? Why?"

"Because they hunt us."

Her mouth formed an O and she was quiet for a moment, though it was not the answer she had expected. "So, you can sleep now that it's raining," she said, bridging the silence.

"Tamsin stubborn," he said, like he was speaking to himself, "like Ysallah. I not sleep when night."

She raised an eyebrow. "So do you sleep at all?"

She saw the corner of his mouth turn up slightly before he took another bite.

She wanted to ask him more questions, but she let him eat instead. She watched the rain come down in front of them, the steady hum of it beating the canvas lulling her into a daze. She hadn't realized she had dozed off until a loud clap of thunder boomed overhead. She blinked a few times, getting her bearings, and wrapped her cloak tighter around her. The rain had brought in the cooler air and it was still coming down heavily. She looked over at Haven and found that he had fallen asleep, still holding a biscuit in his hand. It was the most relaxed she had ever seen him. In this moment, he wasn't a Ma'diin or a hunter. He was just a man. She smiled at the sight, but felt bad that he was forced to stay out here when she had a nice, dry bed waiting for her. But she knew there would be seven hells to pay if her mother found her out here in the morning.

She reached over to take the biscuit before it turned into a pile of mush against his wet clothes and saw that the cloth around his fingers was stained red. Careful not to wake him she started untying it. The cuts on his fingers were mostly healed so she stuffed the old cloth in the pocket of her cloak. Something caught her eye on his wrist and she tentatively pushed his sleeve back. Some kind of scar snaked its way up his skin, but the coloring was off. It was light and silvery, like the stars. And there was another that ran alongside it. She ran her finger along the lines. They were smooth, like new skin, but there was no raised edge to them. While wondering how far they went up his arm she realized that she had never truly seen his face. Did he have scars there as well? Was that why he kept his face hidden? His breathing hadn't changed; he was still asleep so she reached forward towards his hood and lifted the edge slightly. His head was tilted away from her, but she saw the curve of his jaw and the veil that covered the upper half of his face. The blood drained from her face as the thought popped into her head: what if he woke up and saw her? She dropped his hood and scrambled to her feet, backing away. She stood with her back pressed against the column. *What was the matter with her?*

She tried to make as little noise as possible as she tiptoed away and up to her room. She couldn't get back to sleep, though the sound of the rain had slowed to a soothing hum. Every time she dozed off she would see the stone creatures from the main gate hunting her and the panic she felt would snap her awake again. It was easy to return to the nonsensical fears of childhood when she was alone, in the middle of the night in a place she was not used to yet. She wanted to go back and check on him, and to feel that brief comfort she had felt with him, but she was too embarrassed by how intrusive she had been. She drummed her fingers underneath the blankets and tried to find patterns in the rough sandstone ceiling to keep from thinking about it, but listening to Haven's comments about the amon'jii had made her edgy and her mind would not be quieted. She wasn't even sure she believed that creatures like the ones at the gate existed, but hearing the caution in Haven's voice made her uncertainty waver. Haven was perhaps the most dangerous and skilled person she had ever met. He had faced a desert sandstorm with barely the blink of an eye, had challenged more than a dozen trained soldiers single-handedly and escaped, and had turned the Empyrian lords into a quivering mass of frightened children with only his shadow. If Haven was wary of the amon'jii, then what exactly were these creatures capable of? And if Haven hunted them in return, then what was he capable of?

Listening to him talk certainly made the marshlands sound like a much more strange and hostile environment than she had originally entertained. She wondered how long he had been doing this, hunting the amon'jii. She had so many questions for him she didn't know where to begin, and was impatient for the next day to start. And soon her mind told her enough was enough and sleep finally overcame her, though in her dreams she felt hot breath on the back of her neck and a forked tongue smelling her. Darkness surrounded her and all she could see was a glowing blue pool ahead of her, but the harder she tried to move her legs the more paralyzed she became. Then she realized the glow was coming from the woman standing in the center. It was the blue woman and she was holding an S-shaped sword. She swung it in an arc through the air and brought it down in the pool, sending waves bursting out in all directions. Only then did the beast behind Tamsin flee and she was alone in the dark.

CHAPTER THIRTEEN

Tamsin took one of the seeds out of the drawstring bag and held it up so she could see it more clearly. It was long and narrow and concave on one side like the canoes she had seen some of the fishermen use in the river, but it was no bigger than the tip of her ring finger. "And does this one grow into a grain? Or a fruit maybe?"

Haven shook his head no. "Pla'naii. Colors only."

"A flower," she said smiling. Most of the seeds he had shown her from his little bag had been for growing food or herbs. Some of them grew to their full potential in a matter of days, he explained, which was good if one ran out of food in barren terrain. It wouldn't sustain you indefinitely, but it might keep you alive long enough to get to more bountiful lands.

Tamsin was quickly learning that knowing how to survive was something Haven was quite adept at. That morning she had woken up well before her usual time, but not knowing if Haven was still there or not made her anxious and she threw on the first dress she could find and braided her hair simply down the side before flying down the stairs and out onto the veranda. He was exactly where she had left him, only now he was awake and leaning against the veranda wall, watching the clouds roll across the mottled grey sky. He straightened when he saw her and flicked his fingers off the back of his hand. He told her he didn't remember the last time he slept through the night; he and the other Watchers were nocturnal Tamsin figured out. Then he asked her what people do during the day and she had smiled, feeling relieved knowing that she would have the opportunity to get her questions answered.

They walked around the compound a little while her mother was still being prepped for the day in her rooms, but Tamsin was eager to explore beyond the compound walls so they had spent the rest of the morning wandering through the city, and even though he only made kind suggestions to their route, Haven seemed to have an innate sense of direction She couldn't help but compare Empyria to the Cities and he listened politely as she talked about her old home and haunts, but his attention seemed to be fleeting as he was constantly glancing behind them as if they were being followed. And his hand flexing over his weapons did not go unnoticed by her. The threat of more rain had left the open streets fairly deserted, but people still milled about underneath stone arbors and exposed hallways and cast curious and sometimes suspicious glances their way. He was not used to being out in the open like this for everyone to stare at, she realized, and his passing attention was only a result of his discomfort and wariness.

She adjusted their course and it wasn't long before they found themselves on the banks of the Elglas, the mighty Armillary standing guard in the distance. There were few boats on the water today and none paid them any attention, which seemed to ease Haven's apprehension and he crouched down at the edge of the water, his cloak rippling about him in the gentle wind like the currents in the river. The bank itself was mainly moist sand, with a few scattered rocks and some larger boulders. A few tan-colored reeds had taken root in small, protective bunches in the shallow water, but other than that there was no other vegetation. In fact, it was the only plant life she had seen in Empyria that wasn't in a vase or trellis. Even the large palm trees that adorned the bases of the compounds and the courtyards of the Armillary were firmly buried in large, clay pots. Tamsin mentioned this and that was when Haven had shown her the bag of seeds he carried with him.

This particular seed, the pla'naii seed, seemed out of place amongst the others. Haven didn't seem to be the type of person to carry around anything that wasn't necessary. "What is special about this flower?" she asked.

The corners of his mouth tightened and the tips of his nostrils flared. He stood up and faced the river and the silence that followed made Tamsin realize that this seed *was* special. Its importance wasn't in bearing fruit or healing powers; it was sentimental to him. "I'm sorry," she said, standing up next to him and holding the seed out in the palm of her hand. She didn't understand, but she felt the need to apologize anyway, feeling the cultural barrier between them rising up.

But he closed her fingers around the seed. "You keep," he said, not unkindly. "It be pla'naii sun hasafein, flower of woman. Woman should have it. You have it."

"Did someone give this to you?" she asked softly.

"Yes," he replied, his voice gruffer than usual.

She asked no more questions about it, not wanting to pry, though she could not deny her curiosity was smoldering. If it was the flower of women then she had no doubt in her mind that another woman had given this to him. She felt the small seed pressed into her palm and had an idea. She walked over to a scraggly patch of reeds that looked more like a few struggling blades of grass at the edge of the water and dug out a little hole next to it. She sensed Haven watching her as she placed the seed in the hole and covered it back up. "It should be given a chance to see the sun," she said.

Her only approval was a slight nod of his head, though she saw his lips curve up briefly and she knew she had done the right thing. The harsh environment of Empyria was not friendly to natural plant life, but with a little faith and a lot of luck, the little seed might actually make it.

She stood up and wiped her hands together. "I think I've asked you enough questions," she said, deciding to give him a reprieve. "Your turn."

His grin widened. "Why you not learn to be in water?" he asked, his voice purring again like rough velvet.

"Why I never learned…?" She didn't understand for a moment and then her lips parted as she realized he was teasing her about not knowing how to swim. She pointed her finger at him and tried to keep a straight face, but with one of his rare smiles beaming at her she wasn't very successful. "That's not fair. I was unconscious," she said, referring to the night they had found her. "And swimming isn't something a lady of my station is taught. We are better suited to tasks indoors." She blinked in surprise at herself, thinking that sounded like something her mother would say. She recalled a time when she would climb trees and wait in the branches just out of Sherene's reach whenever she was threatened with being put inside for an extended period. She hadn't realized until now just how much she missed the little girl she had been then.

"You should learn," Haven continued seriously. "All Kazserii know how and also fight."

She was about to tell him that her five year old self would've loved the idea, but she heard a noise and looked up and saw a group of soldiers heading their way. She tensed, remembering she had forgotten all about Cornelius's wish to see Haven.

Haven turned to see what she was looking at and then put himself in front of her, facing the soldiers.

They stopped a few yards away, clearly uncomfortable with being so close to Haven.

Tamsin saw Haven's hand move slightly at his side and she was afraid he had misinterpreted her nervousness. She stood up next to him before he could reach for his weapon. "It's okay, Haven. They just want to talk."

The soldiers looked at each other before one of them spoke. "Captain Saveen requests your presence at the Armillary," he said. "If you wish we can escort you there now."

Haven looked down at her, and she realized he was waiting for her to decide. "You can go," she said. "I can find my way back on my own."

"Actually, my lady, Captain Saveen requested your presence as well. He assumed you would be with him."

Tamsin pursed her lips. She really didn't like Cornelius and his assumptions. She knew she had to tell him how she felt, but she felt like she was being watched by him and it put her teeth on edge. And she definitely didn't want to be a pawn in whatever angle Cornelius was trying to play now. "You can tell him I had a prior engagement," she lied. She caught Haven's questioning expression, even under the brim of his hood. "I'll explain later," she whispered. "Go with them. I'll see you later."

She could tell he wasn't happy, but he nodded once and let the guards lead him away.

Tamsin watched them go until she couldn't see them anymore and then let out a deep breath. She stayed by the water a little while longer, letting her mind wander south along the shoreline and inevitably to how her father was faring. Then when the sky looked like it would turn its threat of rain into reality she followed the path back the way they had taken, but turned in the opposite direction away from the Armillary and walked through a bowered hallway to one of the courtyards in between the compounds. Servants in pale blue and men in tan shirts were working together to prepare for the next wave of rain, setting up jars in rows underneath the eaves of the buildings to collect the rainfall.

She kept thinking about what Haven had said about the Kazserii, about how they could swim and fight and she couldn't help but compare it to her own skills. Knowing how to needlepoint or play Paradesium's Symphony on the piano didn't seem as important here as it did in the Cities. In the marshlands, and even here in Empyria, basic survival skills were the most valued of all. Tamsin couldn't hunt or fish, let alone cook anything for herself. She knew for certain if Haven hadn't come along when she was lost in the desert she wouldn't have been able to fend for herself. She could study geography or astronomy as much as she wanted, but none of it mattered if she couldn't apply it to use. Watching the people around her, she realized the things she was good at did nothing to contribute to what was really important.

She saw an older man struggling with a long, wooden box and went over to help him. He had shoulder-length, silvery hair and his posture was slightly hunched as if most of his work consisted of leaning over a desk, but his face lit up when she took the other end and together they maneuvered it so one end was propped up underneath the corner of two eaves and the other was angled downwards into a plant box on the inside of the walkway laden with vines and other leafy plants. The inside was hollowed out so when the rain started a little stream flowed down it and into the plant box. She helped him with three more, one for each corner of the courtyard, and others even pitched in as the rain began to increase.

Though the sky had been overcast most of the day, they were still in the middle of the desert and the heat of it had persisted, but the rain offered cool relief and Tamsin laughed as she held her hands out from underneath the eaves and let the water cascade across her skin. A group of children had found a puddle and were now jumping in it and splashing themselves, their shrieks of delight contagious. Others too were smiling and some even ran out into the courtyard, dancing and hollering, the rain seeming to have lightened their cares.

Tamsin heard a familiar voice and turned around to see Georgiana among the other servants. She made her way over there and was greeted with a huge smile. Stray strands of Georgiana's golden hair clung to her face and neck and she held a small basket in the crook of her arm.

"Tamsin! What are you doing out here?"

"I was just helping—," she looked around, but the older gentleman had disappeared. "Just helping," she said.

Georgiana's face was delightfully puzzled and Tamsin could only imagine what she thought of her, a lady from the lording class, helping the servants collect rainwater. "I was just getting some things from the market for dinner tonight." She lifted her empty basket. "Would you like to join me?"

Someone walked by in a dark cloak and Tamsin glanced over Georgiana's shoulder, her thoughts drifted back to Haven, wondering how he was faring.

"Are you meeting someone here?" Georgiana asked, looking around. "Are you meeting Captain Saveen?"

Tamsin turned back to her. "Why would you say that? I mean, why him?"

"Oh, someone saw you at the Saveen compound last night and apparently Captain Saveen has moved back in there. I don't mean to pry, but are you two...?"

Georgiana was clearly excited, but Tamsin felt sick. "Apparently rumors escalate quickly here."

Georgiana's smile quickly vanished. "I'm sorry, I shouldn't have said anything. If you don't want to have dinner with us, that's alright. I understand."

"No, that's not it," Tamsin said hastily, fearing she had insulted her. "Of course I would love to come."

As Georgiana led Tamsin away from the courtyard, Tamsin explained what had happened the previous night with Cornelius, though she left out the parts about her father and later with Haven. She trusted Georgiana well enough to keep her feelings about Cornelius to herself until she talked to him directly, but her other secrets she would keep hidden for now. The underground market was in full swing due to the rain, though it wasn't really underground, only under the wide hallways below some of the connected buildings. Tamsin followed along, amazed at Georgiana's skills of negotiation. Everything could be bartered here and no price was set in stone. When they were done, Georgiana took her to her home, which was on the ground level of a street composed of what looked to Tamsin as a maze of doorways, all carved out of stone arches and staircases. Most of the servants for the compounds lived on the east side, Georgiana explained, but her father was a scribe for Lord Regoran so they were able to have a residence nearby. Inside it was small; Tamsin could only imagine what her mother would have to say of such a place that was the size of her bedroom, but it was well kept and tidy. She took a seat at the table in the main living room, which also looked to act as kitchen and dining room and folded her hands in her lap while Georgiana got a kettle of water boiling in the fireplace.

A tall man with shoulder length silvery hair came sweeping out of another room and smiled when he saw the two of them. It was the man she had helped with the rain trellis, Tamsin realized.

"Well hello there," he said, shaking Tamsin's hand. "We meet again."

"You know each other already?" Georgiana asked, bringing the kettle over to the table.

"Not at all," the older man shook his head with a wide grin.

Georgiana rolled her eyes. "This is Tamsin, Dad. Tamsin, this is my father."

"It's nice to meet you sir," Tamsin said.

"Please, call me Mr. Graysan. Are you making tea Georgiana? Could you pour me some?"

Georgiana brought three cups over to the table, the smell of chamomile rising from the warm liquid. "I thought you were working at the Armillary today?"

"I was, but Lord Regoran sent me home early. Something came up he said. So I was helping at the compounds before the rains came. Which I am grateful for your help Tamsin."

Tamsin smiled and sipped her tea, thinking she knew exactly what had come up at the Armillary. Despite the soothing aroma her nerves were still on edge. Why would they send people home if Haven had been summoned there? His existence here was no secret. Unless—the guards had said Cornelius had summoned him, not the lords. If the lords hadn't known Haven was coming…Tamsin could see how that might rattle them enough to send people away. But why would Cornelius do that?

"I see you went to the market today. Did they have any fresh tahini?" Mr. Graysan asked.

"Yeah. I was going to make it for supper tonight. I invited Tamsin. I hope that's okay."

"Of course it is. Our guests are few and far between these days," he said almost apologetically. "Here, why don't you come help me with the soup while Georgiana starts the tahini. She makes *excellent* tahini."

Tamsin was able to lose herself for a while helping Mr. Graysan. He was patient with her, showing her which herbs were best to use and how to thicken the soup. Amidst telling her why the basil leaf was good for flavor he veered off into a story about how he spilled a plate of garlic all over Lady Regoran's lap once, which ended his servitude there, but Lord Regoran had found it so amusing that he made him his scribe at the Armillary instead. Mr. Graysan had many stories like this and would often get ahead of himself and confuse his stories together, but he was very animated. Georgiana would just smile and shake her head, as if this was how he was all the time. Tamsin couldn't help but notice how grown up she seemed here, almost like she was the adult and her father was the one that needed looking after. Tamsin wondered what had happened to Mrs. Graysan, but she didn't ask.

Once dinner was ready, they sat down at the small table which was just big enough to seat the three of them comfortably and Georgiana recanted the story of the night of the winter solstice when Mr. Graysan enquired how they met. Tamsin took over the telling from the point she had fallen in the river.

"I'm very lucky that Haven was there," Tamsin said after she finished telling them about making it through the sandstorm.

"I don't think I've heard that name around here. Is he with the High Guard?" Mr. Graysan asked.

"Not exactly," Tamsin said. "He's with the Ma'diin."

Mr. Graysan's eyes grew wide. "The man who saved you is one of the Ma'diin?" He sat back and put a hand over his mouth in disbelief. "That is incredible. I heard it was some soldiers who found you. I didn't realize that the Ma'diin were a part of that."

It took Tamsin some time to tell them what really happened. She explained how the soldiers had shown up at the cliffs and went up until when the Ma'diin had left with her father and by the time she had finished their meal was finished as well. Georgiana had to politely remind her father to eat several times as he seemed too enthralled by her story to focus on anything else. But he stayed strangely quiet when she had finished.

"Your father is Lord Urbane?" he asked after a long pause. "You're Tamsin Urbane?"

"Don't be rude, Dad," Georgiana said.

"Forgive me," Mr. Graysan said with a shake of his head. "I mistook you for one of Georgiana's friends from the compound. I didn't realize you *lived* there. Forgive me."

"It's quite alright," Tamsin assured him, though it confused her a little as to why that was the fact he was stuck on. She knew the lines between the lording class and the working class were drawn, but she didn't think that it warranted that kind of reaction from Mr. Graysan, especially after the lovely meal they had shared together. "Georgiana said you had been to the marshlands before," she said, hoping to change the subject.

It seemed to have worked because Mr. Graysan began talking excitedly. "Yes! And in fact, if it weren't for the Ma'diin, we'd probably still be wandering around there completely lost!" He laughed. "To this day I still can't figure out how they navigate down there. You see—," and he continued on, disappearing into another room as he explained to them the complexity of the marshlands, reappearing with hand-drawn maps with his own notes scribbled in the corners. The Elglas snaked its way south until it ran into range of mountains and then began to split into many different lines until Mr. Graysan's handwriting took over. His excitement was contagious; even Georgiana, who had probably heard these stories a dozen times, paused from her cleaning up to listen. He brought out more pieces of parchment with drawings of long-beaked birds with tall legs, sharp-toothed fish, of huts that were suspended on floating beds of reeds and mud, and people. None of the portraits looked like Haven or his companions though; most of the Ma'diin in the pictures wore very little clothing.

She noticed they were all men. "How come there are no women in your drawings?"

He ruffled through the papers for a moment and then selected one, pulling it out for her to see. "This was the only portrait I was allowed to keep," he said. "They protect their women very well."

Tamsin studied the drawing. It was not what she had expected. The woman wore a tight, bustled garment not unlike the ones the dress maker had shown her. The dress seemed out of place, almost like it was too conservative. It was nothing like what she had seen Ysallah wear. But what was strangest of all was that she was wearing a veil that covered her whole head, with only a slit for the eyes. It reminded her of the face veil that Haven wore underneath his hood that hid the upper part of his face, only the woman's was made of dark lace and revealed nothing about what she looked like.

"A war was nearly started over her," Mr. Graysan said quietly.

"What happened?" Tamsin asked.

He wrung his hands together nervously as if he didn't want to talk about it. "She came back with us. I don't know much about how it started," his eyes flicked up to hers for a moment before looking away, "but it happened about a year after we came back from our expedition." He swallowed thickly. "Some of the Ma'diin had come to see her."

And suddenly Tamsin knew who the woman in the picture was. "She died, didn't she?" she asked.

His light, intelligent eyes flickered in surprise.

"I know about my father," Tamsin said reassuringly, though saying it aloud did nothing to reassure her own anxieties.

"You do?"

"Yes, I know he had an affair with one of them. She's the same woman as the one in this picture, isn't she?"

He looked hard at her for a long moment. "Yes, she was," he said slowly, carefully.

"How did she die?"

"There were many sorts of rumors about it. The Ma'diin claimed she was murdered, some said she caught a foreign disease, and others thought she was poisoned. I never found out which one was true."

"Does your father know that you know?" Georgiana asked Tamsin.

Tamsin shook her head no. "He left with them before I could ask."

There was a pause in the conversation before Mr. Graysan continued. "It happened the same night she died." His eyes grew dark with the memory. "I said the Ma'diin protect their women, but nobody knew how they avenged them, until then. It was just after you were born," he said to Georgiana. "You had a fever in the middle of the night so I took you to the healer's, but his wife said he had gone to Lord Saveen's compound, so that's where I went. They weren't going to let us in, but that's when the shouting started. While they went to see what was going on, I got us inside. Even from the highest level I could still hear the screaming in the streets." His forehead creased and his eyes glazed over for a moment, as if he was seeing it all again as he was retelling it. "We were lucky," he said, drawing a deep breath. "The guards were able to safeguard the compounds, but by the time they got organized enough to fight back it was too late. The Ma'diin killed most of the men who had been on the expedition."

Tamsin was horrified. It wasn't justice for one woman's death, it wasn't an eye for an eye retribution; it was a massacre.

Her father's and the other lords' concerns about the Ma'diin seemed legitimate now.

Georgiana put a hand on her father's arm consolingly, protectively. "You never told me that."

"It is not a night I like to remember." He gave her a small, sad smile.

"What happened to the Ma'diin?" Tamsin asked. The answers seemed more important now than ever.

"Some were killed in the fighting, though the visiting Ma'diin reached a truce with the lords for the others' lives. They were sent into the desert, but being exiled to the Sindune is as good as a death sentence."

"And my father?"

"He was gone before the sun rose the next day. They kept the reasons behind what happened well hidden from the masses," he said. "There were only a few of us that actually knew the truth." He gathered up his papers and sketches and started putting them away.

Tamsin helped Georgiana finish cleaning up, impressed that Mr. Graysan had managed to maintain an avid interest in the Ma'diin after what had happened, and only when she had to light another candle did they realize how late it was. Mr. Graysan offered to take her home. There was no cart waiting for her this time and she had not expected one. The time it took to walk gave her time to process the evening and everything she had learned. Mr. Graysan said little on the way back, but when they reached the compound he stopped her and pulled something out of his pocket.

"I thought you might want to have this," he said and handed her a piece of parchment. It was the drawing of the Ma'diin woman.

Tamsin knew he meant no harm, but she had to bite her lip to keep her emotions in check. So many lives had been lost over this woman, over a woman her father had kept secret from her. There was no reason she should keep it, but she took it anyway and thanked him.

"It was a pleasure to meet you, Tamsin." He patted the side of her head and kissed her on the forehead in a rather paternal way and started walking back.

"Wait, Mr. Graysan," she stopped him and he turned a half-step, but didn't make eye contact with her, as if he was afraid of what she might ask.

"You had to have talked to her. You drew this picture." She didn't know what more she wanted from Mr. Graysan. There was something almost forbidden about knowing her father's past, but it was equally alluring and she could not let it go.

He seemed to understand her conflict. "Do not judge your father too harshly," he said. "She was a force to be reckoned with. I can understand why the Ma'diin were so upset by her death."

Tamsin wondered if Ysallah had known her. Had Haven known her? "Mr. Graysan, were any of the exiled Ma'diin Watchers?"

His silvery hair shimmered around his face, giving him the ethereal appearance of a ghost in the darkness. Before he walked away he said, "The only Watcher that was ever here died."

CHAPTER FOURTEEN

"You must be able to defend you," Haven said.

"You must be able to defend *yourself*," Tamsin corrected him, and then, "From what exactly?" Tamsin had been processing what Mr. Graysan had told her the other night and was trying to reconcile that her father had been a part of it, which was why she hadn't foreseen what Haven intended to do when he showed up in the gray hours just before dawn the next morning and took her to the sparring yard just off the compound's lower level. She remembered what he had said about Ma'diin women and their abilities, but she was neither Ma'diin nor had she been raised in a survivalist culture so she didn't know why Haven wanted her to learn how to fight. She had never touched a sword in her life and the thought of it made her stomach turn. Here in Empyria had been the first time she actually saw one used for something other than a military accessory. Her father would only take his down from above the mantel in the Cities when he attended a function that required he wore his dress uniform.

His lips were set in a serious line. He popped a blade out of its sheath in one swift motion and held out the handle towards her. "From enemies. Take it."

She shook her head and took a nervous step back. "I don't have any enemies, Haven. Nobody here is trying to hurt me," she said, though she was less sure if she believed it now than before she came to Empyria.

"They hide in shadows."

"What do you mean by that?"

He sighed and lowered the sword. "Because you with me, you be target. People try to hurt you to get me. If I not be here, I need to know you able to protect yourself," he said the last word slowly.

"But nobody wants to hurt you either, Haven. There is a truce." She didn't understand why he was thinking like this, like he had done something terrible and was waiting for the backlash. Unless somebody had already threatened him. Mr. Graysan had said there were only a few that knew about the massacre, but was it possible that one of those people still held a grudge against the Ma'diin? Mr. Graysan had also said the only Watcher involved had died, but did that make a difference to one who lost someone? "What did Cornelius say to you yesterday? When you went to the Armillary?" she asked. Was it Cornelius that held the grudge? Or had the need for revenge been passed down from his late uncle, who he said had also loved the same woman as her father. The woman that died.

Haven tilted his head slightly to the side, but didn't say a word. Instead, he took a step closer almost as if to intimidate her. "No give trust until it earned. Not even me," he said. "And when you do, be sure you able to trust with your life." He held out the sword again and this time she took it.

It was much heavier than she imagined and though it looked small in Haven's hand, it seemed quite large in her own. The leather around the handle was worn almost exactly to Haven's imprint, the weaving design on it visible only on the ends, but the blade was in perfect condition, reflecting her face as clearly as if she were looking into a mirror. She could tell he took very good care of it. But she could tell from the cuts in the handle that it had seen battle before and that she should not be deceived by the shiny blade. Haven *killed* with this sword. It was suddenly too heavy and she gripped it with both hands to keep it from shaking. She couldn't imagine ever using this against someone.

"I don't think I can do this," she said.

But Haven did not seem to share her concern. He wrapped his hands around hers, shifting them slightly and then told her to move her feet apart to help her balance. He pushed the blade up with his fingers and then, pleased with her stance, pointed to the burlap dummy on the post. "Try," he said.

She took a deep breath and then swung the sword, arcing it over her shoulder and hitting the target at the cross where the neck would have been. The sword bounced off the post with a jarring thud and it almost slipped from her grasp. She looked at Haven, feeling the blood rise to her face, but the darkness under his hood revealed nothing. He walked over and stood behind her, pressing his body against hers. He wrapped his arms around her and put his hands over hers and raised the sword again.

"Like me," he said, bending her elbows.

She took a few more deep breaths, thinking he smelled of lilacs and smoke, and forced herself to relax, though it was difficult to concentrate with his sweet, fiery scent so near. Then, with his hands guiding hers, he swung the sword to the right and then to the left. He went slowly, letting her get the rhythm of the movement, the edge of the sword barely touching the burlap. He swung low, and then high, back and forth, until her body moved with his. Then he went a little faster and let the sword dig a little deeper. They kept going like this until she could anticipate where he was going to strike by the way his body moved. Faster and faster they went until her arms trembled from exertion. She struck again and again and then delivered a blow that severed one of its arms off, sending tufts of cotton floating to the ground.

She cried out triumphantly and then turned around when she realized Haven was no longer behind her. How long had he been gone? But then she saw him, only a few paces away, like he was just a shadow, watching her with his arms crossed over his chest. His lips were slightly curved. He was smiling.

"Again," he said.

By the sixth day, Tamsin couldn't get to the courtyard fast enough. She excused herself from afternoon tea with her mother and Lady Allard early just so she could get some extra practice in before Haven showed up. He would come early in the morning while the yard was shadowy and still and then again in the afternoon after the sun dipped below the wall, disappearing during the hottest parts of the day. What had once been unthinkable was now all she could think about. After the first couple of days, every muscle in her body ached, but when she was in the middle of it, everything else was forgotten. It was kind of like dancing. When you were in that moment, nothing else mattered. And she felt *empowered* by it. She felt like she could do anything…that was until the first time Haven knocked her right to the ground. She was so surprised she hardly knew what had happened. And that's when she realized had it been an actual fight she would have been finished. That's where the comparison to dancing ended; at a ball when the music finished nobody died. Haven was gentle with her and patient, but he wanted her to get better and the only way to do that was to push her. She realized she wanted to get better too and that meant she had to take it seriously. She thought she was no stranger to hard work; it had taken her three months of practicing every day before she learned the waltzes of each of the seven Ruling Cities back in Delmar, but this was the most physically demanding thing she had ever done and as long as

Haven was willing to teach her she was willing to learn. And though he would never admit it, she thought Haven enjoyed it as well. It gave him something to do and allowed him to flex his skills.

She made it to the sparring yard that afternoon and was surprised to see a small group of soldiers gathered by the practice posts. This courtyard was usually unoccupied during the day, save for a few servants or stable hands that walked through the arches to get from the compound to the stable. Occasionally, Tamsin spotted a curious servant on the second level who would pause from hanging wet clothes or planting seeds in the herb boxes to watch them, but for the most part they remained undisturbed during their sparring sessions.

The soldiers noticed her and one of them walked over. It was Cornelius. She hadn't seen him since their dinner, since he had kissed her, and she felt an unwelcome heat rise to her cheeks.

"Cornelius, what a surprise it is to see you here." She looked around, but she was early and Haven was not here.

"Lady Tamsin," he said, kissing her hand. "I hope it is a pleasant surprise. I was hoping to see you and my men said I could find you here."

"Why were you looking for me?" pulling her hand from his. She thought she had made her feelings quite clear to him.

He gave a short, incredulous laugh. "You're not the first woman to insult me. Though it wounds me that you think I would give up so easily." He leaned in closer and whispered, "Have you missed me?"

She shifted her feet. "I've been too busy to miss you even if I wanted to."

"So my men tell me. They say the Ma'diin man has been teaching you how to use a sword. Is this true?"

"There's no law saying a woman can't use a sword," she said defensively.

"I'm not saying there is. It's just unusual, that's all. If I had known you had an interest in it, I would've been glad to teach you myself."

"I didn't, at first. But Haven insisted that I be able to somewhat protect myself if the need ever arose," she said. "He says that where he's from, all the women know how to fight."

"Well, I don't know the style of Ma'diin swordsmanship, but if you would care to spar with me a round or two, I'm sure I could teach you how to properly wield a sword." He took out his saber and swung it in a circle.

But Tamsin was not impressed. "Haven says you should not reveal how you fight to someone unless you are fighting them for real."

Cornelius chuckled. "Did he now? Well, I must say, it would be quite interesting to see you fight someone for real Tamsin. I'm sure you would make a fearsome competitor."

One of his lieutenants stifled a laugh. Tamsin bristled. "Give me a weapon and I'll show you," she said through her teeth. Haven had told her to be careful not to let her emotions control her when she should be focused, but she was finding Cornelius's mocking tone hard to ignore. Not to mention the fact that his men had apparently been spying on her.

"On the contrary," he replied and then he looked past her and said loudly, "Should we show her how men really fight?"

Tamsin turned around and saw Haven walking towards them, his cloak billowing out behind him, almost snapping with how quickly he was approaching.

Cornelius pointed the end of his saber at Haven. "Unless you only spar with women and straw posts." Some of his men chuckled nervously behind him.

She could almost feel the energy crackling from him as Haven reached her. "You don't have to fight him Haven," she whispered, feeling terrible knowing that he had come here expecting to spar with her and instead was being challenged by the Captain of the Empyrian High Guard, whom she suspected had not gained that title through any lack of skill with a blade.

But Haven held up his hand. "Watch his mistakes," he said softly. "Learn from this."

She backed away and he crossed his arms around his waist underneath his cloak. When he drew them out again he held two long knives. A murmur went through the soldiers. It was not like the one he used to teach her with. These ones had bone-white handles and sinister S-shapes to them. They weren't as long as Cornelius's saber, but they looked just as sharp. And strangely familiar…

Cornelius's smile vanished. He handed off his saber to one of his men who in turn gave him a larger, double-edged broadsword. "Let's see what other tricks you have up your sleeve," he said.

They circled each other for a moment in the middle of the square and then Cornelius lunged, forcing Haven on the defensive. Cornelius swung his sword faster than Tamsin could keep track of, again and again, but Haven blocked each one, almost casually it seemed. They moved around the courtyard, Cornelius attacking while Haven parried, until Cornelius nearly had Haven backed against one of the walls. Cornelius swung down, but Haven twisted out of the way and the clang from Cornelius's sword hitting the stone echoed around them. But Haven didn't attack while Cornelius's back was exposed. Instead, he moved back to the middle of the courtyard and waited for Cornelius to join him. Cornelius rushed him with a howl and Tamsin feared Haven was going to be seriously hurt. But her fears were unwarranted it seemed. Cornelius got two swings in and then it was Haven's turn to go on the attack. He moved faster than Cornelius had done thus far and Cornelius could barely get his sword up in time to block. Their swords clashed three times and then Cornelius's was suddenly flying through the air. Everyone watched as it landed abruptly at his men's feet, everyone except Haven, who had both his blades crossed over Cornelius's throat. Cornelius eyed the knives warily as Haven paused there for a long moment and then slowly backed away.

"That was most excellent," Cornelius said, breathing heavily through his nose, but the scowl that lingered on his face revealed he was not happy at all with the outcome. "I insist on a rematch."

"No," Haven said bluntly and walked over to Tamsin.

She was still trying to process what had just happened that she didn't hear when he asked her a question. "What?" she asked.

"What you see?" he repeated.

She took a few breaths. "I saw, umm, you," she said, figuring out what he had done. "You let him attack first. You discovered his weaknesses without revealing any of your own and you let him get tired."

He nodded and that was all the praise she needed.

Cornelius, having retrieved his sword, stalked back over to them. "I demand a rematch! You can't refuse! The laws of dueling state—."

Haven turned around to face him. "Laws mean nothing when fighting. This...*play* fighting mean nothing. Tamsin sees and that is enough."

But Cornelius did not back down. He marched right up to Haven and swung his sword.

Tamsin screamed, but Haven had already blocked the blow. Using his free hand, Cornelius reached out and ripped Haven's hood back.

Everything stopped. Cornelius lowered his sword and backed away like he was looking at a ghost. His men had taken pause, their swords half out of their sheaths.

Haven yanked his hood back over his head and in one fluid motion hooked his knife behind Cornelius's boot, sending him reeling onto his back, and kneeled on his chest with the tip of his knife pressed against Cornelius's cheek. He said something to Cornelius that Tamsin did not catch and gave him one last shove before he stood up and stalked away.

Tamsin called after him, but he did not seem to hear and then disappeared out of the yard. She looked over at Cornelius, whose men were already helping him off the ground and asked if he was alright.

He nodded, but his face was red as he was trying to get his breath back.

"Should we go after him, Captain?" one of his men asked, almost eagerly.

But Cornelius shook his head. "Follow him if you wish, but keep your distance."

He nodded and a couple of them took off.

"Why would you do such a thing?" Tamsin demanded. She would have knocked him on the ground herself for being so foolish had Haven not already done it first.

"I wanted to see the face of my opponent," he said, still breathing heavily.

"I wish you hadn't," one of his men said.

"Why is that?" Tamsin asked. Haven had had his back turned to her when Cornelius ripped his hood off, but she remembered the look on the soldiers' faces.

"His eyes," the man said. "I've never seen eyes like that, on man or beast. They were like twin moons."

Tamsin knew that if Haven didn't want to be found, then he wouldn't, and the Empyrian guards would be searching in vain for him, but she hoped he would reveal himself sooner rather than later. She was angry with Cornelius for ruining their practice time, but she was even angrier with him for alighting her curiosity. She had listened to what her father said, about the Ma'diin's robes being akin to a uniform and she had wondered about what his face looked like, but she never would've been bold enough to ask him to let her see his face. She had put it in the back of her mind. After all, it didn't matter what he looked like. But after hearing what Cornelius and his men had to say, she couldn't get it out of her mind.

"Did you hear the news, Lady Tamsin?" Sherene asked, who was sitting next to her on the west veranda the next morning, stitching together a tear in one of Tamsin's skirts.

Tamsin had gone to the sparring yard that morning and waited, but Haven had not come. "What news?" she asked absently.

"Your mother is hosting a dinner tomorrow night. She's not only invited the Lords and their wives, but I also heard she was inviting the Commander's wife and a few of his officers as well."

"So?"

Sherene scoffed. "So? I know you're not keen on social affairs, but really Lady Tamsin, I thought you would be a little more excited."

"And why should I be?" Tamsin asked. Sherene was only like this when there was some scheme afoot, and that usually meant Tamsin wasn't going to like it.

Sherene smiled mischievously. "Because Captain Saveen is going to be there and don't think I pay attention to the gossip in the maids' quarters, but…"

No, she was not going to like this one bit. "But what?"

"Well, there is a rumor that the Captain of the High Guard has made inquiries about a certain Lord's daughter." She held up the finished seam on the skirt to the light to inspect it, still smiling. "You must have enchanted him the other night at dinner."

"I don't know what his game is, but he's not interested in me," Tamsin said, rolling her eyes. More than likely Cornelius was still keeping tabs on her because Haven could usually be found with her. "I would rather not have him come to dinner at all."

Sherene stood up and folded the skirt over her arm. "Honestly, Lady Tamsin, I don't know why you are so bull-headed sometimes. Captain Saveen would be a great match for any Lady. Just because he isn't a lord yet—."

"Wait, what do you mean by he isn't a lord *yet*? His uncle was a lord, not his father."

"His uncle never had a son," Sherene explained. "Every city has no less than three governing lords. Empyria has Lord Regoran, Lord Allard, Lord Wohlrick, and your father. When Lord Wohlrick passes, your father will take his place. Eventually, they could vote in another lord if they wish and because Captain Saveen is the only living heir to the Saveen estate, he is the only candidate, unless they wanted to bring someone in from the Cities like they did with your father. And if you and Captain Saveen were to be wed, then I'm sure your father would present him with a lordship that much sooner."

Tamsin had a sour taste in her mouth at the thought of being wed to him. She asked one of the servants for a quill and piece of parchment after Sherene left. She scribbled the names of the lords on it and then put Cornelius's name underneath them. She thought it was a little odd that he had never mentioned this to her. She crossed off Lord Wohlrick's name. The other lords didn't have to name another lord if they didn't want to and after what Cornelius pulled at the council with the Ma'diin, she doubted if her father would approve the vote, let alone them being wed. At least she had him on her side in that. Her brow furrowed, the conversation she had overheard in the kitchens between the two mystery men coming back to her. She still hadn't figured out who they were, but she couldn't forget the sense of duplicity that emanated from them. As long as her father was friendly to the Ma'diin, he was not their friend, and from the sound of it whatever they were doing Cornelius didn't know about it. But they had questioned whether the *Master* they had spoken of wanted Cornelius to take his uncle's title. What if Cornelius wanted that too?

She put the quill to the paper and slowly drew a line over her father's name.

"What are you composing there, Lady Tamsin?"

Sherene's voice startled her and she dropped the quill, splattering ink over the page and her sleeve. She grabbed the paper and crumpled it into a tight ball. "Oh, it was nothing," she said hastily, trying to wipe the ink off her dress, but only managing to smear it even worse.

Sherene placed her hands on her hips and shook her head. "I've had to mend more of your dresses lately..." She sighed heavily. "Oh never mind. Let's get you upstairs and changed before your mother sees and I'll put that to soak."

Tamsin led the way up to the bathing room, trying to shake the foreboding feeling her wondering had caused, but it all disappeared when she saw Haven waiting at the top of the stairs. Sherene, who had been jabbering about some time when Tamsin was younger and had mended three of her dresses in one day, stopped and leaned against the stair wall. She looked a little surprised to see him there, but seemed too winded from the climb up the stairs to make a fuss.

"Well don't just stand there, Mr. Haven." She held out her arm and Haven promptly glided down the last few steps and took her arm, letting her lean on him as he helped her the rest of the way.

Tamsin raised an eyebrow. "I didn't think you two had met."

Sherene released his arm and turned back to scoff at Tamsin. "Just because you have been too neglectful to introduce us doesn't mean I don't know every single person who steps foot in this house. And at least one of you has the decency to help an old woman." She patted Haven's arm and went inside.

Tamsin shook her head.

Haven stepped back down so he was next to her. "I say apology," he said, his hood and veil fully in place. "Yesterday, I not act…right."

"Neither of your actions were appropriate," she said, "but I don't blame you. If I could have I would have knocked Cornelius down myself."

His lips twitched into a grin. It was not easy to get emotion from him, but when he did smile or show pleasure it made her feel like she had accomplished something.

"We practice tomorrow then?" he asked.

She bit her lip. "As much as I want to, I can't. You see, my mother is hosting a dinner…" And then she had a brilliant idea. "Would you like to come?" she asked him, before she even finished thinking it.

"I come," he said. "I keep watch."

She smiled at his misunderstanding. "No, I want you to dine with us. I don't want you lurking in the shadows, I want you out in the light."

He cocked his head, hesitating, and she didn't blame him. She had been to enough dinners with other lording families to know how tedious they could be, but she felt Haven belonged there. If she treated him like any other foreign dignitary, then maybe the others would follow suit.

Sherene called for her impatiently.

"Will you come?" Tamsin asked him again, hopefully.

He nodded, even though he didn't seem thrilled about the idea.

"Good, wait here a moment," she said and ran up the rest of the stairs to the bathing room where Sherene was pouring hot water into a large basin for the dress.

"Well you seem positively cheerful," Sherene said. "What's gotten into you?"

"I invited Haven to dinner tomorrow night," she replied. "And I need your help."

Sherene set the pitcher of water down and a stern look crossed her features. "Lady Tamsin, why must you vex me so?"

"But I thought—I thought you liked Haven?" she said, pointing her thumb back at the stairs.

"There's a big difference between like and tolerance, my lady, and I only tolerate Mr. Haven because he seems to have your well-being in mind."

"I still don't see what the problem is," Tamsin said.

"Your mother is the problem," she said, "and all those other lords and ladies. They will not approve."

"I don't care if they approve! Why does nobody seem to remember that he saved my life? That must count for something!"

"Of course it counts, my lady, but it's overshadowed by the fact that he is not from their world. They see him as trouble, Tamsin. If they knew he was staying here—."

"He's not," Tamsin countered. "He hasn't slept here in a week."

"—they would associate your mother with him and that would make *her* an outsider," Sherene continued. "And he's been sleeping on the shade eaves during the day, like it's some kind of hammock," she added with an incredulous roll of her eyes.

Tamsin blinked in surprise, but noted it for another time. "Please, Sherene, will you help me?" She explained her idea and in the end Tamsin convinced her that if Haven were to come, then it would go a long way in helping the others accept him.

When she finally agreed, they both went outside and asked Haven to come with them. He followed them down to the ground level and a less-used part of the compound just outside the servants' quarters. They waited under a square pagoda with cracked tiles and dead vines still clinging to the stone support columns in the corners while Sherene went to fetch a seamstress. Tamsin explained to him that she wanted to make him some new clothes for the dinner tomorrow night. Haven openly balked at the idea and crossed his arms over his chest. She wondered if he was being reserved because of the reaction from Cornelius and his men when they saw his face. She walked over to him and put her hand on his arm. "You don't have to feel nervous around me, Haven. I won't run away screaming," she said with a smile, hoping to lighten his mood. But he refused to take the bait.

Just then Sherene came back with the seamstress, who could do nothing to hide her anxiety at Haven's presence. And Sherene could not hide her obvious disapproval at Tamsin and Haven's proximity to each other. "You're going to have to take that cloak off," Sherene said. "I'll have it washed in the meantime." She told Tamsin to move away so the seamstress could take his measurements, but it was Haven who actually took a step back.

"Haven?" Tamsin asked, concerned.

"I not need new clothes," he said.

"It will go a long way towards earning the lords' respect," Sherene said.

"No."

"It's not about the clothes," Sherene said, in that chastising voice Tamsin had heard often enough as a child. "It's about making an effort. These people can be ruthless, Mr. Haven, and unless you play along with their rules, they will tear you apart."

"You make us sound like a pack of wolves," Tamsin said.

"Excuse me, my lady, but you I do not include in this, and you know that. There's not a mean bone in your body. Highly unusual for a lord's daughter, but that's beside the point. Now Mr. Haven, if you won't do this for them will you do this for Lady Tamsin?"

Everyone was quiet for a minute. The seamstress looked just as uncomfortable as Haven did. She held her measuring rope tight to her body as if it were a shield. Sherene tapped her foot impatiently.

Though she couldn't see them, Tamsin knew his eyes were locked onto hers and something in the way his jaw clenched told her it was more than just nerves or stubbornness that was holding him back. Something wasn't right. "Could you give us a minute?" Tamsin asked.

Sherene was clearly fed up with the whole situation. She put her hands up and stalked away, mumbling something about only trying to help.

The seamstress gratefully handed over the rope, gave her a quick smile, and left. Tamsin doubted if she would ever see her around here again. As soon as she was gone, Tamsin walked over to him. "Okay, they're gone. Will you tell me what the matter is?"

The edges of his cloak ruffled uncomfortably, like a horse's skin irritated by a fly. "I not need new clothes," he repeated.

She pressed her lips together. Her mother would probably banish him from the grounds if he refused to dress in a fashion she deemed acceptable. "I know you don't need new clothes, but it will help make people feel more comfortable around you. It will only take a few seconds."

He turned his head away, the lower half of his face hidden from the sunlight by the shadows. "If you knew why, you not ask me," he said quietly.

"Is it because of your scars?" Her hand flew to her mouth, but the words were already out and she couldn't take them back.

His whole body stiffened.

Immediately, she felt sorry for trying to push him into it. She should've never said anything, nay, she should never have looked that night in the first place and she felt even worse because a little piece of her was disappointed that she wouldn't be able to see his face. She was starting to think that this whole idea had been a selfish one. "I'm sorry," she said, turning and walking quickly away. She was too ashamed at herself to look at him anymore.

"Where are you going?" Sherene asked as Tamsin brushed past her. She didn't stop. She didn't want to face anyone, but by the time she got back up to her balcony and looked at her still ink-stained sleeve, she realized it was only herself that she didn't want to face.

CHAPTER FIFTEEN

Everything glimmered in the fading evening light and the last of the large clouds, dark grey in the middle but pink around the edges, rolled towards the sunset after a long day of rain over the city. A lingering breeze alleviated the balminess after the rains had lifted, sending little shivers up Tamsin's arms as she touched the water droplets on the veranda wall. The droplets were everywhere, tiny prisms reflecting the light as clear as the crystals that hung around her neck. It was a beautiful evening, from the candelabras that adorned the tables, to the chandeliers that hung beneath the arches and the white, gauzy curtains that framed them. But Tamsin felt like she belonged with those dark clouds that were slowly stealing away. If only she could do the same.

She walked around the veranda, catching glimpses of the party inside between the draped curtains, and heard the butler announce dinner and she knew she could no longer delay. She parted one of the curtains and walked through to the dining area, where the other guests were mingling around a long table that had been set up for the night. A feast lay before them of different roasted birds, basil soup, red potatoes, and a variety of fruits and breads. It was comforting to see some familiar food, since the Empyrian palette was taking some getting used to. Everything here seemed to be cooked with dates or a spice they called *bahara* that had a robust mix of cinnamon and paprika flavors.

Everyone took their seats and once the servants had finished pouring the wine, her mother stood up to thank them all for coming. No sooner had she raised her glass then there was a loud thud on the table and a clattering of silverware. Madame Corinthia let out a small cry and everyone stared at the pile of large, raw fish that now occupied the place in front of her on the table…and then to the man standing next to it.

Haven spread his hands out towards the fish. "I bring food."

As everyone else gaped and stuttered, Tamsin couldn't help but smile. Instead of wearing his usual dark cloak, Haven wore something similar to what she was accustomed to seeing on riders. He wore leather boots that came up to his knees and a light fitted beige jacket and tail with a dark green sash that wrapped around the middle. Had there not been the belt, wrist guards, and straps that crisscrossed his legs, arms, and chest that held his weapons, he would've almost passed for a gentleman. And the hood, which was the same color as the jacket and came to a point just over the bridge of his nose. The seamstress must have added that for him.

But Tamsin didn't care that she couldn't see his face. He had shown up.

Lady Regoran was the first to recover. "I didn't realize we needed to bring our own food, otherwise I would have brought a hen from the coop."

Lavinia's face had gone white. "I must apologize," she said hastily, then, taking a moment to calm herself, said, "Haven, we weren't expecting you. May I help you with something?"

"I bring food," he said again, holding up the fish as if Lavinia had not seen them. They were still wet from the river and dripped onto the table. "I go get more if not enough," he said, his head turning to take in the other guests.

"Haven, thank you for your…contribution, but we are quite well stocked, as you can see." She waved over the stunned servants, who warily took the fish from Haven and began wiping up the small puddle on the table. "They'll just take those down to the kitchens. Was there something else I could do for you?"

"I invited him to dinner, Mathri," Tamsin said. She turned to the servant behind her and asked him to set another place for Haven.

Her mother must have suspected this because the look on her face was not a kind one, but Tamsin knew she wouldn't cause a scene in front of everyone.

"Lavinia, who is this man?" Lady Regoran asked.

But it was her husband who answered. "This is Haven of the Ma'diin from the tribal lands to the south," Lord Regoran answered. He stood up from his chair. "We are honored to have you."

The women did a double take. The news of the Ma'diin's presence among them was not a secret, but most of them had not seen him in person. The men were a little more reserved in their reaction, having full knowledge of what Haven was capable of.

While a place was set for Haven, Tamsin waited to see if any of them would get up and leave, offended by the unexpected guest. Haven sat down and nobody moved, except for Lord Regoran who slid back down in his seat, acknowledging accusing glances from the other men with a subtle, but stern shake of his head. Even the servants seemed a little unsure of how to proceed and were slow to ladle out the soup.

But then a curious thing happened: the ladies started taking an interest in the new guest. Lady Allard, who was sitting next to Haven at the end opposite Lavinia, picked up a plate of thin biscuits and offered it to him.

"It's to dip in your soup," she said politely.

Haven took one and nodded his thanks.

Lady Wohlrick commented on his attire, calling it "quite modern." Tamsin saw Haven's jaw twitch slightly at this and she had to stifle a smile. She could only imagine how uncomfortable he was, but she admired him for coming anyway.

"Do you think he can see us from under there?" Madame Corinthia asked, waving her hand in front of her towards Haven as if she were trying to get the attention of a blind man.

Tamsin pressed her lips together so she wouldn't smile.

Lady Regoran rolled her eyes. "Of course he can. It must just be a cultural oddity. Stop waving about. You're not in a street parade."

Madame Corinthia returned her hands to her lap, her cheeks flushing bright red.

"I would wager it's to hide something," Cornelius put in. "To cover up a deformity perhaps?" He took a sip of wine then, but Tamsin saw the corner of his mouth turn up slightly.

She was about to cut in with a sharp remark in Haven's defense, but she should've known he didn't need her protection.

Before she could speak, Haven said, "I not hide behind mask or…metal skin," he said, his head turning in Cornelius's direction.

Tamsin noticed Cornelius straighten next to her.

"It help me see," Haven continued, though he looked just as uncomfortable speaking there as Cornelius did.

"What do you mean?" Lady Allard asked.

Haven took a deep, slow breath as if to give himself some time to prepare his words. Then, "I see night like you see day. Dark not hide things, it show them to me. It—," he paused, searching for the right word. He picked up a butter knife from the table, making the men's eyes widen slightly, but he only drew it back and forth through the air to imitate the word he didn't know.

"It…*cuts* things?" Lord Allard suggested, shrugging his shoulders at the disapproving look he received from Lavinia.

"It sharpens things!" Madame Corinthia cried, clapping her hands together, obviously pleased that she had guessed what Haven had been trying to say.

"And now it looks as if we'll be playing charades tonight as well," Lady Regoran said haughtily.

Haven put the knife down and gave a rare smile to Madame Corinthia. "Yes. Sharpens. World awake for me at night."

"And during the day?" Lady Allard asked.

The corner of his mouth pulled back slightly. "Day not like before. Day be…be very bright."

That earned some quiet chuckles around the table.

"Most time colors be bright and fast, then hide," he said. "But sometime they stay."

Though she couldn't see his eyes, Tamsin felt as though he were looking right at her when he said this. She wondered what she looked like to him, if she were dull and grey or if she was bright and colorful. She hoped he couldn't see her cheeks flush.

"So it's similar to looking at the sun a touch too long and pink rings dance before your eyes when you look away," Lady Allard offered.

Haven nodded in agreement with her assessment, though Tamsin assumed it was to quell further questions about it.

"Well no wonder you wear that hood all day," Lord Regoran said. "That would give me a headache as well."

Another round of chuckles, easier forthcoming this time, went around the table. Looks were exchanged between the men, but the other women seemed quite curious about him. Lady Regoran seemed curious as well, but not the polite kind that the other ladies displayed, rather, she studied him as one would a spider before they squashed it. And she studied Tamsin as well. Whenever Tamsin and Haven shared a smile, Tamsin would catch Lady Regoran looking at her with one eyebrow raised. And

Lavinia's eyes would dance back and forth between the three nervously. Lavinia was tight-lipped throughout most of the evening, especially when the ladies asked Haven about how he was getting along in Empyria or how he spent his time. But Haven was more discreet than she gave him credit for and never mentioned staying at the compound or his time with Tamsin.

But then there was Cornelius, who took it upon himself to slip in any undermining comments he could. Tamsin figured his pride was still wounded from the other day when Haven had bested him with the sword, but it still did not excuse his behavior.

"Has there been any news from Lord Urbane or the Commander?" Lady Allard inquired.

Lord Regoran shook his head. "We haven't heard anything yet, but once they've reached their destination they promised to send a courier. It is a long journey, but I suspect we will be hearing something within the next week or two."

"That is good to hear," she said. "I can't imagine spending any amount of time out there in the sand and heat."

"That is why we have husbands," Madame Corinthia said. "Rather the men sweat it out in the desert instead of us." There were a few chuckles around the table, though Tamsin noticed Madame Corinthia's smile was a sad one. She must be missing her husband as much as Tamsin missed her father.

"I quite agree," Cornelius said. "The woman's place should be in the home, not out riding horses or say sword fighting. Though I don't think Lady Tamsin would agree."

Tamsin put down her fork and gave him a look that said *not now*. Her mother was ignorant of her activities with Haven and that's how she wanted to keep it, but he persisted.

"Why would you say that?" Lady Regoran asked.

"I don't know how they're bringing up girls in the Cities these days, but I'm pretty sure they don't include swordsmanship with foreigners in their studies."

Tamsin glared at him, though she could feel the other's eyes glancing between her and Haven. She felt her cheeks and her anger flare. "Well, apparently they don't teach swordsmanship here either, since Haven beat you with ease the other day."

"Tamsin!" her mother hissed at her. "Where are your manners?"

"Where are his?" she countered. She saw Haven out of the corner of her eye, but he wasn't smiling.

There was a deadlocked silence for a moment and Lady Allard spoke, trying to ease the tension. "Is it natural for women to learn how to use a sword where you're from, Haven?"

Haven nodded. "All learn to fight."

Nervous glances were exchanged around the table at his comment, even among the women, but Lady Allard, rather diplomatically said, "I must praise you then, Lady Tamsin, for taking the initiative to understand his culture a little better. Lords know we see very little of it here."

"I don't think first-hand knowledge is required however," Lady Regoran said, effectively ending that line of conversation. Tamsin threw a grateful smile towards Lady Allard before talk turned to the rain and less controversial topics.

The stars were hovering over the dark horizon by the time the last course had been served. Cauldrons of fire had been lit throughout the level to stave off the night's cold and everyone mingled yet, except Cornelius, who had stormed off with his lieutenants after dinner was over instead of joining the lords for cigars on the veranda. Tamsin watched as Lord Allard tried, unsuccessfully, to convince Haven to try one and she was able to relax a little. She thanked Lady Allard for being so kind to Haven at the table. Tamsin had thought her a demur woman, but after talking to her she found out that she was not only polite, but had a very open mind where other cultures were concerned. She had grown up in one of the outlying sea towns in Delmar as a ship captain's daughter and it had taken many years before anyone accepted her in the Cities when she married Lord Allard. Then they had moved here and had started the process all over. She gave Tamsin a wink and said she knew a thing or two about being an outsider far from home. Tamsin decided she liked her very much.

Lord Regoran pulled Tamsin aside and with troubled eyes apologized for not seeking her out sooner to apologize for his daughter's behavior. The events of that night seemed like a lifetime ago and truthfully Tamsin hadn't noticed Emilia's absence until now. She told him not to worry and that she was grateful to him for all of his efforts to retrieve her. She was more concerned that he had held onto these feelings of guilt for so long rather than the fact that Emilia had not apologized herself.

Tamsin lowered her voice and asked him something that had been on her mind during dinner. "What will happen when they get to the dam? Do you think my father can persuade them to see that it's a good thing?"

"If there's anyone that could, it would be your father," he said, giving her hands a reassuring squeeze. "You're just like him, you know. Between you and me, I think what you're doing with Haven is very smart. What you did tonight was brilliant. He's not a threat when he's with you."

She gave him a funny look. "But he's not a threat at all. If anyone besides myself tried to get to know him even a little they would see that."

"As long as the negotiations hold. If they fail, then that would change things entirely."

"But they won't fail, will they?"

He sighed and looked over at Haven. "That's up to them I suppose."

After the cigars had been smoked and farewells had been exchanged, Tamsin sought out Haven, but he had disappeared amidst the departure of the other guests. Her mother retired for the night and Tamsin told Sherene not to wait up for her. She wandered around the veranda for a little while, the moon being only a sliver of its full glory in the dark sky, and mulled over what Lord Regoran had said. It was not the same as her old garden paths she used to wander after parties, but then nothing was like it was before.

Saddened by the sudden nostalgia, she decided it would be best to try and get some sleep and turned to go back inside, but she didn't get past the first pillar when the fire in the nearest cauldron suddenly went out. She blinked, but her eyes were not playing tricks on her. She hadn't felt any breeze, she was sure, but there was no one else around that could have put it out. She took another step and another fire went out. She stopped and waited. One by one, the rest of the cauldrons went out, until the level was completely dark.

She jumped when a dark figure stepped out several yards in front of her, but then she recognized him.

Haven came closer. "You afraid?" he asked.

She put her hand over her heart, trying to steady it. "No, you just startled me." Lord Regoran's words came back to her, but she pushed them away. Had their paths crossed differently, she may have been intimidated by him, but even after she learned about the massacre she found she still was incapable of being afraid of him. Though she was a little anxious to hear what he had to say after their last conversation, which she still felt guilty about. He walked past her to the veranda and she caught the slightest upturn of his mouth. He was probably pleased with himself that he had caught her off guard, she mused wryly, though she didn't know him well enough to know if that should've made her more or less uncomfortable. She joined him on the veranda, steeling herself for what he would say.

"The men still afraid of me," he said.

"Yes, but a few of them are coming around I think." Lord and Lady Allard seemed to be leading in this endeavor, with Lord Regoran and Madame Corinthia following. She frowned, thinking of Cornelius and Lady Regoran. They were only two, but more vocal than any of the others and she was afraid the scale could tip in their favor with one wrong move.

Haven looked out towards the desert. "Sand not be here always, you know this?"

Her frown deepened, really caught off guard now. She shook her head.

"The green be here. Long time ago."

She didn't know why he was telling her this, but she went along with it for the moment. "You're telling me there used to be grass here? Trees?"

He nodded.

"Why does it matter?"

He paused. "It matter," he said in a way that reminded her of being scolded by her tutor whenever she questioned his methods. "It matter because amon'jii make it like that."

She looked up at him, surprised. She remembered him mentioning them before, but she didn't know why he was bringing them up now.

"When it be green here, amon'jii come and green disappear. Ground become green ash. Dead. When no more green, amon'jii move south to Ma'diin land. Thousand years Ma'diin not let amon'jii any farther."

"The amon'jii destroyed all the plant life? How?"

"Demon fire."

She tried to make sense of what he was saying. She had an uneasy feeling in her stomach.

He watched her. She knew there was a connection here that she was missing, that he wanted her to see, but she didn't know what it was.

"You protect your homeland from becoming like here."

"Yes."

She bit her lip. An image she had seen as a little girl in a fairy book, of a dragon that could spew fire from its mouth, flashed before her. And then she remembered the stone lizards at the entryway, the ones Haven had so carefully studied. If the amon'jii were like the dragons in the old nursemaids' tales and could indeed breathe fire, then what was the one thing the Ma'diin needed to put the fire out?

Water.

Like a clock striking midnight it all clicked into place. The Ma'diin weren't just concerned about what the dam's constriction of water would do to the plant life, but they were concerned about the amon'jii.

Her father had said that water was more precious than gold. "What will happen if the dam stops all the water?" she asked tentatively.

"Water is only thing that amon'jii are afraid of," he said. "If water is gone, Watchers not be able to stop all of them."

The weight of his words and why they had come to plea with the Empyrians started to sink in. Ysallah would not leave the dam without ensuring that it would come down.

Haven nodded, as if reading her thoughts, though he seemed neither relieved nor satisfied that she knew. It was a grim prospect, one that could easily turn into a reality for him.

"Why did you not tell me?" she asked.

He didn't answer her right away, but seemed to be contemplating something. What to tell her? Or if he wanted to tell her? Then he said, "I not tell you because then you ask questions that I not know how to answer."

"Questions about wh—?" She didn't even finish her question before she knew exactly what he meant and she felt her shame sink a little deeper. Haven and his brothers hunted the amon'jii, the beasts that could breathe fire, and she remembered the markings she had seen on his arm that night on the veranda. Certainly one could not fight fire-breathers without getting scathed.

"The other night, you fell asleep and I saw—I saw the scars, on your arm," she confessed, though he already knew this now, but she felt the need to do it properly and the words started pouring out of their own accord. "I'm so sorry. I never meant … and yesterday, when Cornelius and his men saw you...they were afraid." Then, to stop her jumbled babbling, she reached over and slid her fingers through his before she had even thought about it.

His head snapped towards her, but he didn't let go so she took a deep breath and gathered her words.

"You don't have to tell me if you don't want to," she said slowly, her confidence overcoming her embarrassment, "but I'm not afraid of who you are. Or what you look like. That's what I wanted to say."

His jaw clenched and she felt his hand flex against hers. For a moment she thought she had made a mistake, had crossed some cultural boundary that she shouldn't have, but then he brought her hand up and placed it on his hood. She looked up at him, taken aback, but he just nodded. She hesitated, not because she was afraid, but because this was the moment she had imagined a hundred times in her head and now, when it was actually about to happen, she found herself unprepared. Like a rare painting about to be unveiled and what had she done to deserve it? She took a deep breath and pushed his hood back, and the n'qab slid slowly back over his head.

She did not gasp or take a step back. Her gaze did not waver from his as she finally looked upon the face that had been hidden from her for so long. He was not the monster that Cornelius's men claimed him to be, though she knew now why Haven had been reluctant to show her and why the others had reacted the way they did. His eyes *glowed*, like the sun and the moon, side by side against his fawn-colored skin. They were as bright as blue ice, making everything else appear colorless, as if they had absorbed all the light and now were the sole bearers. But she could see every detail, like the eyes of the snow dogs she had seen in the northern city of Ireczburg: crystal blue against grey fur and white snow. They watched her under his long, dark brooding brows, carefully studying her reaction.

His hair had not been cut in some time and brushed the tops of his ears, giving him a slightly disheveled look, and there was a natural edge about him, as if his cheekbones had been chiseled from the sand, his long nose shaped by the wind. His lips and jaw, the only things she had grown to recognize him with, had only hinted at the strength the rest of his features beheld. Such a face should not be hidden, she thought.

There was another mark, like the one she saw on his arm, that crept up just above his collar and as her eyes lingered there his hands came up and unfastened the buttons of the beige jacket. He shrugged it off and untied the strings of his tunic underneath so it opened down the middle.

Tamsin reached out, already desensitized to bare skin from the servants who worked in only vests around the compound to be scandalized by his immodesty, and touched his bare chest. He didn't have just the ones on his arm, but dozens, maybe hundreds of scars covering his body. They were unlike any scars she had ever seen though. They wound up his shoulders and across his torso like long, thin rivers, blazing a silver map across his skin. They weren't grotesque, but had a kind of mesmerizing symmetry. They didn't even feel like normal scars; his chest was smooth. Then she realized they were underneath his skin, just below the surface, and had that same glowing quality that his eyes had so she was able to see them in the dark, but they also seemed to pulse along with his heartbeat, shimmering like a ripple down his body. The silver seemed to originate from the space over his heart, for it glowed the brightest there. It didn't seem to be affected by her touch, but she could feel his heart beat just a little faster.

She blinked, suddenly aware of his frozen stance under her innocent examination, and took her hand away. She hadn't meant to let her gaze or her touch linger that long. "The amon'jii gave you these marks," she said, unsure if she was more awed or horrified by what the scars meant. "Why didn't you show me sooner?"

But he didn't answer her question. "I used to love the hunt," he said instead, those dark brows knotting his forehead. "I lived for it. Sometimes I not kill them right away just so we could keep playing." The muscles in his jaw twitched. "Are you not afraid of me now?"

She set her gaze on him. His hesitation to show her was deeper than skin. The markings were a part of him and his choices. "But that was in the past. That's not who you are now."

"No. I still in it. My world is darkness, where demons of sleep are real and any moment could be last. Where painful death is certain and your enemy is your only companion. I not wish that kind of world on you. You are too…good."

She didn't know why he was trying to scare her, but she was determined not to let him. "But you are good too, Haven. You've already proven that to me. You don't scare me." But what did scare her was the thought that he was pushing her away because he thought the negotiations would fail.

Those intense, glowing eyes watched her for a long minute, but she did not look away. Then his lips curved up into that crooked smile, breathing youthful humanity back into that intense face. "No fear?"

Footsteps could be heard coming up the stairs then and the faint glow of a torch grew brighter.

Haven picked up his jacket and pulled it back on. He flipped his hood up and backed into the shadows just as a guard appeared.

"Is everything all right my lady?" the guard asked.

"Yes, I was just heading to bed, thank you." She looked into the darkness, but Haven was gone. "No fear," she whispered into the emptiness.

CHAPTER SIXTEEN

She was learning how to fight like the Ma'diin and about their different plants and animals and a little of their culture and she found it all fascinating, but she wondered if there was any reciprocation on Haven's part. "Aren't you curious about the Empyrians?" she asked him the next afternoon as she watched him move against the straw dummy in the sparring yard. She was conscious of the eyes of the servants as they passed on the outskirts with their baskets and trays, no doubt reporting her activity back to her mother, which was why she chose not to participate in the swordplay today.

"You speak as if you not one of them," he said, circling the unsuspecting wooden post with the deceptive nonchalance of a feline.

She imagined those dark brows raising. It seemed his patience for experimenting with clothes, on his body or not, had run out. He was garbed in his usual black hood and robes again, his features hidden from all. Though she was not likely to forget that face anytime soon. "I'm not," she said simply. "I've been here three days longer than you have."

He paused and lowered his sword in a rare display of surprise, turning to face her. His mouth tightened as he contemplated his next question, then, "This not your home?"

"Technically, yes, but actually…I don't know. Sometimes I feel like I've never had a home. I've been to many places, but I've never felt like I belonged to any of them. Even here, nobody seems to understand me." She had never let her standing amongst society get to her before, but she was beginning to wonder if a place even existed where she felt accepted.

"My father told me everything I need to know about the northerners." He didn't say it with contempt, but with enough conviction that told her he didn't want to share what he knew, or thought he knew, about the Empyrians. Or maybe he had made his own conclusions (or confirmations more likely, she thought afterwards) from what his father told him. In any case, he made it sound as if she wasn't missing much by not fitting in here.

But whatever it was, she was too stunned to question him further. "You know that's the first time you've mentioned one of your parents," she said.

He made a sound in the back of his throat that fell somewhere between a growl and an *hmph*. He resheathed his sword. "Your language and his footprints are about all I remember of him. I be very young when he left and the Watchers took me."

"And your mother?"

He shook his head. His mouth opened several times, but he didn't speak. Instead, he went over and grabbed a tall, skinny pole that was leaning against the wall and went back to the straw dummy. For the next few minutes he circled the dummy again, spinning the pole in his hands, occasionally striking it with a quick flick of his wrist and sometimes landing a heavier blow that sent tufts of straw sailing to the ground.

He was recollecting himself, she knew, finding his center again. It usually took her asking a few questions before he would extend his one or two sentence answers and he felt comfortable speaking with her. But there were some things, she was beginning to realize, that he did not speak of at all. He usually did a good job of deflecting any personal questions, but she was still learning that there were some things that he would not tell her, no matter how curious she was. She respected his privacy, but she couldn't deny that she deeply wanted to understand where his need for secrecy came from.

When he had sufficiently battered the dummy to his satisfaction he returned the pole to the wall and then to her, his breathing only slightly faster.

"You have my trust," he said quickly but evenly. "But it not an easy past to share. I am curious, though, about where you come from. Before the Empeerians."

She smiled and narrowed her eyes. A good deflection indeed, but she would ignore it since he was being honest with her and had revealed his trust in her. It was a good place to start at least. Maybe eventually he would tell her why his father left and why the Watchers took him, and about his mother, but for now she would bite her tongue.

She recalled Lady Allard had mentioned an archive building last night at dinner and sought out to find it, thinking it the perfect place to distract themselves for the afternoon and to assist in Haven's geographic and historical education. As they walked through the city streets, she told him all about the known world and her journey through it thus far. She talked about her childhood, how she had gotten to see many of the major cities that made up Delmar because her father travelled frequently as a diplomat throughout the region. She had been to the twin cities of Ireczburg and Socham in the far north, where their castles were as cold as the snow that fell without relief and they wore clothes made of thick animal fur. There were the cities of the lakes: Blaudston, Gemonia, and Fairmoore, that controlled the central lands where serene bodies of freshwater lay nestled in green valleys and tree-covered hills. The coastal cities of Sylvaga and Alstair were the farthest west, the former ruling over the rocky fjords of the northern coast while the latter boasted the most exotic white sand beaches in the south where dolphins could be seen leaping in the Terraz Sea.

"And which of these do you come from?" he asked her.

"Jalsai," she answered, waiting for the waves of nostalgia to wash over her as she remembered her old home. But they never came and she was pleased to find that she could speak of it fondly. Perhaps Empyria was growing on her after all, she mused. *Or perhaps the company is growing on you,* a voice in the back of her mind whispered. "It is near the lake cities, in the harbor of Leis Amaena, though the beauty of the city itself is just as extraordinary as the nature that surrounds it." She described the cobbled streets, the buildings made of white marble, and the garden in her backyard with its meandering paths and sculpted hedges that could make her forget that she was in the center of the most modern city in Delmar.

She had just finished recanting their time in the Ardent Mountains on their way to Empyria when they reached the archive building. It was a miniature version of the Armillary, spherical in shape with a domed ceiling, but had the feel of one large balcony for the main level was a series of support columns and open-air sitting rooms. There were a few people reading in the shade, but Tamsin and Haven made their way up one of the curving staircases to the second level where they entered a large room in which every last available wall space was filled with books and scrolls. The shelves extended higher than even Haven's reach. There were a few desks in the room with stacks of parchment on them weighed down by heavy brass figures. And there was one elderly man in there who glanced up once from his piles of scrolls over the top of his spectacles, but thought what was on the parchment was far more interesting than the two of them, essentially leaving them alone with the aging scripts and salty smell.

"What is this room?" Haven asked, turning in a slow circle as he looked up and down the shelves.

"It is a library," she said, already searching the volumes trying to discern what methods they were sorted by. She cast a disapproving eye towards the old man at the far end of the room, for he was most certainly the caretaker, but it seemed that he liked to spend his time reading the manuscripts instead of making sure they were organized. "Though it's not as grand as the one in Jalsai or even Fairmoore," she said, finding a book on blacksmithing next to a children's nursery book. "Do you have a favorite?"

"Favorite?"

"A favorite book." She turned around when he did not answer.

His mouth was turned down into a slight frown.

She pulled one from the shelf at random and brought it to him. She untied the soft leather binding and opened the cover. She had never considered a book to be a 'modern' development, but perhaps they only used the older, but still common, scroll form. "A book contains information and stories about people and events. This one is about…the application of sewing and the correct techniques used for different garments." She wrinkled her nose as she read it.

But something had sparked Haven's interest and he placed a hand on it before she could put it back. "You know this? You can *read* this?" he asked incredulously.

"Of course, it says so right here," she said, pointing to the title. "Though it would make for very dull reading I'm afraid." Had someone from the Cities asked her that she probably would've taken slight offense, thinking the person thought her unlearned and illiterate. But seeing Haven's look of astonishment as he touched each of the letters (backwards, she noticed) she realized it was the complete opposite.

She paused, but decided to ask anyway, seeing as how this was the first thing not related to swords or fighting that he had taken an interest in. "Can you not read, Haven?"

He was not put off by her question. He merely shook his head, confirming her question.

"Do you not have books either?"

"Books, this," he said looking around at the shelves, "No. But stories, yes."

Tamsin had never been one to enjoy leisurely reading, except when a curiosity overtook her or it was one of the many volumes in her father's study. As a girl, she had wanted to impress him by being able to converse with him about the boldness of the Terrazi explorers or the philosophical tendencies of Shavad's "Astrological Theories." But the more she consumed his favorite literature, or rather what she thought was his favorite, the more she learned that the man she called fathri and the man the people called Lord were two very different people.

She was slowly learning that there was a similar duality with Haven: the man the people called Watcher and hunter and then the man who had revealed his face to her last night. Perhaps she could unveil a little more. "I could teach you, if you like?"

At this, the wonder flickered and receded and the stoic set of his jaw returned. "No," he said and then explained how stories were passed down verbally through the sh'lomiin, the story keepers, and if there were any ancient scripts that remained they would be in their care, though he had never seen one. "Even the kazserii not know the written language."

Tamsin had never heard of a culture without a written language before. Even the fishing villages scattered along the coast had written manuscripts, even if just to keep track of their catch and how much was shipped inland. But the Ma'diin were somehow able to preserve their culture orally. It was an intriguing notion if not a downright baffling one.

"And what good be learning when there is nothing to read in the marshes?" he added. He shrugged it off with a crooked smile.

Even though she couldn't see his eyes behind his n'qab she knew that they did not match his smile right now. She had only seen that smile a handful of times, but she knew that this particular one was not genuine.

She decided to gamble on the chance that he did want to learn, but was too proud or afraid to admit it. "I've often found that what a man reads says more about him than what's in the actual pages. So what does that say about you? A man that refuses to learn something that is taught to children."

His head snapped up and his spine stiffened a little at the implied slight to his character.

She could just make out the glow of his eyes behind the n'qab and she held his gaze.

He breathed out sharply and took the book. "Teach, then," he said.

She smiled at her little victory. "Let's find something a little more interesting then," she said, taking the book of sewing from him and placed it back on the shelf.

It took her a few minutes of searching to find the manuscripts she wanted, but once she had them she put them all on a large desk near the center of the room and they began to go through them. It didn't take him long to get over his pride and she was pleasantly surprised to find him a most eager student, and though it was a little amusing to see a hardened warrior struggle with basic grammar she never teased him. It was a strangely exciting feeling to be the teacher for once and him the pupil and the longer they went on the more she was confident that her interest in his culture was not unrequited.

"Are there pictures like this of you? Of your family?" he asked, studying a portrait of a serious looking lord. Many of the books had hand drawn illustrations that accompanied them, pictures of modern wheelhouses, scenes from important historical battles, maps, and portraits of the lording families throughout the years which were helpful.

"Not here or in these books," she said with a very unlady-like snort. "Maybe a hundred years after I'm dead and just because I'm my father's daughter. There are already stories about him in the Cities, you know."

"Are there stories about you?"

"Me? Lords no!" She laughed aloud. "Though a lord's daughter is a good title to have, it does not merit the scribing of a book about me, especially when I have not accomplished anything of worth. Why, are there stories about you?" she asked, suddenly intrigued.

"One or two, maybe."

She raised an eyebrow. "Really? And what do they say about you?"

The corner of his mouth twitched sideways. "Nothing that I would like to tell."

But he had thrown the bait and she would not let go of the hook now. "Do you think I would think less of you for it?"

He shook his head. "No. If you knew, you just keep seeing past how dangerous I be and try to find good in it when there be none."

She did not know whether to take that as a compliment or an insult, so she kept silent and waited for him to decide if he really wanted to tell her or not.

After a complete minute of silence he finally caved and sighed deeply. "You are stubborn, you know?"

She smiled. "It sounds familiar."

He still had an air of reluctance around him, but she saw his shoulders relax a little. "A Watcher be a good hunter if he kill fifty amon'jii in his life. The Ma'diin say in one moon cycle I kill a hundred."

She felt her eyebrows lift a little despite herself, but then she recalled what Haven had told her about the amon'jii. "You were just protecting your people. Most would say that's a noble cause, not one to be ashamed of."

"Yes, but it not noble cause that led me to do it."

"So it's true then?"

His lips quirked at her cleverness. "It was almost one harvest cycle, not one moon."

So almost a year, instead of a month. It was still pretty impressive, but she could tell he was still not proud of it for some reason. Despite his best efforts to convince her that he was dangerous, she wondered if those rare, youthful glimpses she caught of him only hinted at a gentler soul that lay in his past. Though she did not know the cause, she thought she may have inadvertently discovered the wedge that divided Haven the hunter and Haven the man. "Does killing change you?" she asked softly.

His mood darkened in that moment and she knew she had gone one question too far. She would not question him about it further. He would not be so willing to open up with her in the future if she punished him for it by asking more questions about a topic that was clearly uncomfortable for him, like the topic of his parents. "I'm sorry," she said. "That was extremely insensitive of me. Let's just get back to the manuscri—."

"You not come back from death," he said, making her pause. "No matter what side you on."

The shadows had lengthened across the room, harkening in the time of day Haven was more accustomed to and as Tamsin digested his words she could almost see the Watcher in him emerging with the growing darkness around them. His cloak seemed blacker, the muscles in his jaw firmer, his demeanor a little more distant. He looked like he belonged in a library as much as a bird belonged in the sea, but unto himself he looked steady, daunting even. She realized she was starting to equate the Watcher in him with his formidable, fiercer side, but she couldn't define the boundaries quite so clearly. After all, was it the man or the Watcher in him that had saved her in the desert?

He untied a bag from around his belt and set it on the table. "I want to show you something," he said, his voice gruff.

"What is it?"

He pushed the bag closer to her. "It from my first amon'jii kill."

She hesitated as she reached for the bag, wondering what kind of souvenir he had kept from his first kill and not sure if she wanted to know. Mentally preparing herself, she took the bag.

He stood up suddenly and she jumped as the wooden chair screeched against the floor and dropped the bag on her lap. She turned to look as he moved around to her other side and saw five soldiers emerge in the entryway.

They didn't look surprised to see the two of them there at all, and as Tamsin recovered from her own surprise she realized that she and Haven were exactly why they were there.

She saw Haven's hands creep slowly to his belt and she stood up quickly, moving to his side and shoving the bag in her pocket. She gently brushed his hand with her own, the movement hidden from the soldiers by her billowing skirt. His hand froze and she nodded imperceptibly to him. She knew some of the soldiers still held animosity towards Haven from that first night and she wanted to diffuse any unnecessary conflict if she could.

"Here for a bit of reading gentlemen?" she asked humorlessly.

There were mixed expressions, from smirks to scowls to outright disdain for Haven, but the one closest to them remained stoic. "We are here to escort you out," he said.

"Is there a curfew?" Tamsin asked.

"Not for you, my lady, but *he* must go. It is unsuitable to be here alone with our…guest as the hour grows late." He looked towards the now empty desk at the other end of the room.

Tamsin followed his gaze and saw that the caretaker had disappeared. There was no doubt now as to who had tipped them off.

"I would be happy to remain with you if you desired to stay, my lady," the soldier continued.

"No. We finished," Haven spoke sharply. He took Tamsin's hand and pulled her closely behind him as he moved to leave.

The soldiers parted quickly before him, their previous bravado evaporating in the face of Haven's intimidating proximity. But the one grabbed Tamsin's arm, forcing her to pause, and gave her a questioning look.

"I'm fine," Tamsin said, guessing his question. She put as much calmness into her voice as she could, highly aware that Haven's protectiveness would soon win out over his self-control and she was sure the soldiers wouldn't waste the opportunity to provoke him. She squeezed his hand. "Haven will see me home, but send your men along if it suits you."

The soldier studied her for a moment and then nodded to two of his men. He released her arm.

"Good night, gentlemen," Tamsin said and continued after Haven, followed by her two extra escorts.

She glanced back just before they descended the stairs and saw the remaining three hovering around their desk looking at the scattered scrolls and books, like vultures circling a carcass, about to pick apart the bones.

The next morning she didn't see Haven at all and she understood he was free to go where he wanted, but he had departed as soon as he had seen her home last night without so much as a goodnight or indication to where he was going. Granted, the lingering presence of the two soldiers didn't help ease the tension around them, but she had seen him take on more than that before without batting an eye so she doubted his hasty exit had anything to do with them. Which only confirmed her belief that she had gone too far with her questions last night and he did not wish to be made uncomfortable by the thoughtless curiosity of a young woman.

Her disappointment at his absence nagged at her though, so she went back to the archive building, but found no information on the Ma'diin, dragons, the amon'jii or the marshlands so after several hours searching through the unorganized manuscripts she went back to the compound to her father's study, hoping to find something from his travels that mentioned them. She didn't know what she was looking for, but the more she didn't find anything the more she wanted to know why there wasn't anything. She found herself glancing at the door as if he were going to walk in at any moment. His secret was always at the edge of her thoughts and she was nervous of what she would find. But his study was just as unorganized as the archive building. He had had no time to unpack after they arrived and she found nothing.

She folded her arms across the pile of scrolls she had just finished going through on his desk and sighed. Nothing but dead ends. She had an idea to go back to the Graysan's, but she didn't know what she would ask him. She was about ready to give up when she pulled open one of the drawers in his desk and saw a single, folded piece of parchment. She picked it up and turned it over in her hands. The red wax seal on it had been broken, but the emblem was still intact. It was a single letter S.

"Tamsin, what are you doing in here?"

Tamsin looked up and saw her mother in the doorway. She put the parchment back and closed the drawer. "I don't know. I just—." She shook her head.

Her mother smiled sadly. "It will be nice to see your father in here when he returns." She looked around the room as if she were imagining Eleazar in there now. Then she straightened her shoulders. "But it won't make him come home any faster by dwelling in solitude. Come, let us go have tea." Then she informed Tamsin that they were going out for tea, to the Regoran compound. Tamsin balked at the idea. Lady Regoran had not been overly warm at dinner the other night and she had no desire to see Emilia anytime soon. But her mother brought up the topic of Tamsin's secret sword fighting sessions with Haven so she thought she owed her mother this much and as the mid-afternoon bell tolled in the main square they arrived at the Regoran compound.

The atmosphere was much different than it had been the other night. Lady Regoran's coldness then was nothing compared to the chill in the air in the lavishly erected tea room. Tamsin felt like a leper under Lady Regoran's scrutinizing stare. None of the other ladies had arrived and Tamsin was beginning to wonder if they had even been invited. Even Emilia was absent. She had a sinking feeling that this was not going to be a pleasant afternoon.

Lavinia broke the silence, stating her surprise on the amount of rain they were getting, but Lady Regoran interrupted almost immediately.

"Emilia told me all about your accident outside of the wall." She paused, like she was waiting for Tamsin to deny it.

Tamsin didn't know what stories Emilia had fabricated to her mother about what happened that night or how she even knew what had happened afterwards, but for her own mother's sake she thought it best not to start an argument with Lady Regoran. "I am quite recovered now. Thank you for your concern," she said, without a smile.

"Your health is the least of my concerns dear." Her eyes were like those of a feline, toying with its prey before it made the killing blow. "I'm more concerned with why you would invite the same man who kidnapped you to dinner. Is it true that the foreigner resides in your home?"

Lavinia went rigid, but Tamsin had been prepared for this. She answered in as calm a voice as she could, "Haven did not kidnap me, no matter what else you may have heard. He was the one who saved me. My mother was good enough to repay the kindness, by offering him a place to stay."

"He sleeps outside," Lavinia added quickly.

"As a dog should," Lady Regoran scoffed, "though it is still troubling that he be allowed in the presence of young, impressionable lady like your daughter, especially with your husband away. I suppose, Tamsin, that what was said the other night was also a lie then? That you have been crossing swords with him, in public and unsupervised?"

"I assure you Lady Regoran," Lavinia started, "that they've hardly been unsupervised. In fact, Cornelius—."

"Ah yes, I do remember hearing that Captain Saveen was present. Thank goodness."

Tamsin stared at Lady Regoran, not able to believe that one woman could hold so much malice against a man she had barely met. She realized then that no matter what she said or how she defended herself, Lady Regoran's mind was fixed in its prejudice. It was not Haven that needed to be proving himself to anybody, especially to this woman.

"It would be a shame to have your family's name ruined by such behavior," Lady Regoran continued unblinkingly. "Perhaps you should get an etiquette instructor, Lavinia, before the damage is irreversible."

"Tamsin has had the best tutors the Cities have to offer, I assure you."

"I assumed as much, though it would seem then that the problem lies deeper than her upbringing. If you want my advice, Lavinia, I would suggest you keep your daughter on a tighter leash."

"Like a dog," Tamsin said humorlessly.

Lady Regoran squinted and smiled, taking another sip of tea.

Tamsin looked over to her mother, who was pale and staring at her cup. *This* was how she was expected to behave? To have insults thrown right in her face and just sit there and take it? A year ago maybe she would have, but to hear the insularity and superiority dripping from Lady Regoran's lips was too much for her to bear silently. She was an Urbane for lords' sake. The pressure was building behind her eyes and she had half a nerve to stand up and slap the condescending scowl off that hateful woman's face.

Tamsin put her own cup down, before she had the thought to dump it in Lady Regoran's lap. She stood up slowly. "Your advice is greatly appreciated," she said. "Especially from someone who's raised such a kind, considerate girl like your daughter." She stayed just long enough to see the flash of contempt in Lady Regoran's eyes before she spun on her heel and walked out without a backward glance.

"Can you believe the vile things that old witch was saying?" Tamsin said after she finished recounting what had happened to Sherene, who was busy taking clothes off a line back at the Urbane compound.

"You should be more careful with your words Lady Tamsin. Lady Regoran has a point, however terrible she might be. Ever since that man came here your behavior hasn't exactly lived up to the level your status requires you to."

Tamsin stared at her, shocked. "You can't seriously be taking her side."

"I will always be on your side, Lady Tamsin. Believe me, I want to give her a piece of my mind for ambushing you like that, but there comes a time when what you want isn't always in your best interests. You should tell Mr. Haven to leave this family alone. He needs to find a new place to haunt."

"He saved my life. The least we could do—."

"The least we could do is thank him and move on. But we have given him shelter and food and more than enough gratitude from you. You don't owe him any more than that."

"I never owed him anything, that's the point; he's too noble for that. He's showed me and this family nothing but kindness, which is more than I can say for anyone else."

"You're not understanding, Tamsin," Sherene said. "What happened yesterday at the archive building can't happen again."

"The archive building? How do you know about th—?"

"Never you mind how I know," Sherene snapped, flicking a towel off the line and folding it into a neat square before placing it in the wicker basket next to her. Then she sighed deeply. "It's been my job to protect you far longer than it's been his," she said.

She held up her hand as Tamsin was about to interject. "And that includes knowing where you are and who you're with. What were you thinking taking Mr. Haven there?"

"I was teaching him to read," Tamsin said bluntly.

Surprise didn't even register on Sherene's face. "The lords won't see it that way," she continued. "If things go badly with the Ma'diin for your father, then they'll look at you as a possible conspirator."

"A conspirator? That's absurd!"

"A sympathizer at the very least then. They won't look kindly on you showing Mr. Haven anything about the Cities or Empyria that they don't sanction. No matter how harmless your intentions were," she added softly.

Tamsin put her face in her hands and groaned, wondering how she could be that naïve. At least Lady Regoran hadn't known about that, not yet anyways, but it was only a matter of time before her mother found out. And after the disastrous afternoon, Tamsin knew her mother wouldn't be so hospitable towards Haven anymore.

"What's this?" Sherene asked aloud. She pulled something out of the pocket of one of Tamsin's skirts she had taken off the line. It was a small, leathery pouch.

"It's nothing," Tamsin gasped, recognizing it as the bag Haven had given her the previous night just before the guards interrupted them. She took it from Sherene before she could open it. She remembered Haven telling her it was from his first kill and whatever it was she didn't need Sherene discovering it. "Georgiana gave it to me."

"Oh, the Graysan girl. How nice," she said, though she eyed Tamsin strangely before returning to folding the clothes. The wheels of the cart bringing her mother home could be heard then so Tamsin went to leave, but Sherene placed a hand on her shoulder before she could go. "Promise me you'll consider my words," Sherene said.

"I promise," Tamsin said, kissing her on the cheek and then rushing off to her room before she could get into a confrontation with her mother. She went behind the changing partition in case her mother came upstairs looking for her. She looked at Haven's small pouch in her hand, debating whether to look inside or wait for him, but who knew when he was coming back.

She leaned back against the wall, readying herself for what it might contain…and fell back as the wall caved in behind her. The sudden sensation stole any scream she had and the rest of her air left her lungs as she landed hard on her back. She gasped and coughed as little clouds of dust settled around her. Once she could breathe again she pushed herself onto her elbows and looked up at the wall that had given way. It was still intact and still showed the faded painting of the woman with the silver vase, whose upright hand was now parallel with the edge. She hadn't fallen far. She stood up, gingerly, and inspected the opening, which was a perfect rectangle and revealed her changing partition on the other side. She remembered the crack she had seen when they first arrived, but had forgotten about it since. The lines were too straight to be accidental and the door, which she now knew that was what it was, had swung open too easily to be anything but intentional.

The room she now stood in was dark and had a musty smell, as if it hadn't seen fresh air in years. It was barely the size of her bed. Cobwebs bowed low from the ceiling and draped over an empty torch bracket on the opposite wall, which her head had only avoided hitting when she fell by inches. There was a cold draft coming from another opening to her right and she walked cautiously over to it. From the faint light that came from her room she could see stairs descending down into an endless dark.

She shivered, but she couldn't help herself. Secret passages were something that only existed in stories. The servants had back passageways that they used to avoid the main halls, but this was different. This either wasn't known to the servants or had long been forgotten about. It was a true secret and it was hers alone. She shoved Haven's bag in her pocket and stepped down to the first stair and then the next and the next, blinking rapidly in the dark and letting her hand graze the wall for some sense of support. The air became thicker the farther she went down and there were some spots where the walls were quite close together. Her eyes were quick to adjust to the dark, but it was still slow going because the stairs were uneven and some of the edges crumbled underneath her feet. A part of her told her this was dangerous; if she got hurt down here it could be a long time before someone found her. But on the other hand, it was thrilling not knowing where she would end up.

She finally came to the end of her descent and there was a long stretch of level, solid ground. This was even darker and took a longer time, but was less confining. The tunnel was wide enough so she could stretch her arms and brush the walls with her fingertips. It turned right once and after that she could hear a heavy rumbling. But it wasn't imminent; it didn't get louder as she went. It was just constant. There were holes about the size of her fist at regular intervals along the walls and she put her ear up to one and the rumbling echoed more loudly. Then she noticed water dripping from places in the ceiling as she passed underneath.

She was underneath the Elglas.

The voice that told her this was dangerous screamed louder at her and she was just about to turn around when her hand touched something cold. Something metal. A hinge of some kind and then a wooden door as her hands felt in front of her, its boards partially rotted. She pushed it open and it creaked on its hinges. There were several diagonal holes carved in the ceiling that allowed a small shaft of light to illuminate the room, which was circular unlike the first, but how far it was between the room and the outside she couldn't tell. In the center was a round metal grate and by the wall was a large spool of dust-covered rope. One end was securely fastened to a rock protruding from the wall like a handle while the other end had several knots in it and snaked away from the main pile.

She thought the empty room quite peculiar. Was this where the wealth of the compound had been kept in the early Ottarkin years? It was the only thing she could think of, though there was nothing in the room to support it. It did not appear to have been looted. There were no telltale signs, no little artifacts that would have been left behind, deemed to have no worth to thieves. And she couldn't imagine hauling anything of worth back up those stairs.

She walked over to the grate and knelt down next to it. She peered into it and could see the ground several meters below, but it was illuminated in such a way that appeared as if there was a gap between the end of the tunnel and the ground below. She hooked her fingers through the holes in the grate and pulled up, testing it. It moved slightly, and she pulled again. It took all of her strength, but she was able to lift the grate off the hole and slide it over. She made sure the rope was secured around the rock and then gathered the rest of the rope and threw it down in the hole.

It was obvious now that was exactly what the rope was for, but why? What was down there? She rubbed her hands on her dress to get any extra moisture off them and took a deep breath, deciding to go forward until she discovered exactly what was worth going through all these secret places for. A sudden thought struck her and she wondered if this was how her father had felt all those years ago when he had been an explorer, the excitement of new discovery buzzing through his body like a hummingbird. She missed him.

She brushed the thoughts aside and took the rope in both hands. She backed up to the hole slowly and gave the rope a few hard tugs to make sure it would hold her weight before she leaned back. Inch by inch, she worked her feet down over the edge and then slowly shuffled them down, clinging to the rope as tightly as she could. She worked her way down until she could no longer see above the edge of the hole and she was completely surrounded by the dark tunnel. Her arms and knees began to tremble and she had to pause to take few deep breaths and calm herself, like Haven had taught her when using the sword. It was no use letting fear control your movements, he had said. Fear was a paralyzer and you needed all of your senses working when confronted with a dangerous situation. So she steadied her breathing, tightened her grip on the rope, and repeated *no fear* over and over again.

She took another step down and screamed when the rope snapped underneath her fingers.

CHAPTER SEVENTEEN

The world was blurry and filled with a loud throbbing that made it difficult to focus on anything else but the feeling that her heart was going to jump out of her throat. Tamsin remembered that she had fallen and as her sight cleared she saw the tunnel that she had come from right above her in the ceiling. She fought back the sick feeling creeping up her chest and slowly moved her fingers and toes. Immediately the throbbing increased and she hissed as she located its source. She couldn't move her left ankle without a wicked stabbing pain and another wave of nausea threatening to overwhelm her.

She closed her eyes and lay still, letting the pulsing between her ears subside before she started figuring a way out of there. But as the pounding eased, a different noise took its place, growing louder by the second. It sounded like…laughing?

Tamsin opened her eyes and slowly eased herself up into a sitting position. She was in a small alcove which opened up to a long, wide hallway, crudely made with larger alcoves dispersed on either side down its entire length. One of the alcoves was in front of her, just to her right, and this one was the origin of the laughing, nay, the cackling. In it, with shackles around her wrists and ankles that were chained to the wall, was the seer, Mora.

Tamsin felt that old panic return to her, the same she had felt that night that had set a thousand things in motion. She remembered the possessed look in the old woman's eyes and how she had raved about hellfire and madness and betrayal. She rubbed the backs of her hands, which had suddenly started to itch.

But the look in Mora's eyes now were not the same as they had been that night. They were alight with intrigue and amusement, despite the wretched situation she found herself in.

Tamsin wondered: had she been down here since that night?

Mora licked her cracked lips. "So you have come back to see old Mora?" She laughed again. "It is good to see you are still alive."

Tamsin knew she was being baited. "I have nothing to say to you." She used the wall to support herself as she stood up.

"Really? Nothing? You don't want me to explain what I told you before?"

"I don't care what you *claimed* to have seen." Tamsin started limping away.

"You would care, if you knew what it all meant. It has begun. You are in the midst of it even now."

Tamsin rolled her eyes. "Oh yeah, it has begun. How could I forget," she muttered under her breath.

"There are traitors among you little Urbane. I would tread carefully if I were you. They are closer than you think."

"Well, you're the closest one to me right now, so if I should believe you then that would make you the traitor."

Mora cackled loudly then, her laugh echoing down the hall and then breaking into a fit of coughing. "When you find one, you will come back to me, and you will realize I was telling the truth. Just like your father did."

This stopped Tamsin in her tracks. She turned around, though she didn't take any steps closer. "You knew my father?"

Mora's eyes glittered with mischief, like a small child, and she caressed the shackle around her wrist as if it were a pet.

Tamsin's brow furrowed. She knew she shouldn't be asking; it would only feed Mora's delusions, but she was too curious. "What did you tell him?"

"Ask him," Mora said with a sly smile.

"I can't. He's not here."

This seemed to surprise her, which, Tamsin thought, was strange for a so-called seer.

"Where is he?" she asked slowly.

"You're the seer. You tell me."

Mora let out a shriek then that made Tamsin's skin crawl. "How am I supposed to see anything when I've been in this cave!" she wailed, straining against the chains that bound her to the wall. She panted for a few moments until she slumped back against the wall, raking her black nails over her face. Then she looked at Tamsin again. "Your father knew the cost of coming back here. It is a shame he will not be here to see it."

"See what?"

"The moment he loses you."

Tamsin had had enough. "He won't lose me. Ever."

Mora started to laugh again, low and breathy with long pauses in between, and her pale lips curved up in amusement.

"Tamsin?"

Tamsin twisted around, surprised to hear another voice. A guard was coming down the hallway towards her, but she knew his face. "Enrik?"

"Tamsin what are you doing down here? Are you okay?" He rushed over to her when he saw her start to limp towards him.

"Leaving so soon?" Mora's words hissed through her teeth like steam. "Don't you want to know when you will die?"

Tamsin felt her bones go cold, as if Mora's words were frost, slowly creeping up her spine, taking root and turning her limbs to white ice.

Enrik seemed to notice Tamsin's reaction and quickly slipped his arm under hers and led her away. "Don't listen to her," he said lightly, but sternly. "She hasn't had a sane thought in years."

Tamsin tried to shake the feeling of dread. "She seems pretty convinced that I'm going to die a horrible death surrounded by traitors and hellfire."

Enrik smiled. "I think everyone gets a version of that. She once told Gia that she would bring about the destruction of the city and be buried underneath it when it crumbled. And she told me I was going to be killed by a man who will come back from the dead. Pretty messed up huh?"

Tamsin nodded. "Enrik, what are you doing here?"

"Captain Saveen sent me to fetch Mora," he said. "He doesn't like coming down here himself and he wanted to question her."

"No, I mean, what are *you* doing here? I thought you didn't want to join the army."

"Oh, that." He shrugged like it wasn't a big deal, but she could see the disappointment in his face. "I didn't really have a choice." He gave a quick smile. "I'm sorry by the way. For that night. I tried to get help when we realized you weren't with us, but…" He shook his head. "I'm just really sorry."

Tamsin squeezed his arm. "It's okay. Georgiana told me what happened. Don't give it another thought okay?"

He scratched the back of his head like he was uncomfortable, but he nodded anyways, though she knew he would probably feel guilty about it despite her words. "Well, how about we get you out of here," he said and she gratefully accepted his help. He put her arm over his shoulders so she wouldn't have to put any weight on her ankle and she was able to slowly hobble down the hallway with his support. "By the way," he asked when they had rounded a corner and now faced a daunting flight of stairs. "How did *you* get down here?"

She bit her lip, unsure if she should tell him now that he was working under Cornelius. "I, um, got lost," she said and then laughed. "It seems to be a reoccurring problem."

Enrik laughed too. "You found one of the slave tunnels didn't you?"

This took her by surprise. "The what?"

"The slave tunnels. When the people from the Cities took over Empyria from the Ottarkins, they forced them to work, building most of the west side, aside from the temples, I mean— the compounds. But they were also forced to build the catacombs below ground as well, most of which were used to imprison the very men who built them. But what they didn't know is that when the Ottarkins were building the city, they also built secret tunnels to the temples where the priests would help smuggle them out."

"Weren't they ever found out?"

"Of course and when they found out the priests were giving *their* prisoners sanctuary they disbanded the religious order and took over the temples and converted them into, well, you know, the lords' residences. But the Ottarkins built other secret tunnels throughout the city too."

"That's incredible," Tamsin said. "How many people know about these tunnels?"

"You mean should you be worried about anyone sneaking into the compound?" He chuckled. "No. I mean, I don't think hardly anybody knows anymore. My great great great," he made a large sweeping motion with his hand, "great grandfather was one of those slaves and the knowledge has been passed down through the generations. But I didn't know about the one from your compound."

Tamsin then described to him how she had found it and the tunnel that had led to the room with the rope and how she had tried to climb down but the rope had snapped.

Enrik made a whistling sound. "You're lucky you didn't break your neck. That rope is probably hundreds of years old. They must've disguised it as one of the ventilation shafts…" His words trailed off as he became lost in his thoughts.

"I'll show you sometime," Tamsin promised and then winced when her ankle smarted.

Enrik helped her up the last set of stairs and she was surprised to see the ornate style of the Armillary around her. Enrik led her to a quiet room and over to a chair so she could sit for a minute. He was about to go fetch a healer when the doors burst open and another man walked in. For a moment, he looked just as surprised as they did, but then a scowl replaced it and he marched over to them quickly. Enrik's face grew dark red.

Tamsin recognized the man from dinner the other night, one of Cornelius's men, though she had not spoken to him directly. Lieutenant Riggs she thought his name was.

"Enrik, what are you doing here?" he asked. "Captain Saveen said he asked you to retrieve the prisoner." Then he must have spotted Tamsin because he stopped. "And what are you doing with Lady Urbane?"

"I'm sorry Dad, I was going to—."

Tamsin felt her mouth drop open a little, but she couldn't help it. Lieutenant Riggs was Enrik's *father*? The one who had been pushing him to join the Empyrian army.

"Lieutenant Riggs, it's nice to see you again," she said cheerfully, though she already resented him a little for forcing Enrik to be a part of something he had never wanted. "I'm afraid this is my fault. I fell and hurt my ankle and Enrik was kind enough to help me. I hope he's not in any trouble because of it."

"He will be if he doesn't bring the prisoner up for questioning." He raised his eyebrows at Enrik expectantly.

Enrik gave Tamsin an apologetic look before he shuffled off towards the door and out of sight.

Lieutenant Riggs shook his head. "He just doesn't have the stomach for this I guess." He sighed heavily.

"He was just trying to help me," she said, not understanding why he didn't seem to think his son had done a good deed.

Lieutenant Riggs stared at her for an uncomfortably long moment, as if he was just now seeing her there. "Yes," he said slowly. "That seems to be the root of the problem now doesn't it?"

Tamsin thought that was an awfully strange thing to say, and it also didn't sound like he was talking about what had just happened. She didn't want to bring up the fact that Enrik had been with her that night in case Enrik hadn't told him. She wouldn't blame Enrik for not wanting to get in trouble, but it didn't make sense because Enrik had said he went to get help when he realized she was missing. And if his father was part of the Empyrian army he would've been the perfect person to tell who could help. Something just didn't seem right.

Lieutenant Riggs watched her as all this went through her head. He walked towards her, an unreadable look on his face, and she sat up a little straighter. He reached for something in his pocket.

Tamsin backed against her chair, her heart pounding against her chest as if it wanted to break free and run away as fast as it could.

He pulled out a handkerchief and pressed it against her head. When he pulled it away, there was a dark red streak on it. "Looks like you hit your head when you fell," he said.

She touched the spot on her head, just below the hairline, and winced. She did have a cut there, but it didn't seem too deep. She looked at him, unable to hide her confusion. But she wasn't just confused about him. She was confused about why she had reacted like that. Her instincts were telling her he was dangerous, but he had given her no reason to believe that.

"Are you alright?" he asked.

She shook away the strange look she must've been giving him. "I'm sorry. I must've hit my head harder than I thought."

He folded up the handkerchief and put it in his pocket. "I'll go get the healer. You stay right here." He walked out of the room then, his boots clacking sharply on the floor.

It was like a burst of lightning through her mind then and her senses screamed at her as loud as thunder. She now knew why he had put her teeth on edge.

He just doesn't have the stomach for this…

She had heard him say those words before, only he hadn't been talking about Enrik. It was that night she had hid under the table in the servants' kitchen and he and another man had been talking about Lord Saveen and Cornelius—and her father.

She gripped the edge of the chair as her mind replayed what she had heard that night. Her instincts had been right. Lieutenant Riggs was not someone to be trusted. She still didn't understand what he was talking about, but he was definitely not on her side, nor was he a friend of the Ma'diin. She got up and as quickly as her ankle would allow her, hobbled across the room, not wanting to be here when he returned, but she was not quick enough. She heard footsteps coming rapidly down the hallway and a moment later the healer was there. And so was Cornelius.

"Tamsin, are you alright?" he asked, bridging the distance between them. "Here, let me help you," and he let her lean on him as he led her back to sit down.

She never thought she'd be relieved to see him, but his presence helped ease some of the panic that was building. She looked past him to the door, the throbbing in her ankle seeming in unison with her heart, but nobody else was there. "Where is Lieutenant Riggs?" she asked.

"I don't know," he said. "He said you fell?" His thumb brushed the spot over her forehead. He motioned the healer over, but Tamsin shook her head.

"No, I need to talk to you." She glanced at the healer. "Alone."

"You need to let the healer take a look at you."

"No! I won't let him near me until you hear what I have to tell you. It's important."

The look of concern on his face was replaced by controlled patience as if he were indulging the whim of a small child. After a moment he told the healer to wait outside. Then he took Tamsin's hands in his own. "I'm sorry for the things I said at dinner."

She barely noticed her hands in his. "What? No, that's not—it's forgotten," she said. What she had to say was too important to get hung up on the other night. She watched the polite attention give way to seriousness as she described what she had heard that night in the kitchens. She told him everything she could remember, how Lieutenant Riggs sent the other man in his place so he could keep Cornelius occupied because there might be something at his compound that he didn't want him to see. She told him about how they kept talking about a "master" and he needed to know that the Ma'diin were in Empyria. And she realized that whoever this "master" was had to be the same one that sent him the box and he didn't know his uncle was dead.

At the mention of the box, Cornelius's eyes widened. "Did they say what was in the box?" he asked her.

She shook her head. "They left before I could hear any more. Cornelius, I know you trust him, but—."

He held up his hand, cutting her off. "I believe you," he said. "Undoubtedly Riggs is hiding something."

"What are you going to do?"

He squeezed her hand and she let him. "I'm going to get to the bottom of this."

He persuaded her then to let the healer take a look at her and, after her ankle had been wrapped and it was determined that she would be fine in a few days, he escorted her home personally. He explained to Lavinia what had happened, save for what Tamsin had told him about Lieutenant Riggs, for which she was grateful, though she had to decline his offer to let her keep a few of his personal guards. She was more worried about her father than she was for herself. And strangely enough, Cornelius. As annoying as she found him to be sometimes, she didn't want anything bad to happen to him. She hoped he would get the answers he needed soon and that she hadn't been too late in her revelation.

CHAPTER EIGHTEEN

Cornelius waited in his uncle's old study, swirling a glass of untouched Arak between his fingers, his thoughts drifting back to the past. His uncle had been a strange, obsessive man, though despite his oddities he had been very smart. He was strategic and never missed an opportunity to teach Cornelius about cause and effect, about moves, counter-moves, and how to anticipate your opponent.

The sounds of boots clicking against the stairs alerted him to someone's presence and a moment later, Lieutenant Riggs appeared in the doorway. Cornelius waved him in and bade him to sit.

Riggs sat opposite him across the desk. "You wanted to see me sir?"

Cornelius didn't say anything right away, still watching the dark liquid swirl around in his glass. Then he reached across the desk and set the glass down in front of Riggs. "Drink," he commanded.

Riggs looked at the drink and then Cornelius, confused. "I'd rather not, sir," he said. "I'm on duty until—."

"Drink," Cornelius said again, his steely gaze unwavering.

Riggs hesitantly picked up the glass and took a slow sip.

As he did so, Cornelius reached underneath the desk and pulled out the long wooden box. "How does Tamsin Urbane know about this?" Cornelius asked him calmly. Of course he had shown her the night he kissed her, but Riggs didn't know that and

Tamsin had not connected the conversation she had overheard in the kitchens to the box in front of him.

Riggs' eyes flashed with suspicion before he adopted a confused expression. "Tamsin Urbane? I have no idea."

Riggs had been the one to give Cornelius the box, though Cornelius would not let him pretend to be ignorant about its meaning any longer. Cornelius had not risen quickly through the ranks of the Empyrian army by being soft and forgiving. Riggs was fifteen years older than Cornelius and had been a loyal guard under his uncle for much of that time, so Cornelius had extended the courtesy of having this conversation in private, but that's as far as it went. Disloyalty was not something he tolerated among his men, no matter how old they were, and until now he had thought Riggs of like mind where secrets were as dangerous as swords.

"Well let me tell you," Cornelius said, opening the lid to reveal the cleaned sword, one that he now knew after sparring with Haven belonged to the Ma'diin. "She overheard you talking about it and from her rendition of what was said, I got the distinct impression that you know exactly where this came from and who sent it. Now, tell me who the Master is."

It would go better for Riggs knowing he had been caught, and judging from the thin line his lips were pressed into, Riggs must've known there was no talking his way out of this one.

There was a loud commotion downstairs then, catching both men's attention and one of the servant's came running up the stairs and into the study, though the shouting continued below.

"What is it?" Cornelius asked, though he kept his eyes on Riggs so he would know their conversation was not over.

"There's a man demanding to see you," the flustered servant replied. "He says his name is Jediah Harvus."

The name wasn't familiar and normally Cornelius would tell the servant to send him away, but the way Riggs' knuckles turned white and how the veins in his neck bulged made him pause.

"Send him up," he said.

Jediah soon emerged, his face red as if he had been running and his clothes were streaked with dirt, sweat, and horse hair. He was about to speak, but then caught sight of Riggs and stopped.

"Your timing is impeccable," Riggs said drily, downing the glass of Arak with a to-hell-with-it-all abandon.

Cornelius smiled. "Lieutenant Riggs was just about to explain this," he splayed his hands over the sword.

"You were?" Jediah looked incredulously at Riggs. "Well that's good because if you didn't I was going to. We have a problem."

"What kind of problem?" Riggs asked.

Jediah's eyes flitted over the sword. "Monstran is coming."

Riggs' eyes grew wide and the glass clattered on the desk as it slipped from his hand. "Monstran is coming here?"

Jediah nodded and Riggs ran his hands over his head. They seemed to have forgotten that Cornelius was there at all.

"Someone better tell me what in the seven hells is going on before I have you both arrested." He recalled what Tamsin had told him. "Is this Monstran the Master?"

"No," Jediah shook his head, "but he speaks for him."

Cornelius indicated the other chair. "Have a seat Mr. Harvus," and when he had, Cornelius told them, as calmly as his waning patience would allow, to explain everything or he would have both their heads on spikes in the main square before the sun rose.

It was late in the evening before they had concluded and what Tamsin had told him finally made sense, though he wished for a moment that it was all an elaborate lie. But when Riggs poured himself a second glass of Arak Cornelius knew the story was not fabricated. He leaned forward in his chair, putting his elbows on the hard wood and clasping his hands together. He didn't know how his uncle had gotten himself into this mess, but he had left the pieces for his nephew to clean up.

"When?" he asked.

"Soon," Jediah replied.

Soon. Cornelius entertained for a moment the idea of going to the lords with all of this and letting them handle it, but he knew if it was left to them they would just scoff and say their walls were impenetrable and by the time they realized they were wrong it would be too late.

"Your uncle tried to call it off," Riggs said, "and I don't know what changed his mind, but he said construction needed to be resumed. That was only a few days before——."

"Before he killed himself," Cornelius finished.

Jediah and Riggs exchanged a look. "The Master's true intentions lie with the Ma'diin," Jediah said. "If we continue what your uncle started, then we might get out of this unscathed."

"How do you figure?" Riggs asked.

"Think about it," Jediah said, tapping his head hard. "The very thing that could be the Ma'diin's undoing could be our salvation."

Riggs snorted. "You're dreaming if you think the Master will leave us alone after this is over."

"I thought you wanted this? Why the sudden change of heart?"

"Because they were supposed to stay far away! The Ma'diin, Monstran, the Master, all of them!"

Cornelius listened to their argument with conflicting thoughts. The notion that someone had been pulling the strings behind his back all along infuriated him. His uncle had allowed himself to be played like a puppet by someone who wasn't even here and Cornelius didn't want to fall into the same web. But seeing these two grown men tremble at just the thought of this Mr. Monstran coming here gave him reason to pause.

He looked at the sword still sitting in the box, remembering the blood that had been caked on it. He thought about his duel with Haven, how the Ma'diin had toyed with him, making him believe that he had a chance when really Haven could have easily finished him right away. Cornelius had never met someone whose skills surpassed his own at the sword, but Haven had made his attempts look like child's play, a truth that was hard to swallow, but undeniable all the same. If the sword in front of him belonged to someone like Haven and the blood that covered it was its owner's, then what possible chance did the rest of them have against someone who could turn a Watcher into nothing but a red stain?

His eyes slid over the edge of the blade. He had the blueprints for war in his hands, but the only question was whose side he would be on. His loathing for Haven could not be tempered despite his misgivings about an alliance and the thought struck him that there was someone out there that wanted Haven and the rest of the Ma'diin dead.

The room had gone suddenly quiet and Riggs and Jediah both looked at Cornelius with concern, as if the hour of judgment was upon them.

Cornelius unlaced his fingers and flexed his hands. "You still haven't told me exactly who the Master is."

"You wouldn't know his name," Jediah said. "But you would feel his wrath. Ask Monstran when he arrives. He will show you. Then you will believe."

Cornelius still wasn't sure if he would. He would be wary. He would watch. Then he would make his decision. "Tell the servants to prepare the second tower. We wouldn't want our guest to feel unwelcome when he arrives."

Tamsin lay in bed, wrapping, unwrapping, and re-wrapping a shawl around her hand absentmindedly. It had rained relentlessly for the last three days, successfully confining her to her room. Her mother had been adamant that she didn't need a daughter with two bad ankles if she were to slip on the stairs, so she arranged for meals and anything else she might need to be brought to her. Sherene made sure she had plenty to keep her occupied, though Tamsin quickly wearied of stitching patterns into canvases and reading about the settlement of the western Sea Islands. Her most recent venture had been to study the murals around her room, though after a few maddening hours she realized that she was no closer to discovering what they actually meant. Maybe they meant nothing. Maybe they had only been painted there to cover up any remnants of the temple that remained after they had been dissolved.

When Sherene was busy with her own chores Tamsin spent her free time practicing the motions Haven had taught her. She was careful not to put too much weight on her ankle, but she didn't want to forget everything he had taught her, so she gripped her hairbrush and imagined a long, silver blade on the end. But imagining a sword was much different than actually holding one and feeling the weight of it pulling against her muscles. And she had not seen Haven once since the rain started. She gathered that the Watchers were nocturnal, by nature or necessity she wasn't quite sure, and she knew he had spent a lot of time with her during the daylight hours lately. He more than deserved to rest and she hoped he had found a nice, quiet place to sleep, but his absence still bothered her.

And Cornelius's silence bothered her as well. She had hoped he would find answers quickly and would have the decency to update her, but she had not seen him since that day at the Armillary. She wondered if Cornelius's offer to leave guards with her had raised alarms with her mother and the rain was only an excuse to keep her within the compound. She didn't want to believe that Lieutenant Riggs was dangerous, for Enrik's sake, but she kept replaying the conversation she had overheard with him. And even if Cornelius had taken Enrik's father into custody, there was still the other man she had overheard as well. Who and where was he? She wanted it to be enough that Cornelius believed her and to leave it in his hands, but the more she tried not to think about it, the more anxious about it she became.

So now here she was, listening to the sound of the rain as it drummed against the stone and playing with her shawl, twisting it so it resembled a small pouch.

The pouch!

She had forgotten all about the bag Haven had given her the other night after everything that had happened. She untangled the shawl from her hand and got off the bed. She knelt down and retrieved it from where she had hidden it under her bed before. She sat on the ottoman near her balcony and, setting the bundle on her lap, slowly spread the drawstring apart to open the pouch.

It was strange looking, glossy black and shaped like a diamond whose points had been broken off. It didn't look completely solid either, as if it were a gem, slightly translucent. It reminded her of the paperweight her father had in his old study back in the Cities, though he had kept it on the shelves with the rest of vases and artifacts he had collected from his adventures, safely out of reach of a curious young girl. She turned it over in her hands and every now and then she thought she caught glimpses of color, tiny flecks of crimson, green, or sapphire. The more she looked at it, the more convinced she became that there was something *inside* it, but it was too dark to make out what exactly. And it was warm, which puzzled her immensely. It was almost as if it was…alive.

The thought made her nervous, but she couldn't look away. The darkness within the stone deepened, but brightened at the same time, making everything else around her seem dim. Her bed, her wardrobe, the murals, the sound of the rain—it all disappeared into the abyss. There was a hollow, pulsing sound that grew louder and louder in her mind and she realized it was coming from the stone. The hairs on the back of her neck stood up and her instincts told her to look away, but she couldn't tear her eyes away from it. She stared in wonder and trepidation at the object in her hands, compelled by a force terrifyingly foreign to her. It coaxed her closer, deeper, its presence wrapping itself around her mind with persistent curiosity.

Then it shrieked, a high-pitched wail that sounded as if it came from the very pit of the earth.

Tamsin dropped the stone, covering her ears and closing her eyes, and prayed for the ear-piercing attack to stop.

When she opened her eyes again, she found herself on the floor, with her forehead pressed to the cold stone. It was startling, how quiet it was now. With trembling hands, she pushed herself up and paused when she saw the stone lying only a few feet away. Her connection to the stone was severed, but a lingering numbness resounded through her mind. She grabbed her shawl and threw it over the stone, not wanting to look upon it anymore. She pushed herself the rest of the way up and staggered over to the balcony. The rain was cold and bounced off her skin lightly, fracturing into tiny droplets. Her clothing was soaked in a minute, but she didn't care. She lifted her face to the sky and let the abruptness of the rain drops awaken her senses again. She stood there until any remnants of the stone's power had disappeared and she felt she had control again. She returned inside, rung out her hair, stripped off her wet clothes, and laid them by the fire to dry. She redressed into something looser, took a seat next to the fire to stave off the chill, and waited.

She glanced at the shawl-covered stone on the floor and wondered why Haven had given her such a deceptively evil object.

Haven's feet barely touched the ground as he ran along the roofs and over the tops of arches that served as useful bridges between the buildings. He jumped over alleyways and ducked under windows, avoiding the main streets that would get him noticed, though most people seemed to have holed up in their homes to avoid the deluge. He grabbed hold of a ledge and hoisted himself up to the next level, making sure his footing was secure on the rain-slicked stone before continuing. He ran along the narrow stretch as fast as his feet would go and when he came to the edge where the wall turned, he pushed off of it and leapt. Arms outstretched, he flew through the air until his hands clasped around his goal: a long, wooden flagpole that protruded from the next building. Using the momentum from the jump, he was able to swing himself up and once he was balanced on the pole, he found the cracks in the wall face and started climbing up. He pulled himself up once he had reached the top and dropped into a crouch, searching for movement between the strings of rain coming down. But there was none, so he moved on. The canvas flaps to keep the rain out were all secured around the compound so all he had to do was run over to the stairs and up to Tamsin's room. He finally stopped once he reached her doorway and scanned the room. She was alone, sitting by the hearth and staring into the flames as if she were trying to work out a puzzle, her eyebrows furrowed in deep concentration.

The tension in his shoulders eased now that he saw for himself that she was okay. He had come as soon as he had felt it. It had awoken him from a dead sleep and it felt as if all the air had suddenly been sucked out of his lungs. He hadn't known what it was at first, but then he realized it was the same pressure he felt when he touched his firestone, only ten times stronger.

And Tamsin had his firestone.

Even at a distance, he could feel its presence and control it. Even when he slept, there was always that tiny part of his mind that kept it subdued. But there were a few moments of panic after he recognized what it was and tried to harness it again that he realized he hadn't lost control, he was still connected. It was as if something else, something much stronger, had pushed him aside and was using it. That's when he had started running and somewhere between him leaving the Hollow Cliffs and reaching the city, it had suddenly stopped.

He took a few steps inside, leaving little pools as footprints. Tamsin's eyes slowly moved away from the fire and focused on him. She didn't look surprised to see him, but she seemed angry. Whatever had happened to the stone, it had affected her too.

She stood up and crossed her arms. He noticed a small, pink mark just below her hairline. A cut that was healing. Something else had happened, but that would have to wait. She took a few deep breaths, her eyes darting suspiciously to a bundle on the floor.

Haven guessed the firestone was underneath it. "What happen?" he asked her cautiously.

"What happened?" she asked incredulously. "Why don't you tell me? What in the seven hells of old is that thing?"

He crossed the room and knelt down next to the bundle. He slowly removed the fabric and picked up the firestone, turning it over in his hand. It looked just as it always did. He stood up and walked over to her. She took a step back.

He held it up in his palm. "It be cavii'jii, a firestone. It be a—a heart."

"It is *evil*," she said, with more fear in her eyes than he had seen since the sandstorm. "You need to destroy it."

"No," he said.

She looked at him strangely, as if some kind of madness had taken root in her. "Then I will!" She snatched the firestone out of his hand and threw it into the fire. She pushed her damp hair away from her face and slumped back into the chair, breathing heavily.

He knelt next to her, searching her face for clues. "Tell me what happen, Tamsin," he said gently, placing his hand on the armrest next to hers.

She wouldn't look at him, but stared at his hand, her eyes wet with emotion. Her voice shook when she spoke. "I think you should go."

His throat constricted, making it impossible to respond, and he felt the wooden armrest start to buckle under his grip. He released it before it cracked and stood up. He nodded. He reached out with his senses, felt the fire in the hearth, and subdued it until it was nothing but embers. Tamsin's head snapped up, her eyes wide. He reached in and plucked the firestone from the coals and then released his hold on the fire, letting the flames climb back up.

He wished he could destroy it along with the sting in his chest. But he was bound to both. He walked over to the arched doorway.

"That night at the Armillary, when you attacked the soldiers. That was you, wasn't it?" Her voice stopped him. He looked back over his shoulder. "And the other night at dinner, when all the cauldrons went out."

He pulled back his hood and his n'qab with it and turned around to face her.

"You can extinguish fire and bring it to life without even blinking," she said. "How is that possible?"

"We not make fire where none exist," he explained to her, "but we able to keep it under control. We able put it out if we must."

"The stone has fire in it," she breathed, still struggling to understand. "Is that what I felt before?"

Haven's eyes darkened. "I not know what that was."

"But you felt it too? Is that why you came back?"

"I felt…something. Like something be trying to take control away from me."

"So it wasn't you?"

"No, but I promise Tamsin, I find out what." Or who, he thought silently.

She bit her lip.

He looked down at the firestone in his hand. He should have never given it to her. How was she supposed to understand? He went to put the firestone back in his pouch, but her hand reached out and stopped him.

She had gotten up and bridged the distance between them. Her glistening eyes slowly focused on the firestone. "I was looking at it and—and at first it seemed, I don't know, beautiful, but then it changed. Everything was dark and twisted and it was screaming inside my head." Her hand gripped his arm tightly, turning her knuckles white, but he didn't mind. Her fear was justified. She stared at the firestone, but Haven knew she wasn't seeing it. She was re-seeing what she had seen with the firestone. "You said— you said it was a heart? Of an amon'jii?" She blinked a few times and refocused on him, her frightened eyes shredding his resolve to pieces. "Why do you keep it?"

He held the firestone between his thumb and forefinger. His other hand hovered over it and tiny, iridescent flames spiraled up from its core. Once they had reached his fingers he subdued them and the firestone once again lay dormant. "You be right. It has fire inside it. Even when it master be dead. Fire not be destroyed." Not until…no. He would not tell her that.

"So you control it," she said.

He would let her think that was all. The rest of it, the truth of it would be burned with him on his funeral pyre. A soul of ash, contained by a body of shadows, branded by flames. Blood was thought to be the strongest tie, but to be bound by fire was a burden of a different beast. One he would share with no one.

"It's a brave thing you do," she said, pulling him out of his thoughts. Then she took a deep breath and held his gaze. "Can you teach me how to control it?" she asked.

He shook his head, not wanting the firestone to be anywhere near her after what happened, and the ability to control fire was something only the Watchers were able to do. Or so he had thought.

But she was persistent, desperate almost. "I could help you figure out what it was," she said. "Can you teach me?"

Haven didn't understand what had happened with her and the firestone and until he did, he didn't want to risk something happening to her. He had a hunch that they had only tested the shallows, that an ancient power lie waiting in the deeper pools, a power that he did not even comprehend. But the firestone had responded to her. She had awoken something and something had awakened in her, something that had lain dormant for many years, something he had not expected. He could see it even now, in her eyes, the echo of the flames still burning underneath those dark lashes. Maybe learning how to use a sword wasn't the only way she needed to learn how to protect herself.

She repeated her question, and he almost didn't catch it, so easily had it flowed off her tongue, but she had asked him not in her language of the north, but in *his*.

If only Ysallah were here now.

That night, after the rest of the city had gone to sleep, Haven took her down to the river and almost to the very spot where she had fallen in, though this time they were underneath the wall. There was a walkway on each side of the river underneath the large, stone arches that covered it. The portcullis came down through each section, but it had been left to the elements unmaintained and there was a massive hole eaten away by rust in the section where it met the walkway. Haven helped her through, though she was able to manage the rest of the way out to the Hollow Cliffs under her own power. Her ankle was not fully healed, but the landscape next to the river was solid, unlike the shifting sands they had encountered on the other side of the cliffs in the sandstorm. They had both agreed that the threat of discovery would be too great at the compound, especially with Sherene and Cornelius's men watching her like hawks, and if Haven were to teach her how to control fire then the less curious eyes there were the better.

Haven had found a set of massive, uneven shelves of rock that formed a crude kind of staircase that led up to a wide ledge halfway up the cliff. The ledge was mostly flat and when Tamsin looked over the edge she could see the Elglas churning a ways below, dividing the cliffs into two separate halves. The other side of the ledge was buttressed by a vertical wall that rose up like a guardian into the cobalt sky. Tamsin could only see where it ended by where the stars appeared. The towering wall and the open space over the Elglas should have made her feel uneasy, but the ledge was large enough where she would have felt comfortable sparring with Haven if her ankle allowed it. Her ankle was still tender however and Haven had to help her up most of the steps leading up to the ledge, the height on some of them almost level with her shoulders. His canvas tent, a *buurda* he called it, was already set up on the far side of the ledge with a few of his things and Tamsin guessed that this was the elusive hiding spot he occupied when he was not in the city.

She was nervous about facing the firestone again and she had to wipe her palms on the sides of her dress when she thought about the darkness she had felt within it, though she did not voice her concerns to Haven. He was still skeptical of this whole arrangement and she knew he would call it off the moment she showed hesitation. She understood that the firestones came from the creatures Haven hunted and that they were foul, vicious beings, and they were dead by the time the firestones were acquired. But she also understood the wary look in his eyes when he dropped his hood. This was new territory for both of them. What she had experienced should not have happened and that was the driving force behind her decision to learn how to control it like Haven could. He explained to her again that the fire was not summoned, it was already inside the firestone, but they sought to contain it there. He told her it wasn't even something he had to think about anymore, it was just a tiny pressure that he felt and his body recognized and responded to it.

So they practiced together, night after night. Haven would lessen his hold on the flames and they would spread from the stone like wings. Tamsin would search for that spot, for that place where she had felt the firestone. After a week of intense focus and no results, Tamsin began to wonder if she was even capable of doing it. But he had more patience than she did, long after her fear of it vanished and frustration replaced it, so he continued to push her. He would alternate between watching the firestone and watching her and sometimes he would get up and circle them until Tamsin thought there must be a path worn right through the stone. By the end of the night, he usually became more and more silent and he would return her to the compound with that look in his eyes when something puzzled him and she imagined he returned to the cliffs afterward and continued to stare at the firestone. The fact that even he was no closer to figuring out its secrets made her even more painfully aware of her shortcomings.

"Maybe we be going the wrong way," he muttered to himself one night.

"What do you mean?"

He took a few pieces of what looked to be thin tree bark or thick parchment out of his bag and arranged them next to the firestone. He lit the small pile from the firestone and stood back.

"Try on this," he said.

She looked at him skeptically, but tried all the same. She tried to push away the frustration and focus on the flames. She envisioned them dwindling down, fading into the ground, but the harder she tried the more they seemed to flicker and laugh at her and the more angry she got. She tried until it was just a pile of embers in front of her, but she could take no credit for it.

Haven took out some more bark. "Again," he said.

"No, Haven, no more. I know you think I can, but I can't do this." She paced back and forth with her arms crossed. She kicked a pebble off the edge of the ledge, but didn't watch to see it hit the water. She knew she was being childish, but night after night of failure was starting to take its toll. What if none of it had really happened? What if she had just imagined it all? And what little sleep she did manage to get during the day was not enough; her mother had noticed the dark circles under her eyes and had asked if she was sleeping well. She didn't know how much longer her mother would believe her excuses.

"We take break," Haven said.

"I'm done. I mean it. I don't know why I thought I could in the first place. Stuff like this, this magic or—or whatever you want to call it, it doesn't make sense to me. It doesn't exist in the world I come from."

"Yes it does and it not be magic."

"Then what is it? Why does it even matter if the fire stays in the stones or not? How am I supposed to control something I don't understand? I don't understand Haven!"

But he wasn't looking at her anymore, he was looking past her.

Tamsin turned around and stared at the pile of ashes, but it wasn't a pile of ashes anymore, it was *burning*. The flames were as bright as any she had ever seen and snapped like whips in the wind, cutting into the darkness with a wild frenzy. And then it was over and nothing remained but a few wisps of dust and a mark where it had scorched the rock.

Haven touched her wrist and a shudder ran through her. She scarcely dared to breathe, staring at the blackened spot where the flames had been. "Did you do that?" she asked, though she already knew the answer.

He shook his head and whispered something in his own language that she didn't understand, but the meaning couldn't be clearer: something amazing had just happened, something unexpected, and she had no idea what it was. He knelt down next to the spot and let his hand hover over the few pieces of dust that remained, but his fingers stopped just short of touching it.

She stood rooted to the spot. "Haven? What does this mean?" She was supposed to be learning how to control fire, not create it.

His fingers curled back into his palms and he stood up to face her. "It mean you be special, Irinbaat," and she only had a moment to wonder what he meant before he asked, "Do you think you can do that again?"

She smiled, all of her previous frustrations evaporating like a dream. She had felt it, just like he said. A tiny burst of energy, but it was enough to leave her fingertips tingling. She tried again to access the source of her newfound power and create another flame. She tried several times, but each time nothing happened and the ground just got colder and colder with the passing night. She started to shake from the effort of it.

"Enough," Haven said and she frowned. She wanted to keep going, to prove not only to Haven but to herself that she could do it. As if reading her mind, he said, "You already be able. You earn your rest now."

The moon was already high in the sky, but she did not feel like going home just yet. It was not unusual for her to stay longer at their little camp after she was done with her lessons for the night. She would watch him in his various tasks as he cooked or mended his clothing or sharpened his knives. She often helped him sew his clothes, for he was not very good, and she got accustomed to bringing thread and needles and other bits of food for when he made their midnight meal, which usually consisted of fish and some kind of grain that he turned into a porridge-like dish. One night he laid out all of his weapons to clean them. She counted eleven, each one a different shape and size. Only a couple looked like actual swords similar to the kind the Empyrian guards carried, but most of the others were strange to her, looking like large animal teeth instead of knives. Where he kept all of them hidden in the folds of his robes she did not know and she did not ask.

He had started teaching her the language of the Ma'diin since their first night in the cliffs, starting with simple words, pointing things out in their surroundings and telling her their names. The language was sharp and silky all at the same time, like it was a piece of chocolate flecked with spice. She would practice during the day and she couldn't hide her pleasure when Haven would smile and comment on how good she was getting.

Her favorite thing though, was when he told her stories of the Ma'diin. He never told her stories about himself, but once in a while he would share tidbits of information about his home and his people. It wasn't exactly fondness with which he spoke, but rather familiarity, and he seemed to relax when he told her about these things.

Tonight was one of those nights.

She sat on the edge, taking a break from their attempts to create fire, and dangled her legs into the air above the large expanse above the river. The water reflected the light of the moon up onto the sides of the cliff walls, blue and silver rays swelling and ebbing with the motions. Haven settled in next her, his eyes glowing fiercely as if they were absorbing the light from below and radiating it back into the night. His gaze wandered from her face to her neck and the top of her shoulder. With a curious look on his face he brought his hand up and gently brushed the hair away from her shoulder and slowly pulled back the collar of her shirt.

She trusted him, but her heart still jumped with an extra beat when his fingers touched her bare skin, tracing a line down her neck. She sucked in a tiny breath of air, but it was enough to make Haven blink, as if he hadn't been aware of what he was doing, and he quickly withdrew his hand.

She glanced at her shoulder and realized it was her freckles he had been studying. She gave him a questioning look.

"Your markings be unique," was all he said, refusing to meet her gaze for more than a second.

It was always her face that people said was unique, with her wide eyes and smile on an otherwise narrow face, not her freckles. "More unique than yours?" she pried.

He met her eyes and then glanced down to her neck again, though still clearly embarrassed by his actions. "They look like the stars, like Lumierii before they be broken." He pointed up to the sky, to a constellation Tamsin recognized.

"Broken? But it is whole. We call that the constellation Dracao, the great serpent."

"It be broken long before your people name it." He touched one of her freckles and moved to the next, naming each star as he went. Tamsin watched the sky, her eyes drifting from star to star along with his movements until he continued down her shoulder, still naming each one though Tamsin had run out of stars to follow. When he had finished, and her skin had stopped tingling, he said, "Every Ma'diin know this story. In time before beginning, there be Mahirii and Bherun. Mahirii ruled over ground and it be she who made Edan, the green mountain. Bherun ruled over water and he made the rivers. Together they able to make Edan beautiful and they lived there many years. They had two children: Baat, daughter, and Ib'n, a son. They were the first, the *Q'atorii*. As gift, Mahirii and Bherun give Baat and Ib'n power over the sky. To be pleasing his parents, Ib'n made the moon and the stars, but none of them burned as bright as Baat's sun and he became jealous. One night, while the others be asleep, he stole a piece of the sun."

"Ib'n made fire from the sun. He became fixed on it, but he not able to control it. He became angry and almost burned Edan to ashes. When Mahirii and Bherun found out what happen, they punished him. They capture him and put him in the moon. For a thousand moon seasons he watched from the sky as his family made the Ma'diin on earth. Mahirii mold them from the clay ground and Bherun give them red water in veins. Baat give them light so they able to see the beautiful world. Ib'n hated the Ma'diin and his hating only grew the longer he stay in the moon. When his anger grew too bigger to be contained any longer he broke free, splitting the moon in half. He fell to the earth, but no longer he be Ib'n, one of the Q'atorii, he be a monster. His anger made him be cruel on inside and outside. He have horns like *santaari* and his heart be turned to stone, but all the seasons trapped in the moon he learned how to control fire. He unleashed his fire on the Ma'diin, destroying the people his family loved so much."

"Mahirii and Bherun tried to protect the Ma'diin, hiding them in Edan. Bherun built huge lake around it, for water be only thing that able to stop Ib'n's fire. But Ib'n's anger not be stopped and he went on and burned down all trees and life around the lake, leaving the earth dead and only green ash. Mahirii died soon after then, not able to endure loss of her creatings; she feel each blade of grass, every leaf as it be turned to dust. Bherun went out to face Ib'n, to be avenging Mahirii's death, but Ib'n's anger made him be more powerful than Bherun and it be soon clear that Ib'n not be defeated."

"Baat see all of this and went to the sky. She seek the stars' help to defeat her brother and they agreed, feeling abandoned by Ib'n. Twelve of them," his gaze flickered over the freckles on her skin, "the Lumierii, flew down to the earth with her and when Ib'n see them coming out of the sky towards him he be afraid. Ib'n unleashed his fire on them, but fire not destroy light. They be made by him, they not die. Instead, they be able to control the fire and Ib'n no longer be using it against them. It be Baat who struck the final blow, ripping out his stone heart."

Haven let out a deep sigh and then was silent.

Tamsin blinked. Though his grammar was not yet perfect, she envisioned everything he told her perfectly and seeing the cliffs around them and the river below once more was a little jarring. "Is there more to the story?" It was a story of their creation, she realized, the creation of the world and of the Ma'diin and she wanted to know more.

He smiled, and years of hardship evaporated from his face. "Yes, much more, but I not be able to tell it good."

"You told it beautifully," she encouraged him.

But he was finished for the night, she could see. "You should hear it from the *sh'lomiin*, the story keepers," he said.

"Will you take me there someday? To hear the stories?"

His voice was soft when he answered and he spoke in Ma'diinese. *"I would want nothing more."*

Their eyes met briefly, but he looked away quickly, gazing down into the shifting water. "But it not be safe place," he said, the gravel in his voice returning as he switched back to the common tongue.

"But you would be there to protect me," Tamsin nudged his shoulder with her own playfully, but the shadows in his eyes remained.

"It be easy to protect one person, but when there be many..." his words trailed off.

She knew that he was not going to pursue the topic any further. "Well, I am glad I get to know a little of your world at least," she said. "You are as good a storyteller as any I've heard."

His brow furrowed and he looked as if he was about to ask her a question when his expression changed entirely. In an instant he was alert and pulling her back from the edge. The speed at which the Haven who told her stories disappeared and Haven the Watcher and hunter emerged was startling.

"What is it?" she asked, but he was crouched down and peering over the edge into the river, still and silent like a bird of prey. She inched closer so she could see what he was looking at and he held a finger up to his lips.

She looked over the edge and saw two men, dressed in Empyrian military garb, rowing cautiously in a wide boat. She thought for a moment that it was part of the dam party returning, but she remembered that they had not taken boats. Then she saw the glint of steel reflected in the moonlight and two helms sitting on the floor between them.

"What are they doing?" she whispered.

"They be tracking me," he said. "Or trying at least."

Tamsin felt a spike of fear in her stomach. If they found them and she was with him…

Haven must have sensed her concern. "They not find us," he said, getting up and walking over to the buurda. He started re-sheathing his knives and tightening the straps for his swords. "But we be going."

Tamsin watched the boat a minute longer. "I can't believe Cornelius still has his men following you."

"They've redoubled their efforts lately. I stay as vigilant as I can, but I can't keep track of all of them." He thrust the last knife into its holder with more force than was necessary. If they had come all the way

out here looking for him, then it meant that he was right and some were slipping through without his knowledge.

Now that she was learning the Ma'diin's language Haven often slipped into his native tongue more often and she did her best to keep up. *"You think maybe they just want to talk? Maybe the lords have something important they need to talk to you about."*

"They said everything they wanted to the other day."

Tamsin thought back to that day when the guards had escorted Haven from the river to the Armillary. *"What did they say to you?"*

But he just shook his head and pulled his hood up. *"I've been a hunter long enough to know when I'm being hunted."*

Tamsin knew he was right. Every day that the dam party was gone only strengthened the tension between the Ma'diin and the Empyrians. Everyone was getting edgy, waiting for an answer one way or the other, but as she and Haven made their way down from the cliffs she knew that once the dam party returned, her time with Haven would be over. She wasn't sure she was ready for that. She looked over at him. His eyes were like arrows in the night, sharp and precise, and she felt the goosebumps on her arms emerge as if his gaze was like claws lightly raking against her skin. She remembered her neck tingling when he had touched her.

He knew what it felt like to be hunted.

So do I, she thought.

CHAPTER NINETEEN

Tamsin found herself growing accustomed to being awake at night so it was hard to keep her thoughts at bay when Haven didn't show up the next night. She grew more restless as the night inched by, worrying that he had gotten into trouble with the Empyrian soldiers. She wrapped a cloak around her shoulders and wandered down to the third level with a single candle, hoping the open air would calm her spirits. She could see tiny lights moving along the top of the wall in the distance as the guards went about their posts, but there was little activity besides that. Even the Armillary was dim tonight, allowing the stars to shine more brightly overhead.

She stopped at the veranda wall and located the candle's tiny presence in her mind and focused on quenching the small flame. She smiled as a thin wisp of smoke floated up, taking the place of the flame. It was getting easier to extinguish fire with just her will; once she stopped thinking of it as a solid thing and started feeling its movements as if it were a live entity she could locate its presence nearly every time, though she still couldn't fathom how she had started the fire the other night with just a few embers. She tried that now, seeing if she could bring the flame back to life from the hollow spot where its pressure had been, but the candle stayed dark. She frowned. She had been angry, angry with Haven, angry with her own shortcomings, but most angry that there were forces at work that she couldn't explain. Forces that Haven took for granted and could tap into and summon without even breaking a sweat. She wasn't angry now, and she hoped her ability wasn't limited to when she was emotional, but she was curious. Haven hadn't given her much time for questions in her training, but now she found herself thinking about it. What kind of power did one possess that allowed them to control a natural element? Was it bestowed by some heavenly deity or dredged up from some earthly source? For the first time she wondered if there was a cost for possessing such power.

A light sparked on the wick.

She remembered when Haven had first shown his face to her, of the story he had told her about the desert they lived in, how it used to be a jungle of sorts. The amon'jii had turned it into the desert it now was. She remembered when she first realized his scars were from the amon'jii.

The flame crackled with heat.

Haven and his brothers hunted the amon'jii. His brothers wore the same robes and hood that he did. If they had similar markings, then…could they control fire as well? Did their ability to control fire somehow come from the amon'jii? The same creatures that *breathed* fire? The same creatures that had burned them and turned this land into a desert waste?

She drew in a sharp breath as the melting candle dripped on her finger. She extinguished the flame and wiped off the wax, pressing her finger to her lips. She was close to something, an answer. She just needed a little more light to see…though there was a bigger question looming over all the others, one she was afraid to even think about.

The next day she visited the Graysan's dwelling. Georgiana was out, but it was Mr. Graysan who she wanted to speak to. He graciously, if a little nervously, let her in and offered her some tea. He forgot to warm it, but she paid no mind.

"What do you know of the Q'atorii?" she asked him.

"The Q'atorii?" he said, raising his eyebrows. "I haven't heard that name in years. Why do you want to know about the Ma'diin gods?"

"Haven told me a little about them, but I was hoping you could tell me more."

"What would you like to know?" he asked, obviously pleased to have someone interested in what he knew and eager to divulge. And probably happy that she wasn't asking about the Ma'diin woman.

"I was wondering what happened to the twelve. The stars that helped Baat defeat Ib'n."

His eyes flicked back and forth as if he were searching deep within his memory for the information. "They were the Lumierii, yes, that's right. Ib'n had created more like him before he was defeated so the Lumierii stayed to protect the Ma'diin. They are believed to be the first of the Watchers."

"So the amon'jii supposedly came from Ib'n and the Watchers from the Lumierii?"

"That is the gist of it, yes."

She placed the small bag she had brought with her and set it on the table between them. At her encouragement, Mr. Graysan reached inside and took out the firestone. His eyes grew in disbelief as he turned it over and over in his hand like it was a precious gem.

"Where did you get this?" he asked.

"It's Haven's. He's letting me look after it." In truth, she had asked him to let her keep it for a while so she could practice.

Nothing had happened like that first time she held it, though she was still cautious when she practiced with it.

He gave her a strange look, but his eyes quickly wandered back to the stone. "He must trust you a great deal."

"Have you seen one before?"

He nodded and gave the firestone back to her. He rubbed his hands together. "I don't know where they come from originally, but every Watcher has one."

She put the firestone back in the bag. "Did you ever talk to them?"

"The Watchers? Only a few times did we see them, but they never spoke to us." He paused before continuing. "There's a complicated arrangement or relationship between the Watchers and the rest of the Ma'diin. For instance, the Ma'diin worship their sun god, Baat, but it's forbidden to have light around the Watchers, their protectors."

Tamsin ran her thumb over the spot where the wax had burned her. "Why is light forbidden?"

"It all goes back to the story of the Lumierii, I suppose," Mr. Graysan said. "They soon discovered that they were bound to the night, that Baat's light burned them. Though we came to learn that if the Watchers were around, it usually meant they were hunting and the animals they hunted were attracted to fire, and nobody wanted those around," he explained with a half-humored smile.

But Tamsin was thinking about the Lumierii. What if it wasn't just a story? "So the Watchers aren't nocturnal because that's when the amon'jii are active, but because they can't go into the light?"

He gave her an approving look at her knowledge of the amon'jii. "According to their stories. Ib'n was the god of the night in a way, and he created both the amon'jii and the Lumierii so it serves to explain why they both live at night, I suppose." Mr. Graysan shrugged his shoulders, but even as he did so Tamsin's eyes went wide.

"Are you alright dear?"

She blinked. "Yes, yes, it's just, my tea's gone cold. I should probably be getting home now." She thanked him, told him to say hello to Georgiana for her, and rushed out, her mind turning faster than she could keep up with.

She didn't even realize she was running until she reached the outer wall. She climbed the stairs onto the southern walkway and stopped in between two columns at the top to catch her breath. She pressed her palms into the rough stone and looked out across the desert to the Hollow Cliffs. Heavy clouds were rolling in from the south, casting a shadow over the Cliffs like a dark halo, cracks of lightning illuminating their cores. She had a vision, of a vast green plain with flowers and trees and vines, stretching as far as she could see, from the great mountains in the west to the enigmatic regions in the east. But then a storm thundered in and it wasn't a storm of rain, but of fire. When the storm passed, the charred remains of what had been crumbled and dissolved in the wake of the sun's light until there was nothing left but a great sea of sand.

Haven had laid it all out for her the other night when he told her the story of the Q'atorii, of Ib'n and Baat and the Lumierii. Whether it was true or not, it made sense. Ib'n had created the amon'jii and with Baat's help, the first of the Watchers. But the words Mr. Graysan told her gave the story a new, punishing meaning. *Baat's light burned them.*

She leaned against the column, feeling the paralyzing creep of fear move to her heart. That was the cost. Haven and the other Watchers were confined to the shadows, to the darkness of night not only to hunt the amon'jii, but because they could not go in the light. If they did, would what happened to the Sindune happen to them? Every day that passed without seeing Haven made her wonder if something had happened to him. She didn't think Cornelius was bold enough to do anything while the truce was still in place, but now that she was aware of a much more constant threat looming bright in the sky she could only console herself with the knowledge that Haven knew how to look after himself.

Haven looked toward Empyria from the top of the Hollow Cliffs, his dark cloak silhouetted by the storm growing behind him, creeping up from the south like a massive shadow. It rumbled impatiently, as if in annoyance that the Watcher's attention was directed elsewhere, echoing Haven's keen awareness that his thoughts should be to the south. Like an invisible tether turning his head away from the marshes and the wall in the river, his thoughts kept pulling him back to the northern city. It was as if Oman had predicted this: the distraction. It was a feeling opposite of focus, and anything that took away his focus was dangerous. Experience had taught him that lesson many times.

But this was not like the other times. He could not sever the hold this tether had on him, as much as he wanted to protect them both. It didn't matter whether he was here or in the marshlands. He was a hunter and the hunted, and if Tamsin was near him she was bound to get caught up in the vicious circle. He had never felt this helpless to his own emotions before and being at their mercy made him shake with rage. He had thought he was protecting her, but his presence only put her more at risk.

Every time he was with her images of a future, a different future than the one his life had set him on, flooded his mind, stirring up a longing that grew with each brush of her hand or glimpse of the sunlight sparkling in her eyes. Her gentleness, her beauty, her resilience, her fearlessness…it made him forget that their shared world was only temporary. But he was reminded of their reality with each sunrise, and every time they parted. Then the cruel truth sharpened before his eyes again: that she was safer the further she was from him and if he loved her the best thing for her would be if he left.

His chest heaved at the thought, and he knew he had let that tether become too intertwined within himself to ever untangle. Not without causing himself unthinkable pain. Even staying away for this long felt like water rising over his head, making it difficult to breathe. Being alone was not something that had ever tortured him, in fact most of the time he preferred it. But now it seemed an unbearable punishment.

But would he only bring about worse pain if he stayed? Would his attachment pull her under the surface with him?

He turned away from the sight of the city and headed back to his encampment within the cliffs, but the storm stirring inside him only seemed to build and darken with his thoughts. It blurred the space between past and present, flashing images of another soul who had hooked his affection back in the marshlands…and had paid with her life for his failure.

It had been almost a year ago, he realized. His attachment to Lu'sa had been innocent, pure, a friendship that had held him since the day she was born. She had been unafraid of him too.

He started untying the straps that held the pieces of his buurda, as he tried to quell the forge roaring inside him. Then his eyes caught a glimpse of the bracelet underneath his sleeve, the one she had given to him. He gripped the pieces of his buurda and flung them against the wall. His shoulders quivered from the weight of the memories, pent up inside like a knot of snakes. They tried to slip through his fences and each time he put one back in place another one snuck out, striking with a venom that turned his blood black and cold.

But Tamsin took the sting away. She lifted the weight without even realizing the effect she had. Did she even feel the same? Was she daydreaming of a future with him or was she firmly awake and knew these dreams should be buried in the ground? She was here, living a life in the sun and he could never escape the darkness. They each belonged to different worlds, ones that never should have collided.

And yet, they already had, long before they had met.

But Tamsin had no idea, so it didn't matter. *Irinbaat* he had called her the other night, and she hadn't even blinked. The gods had chosen to keep her far away from his world and maybe it was time he listened to them.

CHAPTER TWENTY

Lavinia Urbane was in good spirits, albeit a little puzzled as to her daughter's peculiar behavior lately. She confronted her at the dinner table one evening, asking her if something was on her mind, but Tamsin continued to push the food around on her plate with her fork, seemingly oblivious to everything else around her. Concern replaced curiosity and she tried to coax whatever it was that was troubling her daughter out of her. She knew she had not been sleeping well lately, but now she began to notice other things too, like how pale her skin had become and how any conversation with her these days was usually one-sided. This new level of despondency was alarming and the next morning she sent for a healer, who examined her despite Tamsin's protests, but could not ascertain any physical ailment. He explained that she seemed to have a preoccupancy and whatever was causing it was giving her an unhealthy level of nerves. He gave her some herbs to mix in with her tea and instructed she rest until the preoccupancy had resolved itself or her strength return.

While Tamsin lay at home in bed, Lavinia visited Madame Corinthia, whom she had run into while at the dress makers. Both their spouses were gone and she felt a certain connection with the Commander's wife, even though she found her to be lacking certain sophistications. She was not much older than Tamsin; no doubt a factor in the Commander's decision due to his age and the fact that his first wife had left him childless. She had an obvious eagerness to fit in with the lording ladies and her welcoming disposition was genuine, albeit a little simple, so when she invited Lavinia for tea, Lavinia pleasantly obliged.

"When do you expect our husbands will return?" Madame Corinthia asked, setting out a tray of sandwiches.

"When their business with the dam has concluded, I suppose. Though I do wish it was sooner rather than later. I know Tamsin misses him more than she's letting on. And something has been troubling her. She has been rather closed off and I don't know how to reach through to her."

"I do hope it's nothing serious." Madame Corinthia said, genuinely concerned. "Tamsin seems like a girl with a good head on her shoulders. Is there anyone you could talk to? Someone Tamsin confides in perhaps?"

Lavinia shook her head. "I have seen her with no one." Tamsin had always been close to Sherene, but even Sherene could not give Lavinia any answers.

"Not even that strange tribal man from the south?" She lowered her voice, though they were the only two in the room. "My maid tells me they've been seen together."

Lavinia smiled curtly and explained that she had put a stop to that, though there was not much to put a stop to in the first place. The Ma'diin man had taken a fancy to her and followed her around constantly, until she had made it clear that this was unacceptable behavior. There were no attachments at all on Tamsin's part.

"Oh my," Madame Corinthia exclaimed, thoroughly shocked.

Lavinia nodded gravely. Madame Corinthia would no doubt circulate amongst the others what Lavinia had told her. This would surely put them back in their good graces.

"And to think, Lady Regoran spreading those awful rumors. Poor Tamsin. I suppose now suitors will be lining up to be with her, now that she doesn't have some barbarian following her around like a puppy. Lady Regoran was right about that at least."

That got Lavinia to thinking and she asked Madame Corinthia for a quill and parchment. She wrote a quick letter and after she had finished, she ordered one of the servants to take it to Captain Saveen. There had been something there, between Cornelius and Tamsin, until they got messed up in all this foreign business. Lavinia partially blamed herself for that, for agreeing to house the Ma'diin man in the first place. She had been wary of him, afraid of the influence he would have on Tamsin, and rightly so, though it was not Tamsin's fault that she was drawn to him. Lavinia blamed Eleazar for that. She had vowed to raise Tamsin as a gracious, well-respected lady and she had done so to the best of her abilities, though the sooner she married her to a powerful and equally respectable gentleman the better. Cornelius Saveen was just the type of man she imagined would be devoted to her daughter and would also be able to control her more imaginative flights of fancy. No doubt Madame Corinthia was right and the rumors Lady Regoran had spread had turned many possible suitors away. Cornelius was a busy man, though, and she would rather think that was the reason for his lack of appearance lately. But Lavinia believed if she intervened slightly on their behalf then she could mend the whole situation and these last weeks would have only been a minor hiccup.

Cornelius Saveen finished reading the letter, folded it, and tucked it back in his breast pocket just as a knock on the door echoed in the chamber. Things were moving along nicely, he thought, and now that he had Lady Urbane's approval there was nothing stopping him from taking the next step with Tamsin. That girl was a potent mix of fire and beauty and her indifferent attitude towards him only made his interest in her stronger. He didn't even realize the magnetic effect she had on him until he had a moment to think about it and once he did he knew he would pursue her. He had had other affairs before Tamsin, none of which he expected to lead anywhere, but Tamsin was part of the lording class and a member of a family that was highly influential in the Cities. Though he did not care much for her father, a union with the Urbanes would only further his aspirations.

Another impatient knock sounded on the door and Cornelius called him in. Riggs came in carrying a stack of scrolls in his arms. He deposited them unceremoniously on the table and began rifling through them.

"No more letters today," Cornelius said, irritated. He had just finished a dozen from the Cities before Lady Urbane's letter and he still had more to get through before he went to check on the training of the new recruits.

Riggs ignored him and continued to sort through them until he found the ones he was looking for. He plucked two from the pile and thrust them in Cornelius's face, making Cornelius think these weren't just standard reports.

Cornelius took the first and looked at the seal. "This is from Commander Corinthia?" He broke the seal and unrolled it quickly. This was the news everyone had been waiting for. He read the Commander's short, clipped handwriting with bated breath.

"Well?" Riggs asked when he had finished.

Cornelius let out a sigh, but it was not one of relief. "The negotiations were successful," he said. "The Ma'diin are not going to attack. The Commander says they are going to stay a little longer and begin disassembling the dam."

"What?" Riggs replied, incredulously. "If they take down the dam then—."

"I know, I know!" Cornelius slammed his fist on the table.

Riggs pointed to the other scroll. "You should read that one."

Cornelius picked up the other scroll, which wasn't really parchment at all, but the supple hide of some animal, with wariness. He didn't recognize the seal on it. "Where did this come from?"

"It was on your doorstep," Riggs said, the same look of concern in his eyes.

Cornelius opened it and nearly gagged at what was rolled inside. He closed his eyes for a moment, then read the short lines that were written underneath and then turned it around and laid it on the table so Riggs could see. Written in blood, just like on the sword box, were the instructions:

Bring me the she-hunter
Kill the others

Riggs looked at it with a sickened expression. "Does he have to be so damned macabre all the time?"

Cornelius placed his palms on the table. This had gone from bad to worse in the blink of an eye. Monstran would be here any day and when he found out that not only was the dam being taken down, but the Ma'diin he wanted was a hundred leagues away, he would surely be upset. Why he wanted Ysallah, Cornelius couldn't begin to guess, but now he wanted Ysallah's guards and the Watchers dead?

"I want to be notified the second Monstran arrives," Cornelius said, "and double the guards on patrol. I want Haven found."

"We've already doubled the patrol. What are you going to do?"

Cornelius shook his head. "We're going to stall."

Riggs narrowed his eyes. "You think if we give him the Watcher instead of the Ma'diin woman he'll be okay with that?"

"No, but it might buy us some time to get her." He gave Riggs a look that demanded unwavering loyalty.

Riggs nodded. "I'll take a squadron there myself."

"Take only those you can trust," Cornelius said. "If Lord Urbane or any of them try to intervene…"

They shared a grave look. "Understood," Riggs said.

"I'll send a second wave of builders after you. Come find me when you're all prepared. I'll see you off personally."

Riggs turned to go, but when he got to the door he turned around. "How are you going to catch the Watcher?"

Haven was like a shadow, disappearing with the clouds and invisible at night. "I'll have to get creative," Cornelius said, taking the letter from the Commander and holding it over the candle flame. Then he set it down on the animal hide and watched as the flames engulfed the eyeball that had been sent with it, imagining that the murky orb had once glowed bright blue or silver. This would be the last time it ever did.

It was just before dinner when her mother returned from her social excursions. Tamsin was already waiting at the table for her, the meal laid out before them. Her mother paused in the middle of taking a bite, noticing that Tamsin had not touched her food.

"My dear, you have to eat something. The healer said you have to keep your strength up."

Tamsin stared at her then withdrew the letter from her lap that had arrived just before her mother had gotten back. It had been addressed to her mother, but she had seen the Saveen seal on it and had been curious. So she had read it. "Why is Cornelius under the impression that we are to be married?"

Lavinia grinned. "So he did stop by then?"

"No, but he wrote this letter and," she opened the letter and began reading, "is *'most pleased to have received your proposition and am eager to meet to discuss the future joining of the esteemed Urbane and Saveen families.'*" Tamsin placed her hand flat on the table over the letter and repeated her previous question.

"Because you are," Lavinia said blatantly. "Why are you acting like this? I thought you would be happy."

Tamsin shook her head. "Why would you think that marrying Cornelius would make me happy?"

"Because you two hit it off rather well on your date and you've been so discouraged lately that I figured Cornelius's absence had something to do with it."

"And you told him this? Without even asking me?"

Lavinia put down her silverware, a stern expression on her face now. "It is not up to you, Tamsin. The arrangements are being made. Everything is in motion now. It would do you and this family some good to be allied with the Saveens. He is one of the most powerful men in Empyria. You could do a lot worse than him." She held up her glass for more wine.

"I don't want anything to do with him."

"Believe it or not, I had the same reaction when my mother told me who I would be marrying. All I knew about your father was that he had recently returned from the east. My mother knew it would be equally…beneficial for both of us so she proposed a union. I admit, it took some time getting used to, but in the end I accepted my responsibility and have not looked back since."

Tamsin had never heard her mother talk of her marriage to her father before. "I didn't know you and dad had an arranged marriage," she said quietly.

Her mother took a sip of her drink. "There are many things about the past that you are not aware of that has led to this moment right here. Much has been sacrificed so we can live in wealth and privilege."

Tamsin stared at the candelabra sitting in the middle of the long table. "What if that's not what I want?" she asked softly, tears filling her eyes.

Her mother's expression remained hard. "It's time you learned, Tamsin, that what you want and what you live with are two very different things in this world."

Tamsin let out a breath, watching it condense in the cold night air. She wrapped her cloak tighter around her shoulders and looked back and forth down the lane, making sure there were no lurking meddlers in the street. She crossed to the other side and knocked on the familiar door underneath the stone arch. She waited patiently for a minute and was about to knock again when the door opened, letting light stream out into the street.

"Tamsin?" Georgiana rubbed her eyes sleepily with one hand and held a lantern with the other. "What are you doing here?"

"I know it's late, but I couldn't sleep and——."

Georgiana's brows knitted together in concern. "Is everything alright?"

Tamsin's face scrunched together and her throat tightened painfully. She started to say she was fine several times, but she couldn't get the words out. "Can I come in?" she asked instead, her voice cracking.

She didn't have to say anymore and Georgiana ushered her inside and sat her down at the kitchen table and started stoking the fire so she could prepare some tea. She got Tamsin a blanket, but the fire was soon warm enough where she didn't need it anymore and the tea and the coziness of the small room helped calm her nerves some. She explained to Georgiana, as best she could, of the mess that was unfolding around her. She told her of her mother's plans for her to marry Cornelius and how she really felt about it. When Georgiana asked why, she knew it was time to tell someone about Haven. She told her about the lessons with him and what he had been teaching her. And she even told her what she had figured out about why he could not go in the sunlight and how his absence weighed on her. After she had finished, Georgiana sat back, staring at Tamsin in concern. She asked what she was going to do about Cornelius, but Tamsin had no idea. Her father would never approve of the match; he seemed to loathe Cornelius as much as she did, but she wasn't going to underestimate her mother's persuasive abilities. "I'm going to have to figure something out," she said. "Maybe I'll introduce him to Emilia Regoran."

Georgiana laughed aloud and then covered her mouth quickly. The two chuckled quietly together, alleviating some of the tension Tamsin felt and talked in hushed tones after that so as not to wake Georgiana's father, but what the girls didn't know was that Mr. Graysan was indeed awake.

"Could you show me?" Georgiana asked.

"Show you what?"

"You said Haven's been teaching you how to control fire. What does that mean?"

Tamsin allowed a smile to cross her face. She took one of the candles on the table and set it between them. In a moment, the flame disappeared. Tamsin's smile grew. It was getting easier. Before Georgiana could say anything, she let the flame reignite, and the startled look on Georgiana's face as it once again illuminated the space around them gave away her astonishment.

"I'm not that good at it yet, not as good as Haven, but—."

"*This* is what Haven's been teaching you?" She reached out her hand towards the candle, but retracted it quickly as she realized the flame was indeed real and not an illusion. "How is it possible?"

"I don't know. It's just…a feeling. I can *feel* the flame."

"Is it magic?"

"I don't know what it is. It's some kind of power that he and the Watchers have."

Her forehead creased in confusion. "But how are you able to do it if the only ones that can are the Watchers?"

A shadow fell across Tamsin's face. That was the big question, one she didn't have the answer for and she didn't know if Haven did either. She told Georgiana about the first time she encountered the firestone and what had happened.

"Do you think your ability came from the firestone?" she asked.

Tamsin shook her head. "I don't think so. It didn't feel the same."

"Well maybe you can teach me then," Georgiana said brightly.

Tamsin didn't think so and she was even less sure of her ability to teach it to someone even if they did have the ability, but she tried anyways and it served to distract her for a little while. It didn't seem to matter to Georgiana that she couldn't do it, though, because every time the flame went out on its own Tamsin brought it back to life and Georgiana would gape in wonder.

On the other side of the wall, Mr. Graysan held his chin in between his thumb and forefinger, deep in thought. He could not tell Tamsin the truth because it was not his to tell. He assumed the Watcher had figured it out as well, or else why go to such lengths to develop such a gift? But why indeed? Haven might have figured out who she was, but what was he going to do with the information now that he had it? The girl had a gift, one that no one had foreseen, so what did the Watcher intend to do with her?

The next day, Tamsin sat cross-legged in the middle of her bed, playing with the flame of a candle, extinguishing it and then lighting it again over and over until her mind began to drift and she started daydreaming. She remembered when she used to take walks in the gardens back home, in the Cities, whenever she grew weary of the repetition of day to day life. She would roam the winding pathways between the red amaryllis and the larkspur, wander by the little stream that ran parallel to the high wall, dotted with sanguinaria, and smell the cherry blossom trees that surrounded the newest addition to the garden: a willowing manolia tree. She had seen one once before when they had been on holiday in the southern city of Judain. It reminded her so much of her beloved cherry blossoms, with its cascading branches holding the pink and white flowers like the jewels on a chandelier, though the blooms were as big as lilies. Upon their return, her father had surprised her with one of her very own. She only got to see it bloom once, in the spring, before her father announced they were leaving the cities and moving to Empyria.

"You shouldn't play with candles, Lady Tamsin," Sherene said as she walked into the room, carrying a large bundle of clothes. "You will get burned. Or worse, you'll set something on fire."

Tamsin shook her thoughts away and blew out the candle, setting it on her nightstand. "What are all of those for?"

"Your mother ordered these for the ball." She set the heavy outfits down on the bed in front of Tamsin. The Lords' Ball was held throughout the Cities as well and marked the near end of the solstice, but Tamsin had heard mentioned that this one was going to be special, though for what reason she didn't know.

Tamsin lifted one up and then glanced at the others. "Did she buy every single dress in the dress maker's shop?"

Sherene smiled. "She may have saved one or two of the uglier ones for Emilia Regoran." She gave a conspiratorial wink.

Tamsin grinned, but then a frown replaced it. She had still not been able to set Cornelius straight about the arrangement. She had gone to see him at the Armillary earlier, but she had been turned away by the guards, saying he was in a meeting with the other lords. She did not want to have that conversation in a public setting. "Do I have to go Sherene?"

Sherene gave her a stern look. "Do not be childish, Lady Tamsin. It is a privilege to go to such events." She held up a blue one with silver trim around the waist.

Tamsin shook her head.

"And it will do you some good to talk to other people other than your mother and me." She held up another one, which Tamsin rejected like the first.

"But I like talking with you Sherene," she said sweetly.

The maid waggled her finger. "Flattery will not get you out of going this time," she said.

Just then another maid appeared carrying another stack of dresses, making even Sherene raise her eyebrows. But when the maid left, Georgiana emerged from the doorway carrying a basket of ribbons.

"Ah, reinforcements. Miss Georgiana, you are just in time," Sherene said.

"Just in time for what?" Tamsin asked, though she was delighted to see Georgiana.

"To help me convince you to go to the ball. I suspected you would be pig-headed about it."

"Lady Allard said you had asked for some ribbons," Georgiana said, walking into the room slowly.

"Indeed I had. Don't dawdle child, bring them here," she said, but she went over to Georgiana anyways and took the basket. Then she set it on the dresser without another glance. "Now, you don't want to have to explain to your mother or Captain Saveen why a lord's daughter could not attend the Lord's Ball, do you?"

"That's why I don't want to go," Tamsin said. "I would rather not talk to Cornelius there."

"You still haven't told him?" Georgiana whispered harshly.

"Told him what?" Sherene asked.

"Nothing," the girls answered in unison.

Sherene eyed them suspiciously for a moment and then held up another dress.

"That one is beautiful," Georgiana breathed.

Tamsin had an idea then. "You should try it on," she said.

"Oh no. I couldn't," Georgiana said hastily, backing away from the garment.

"I insist. Sherene, would you help her put it on?"

The two went behind the dressing partition and a few minutes later Georgiana timidly emerged, her arms stretched out as if she were afraid to touch the dress. It was a rich cream color with a soft tulle skirt and glittering green sequins swirled around the bodice. It was a perfect match to highlight her curly, golden hair.

"You look fantastic, Georgiana," Tamsin said.

"I've never worn anything so beautiful in my whole life," she breathed, "or so tight." She adjusted the corset.

Tamsin laughed. "Well you're going to have to suffer, because that's what you're wearing to the ball."

Georgiana looked up quickly. "Tamsin, you can't be serious."

"The only way I'm going to the ball is if you come with me. That is my condition."

Sherene smiled. "You look stunning Miss Georgiana."

Georgiana let out a squeal of delight and twirled around the room.

Sherene whispered to Tamsin, "That is a very nice thing you did."

Tamsin smiled, happy for Georgiana, but she knew the only way she was going to make it through that ball was with a little support.

Sherene helped Georgiana change back into her regular clothes and she gave a little sigh as she sat back down, sad to be taking off such a beautiful piece of clothing.

Another maid came in, carrying a velvet-cased, shallow box. "This came for you, my lady," she said, handing it to Tamsin before leaving again.

Tamsin opened the box and gasped. Inside was a dazzling diamond necklace. It formed a circle and came to a gentle V at the bottom. Connected to the bottom of the V was a large royal blue sapphire surrounded by dozens of tiny glimmering diamonds.

"Oh my lords," Georgiana said, her eyes as wide as peaches.

Attached to it was a note. It read:

To the most beautiful jewel in Empyria
Cornelius

Tamsin shut the box. "I can't wear this," she said, her hands trembling. "I can't."

Georgiana smiled sympathetically for her friend, but Sherene let out an incredulous cry. "What has gotten into your head Lady Tamsin?"

Tamsin looked at her maid with a pained expression. "I can't do it. If I wear this, then he'll think…"

"He'll think what my lady? What is going on?" She looked back and forth between the two girls.

"He'll think that I'll want to marry him."

"And why wouldn't you want him to think that? He's a good match, Lady Tamsin. Soon you'll get to know him and then before you know it you'll be head over heels for him."

Tamsin took a shaky breath. "I'm in love with someone else, Sherene."

Georgiana's eyebrows arched up and she looked away as Sherene's mouth opened and closed wordlessly. After the shock passed, a knowing expression came over her face. She put her hands on her hips and shook her head. "It's Mr. Haven, isn't it?"

Tamsin hadn't been able to say it out loud even to herself until now. She had wanted to keep her feelings in check because she knew that nothing could come of it. Haven would have to leave eventually and that would be the end of it. But after knowing the danger he faced every day she couldn't avoid the risk just because she feared the pain that would follow. And with her mother trying to marry her off to Cornelius, she realized she wasn't ready to let go. "How did you know?"

"I didn't. Just like I didn't know that you were sneaking out with him every night." She raised her eyebrow. "He returned you each time just as he found you so I didn't say anything, if only to save your mother's nerves." She turned back and started going through the dresses again.

Tamsin was speechless. All this time, she thought she had been so clever, so *careful*. And now to find out Sherene had known all along. But she had kept quiet. She hadn't given up Tamsin's secret. She climbed off the bed, crossed over to the maid, and hugged her.

Sherene paused and then patted the back of Tamsin's head. "I just hope you aren't loving Mr. Haven to fill the void," she whispered.

Tamsin leaned away, about to question her, but another question filled the room.

"What's going on in here?"

Tamsin jumped back, wiping the tears out of her eyes hastily, and saw her mother standing in the doorway.

"We were just picking out a dress for the ball tomorrow evening, my lady," Sherene said, throwing a reassuring smile towards Tamsin.

"Oh good. I'm glad to see you are up to the task, Tamsin." Her mother's pleasure was icy at best.

Georgiana got to her feet. "I should be going," she said. "I'll see you tomorrow, Tamsin." She curtsied to Lavinia. "It was nice to see you Lady Urbane."

Lavinia watched her go and then turned to her daughter. "You really shouldn't attach yourself to the servant girls," she said, dusting off the chair Georgiana had just vacated.

"Georgiana's my friend," Tamsin said. "And her father is a scribe for Lord Regoran. You could be a little more courteous."

"Would you look at this," Lavinia said, admiring the necklace in the velvet box, ignoring Tamsin's words. "This is remarkable. Cornelius has impeccable taste."

"I'm not wearing it," Tamsin said firmly.

Lavinia rubbed her fingers on her temples. "I've had quite enough of your attitude lately. I am your mother and you will do as I say. Your father would be very disappointed to see how you're treating me if he were here." She ruffled through the dresses and then selected a long, yellow one. "Put this on."

Tamsin did as she was told and then Lavinia placed the silver necklace around her neck and clasped it at the back. She turned to face her.

"Don't cry." Lavinia said. "You'll ruin the satin." She turned to Sherene. "This is the one. Make sure she is ready tomorrow evening." And she walked out of the room.

Tamsin stared down, watching her tears splash against the floor, feeling like they were only a precursor to the storm that was sure to come.

That night Tamsin snuck out of the compound after everyone had gone to sleep and made her way down the river to where it met the wall. There were guards on the wall yet, more than she had seen at this time of night, and she had to be careful to keep to the shadows to avoid being seen, but she needed to find Haven. But when she walked on the slippery ledge underneath the wide, stone arch, she found that the hole in the portcullis was no longer a hole. Someone had replaced the missing metal bars with new ones. There was no way to get through now.

She wondered if that's why she hadn't seen Haven in so many days. Had he gotten trapped on the outside when they fixed it?

She took hold of the bars and pulled. It didn't budge. She pushed and still it didn't move. She pulled on it again and again with all of her strength until she was out of breath and when nothing happened she beat her fists against the metal, letting an almost desperate cry escape her lips.

A hand clamped around her mouth then, stifling her scream. The person behind her spun her around and it took her wide, fearful eyes a moment before she recognized the familiar black hood and cloak. She couldn't see his face, but the relief his presence brought washed over her like a cool breeze. She wanted to ask Haven where he'd been, but he kept his hand over her mouth and pulled her away from the portcullis, moving her behind a large boulder that protruded from the water. He crouched down next to her and held a finger up, indicating she should remain quiet. He removed his hand from her mouth and pointed up the river. She looked where he was pointing and saw a group of soldiers a little ways upstream on the eastern bank pushing several large boats into the river. It was hard to tell exactly how many there were in the dark, but there were five boats and no less than half a dozen men in each.

Before she had time to ask what they were doing, a high-pitched screech sounded behind them, making them both flinch. Tamsin covered her ears against the echoing sound and watched as the portcullis slowly started to rise out of the water. She could feel the slight tremble in the ledge beneath her as the metal gate was lifted and the water sloshed over the edge and soaked her shoes.

When it had risen all the way and the only sound was the water dripping off the spikes they turned their attention back to the boats, which were now all in the water and approaching the tunnel. Haven pushed her down even further until her hands and knees were slick with water. She held her tongue and kept quiet, though his behavior was as cold as the stone beneath her. He even smelled different; not the bittersweet mix of a cooking fire amidst a garden of lilacs, but of salt and fish.

She couldn't see the boats anymore, but she could hear the water lap against the hulls as they went by. Luckily, the soldiers didn't have torches to see by, though Haven could have easily snuffed them out if they had. Once they passed, Tamsin stood up and wiped her hands off, thinking about how she would have to wash it before Sherene saw the dirty water stains on her skirt. She turned towards Haven, but he was already making his way across the ledge after the boats.

"Haven?" She started to follow him, but he stopped abruptly and held his hand out. He did not want her to follow him. He started again and she followed again, confused by his strange actions. When he stopped this time it was with a sword pointed at her throat. She took a step back, alarmed. "Haven? What's going on?"

Just then, the grinding screech of metal against stone sounded again as the portcullis began to descend.

He nodded sharply towards the city and then darted away after the boats.

Tamsin watched him go, her chest constricting painfully, until the portcullis came down between them with a final, echoing thud.

CHAPTER TWENTY-ONE

The morning was a pallid grey yet, with only a few streaks of gold overhead as the sun slowly rose. The air was still cool and she closed her eyes, reminded of the milder climate in the Cities. She could almost see the dew drops, festooning the grass like jewelry. She had loved the view of the sunlight as it emerged through the trees and danced between the leaves. Her favorite time was when the darkness conceded to the light and everything was crisp and alive. She just wanted a few moments to herself before the inevitable rush of preparations began for the ball tonight.

Tamsin opened her eyes and sighed, the view from her balcony transforming once again into the grey-gold rooftops of the eastern city. She turned around to go back in her room… and saw Haven standing in the middle of her room, just on the edge of the light creeping into the room.

She drew in a sharp breath, not expecting to see anyone, let alone him, in front of her. The momentary burst of excitement that usually accompanied the sight of him was there, but the pain and rejection of last night was also there and she hesitated before walking back into the room. It had been a sleepless night for her, filled with unanswered questions and an ache that took her most of the night to identify, and the crippling thought of, not what she would say to him if she ever saw him again, but what he would say to her.

His n'qab was lowered and he studied her distant expression with a precautious eye. He slowly touched his fingers to the back of his hand in what she had come to learn as a sign of respect.

She frowned. He hadn't done that since they first met. "I thought you left," she said in the common tongue, not completely able to keep the edge out of her voice.

"I sorry," he said. "I not mean to leave you alone so long." He switched to Ma'diinese. *There were things I had to do.*

"Like what?" she said, stubbornly staying in the common tongue. She knew she shouldn't pry. He was a free man, able to do what he wished and go where he wanted, but things had been said, glances shared, and hidden feelings revealed in quiet moments. She knew she had no claims on him, but the way he had treated her last night left her inhibitions knocking on locked doors. Maybe he had changed his mind and the things he had said at the cliff that night meant nothing anymore, but she didn't believe that. So she wanted an explanation.

His body language was tense, defensive almost, and his eyes narrowed. "Things you not understand."

"What wouldn't I understand?" She remembered what she had realized when she had finally said what she felt out loud: that she had been afraid. Was Haven afraid now? He was always telling her not to be afraid; did the same principal not apply to himself? "Why are you shutting me out?"

"It not involve you," he growled, clenching his fists. His face contorted like he was in pain. He started pacing back and forth like a caged lion, but he never got more than a few feet from her. It was as if he was reluctant to leave her side, though her questions clearly agitated him. *Why must you know so badly?*

"Because it does involve me when my feelings are involved. You disappear for days after we saw the soldiers and you think you can show up without an explanation? I just couldn't think of—," she choked out. Her vision blurred and she wiped her tears away quickly, embarrassed by her emotions. She could see him searching her face, looking for the words written in her tears that would reveal her feelings. She took a shaky breath. There was no more time to be timid. Despite everything that had happened last night and despite what was unfolding now, she couldn't deny what she felt, no matter what he felt in return. "I can't lose you," she said. "I'm in love with you."

A long moment went by before Haven was able to respond. He stopped pacing, trying to read her face for some indication that she wasn't serious, but he found none. She repeated what she had said in his language.

"It be true?" he breathed.

She nodded.

His heart pounded with such force it threatened to overwhelm him. He walked over to her and slowly reached up and wiped a tear from her lips. He searched for the right thing to say. He had pushed away his feelings for so long it had seemed impossible that he would ever get the chance to tell her how he felt. And now that they were here, together, and she was saying these things, he couldn't find the right words. He could imagine smiling, wrapping his arms tightly around her and never letting go. He could imagine the smell of her hair, kissing her, and telling her how long he had hoped to hear her say those words. He could imagine happiness.

But the old world would not let him go that easily. What kind of happiness could she have with someone like him?

"Why?" he asked.

"Why…?" she echoed. Then, "Because you're alone here, like me."

His hands dropped away from her face and he took a step back. He looked away, not wanting to see the confusion and hurt in her eyes.

"You don't know what it's like to be alone," he whispered.

"What's wrong?" she asked in Ma'diinese.

He clenched his hands into fists, angry with the world for its cruelty, angry at himself for being a part of it. He had let his actions be ruled by his dreams for too long, his dreams of being with her, and he had neglected his duties. Those duties would soon catch up with him and pull him back under.

"What's wrong is that I am a killer. Death is the only thing I am capable of."

"I don't believe you."

He turned back to her. Her soft, angelic face showed neither hurt nor fear, only resolute patience. *"My own people are afraid of me,"* he said. *"Why are you not?"*

Even though her eyes were still wet with tears he could see her stubborn defiance. She was not intimidated by his true nature and it baffled him. His own people treated him with wariness and feared him as they feared the very beasts he protected them from. The attention and affection Tamsin showed him was something he had never experienced before. He was not worthy of it.

"I don't fear you because I'm afraid of life without you," she said.

Even in his anger she captivated him. She dominated his thoughts entirely and he couldn't deny that she made that part of him, the part that was wild and full of anger, a little bit smaller. But he could almost hear Oman telling Kellan that if she was going to be a distraction then he would be sent home. Had they been in the marshlands, he would have been unfocused, undisciplined, and would have potentially make a fatal mistake that would get him or both of them killed. That's why Watchers were rarely chosen as mates, because love ruined them.

"If you knew what my life was like, you would be afraid of it," he said.

"It was you who taught me not to be afraid," she said, an edge to her voice now. *"I would give up the light in a heartbeat if it meant I could be with you."*

Her words startled him. *"Don't speak so casually of things you don't understand,"* he said, even though the look in her eyes was anything but casual.

"But I do understand," she said, taking a step towards him. *"It's what you've been hiding from me. The light will kill you, won't it?"*

His eyes narrowed, wondering when she had figured it out. He had never meant to keep this a secret from her, there were other secrets that he wasn't sure he could ever bring himself to tell her, but he hadn't meant to get this attached to her either.

She switched back to the common tongue. "Is that why you've been so distant? Is that why you pushed me away last night? Are you afraid that I can't handle the truth?"

He was about to rebuke her, but one comment left confusion trickling through him. "Last night?"

She raised her eyebrows. "Last night at the portcullis when I tried to follow you and you pointed your sword at me."

He didn't understand. He had never raised a weapon to her that was meant to intimidate her. *"Tamsin, I wasn't at the portcullis last night."*

Tamsin tried to comprehend what he was saying. His eyes were glowing fiercely. Protectively. A sliver of fear pricked her as she caught the scent of lilacs and smoke.

Her eyes widened. "It wasn't you," she whispered, realizing with dreadful certainty that the man from last night was not the same as the one standing before her. She gripped his elbows to keep steady. "He looked just like you."

Haven told her to tell him everything and she relayed the brief events from last night as best she could amidst the rolling emotions inside her. She told him about going down to the portcullis so she could get out of the city and look for him, about the soldiers and the boats, and about the man who she had thought was him. He let her hold his hand as she spoke and the buzzing it caused in her head actually assisted in calming her. He was quiet, rubbing the back of her hand with his thumb as he listened. The steady touch helped remind her that it hadn't been him last night, that everything she had felt then wasn't real. She let the moments stretch between them, savoring his presence like the last rays of sun before winter.

When he spoke, he told her that until he knew for sure who the stranger was and what he was doing here and what the Empyrian soldiers were up to it wasn't safe. He needed answers.

Tamsin nodded. "You're leaving again, aren't you?"

"I not leave you again unless you tell me to go," he said, his voice so low it was almost a whisper, but his eyes pierced her like thunder.

She didn't want him to go. She wanted to be selfish and keep him here with her where he was safe. He needed to know what was going on though, they both did. It wasn't even a choice, but the fact that he was leaving the decision up to her gave her all the hope she needed to let him go. Leaving was going to be as hard for him as it was for her, even if he couldn't say it out loud.

The memory of her father's departure resurfaced and she realized this was probably how her mother felt saying goodbye to him.

She swallowed the lump in her throat. "Go," she said softly.

He hesitated and then slowly put his n'qab in place, looking exactly as he had when she first saw him. A little breeze drifted in from the open balcony, ruffling the curtains as it moved through the room and out the door, taking Haven with it.

Mora thought she was speaking the words of the gods, telling people their fates and dealing out sentences of doom bestowed by greater power. Tamsin, her father, Georgiana, and Enrik had been among the unfortunate ones to hear such prophecies, though Tamsin refused to believe any of it. But Haven believed in his gods. He believed he was a weapon, to be sharpened and wielded for the gods' own intentions. They had bound him to darkness and choked every piece of kindness and love he had ever known out of him until all that was left was anger and fear.

She had seen it in his eyes, heard it from his lips. Haven believed he was a monster. He believed it because the god who created his ancestors had been a monster, had killed his mother and tried to destroy the Ma'diin forever. But if Ib'n was a part of him, then so was Baat. Haven may have chosen to overlook this part of the story, and himself, but the original Watchers had defied Ib'n, had defied their creator to do what was right. And Haven did that every day by protecting his people, but he was incapable of seeing it because all he saw was the fear and distrust reflected in his people's eyes. Haven was a living reminder of the evil that had almost destroyed their world and it was all because of some stupid myth about how the Watchers came to be. And that was why he had denied his feelings for her for so long. Because all he had ever known was anger and bitterness.

Tamsin was sick of the gods trying to control the people she loved.

The gold-flecked sky of the morning had disappeared all too quickly and soon the preparations for the ball were underway. Tamsin found it hard to concentrate on getting ready when her mind was occupied with questions and worry, but Sherene was diligent and made sure she was presentable to her mother's liking by the time the sun set. Tamsin had stayed while Sherene put the finishing touches on Georgiana's hair, but her mother still didn't know that Georgiana was coming so Sherene said she would bring Georgiana after Tamsin and her mother left. As soon as her mother was ready, Tamsin knew she couldn't put off the inevitable any longer and she climbed into the rickshaw cart with her mother, hoping that the night would pass quickly.

They were greeted in the courtyard and ushered across the bridge leading to the Armillary by a man in pale blue, though soldiers stood at each entrance, silently watching as the guests arrived. Rows of torches lined the outer veranda, making the jewelry on the ladies sparkle like stars and the helms of the soldiers shine like water in the moonlight. As Tamsin and her mother walked the outer edge, stopping periodically to talk to one of the ladies, she noticed there was a guard for every door save for the one that led to the ballroom. She looked to see if Enrik was one of them, but she didn't recognize any of them.

One of the servants came out and announced it was time to go in. The higher officers who were not on duty went in first and the Lords and their families came after, each being announced to the crowd separately. The ball was being held in the main room: a large circular chamber with a ring of decorated columns that supported the domed ceiling which was made entirely of stained glass. The floor was a masterpiece of hand-crafted mosaic designs which shone brightly under the light of the dozens of tall candelabras that were placed between the columns. Two staircases flanked either side of the entrance and led to the second story balcony that encircled the room. Long banners, with the emblems of the Lords' seals on them, hung from the balcony. There was the Regoran's, the Allard's, and the Wohlrick's, and there was even one for the late Lord Saveen, a deep red one with a large S emblazoned in the center of an orange triangle, though there was a thin layer of black tulle that covered it.

Tamsin saw the Urbane banner hanging beneath where the string ensemble was set up. Their emblem: a hand placed in the dark part of a crescent moon, had been stitched in gold against a blue background, similar to the Empyrian flag, Tamsin realized. And hauntingly similar to the blue sapphire around her neck that complemented her yellow dress.

CHAPTER TWENTY-TWO

Haven's plan had been to search for the man Tamsin had seen and if he hadn't found him by nightfall, then he would follow the river south and try to catch up to the Empyrians who had left, but his plan was quickly arrested when the man he was looking for found him first. He had had a hunch who the man might've been, but he was still unprepared to see him in the flesh. Haven had been angry at first for having been deceived by those he thought closest to him, but after talking with him he knew that there were bigger deceptions afoot, mainly with the Empyrians. And a strange sense of pride lingered in him, knowing that he had remained hidden from Haven this whole time.

But the biggest thing for Haven was that Samih was speaking to him again.

One of the Empyrians had left the dam site to deliver a message back to the city and Samih had followed him discreetly, choosing to stay hidden even from Haven. He could be more observant that way, he said, though Haven assumed either Ysallah or Oman, or both of them, were behind this. Samih told him that two pairs of eyes were better than one and it was well because Haven had missed the soldiers that left last night. Samih told him that he had followed them just past the cliffs, but returned to find Haven when he realized they weren't stopping there. The Empyrians were up to something and he didn't know what.

They spent some time discussing what needed to be done and it was soon decided that Samih would leave today and follow the

Empyrian soldiers south and Haven would follow shortly behind and catch up. It wouldn't do to confront the lords here; if they knew the Ma'diin had caught on to whatever plan they had concocted it could put both he and Samih at risk. But there were loose ends that needed tying up. Samih didn't pry for details, though, and Haven didn't offer any.

The afternoon was spent gathering the supplies they would need for the journey. They couldn't afford to stop to hunt or fish on the way because they were already almost a day behind so they took what food they could from the kitchens of unsuspecting Empyrians. Haven would get anything else they might need before he left. And Samih had already seen to their transportation: when he wasn't spying on the Empyrians he had been constructing canoes for them, planning for the day when they got to leave. He hid his boat in one of the caverns in the Hollow Cliffs close to the river.

As they were finishing packing, Samih asked him, "The girl was looking for you last night, wasn't she?"

"Yes," Haven said, checking the cross frame of the boat one last time. Samih had done exceptional work with his limited supplies.

"Why?"

Haven looked at him. "Why was the girl looking for me or why did I not catch the Empyrians leaving?" he asked, guessing his underlying question.

"Both."

"Neither one is your concern," he said, though it wasn't true. He had gone to the cliffs to be alone. And to pray, though it was not something he did often. But Lu'sa deserved his prayers, especially on the anniversary of her death. And Tamsin deserved the truth, but he hadn't been able to summon the courage to tell her when she confronted him earlier about where he had been.

He held the boat and Samih climbed in. "I'll see you soon brother." He paused, then added, "It is good to hear your voice again."

Samih nodded and extended his arm.

Haven, though slightly taken aback at the gesture, reached out and clasped it firmly with his own. Ysallah may have been right, he thought. Maybe getting away from the marshlands had been good for Samih after all.

Haven watched until Samih disappeared and stared at the glittering stars as they dotted the southern horizon, his thoughts lingering in the past. Samih seemed to be accepting his new life and responsibilities. He was putting his old life behind him. Maybe it was time for Haven to do the same. The starlight glowed in his own eyes, seeming to illuminate those doubts which he would try to hide even from himself. He had never questioned his birthright before, never thought about a life other than the one he lived. After Lu'sa died, all that changed. Now he couldn't take a step, couldn't draw a breath without questioning if what he was doing was right. If it was *enough*. It made him hesitate, and in his world hesitating was as good as a death sentence.

The memory of that night was as fresh in his mind as when it happened…

The air was thick and heavy like a blanket soaked in the mud. There were no stars that night, but the crescent moon reflected sharply in the still water through a crack in the clouds. It was not a good omen, especially on the eve of the fire season. The others would be gathered together right now, each clan marking the end of the rainy season with their brothers and sisters with one last celebration. But Haven and the other Watchers could not afford to lose their vigilance, especially this night when the amon'jii would be at their most aggressive. During the water season the beasts were less active, burrowing into the earth and caves while the rains flooded the marshes. But after long months of hiding and scavenging, they would be hungry.

So far, Haven had seen nothing. Not a rustle in the reeds or a ripple in the water. The night was as silent as a bone.

The hair on the back of his neck prickled. They were out there. He could feel it. The water barely moved as he paddled through, scanning the reed patches from beneath the edge of his hood. He came to a narrow section, where the reeds on either side just barely brushed the sides of his canoe, but beyond it was a vast pool with many mud flats dispersed throughout the open water. It was a clan he knew well. The huts on the flats were dark save for the soft ruby glow that emanated from the tops of the smoke openings.

He set his canoe on the edge of the second one to the west and climbed out. Before he had even made it a step, a pair of short legs with wavy brown hair came running out of the hut to greet him. The small girl wrapped her arms around one of his legs tightly, the top of her head reaching just above his knee.

"Well hello little Kazsera," he said, patting the girl on the head affectionately.

"'ello 'aven," she smiled up at him. 'I made you this,' she held up her hand, beaming.

He knelt down next to her, taking the string of beads from her tiny fingers. Though she was small for her age, she surpassed her peers in speech and thoughtfulness. Haven did not much care for children, and they did not much care for him, hiding behind their mother's legs or running away at the sight of him, but this little girl showed no fear and had wriggled her way into his heart.

He pushed back his hood and admired the gift. "It is truly beautiful," he said. "I will treasure it always."

"It will bring you good luck when you 'ave to fight the am'jii," she said.

He smiled proudly at her. "Thank you. I'm sure it will."

The girl's father stepped out of the hut then and nodded in greeting.

"I have something for you too," Haven said, smiling as the girl's eyes got wide in excitement. "It's in my bag. Why don't you get it while I talk to your father?"

The girl darted over to the canoe and began rummaging through his bag.

Haven walked over to the girl's father, Ko'ran, his lifelong friend. "I brought you something as well," he said, handing him a small bag, laden with nofii seeds. "I don't know when I will be back again, but they should last a few weeks."

"Thank you, my friend. It is good just to see your face. How goes the hunt?"

Haven turned back and watched as the girl held her new doll triumphantly over her head, grinning from ear to ear. "It is quiet tonight, but it makes me nervous."

"I'm sure there will be plenty of the beasts to feed your appetite soon enough." His friend smiled. "Can you spare a few minutes? The meal will be ready shortly. I'm sure it's been awhile since you've had hot food."

"I'm afraid I can't stay. I've already lingered too long."

"If anyone has a problem with you, they can take it up with me," Ko'ran said, "or Ysallah. She will defend you."

"I don't need defending," Haven said. "Your Kazsera is honorable and so are you, but I will leave you and the others in peace. I must continue my watch."

"Very well," Ko'ran said, knowing full well the demands placed on those that wore the cloak. "Don't stay away so long next time. She worries about you, you know?"

Haven nodded. "I will be careful."

Ko'ran called out to his daughter to say goodbye.

Just then, someone screamed, the sound tearing through the night like lightening. Both men turned to the sound, just a few flats over, and saw the cause. One of the huts had erupted in flames.

More screams joined the first and propelled Haven forward towards the flames. "Put the fire out!" Haven roared. "Put it out!" He heard Ko'ran yell to his daughter to stay put as he followed, right on his heels over the narrow causeways between the mud flats. Men and women were already throwing bowls of water on the flames as they reached it, but the hut was entirely engulfed in the inferno.

Haven concentrated on the fire, putting all his energy into extinguishing it before the beasts were drawn to it, but as soon as he managed to reduce it another sight caught his attention. He immediately unsheathed both scimitars strapped to his back, leaving the others to put out the smoldering fire.

He rushed forward and slashed at the beast as it swung around to face him. Its lips curled back over its teeth and it lunged at him. Claw met steel in a sickening screech. It tried to unleash its demon fire on him, but Haven quenched it before it could leave its gaping maw. Taking advantage of its momentary surprise that it had not fried its enemy, Haven leaped at the beast and sunk his blades deep into its side. The amon'jii shrieked and twisted, but Haven ripped his swords out and slashed again, severing the creature's jugular. Another scream jolted his senses and he pushed the dead carcass away, turning around to see another beast on the next flat, straddling a young boy who was writhing on the ground below the creature's open mouth.

Haven cursed and ran forward, stretching his will until he felt the amon'jii's fire stone and clamped upon it with all of his power. Others were fleeing the scene, over the causeways and in their boats. Some just dove into the water head first. Haven threw a dagger and hit the beast just above its hindquarters. It whipped around, clawing at its side, and the boy stopped screaming and weakly crawled away on his elbows. Haven ran to the edge and jumped, leaping over the several feet of water that separated the two flats. He landed in between the boy and the beast and crouched low as it turned to face him. It was an older one, Haven could see it in his eyes, which meant it would be harder to kill, but he could also see the hunger which had driven it here, into Ma'diin territory. It's first mistake.

The beast attacked, but Haven was quick with his blades and it retreated again. It tried to swat him away, but Haven made sure he stayed between it and the boy, who was shivering on the ground behind him. Haven risked a quick glance behind him, hoping somebody would come for the boy, but fear drove the people away.

Then his heart stopped.

Beyond the boy, beyond the running people, beyond the smoking hut, drifting slowly in the middle of the water was a little brown-haired girl in a canoe, peering fearfully over the edge at the chaos unfolding on the flats. And just beyond her, waiting in the reeds on the other side in the untamed marshes was another amon'jii. It was watching her, dipping its claws in the water as if to pull her closer, raking at the mud, trembling with half contained hunger.

Haven screamed her name and then felt the breath knocked out of him as he was thrown into the side of the hut, sending shards of dried reeds flying. He staggered to his feet, grasping for his blades, but he had lost them. He saw a flash of teeth between the black spots in his vision as the beast crashed through what remained of the wall after him and was able to grab another knife from his boot just as the creature's jaw closed around his arm. He slashed at its face repeatedly until it let go with a roar of pain, but he did not relent. He struck it again and again, receiving several gashes of his own as the beast tried to defend itself from the onslaught. But it was no match for Haven's fury in the end and caught between him and the water, it had nowhere to run. Haven dealt a final blow to the creature, driving his knife up to the end of the hilt into its neck just behind the jaw. It fell back in the water, dead, with a mighty splash.

"Help me," a ragged voice murmured behind him.

Haven rushed over to the trembling boy and cursed. The boy had been burned by the demon fire.

"Hey!" Haven yelled at a retreating form. The man hesitated from his flight, but stood frozen. Haven yelled again, "Get over here! This boy needs help!"

The man crept closer, agonizingly slow as he fearfully scanned around him for more of the beasts. He cringed when he saw the boy. "The shadow is upon him," he whispered and began backing away.

"Stop! Come here!" Haven yelled and looked over his shoulder. The canoe was drifting closer to the opposite shore. The girl's eyes darted about,

wild and wet. He turned back, but the man was gone. Then he saw Ko'ran running towards them. "Ko'ran! Get the heart and get him out of here!"

He wasted no more time, confident his friend could manage, and ran back across the flat and dove into the water. He swam as fast as he could, trying to keep his eyes on them as much as he could. He called out to her and her eyes locked onto his, a mixture of relief and terror. So did the amon'jii's. Its gaze flicked back and forth between its prey and this new enemy approaching. It clawed the water quicker now, almost in a frenzy, but still the girl did not see the danger right behind her. The boat was only a few feet away. The amon'jii stretched out its arm…

"LU'SA! JUMP!" Haven yelled.

The girl flinched, but before she could react, the amon'jii swung its massive clawed foot down and caught the end of the canoe. The boat capsized, flinging the little girl into the water.

Haven dove underneath the surface. His lungs burned and his head pounded. He searched and searched, now frantic, and then he saw the light glow of brown hair. He swam deeper and grabbed the girl around the waist, hauling her to the surface. They broke into the air and Haven took a huge gulp of it, easing the burn in his chest. But just as he looked to see if Lu'sa was alright he felt a stabbing pain in his shoulder as the beast hooked its claws into him. It ripped him from the water and he felt the tiny girl's body slip through his fingers back into the water as he was hurled into the reeds several yards away.

His vision blurred and it was all he could do to put up his arms as another searing blow knocked him another few feet. He grabbed a dagger from his belt and swung upwards. The creature reared back as part of its horn fell to the ground. It came back down on him with equal force, forcing all the air from his body and pushing him deeper into the mud. He grabbed the beast's jaws and pushed back with all of his strength as it tried to crush his skull between its teeth. The beast snarled at him, a wave of hot, sickly breath escaping its mouth. Haven roared back and with the last bit of energy he had heaved the creature's face away from his own and twisted. The amon'jii was forced to roll on its side to keep from breaking its neck. Haven gasped as the creature's weight was lifted off him, but the mud paralyzed him, trying to suck him back into the earth. He saw the beast get to its feet, fire in its eyes. It turned towards him, its lips curled back in rage. Haven's grip on his dagger tightened, though he could barely lift his arm.

Then the amon'jii whipped its body around and snarled, faced with a new enemy. A considerable amount of water was hurled at it, splashing over its face and sides. It spun around and fled, with more speed than a beast that size ought to. Two more dark figures rushed by in pursuit, but Haven could not see who they were. He was only half aware of being pulled up from the mud. The last thing he remembered was seeing blurry figures pulling a still body from the water…

He closed his fists around the memory. He always stopped there. What happened in the months that followed was a dark haze, cut through only with the sense of loss, but he would never allow himself to forget that night. He could brush his emotions away like dried leaves, let the pieces crumble through his fingers and go back to that place after her death of blind anger and hate, but even as he cleared away the fragments, what lay underneath was etched into his being, like words into stone. Someone told him that time would eventually smooth the edges and make the pain not so great, but Haven didn't want time to help him. The punishment of reliving that night was nowhere near adequate in making up for his failure to save her.

But more and more now he thought of Tamsin. Not just what she meant to the Ma'diin, but what she meant to him. He could not bring himself to let go, even before he knew who she was. She distracted him from his thoughts, from his guilt over Lu'sa and Samih, so he clung to her, clung to the relief she brought him from his inner darkness. She reminded him of a time before everything had changed. Her smile alone was enough to blind his torment. But the respite brought with it a new kind of guilt. He didn't deserve the love he knew she bore for him, nor the reprieve from his penance. He could leave now, go south back to his homelands, while she could still forget him, while she still had a chance at a normal life. But even as he thought it he knew he would never leave her. The relief she brought him had only been a single drop in the river of what he felt for her. They were both in too deep now to think of turning back, whatever the outcome might be.

He had been around the foreigners too long, in a place where the men made all the decisions. If Tamsin had made up her mind, then he could not question it. He would not question it. Not anymore. He had been a coward, afraid to get too close. He hadn't just been afraid of putting her in danger, danger had found them anyways, but he had been afraid that he would not be able to protect her and if something happened to her it wouldn't be like when he lost Lu'sa. Losing Tamsin would be his undoing. So if she was intent on loving him, then he would let her, and love her back as best he could, if only for the selfish reason that he needed her. He might not be able to protect her from everything, but the demons he knew were better than the ones he didn't, and he would be damned by the gods before he stopped trying.

The Urbane compound was nearly deserted when Haven returned. Only a few servants remained in the lower levels and the upper ones, including Tamsin's room, were empty. He searched for any clues that might tell him where she had gone, but there was nothing. He wanted to tell her what he had found out and that he would have to leave again, maybe for good this time. This wouldn't be like the last time he had been gone for several days;

he wasn't sure if he'd be coming back this time and she deserved better than to be left wondering what happened.

He stood on her balcony, quickly trying to think of where she would have gone, when the lights from the Armillary caught his attention. It was lit up like a hundred fireflies floating on a lotus flower in the middle of the dark river. It was like a beacon pointing him in the right direction. He knew then that's where Tamsin would be.

He left the compound and as he reached the outer courtyard of the Armillary, he could see the soldiers lining the walls, bedecked in the hard, metal clothing he had seen them wear when they first met at the cliffs. It was going to be difficult to get inside with all of them watching, but not impossible. He was good at blending into the shadows after all. He skirted around the outside of the courtyard until he came to where the wall connected with the river. It would be simple to swim underneath the bridge and just climb the main support columns to the Armillary, but his wet clothes and footprints would give him away in an instant. Instead, he found a foothold in the side of the wall and climbed up to the top. It was the tallest distance from the ground, but there were less soldiers to get past this way. Once at the top, he peered over the edge and waited until one of the guards walked past and then he pulled himself up the rest of the way. He hid behind one of the pillars that supported the stone canopy over the entrance to the bridge, standing on a piece no bigger than his hand that jutted out from the rest as another guard walked by unawares. But he was exposed to anybody on the bridge if they happened to look his way so he quickly extinguished the torches nearest him. Some of the guards paused and he used the momentary confusion to grab onto the top edge of the pillar and hoist himself up. He flattened himself against the top of the canopy and when he was sure nobody was looking he shifted over to the top of the bridge. The ceiling of the bridge was curved on top and sloped down on either side so he had to be careful to stay in the center, but he was able to make quick time over it to the Armillary. Once on the other side, he dropped down onto the slanted veranda ceiling and stopped himself just before he slid off the edge. He listened for a minute to the conversations below and heard some kind of music coming from inside. It must have been some kind of celebration to have this many people gathered all at once. But with this many guards watching the place, Haven's instincts told him that this was just an illusion. After stepping up their efforts to find him, Cornelius's men had suddenly and unexplainably given up. But now he knew why.

He had been wrong. The Armillary wasn't a beacon, it was an invitation.

His nostrils flared and his hand flexed on his bone-handle knife. They had set a trap for him.

He had half a notion to drop to the floor and slit all of their metal throats so they would let Tamsin and him be in peace, but he was almost sure that Tamsin would disapprove. He made his way back up the slope instead until he came to one of the dark towers protruding through the roof and climbed through the archway. There was a dark staircase to the left that spiraled tightly down and he moved swiftly for he was not fond of the tight space. There was an archway at the bottom that opened into a wide, dimly lit room. There was no one in it, but another archway across from the staircase that revealed a hallway on the other side. He made his way over to it and then flattened himself against the wall as two people walked by through the hallway, but they were too enamored with each other to notice anything. He made sure there was no one else behind them and then followed a little ways behind them around the curved hall until he saw them disappear underneath another arch. This one was outlined by two massive pillars and a man in blue and two soldiers standing outside the entrance. The music he had heard earlier was coming from that room.

He heard footsteps coming down the hall behind him so he ducked into a small alcove showcasing a painted vase on a stone pedestal. That was one thing about the northerners he was grateful for: they walked as loudly as herd of el'phantii through a jungle, with their hard shoes and metal clothes. He stayed hidden there as more people walked by and went into the room with the music. If Tamsin was here, that's where she would be. He just needed a way in.

Going back and finding another way in would take too long, but he had an idea as another man walked by. Haven left the alcove, snuck up behind the man before he could get within sight of the soldiers, covered the man's mouth and hit him over the head with his knife handle. Haven caught the man as he slumped down, unconscious. He would have a wicked headache in the morning, but no lasting damage. Haven quickly carried him back to the dark staircase, setting him on the floor.

Once he had taken his cloak off and replaced his clothing with the man's, he took his ridiculous hat and placed it on his head. It had a pointed ridge running from the front to the back, but the brim was wide enough to keep his eyes at least partially covered. The coat was stiff and uncomfortable and the man's boots were worse, but it was the only way he was going to get in without being recognized.

He rolled his cloak up, pulled the brim of his hat a little lower, and crossed the room out into the hallway. He had to grit his teeth against his instincts, which were telling him that going out in the open was a mistake. He froze as another couple walked by him, the man dressed in a similar fashion as Haven, but they smiled politely in his direction and continued without a backward glance. He took a deep breath, telling his instincts to back off, and followed them. As he passed the alcove where he had hidden before, he took his cloak out and slipped it in the vase. He lowered his head as he got to the pillars, watching the guards out of the corners of his eyes, and tried to appear as if he belonged there. The man in blue nodded in greeting, but the two guards didn't even glance his way.

Haven strode forward, smiling.

CHAPTER TWENTY-THREE

Tamsin rubbed the giant albatross around her neck for the tenth time that evening, feeling the weight of the gem in her fingers and wanting nothing more than to tear it off and fling it into the river. She was in no mood for dancing or civil conversation, and Georgiana was doing her best to bring out the lightheartedness in her, but it only served to make her feel worse about being such a rotten partner. She encouraged Georgiana to go dance when more than a few eager gentlemen asked her, but she was too caring a friend to leave Tamsin to wallow by herself. Her mother's attention never strayed far from her either and it wasn't long before she was ordered to be more sociable.

Luckily, the next dance was a cotillion style, and she was able to escape her mother's scrutiny and let Georgiana partake in the festivity. The men bowed and the women curtsied as they lined up across from each other. Tamsin stood next to Georgiana and leaned in to speak to her as the music began.

"Have you seen Cornelius anywhere?" The Captain had yet to make his appearance and Tamsin wanted to clear the air between them as soon as possible.

Georgiana shook her head. "No, but some of his servants have been watching you all night. I recognize them from the compounds."

They lifted their hands, taking a few steps with their partners, and then circled around and broke away.

"I thought the Armillary had its own set of servants?" Tamsin asked as her path crossed with Georgiana's.

"They do." Georgiana gave her a pointed look and then turned away as the steps took them away.

Tamsin surveyed the crowd as they turned again, trying to see if anybody was watching her, but it was hard to tell who was watching her and who was just watching the dancers. What were Cornelius's servants doing here? And why were they watching her? She knew the guards had been watching her before when Haven was around, but they had left her alone since they started spending less time together in the daytime.

She thought she spotted one and strode off the dance floor before the last note was even played. The servant, seeing her coming, slipped away in between the guests before she could reach him. His hasty retreat was enough to tell her that Georgiana was right and that Cornelius had his men watching her again. The guests clapped as the dance ended and Tamsin lost sight of him amidst the people. She weaved through them, trying to find him again, but there were other servants in blue that crossed her path, making it difficult to tell where he had gone.

She stopped up short then when she saw Cornelius coming out of one of the adjoining halls on the balcony with Lord Regoran, Lord Allard, and Lord Wohlrick. They took turns shaking Cornelius's hand, though the grim expressions they wore didn't match the gestures. Cornelius spotted Tamsin and walked down the stairs and over to her, tugging at the ends of his sleeve cuffs.

"I see you received my gift," he said, his white teeth beaming as he glanced over the necklace. "It suits you."

She scowled. "Tell your vultures to hover over someone else," she said coldly, ignoring his compliment.

His surprise didn't last long. "They're for your own protection," he said.

"Protection from what?" She was rather tired of everyone thinking she needed protection.

He held his arm out. "Dance with me and I'll tell you."

She gritted her teeth, but took his arm anyway. She was the one that had wanted to talk to him after all. He led her back onto the dance floor and they joined the couples already waltzing around in sweeping circles. The music was dramatic, the cellos plucking deep chords as the violins sung a slow, haunting melody.

"Please don't tell me this is about Haven," she said as they took a few turns. "He would never hurt me." But even as she said it, she felt the keen sting of his absence.

"The Ma'diin can't be trusted," Cornelius replied. "I wish you would understand that."

"They've given me no reason not to."

"Have they not?" Cornelius looked away, trying to hide some emotion from her, but she saw it.

"Cornelius, what is it?" The look in his eyes and the crease of his brow scared her.

He sighed. "I didn't want to have to tell you this now. I wanted to wait until after the proposal."

Proposal. The word hit her like a cold slap in the face. She realized she was out of time. She had to tell him now that there would be no engagement, no wedding. But there was something else, something important that he didn't want to tell her and she had the feeling that she wasn't going to like it. "Tell me."

"A messenger arrived," he said, watching her face for her reaction. "From the dam."

Her heart leaped to her throat, momentarily silencing her. "W-what did he say?"

He waited a moment before answering and each second seemed like a lifetime to Tamsin.

"He said they were attacked."

"Attacked? Attacked by wh—?" She froze, though the music still continued to move the dancers around them. "No," she shook her head. "The Ma'diin wouldn't do that."

"They would and they did," he said pulling her back into the rhythm of the dance. "I just spoke to the other lords…"

And that's when she noticed the pins on his coat. One, the S of his family's emblem and the other, a helm with a sword overlaid through the middle. The lords' emblem. They must have made Cornelius a lord, but they only would've done that if…

"…and they have agreed it's best to keep this quiet for now until we've handled the situation," Cornelius finished.

Her mind could only think of one thing right now. "My father, is he alright?" Her mouth felt dry and her tongue heavy.

His expression was firm, stoic almost. "There's been no word on survivors yet. You must keep to this to yourself for now, okay? Until we know more."

The music ended and Cornelius bowed, but Tamsin could only stare in disbelief.

Her mother walked over then, concern on her face. "Is something the matter? You're as white as a sheet Tamsin."

Cornelius smiled. "I'm afraid I let slip that I was going to propose this evening. She's just a bit overwhelmed."

Lavinia let out a delighted cry and hugged him. Some curious onlookers came over and inquired to the commotion and she excitedly exclaimed that she was going to have a new son-in-law. People started clapping Cornelius on the back and shaking his hand and others kissed Tamsin on the cheek, but all she could feel was the mosaic tiles turning to quicksand beneath her feet.

The ballroom suddenly seemed too small and the faces around her started to blend together as her breaths became quicker. Tears stung the corners of her eyes and she reached out to grab something to keep from swaying and latched onto someone's arm. The man gripped her elbow and waist to steady her as her pulse pounded in her ears. She vaguely heard Cornelius tell the man to take her out for some air and then felt the man pull her away from the stifling crowd. It felt like she was floating, not walking, and she closed her eyes to keep the dizziness away.

In a few moments, she felt the cool tingle of night air rush over her skin and sucked it in greedily. It was a few minutes before she could feel the ground beneath her feet again as the immediate panic subsided. The pounding in her ears lessened and she was able to hear the lapping of the river against the Armillary's walls. She blinked and as her vision returned she was able to make out the man whose arm she was still gripping. It was one of the officers.

She looked up under the brim of his hat, an apology on her lips, and saw two glowing eyes staring back at her.

"She's enchanting, Cornelius," one of his officers said, congratulating him.

"She'll look even better in white," Cornelius replied, shaking more hands.

Lavinia was still going around telling anyone with ears about the good news. Having her on board would make things go much smoother. Especially when the news hit about the dam. Any sympathies towards the Ma'diin would soon be squashed and if he and Tamsin were engaged people would be less likely to view her as a sympathizer.

He rubbed the lords' pin on his chest. Having a lady by his side would also solidify his claim to lordship should Lord Urbane somehow return. But his men had their orders and he trusted their loyalty to him.

He excused himself from the crowd of well-wishers, motioning for Lieutenant Pak to join him. They left the main ballroom and made their way to Cornelius's office.

"I don't wish to keep you long," Cornelius said. "You deserve to enjoy the evening." He reached in his desk drawer and pulled out a shallow velvet case. He took the cover off to reveal the Captain's emblem, two crossed silver swords, and extended it to Pak.

Pak looked up, surprised, and then noticed Cornelius's own emblem. "You've been promoted. I'm sorry Captain, I mean my Lord, I didn't know."

"It's alright. It happened quite recently."

"This ball should really be for you, then. It's a big night."

"It's a big night indeed." He pinned the captain's emblem on Pak's coat.

"Are you sure?" Pak asked. "Wouldn't Lieutenant Riggs be more qualified, or Lieutenant Dunbar?"

"Lieutenant Dunbar only looks forward to his next meal and Lieutenant Riggs is indisposed right now. No, I need someone who I can count on to be loyal and someone who I can trust with my life, and my fiancé's life. Can I count on you Captain?"

Pak straightened, looking every bit the devoted soldier, though he couldn't help the smile that twitched at his lips. "Yes, my lord."

"Good. I'll debrief you in the morning. Enjoy the rest of the evening Captain Pak."

But before Pak could reply, one of Cornelius's servants rushed in, looking apologetic for interrupting, but urgent. "I'm sorry," he said, "but you should come with me. We have a problem."

"It looks like your debriefing starts now," he told Pak and they followed the servant down the main hall to the southwest tower entrance. Inside, there were a few other soldiers gathered around another, this one in little more than his undergarments, sitting in a chair and holding his head as if he had a headache.

Cornelius raised his eyebrows. "If you summoned me here to behold the effects of too much Arak consumption…"

"No, Captain," the scantily clothed man said, and Cornelius recognized him as Lieutenant Cazif. "I was hit."

"Explain yourself lieutenant,' Cornelius said.

"I was on my way to the ballroom and someone hit me. Knocked me right out. Then I woke up here without my clothes." He rubbed the back of his head gingerly.

Cornelius wondered who would have done such a thing, but then it clicked. With all of the extra guards and servants he had watching the Armillary, he hadn't expected Haven to get this far. It made his blood boil knowing the Ma'diin was probably inside right now, laughing at how easy it had been to impersonate one of his men. He whirled on the soldiers, telling them to go alert the guards in the courtyards and the tunnel entrances not to let anyone in or out regardless of who they were.

"My lord, what is it?" Pak asked.

Cornelius ordered him and his servant to follow him as he headed back to the ballroom. He told them what he suspected and that they were to alert the other servants and guards on duty about the intruder. "But do it quietly," he said. "It will be easier to find him without everyone panicking."

They made it back to the ballroom and dispersed. Cornelius acknowledged a few more congratulations thrown his way, but kept his eyes peeled for any suspicious activity. He circled the large room, picking out the officers from the rest of the guests and identifying them as his own men. He saw his servants doing the same, going up to the officers and asking if they needed refreshments, but so far none had stood out. Pak came back a few minutes later, telling him the inner halls and rooms had been searched and there were guards on the towers, but there was no sight of him.

Cornelius frowned, having a hard time believing that the Ma'diin would have gone to such lengths to get in here, just to leave again without seeing Tam—.

He felt like he was punched in the stomach. "Where's Tamsin?"

Pak looked at him strangely. "She went out for some air with…" he trailed off, trying to remember, then his eyes grew wide.

"Dammit," Cornelius cursed.

They raced through the crowd, pushing indignant guests out of the way and calling out to the other guards to follow them. The music ended abruptly and cries of confusion swept through the crowd, but Cornelius would deal with them later. Adrenaline and anger coursed through him as the realization hit him that both Haven and Tamsin were slipping through his carefully laid nets.

He started barking orders as his men gathered around him outside the ballroom entrance. "If you're not armed go to the weapons room now. The Ma'diin man has kidnapped my fiancé. I want them both back alive, but if you need to use force, do it. Understood?"

There was a rallying cry and then his men sprang into action.

Cornelius pulled out his own sword. He might just get his rematch with the Ma'diin after all.

He came back. The thought collided with her senses and Tamsin jumped up and flung her arms around Haven, her feet dangling well above the ground. She buried her face in his neck, trying to control the onrush of sobs that shook her and failing. She didn't care what he thought about the emotional display; he was here and it meant her feelings for him were validated. And she wouldn't have to be alone in this.

He held her tightly and it was almost enough to dispel the dark clouds swirling inside her. His presence engulfed her, seeming to absorb her pain and giving her strength all at once. She wanted to stay like that until they were so close nothing could separate them. Like they had been in the sandstorm when they first met.

She almost wished that it had all ended out there in the desert, because they faced a different kind of storm now, one that could tear them apart, and they would've been buried together at least.

She slowly untangled herself from him when her trembling lessened and he eased her back to the floor, his eyes burning with worry.

"What happen?" he asked, the muscles in his jaw tight.

"The dam," she said, her heart pounding in her chest. "Cornelius said the Ma'diin attacked."

He bristled at Cornelius's name. "That not be possible," he said. "Samih said—."

"Samih?" She tried to recall where she had heard that name before. "He is one of your brothers? One of the other Watchers?"

"Yes. The man you thought was me last night… that was Samih. He followed one of the messengers back here. He said the talks went well and the wall was going to be taken down. Ysallah wouldn't attack if she got what she wanted. She wouldn't risk it."

She let it sink in, relieved that it was someone he knew, someone he trusted, but it still didn't make sense. The messenger should have brought good news. "Could Samih have been mistaken?"

"Samih not lie about this or anything."

"Then where were the soldiers going last night? What else could they be doing except going to help?"

"That be what I must find out. Samih be already half day ahead of me."

"Why didn't you go with him?"

"Because you deserved to know what was going on and why I had to leave. If the others are in danger I need to go."

Just then they heard the sound of boots against stone coming closer, not just walking, but running and from the sound of it there were more than just two. In that instant she realized exactly what they were doing: they were hunting Ma'diin. Haven was right and that meant Cornelius had lied to her. The Ma'diin hadn't attacked; that's what he was sending his men for. She remembered what she had heard that night in the kitchens from Lieutenant Riggs and the other man, that if her father was a Ma'diin sympathizer, then he was a target.

"Haven! My father! They're going to kill him!" The panic that her father was in trouble resurfaced again. But the sound of thundering footsteps also reminded her that they weren't just after her father. They were after Haven and he was much, much closer than her father was, in the heart of their snare.

"I not let that happen," he said, his lips curling up. He may be being hunted, but the expression on his face was not that of prey.

"I'm coming with you," she said boldly, making up her mind right there.

The look in his eyes told her he didn't like the idea and was about to tell her how it was too dangerous, but then his eyes flashed past her and she knew they weren't alone anymore. She whirled around and saw a young guard kneeling with a crossbow aimed at them. She sucked in her breath as Haven suddenly grabbed her around the waist and pulled her back just as the arrow went whizzing in front of her face. She didn't have the chance to get her feet under her before she saw more soldiers join the first, one of them yelling loudly and yanking the crossbow out of the man's hands. She caught herself on the wall just before she fell, noticing Haven was no longer with her.

His hands were already at the young guard's throat, lifting him up and throwing him into the soldier who had taken the crossbow. The others, who had taken pause at the Ma'diin's swift advance, now rallied against him, swinging their weapons. Haven realized almost a moment too late that his own swords weren't strapped to his back and had to dodge a wide arc meant to take his head off. He kicked the man's knee, giving him a moment to grab the knives at his hips.

They came after him, two, and three at a time and yet he was able to stand his ground. His strength and speed was a sight to behold, but his fearlessness only made Tamsin more frightened. Not because she was finally seeing what he was capable of, but because the soldiers outnumbered him ten to one and yet he showed no sign of self-preservation. Those odds were enough to make any man turn and run, but not Haven. She watched in growing horror as more soldiers came. Some of them had crossbows and knelt down to take aim, waiting for a window to arise between the combatants.

Tamsin screamed at Haven to run and he ducked another blow. He kicked the legs out from his opponent, sending him falling back into the next man, and rolled away. He sprang up next to Tamsin, grabbed her hand, and together they fled. Her legs felt clumsy though and buckled underneath her. Haven picked her up in his arms without missing a beat.

Ahead, more soldiers started coming at them and Haven swung into the nearest archway, running through the hall at a terrifying speed. Tamsin closed her eyes, not wanting to see the soldiers she could hear only yards behind them. She pretended the sound of their pounding footsteps was Haven's heart beating against her ear. She wanted it to be a dream where she would wake up and realize this night had never happened.

A sudden spin and a jarring collision snapped her eyes open and she cried out as wooden splinters flew around them. The shattered door hung in pieces on its hinges, but no soldiers came through after them. Haven had a good lead on them, but they could still be heard coming. There were two more archways in the room that led to other halls, but Haven carried her quickly up a narrow staircase that spiraled around the outer edge of the room and up to a dark hallway whose arches on the outside opened up to the brisk night. Haven set her on the ledge underneath one of the open arches, climbed up after her, and then lowered her down on the other side. They now walked on a slanted surface that dropped off over the river. Tamsin was reminded of their spot in the Hollow Cliffs.

One of the towers protruded through and they went around it to avoid being seen from the open hallway they just came from. Haven was careful leading them around, making sure there were no eyes looking about.

Tamsin noticed something shining on his neck then. "Haven you're bleeding."

"It nothing," he said. "We keep going."

"Not until I've looked at that," she said, taking her gloves off so she could inspect it.

But he turned around and stopped her. "Leave them on," he told her.

"I'm not afraid of a little blood," she said, though it actually looked like a lot of blood and knowing it was his would've made her hands tremble had he not been holding them.

"Leave on," he repeated, a little gentler this time.

Tamsin remembered back to the sh'pav'danya and the way her skin tingled after he had cut his hand over hers. She realized he didn't want his blood touching her. She conceded, though she didn't understand, and they sat with their backs to the tower. He shrugged out of the jacket and let her inspect the gash that ran along the side of his neck. It didn't look like it cut his artery, but it was deep enough where it needed binding. She wasn't a healer, but she wasn't comfortable letting him continue without that at least. She used his knife and started cutting off strips of her dress.

"You not do that," he said regretfully. *"You looked so beautiful in it."* He winced as she applied the first piece to staunch the bleeding.

"And you look hopelessly bizarre in that uniform," she replied, trying to take his mind off the pain. Somewhere during their flight he had lost his hat too, but seeing him out of his natural clothing made her wonder just briefly how this would've all turned out if Haven had been Empyrian. If he had been born here, grown up here, and become a soldier. Would they still have met? Would they be strolling around the Armillary's veranda in the moonlight, arm in arm, instead of above it? She tried to smile, but her face contorted into an ugly grimace as she tried to hold back tears.

"Hey," Haven tilted her chin up. *"It got me to you didn't it?"*

She nodded, not trusting herself to speak, and wrapped the last strip around to secure the makeshift bandage.

His eyes were troubled as she tied a knot in the fabric to hold it in place. *"You can still go back you know."*

She looked up at him sharply. "What?"

"You're not the one they're after," he said.

She shook her head firmly. *"I'm coming with you. They're going after the people I love and I'm not going to stand by and watch."*

He studied her for a moment, looking for any hesitation, any doubt in her resolve, but she had made up her mind. Something in her tear-streaked face must have hit him then, for his bright blue eyes faltered and the fortress he had built around himself crumbled and he pulled her close, pressing her fiercely against his chest. She felt his arms wrap around her back and her breath hitched as she realized that he was finally letting her in, that this was his confession. She felt his lips on the top of her head. *"Damn you for making me love you,"* he breathed into her hair.

"Then we will be damned together," she said.

He pulled away and unfastened his wrist cuff to reveal something tied underneath it. He cut it off with his small knife, pulled one of Tamsin's, now reddened, white gloves off, and then retied it around Tamsin's smaller wrist.

It was hard to see in the darkness, but it looked to be a bracelet, made from softened hide with flat, colorful beads woven throughout that shimmered in the starlight. She looked up at him questioningly.

"It was given to me by someone I loved," he said. *"I want you to keep it."*

"But I couldn't take this from you," she said, knowing how special it must be to him, especially when he only kept things that he deemed useful.

"Everything that is important is with you now. Keep it safe for me." He held her wrist to her heart. His eyes were tight as they lingered over the bracelet, not from regret of parting with it, but from some memory it dredged up.

She held her other hand over his. *"I will protect it with my life."*

He blinked then and smiled patiently at her, some of the tension leaving his body. *"Not with your life, jha'ii. My heart. You are my happiness now."*

She knew he was still afraid, still afraid that something would happen to her and he would not be able to protect her. Still afraid his fear would get her killed. But there was no resistance, no wall. He was realizing that fear and love went hand in hand. And should his demons return, she would be there to remind him. She would not give up on him. Ever.

A horn blew loudly above them and Haven jumped up, looking at the tower behind them. He carried the knife in his teeth and scaled the wall into the open window before Tamsin could get a word out to stop him. There was the clanging of metal and scuffling sounds and then the horn was silent. Haven climbed back out the window and started climbing down. "More coming," he said. "We have to go."

Another horn blew from the next tower over and an arrow bounced off the stone just above him. He dropped down the rest of the way and almost slid, but Tamsin grabbed his arm and steadied him. They heard shouts coming from the tower above and Haven took her hand.

"Not let go," he said and before she knew what he was doing they were running down the slope. She didn't realize what he had planned until they reached the edge and he yelled for her to jump.

She screamed, not noticing the arrows flying by them or when Haven's hand slipped out of hers, and all her panicked mind could think of was the dark, churning abyss of the river below and the last time she had fallen in. Her cry was cut off as they hit the water. She couldn't see, couldn't breathe, and couldn't grasp anything as the current consumed her. Then something grabbed hold of her and pulled her up. She gasped as she broke the surface, spluttering and flailing her arms as she tried to regain her bearings. It had only been a few seconds she was under, but it had felt like minutes.

"I got you," Haven said, in between spitting water out of his mouth. "I got you."

She clung to him as the current took them further and further away from the chaos of the Armillary. The river was strong, but Haven was able to gradually steer them to the eastern bank. They dragged themselves up, and though her clothes were sodden with water and her limbs heavy, Haven didn't give them any time to rest. The soldiers would be scouring the banks soon enough and they needed to be well away from there by then. They had already passed the docks where the boats were tied up and backtracking now would be dangerous and with the portcullis being shut that means of escape was closed to them. Their only hope was getting out the east gate.

"Once they realize we're out of the city, they'll send horsemen and they'll outrun us," Tamsin said as he helped her climb off the bank and onto a cobbled walkway.

"I have a boat at the cliffs," he panted, leading her up to a wide arch. *"If we can get to it before they realize that, then we'll be safe."*

But something was wrong. Even through her own trembling and fatigue she could hear the rattling in his breath as he helped her.

She put her hands on his chest. "Haven, what is it?" she asked, suddenly afraid, her own heart pounding loudly against her ribcage, but then her fingers brushed against something, something long and thin and cold. Her mouth opened in horror as she felt the feathered edges at the end of it. She leaned away, letting her eyes adjust to the darkness, but she already knew what she would see when they did. She could feel his gaze on her, watching her. Sticking out about a hand's length from Haven's chest was an arrow from one of the crossbows that the guards had fired upon them.

"No, no, no, no," she repeated, her anguished mind unable to articulate anything else.

Haven tried to comfort her, telling her it was okay. "I be through worse," he said, but he had to put his hand on the wall inside the archway for support and this only added to Tamsin's distress.

"We have to get you to a healer," she said.

He shook his head. "No. We have to keep moving."

She was about to rebuke him when his head suddenly snapped to the side and he put his fingers over her lips, silencing her. He was listening to something through the archway and in the quiet she could hear his harsh breathing. The feathered tip of the arrow quivered with each breath he took, but other than that he remained completely still.

Her stomach clenched painfully, the urge to yell and cry too much for her to bear. She wanted to shake him to his senses, embrace him, and comfort him all at the same time.

She didn't have to endure it long because at that moment three guards appeared on the other side of the archway. One of them spotted them and stopped abruptly. His hand had barely grasped his sword and Haven already had his hands around his neck, snapping it cleanly. The other two drew their swords and

Haven took the dead soldier's sword and blocked a blow. He managed to block another and then went on the offensive, swinging hard and quick. He slashed down, cutting the man across the neck and chest. The man fell forward, grabbing onto the arrow sticking out of Haven's chest. Haven pushed him away with a hiss, his lips curling back over his teeth.

The third man threw down his sword and took off running. Haven went to follow him, but staggered, clutching his chest.

The pounding of her heart was the only thing that forced Tamsin's numb limbs to move. She stumbled out over one of the dead soldiers, his lifeless eyes seeming to stare right at her. Death had always been something that seemed far away, like some foreign land that she had read about in books but had never actually visited. But seeing this man, who had been alive only moments before, made death a tangible, visceral reality. And Haven was at its brink.

Haven held out his hand towards her, not for help, but to stop her. She ignored him, but she had not even taken another step before another soldier charged into view, sword swinging. It was not the same one that had fled; this man was bigger, more sure, and he swung hard at Haven, who ducked out of the way and parried with his own.

Tamsin screamed and fell back over one of the bodies. She scrambled away from it, not wanting to see those eyes again, but then her own caught sight of something else: more soldiers flooding into the street.

She backed up until she hit a wall and then she could only watch, petrified, as the soldiers attacked. Haven struck at the soldiers with incredible speed, turning himself into a lethal barrier between the soldiers and Tamsin behind him. Even wounded he was too fast for the Empyrians to parry effectively, moving too quickly for the soldiers to react before he was upon them. It was like watching a deadly, dark tornado cutting down everything in its path. She was in shock and she didn't know where Haven's extra strength was coming from. It made her training sessions with him look like child's play.

One after another the Empyrian soldiers fell, their pain-filled cries splitting the night like shattered glass. The sounds of wounded men ripped through her, making her want to cover her ears and scream at him to stop. All of this death, all of this suffering was almost too much to bear. But she couldn't stop it, couldn't say a word because Haven's life hung in the balance. She knew it was either them or him and despite the agony in her heart, she knew she would choose him, the man she loved more than any other, over a thousand soldiers.

Then, abruptly, the soldiers retreated and it was just Haven standing amidst the ruin.

Tamsin sucked in her breath. For one, hopeful moment she thought it was over and he had won. But then she saw the retreating soldiers give way to a new group at the end of the street and from them stepped forward one figure: Cornelius.

Cornelius wore no armor, but had his sword out. He glanced only briefly at Tamsin before focusing on Haven. "You may have won our last duel," he said, "but unlike you, I finish the job." Then he smiled triumphantly and sheathed his sword.

But before Tamsin could wonder what he was doing Cornelius raised his hand and the archers next to him took aim.

"NOOO!" she screamed, but she was too late.

Cornelius' hand dropped and there was a *whoosh* as another arrow embedded itself in the Ma'diin. Haven staggered back, his bloodied blade slipping out of his grip into the sand. He didn't make a sound as he dropped to one knee, fighting now against his own body that was slowly betraying him.

Tamsin forced her stunned limbs to move, propelling herself away from the wall. "Stop! *Please! Stop!*" she cried.

Haven turned towards her and tried to stand, but another arrow sliced through the air, piercing his shoulder, and he fell back in a cloud of dust.

She reached him as his head hit the sand. She grabbed his arms, his chest, his face, but didn't feel any of it. A muffled 'hold your fire!' sounded far away along with her own cries. His glowing eyes locked onto hers, filled with pain and incomprehension. She screamed at him to stay with her, to hold on, though she didn't know if it was coherent or not. She grabbed his hand, holding it between their chests, willing her strength to flow to him so he could get up. Her tears fell on his face, her eyes never wavering from his own. It didn't seem real. It *couldn't* be real.

Someone grabbed her from behind and tore her away. Haven's hand slipped from her own. She kicked and screamed, desperate like a cornered animal, but the arms around her held her fast and Haven got further and further away until he disappeared completely in a sea of metal and men.

CHAPTER TWENTY-FOUR

Lavinia paced back and forth just down the stairs from Tamsin's room, wringing her hands together. The healer came down after a short while, his long, archaic-looking robes making a scratchy, shuffling sound as he descended the stairs.

She looked up expectantly. "Well?" she asked.

Two days ago, after being corralled in the ballroom like sheep, not knowing what was going on, she had been whisked away by Lord Regoran to another room in the Armillary. It had been chaotic, soldiers running everywhere, some of them wounded, but Lord Regoran seemed just as confused as she and spoke in broken pieces. She remembered him saying something about the Ma'diin and immediately red flags had gone up, especially since she had been unable to find Tamsin. There were anxious looking guards outside the room and Lord Regoran conversed quietly with them for a moment before they stepped aside to let them through. Inside, it was quieter and three more guards turned as they approached.

"Has she said anything?" Lord Regoran had asked.

"Not since the screaming stopped," one of them had replied.

That's when Lavinia had seen her. Sitting near the fireplace with a blanket wrapped around her shoulders was her daughter. She had been drenched from head to foot, her ripped clothing smeared with blood.

A shocked gasp escaped Lavinia's lips and she rushed over, but Tamsin had barely seemed to notice her, her eyes red from crying, her breath coming out in hitched bursts. She tried several times to get a response from her, but Tamsin had only stared straight ahead, her gaze glazed as if she wasn't seeing what was right in front of her. Lavinia asked what had happened, scared beyond her wits. Never had she seen Tamsin in such a state before. Never a look of such suffering. Lord Regoran and the guards had filled her in the best they could, explaining how the Ma'diin man had taken her and tried to flee the city. That's when Tamsin had started crying again, harsh, panting sobs that made her whole body shake, and Lavinia insisted they go back to the compound. Lord Regoran had carried her back, bringing several guards with them, though along the way Lavinia heard that the Ma'diin man had been killed.

A healer was summoned right away and he assured them that Tamsin was physically unharmed, but since she had been brought back to the Urbane's compound, Tamsin had not said a word to anybody and hardly seemed to know even where she was. She wouldn't eat or drink anything and even Sherene, who had always been so close to Tamsin, couldn't bring the girl out of her melancholy. Lavinia had stayed at her bedside for the better part of the last 48 hours, but there had been no change so she called for the healer again.

The healer adjusted his cream-colored robes, the expression on his face difficult to read. "She's very weak," he said, "but she's been through a trauma, in which this kind of behavior is not unusual."

"Is there nothing you can do for her?"

"She will come around when she is ready. In the meantime, try and get her to drink something. I've left some herbs you can put in her tea to help relax her. If her condition worsens though, please summon me again. It would be dangerous to let this continue for too long." He gave her arm a sympathetic squeeze.

Lavinia nodded and thanked him, letting one of the servants see him out. She went back into Tamsin's room and sat on the ottoman near her bed. Tamsin continued to do nothing, to see nothing. She seemed to exist at the most basic level, dwelling in a place too deep for Lavinia to reach her. She fell asleep a few hours later, for that Lavinia was grateful, but Tamsin's face still seemed sad, as if she could not escape what distressed her even in her dreams.

Lavinia just started to doze off herself when one of the maids gently shook her shoulder and alerted her to a visitor. Lavinia begrudgingly left her daughter and went downstairs. She found Lord Regoran waiting on the veranda, a grim expression on his face. He asked how Tamsin was doing and she shook her head, replying that there was no change or encouraging signs. His eyes had a haunted look about them and she sensed that his visit went beyond enquiring about Tamsin. Before she could ask him about it he said, "I have news of the caravan."

She led him inside and told the servants to curtain off a section so they could speak privately. She bade him sit, offering him something to drink, which he declined. She took a deep breath and sat down next to him, gripping the armrest tightly, though she tried to keep the tremor out of her voice as she spoke. "Is—is my husband alright?" she asked, though she already knew the answer in her soul. The fact that Lord Regoran was here and not her husband told her what she had already feared ever since the ball. The death of the Ma'diin meant the truce was over. Her daughter's needs had overshadowed her own fears since then, but now she knew she could not hide from the truth any longer. She listened quietly as Lord Regoran relayed the news, unable to look directly in his eyes. The Ma'diin had indeed attacked the caravan at the dam site. Lord Urbane had not been among the survivors.

"Have they not hurt our family enough?" she whispered, staring up at the ceiling.

Lord Regoran watched her with sympathy. "You have my word: we will do everything we can to protect you and your daughter, and to bring those responsible to justice."

She clasped her hands together, trying to hang onto the last shreds of composure. "Thank you Lord Regoran. If you will excuse me, though, I just need a moment alone I think."

"Of course. If there is anything I can do…" He gave her hands a comforting squeeze and then took his leave.

Lavinia stood up and closed the curtains behind him. She put her back to one of the pillars and covered her mouth with her hand, holding the sobs back.

She let herself have a few minutes, that was all, and then she dried her eyes and went back upstairs. She sat on the edge of her daughter's bed and smoothed the creases in the blanket, wishing she could smooth the troubled lines in Tamsin's forehead even as she slept. "I'm sorry," she said to Tamsin's silent form. "Oh my little orphan, I'm so sorry."

CHAPTER TWENTY-FIVE

They were calling it the Tragedy at the Dam. A week had gone by since news of what had happened to Lord Urbane and the others hit the ears of the Empyrian people. Mr. Graysan went to the Armillary, as usual, to scribe documents for Lord Regoran, but he could not focus for long periods of time for his thoughts kept returning to what had happened. And to the Ma'diin. He fidgeted constantly, spilled two bottles of ink, ripped a large gash through one of the documents with his quill, which he ended up rewriting twice because he ended up writing down his own thoughts instead of what was on the manuscript, and succeeded in nearly setting everything on fire when he knocked over the lantern, all throughout the course of the day. Night had already fallen when at last he finished, and he took the completed documents to Lord Regoran.

"It's a bit late, isn't it?" Lord Regoran commented, taking the stack of papers.

"I'm sorry, my lord," Mr. Graysan said, dipping his head low. "I must confess I've been rather distracted today."

"Yes, well, a lot has happened recently," he said, rubbing his palms over his eyes. "What's on your mind Graysan?"

Mr. Graysan pressed his palms together. "Well, my lord, I was wondering if I could actually speak to Captain—I mean Lord Saveen."

"Cornelius?" Lord Regoran snorted. "What could you possibly have to discuss with him?"

"Just something small, nothing really, it's just, well, my daughter has this friend—."

Lord Regoran held up his hand. "On second thought, I don't want to know." He flicked his fingers out. "I think he's still here. Go talk to him as long as you wish."

Mr. Graysan dipped his head low again. "Thank you. Thank you my lord. Have a good night my lord."

"Hmm."

Mr. Graysan made his way to the eastern wing and Lord Saveen's office. He dabbed the sweat off his forehead with his sleeve and then knocked on the door.

"Come in."

He entered hesitantly. He had never spoken to Cornelius Saveen directly. He had known his uncle many years ago, before the drinking started, and had seen Cornelius rise through the military ranks throughout the years, though seeing him sitting behind his uncle's desk was a strange sight.

"Who are you?" Cornelius asked.

"Mr. Graysan, my lord. I work for Lord Regoran."

"Oh. What does he want now? Why not come see me himself?"

"I actually wanted to speak with you, my lord. My daughter is a friend of Tamsin's, whom I understand you are courting—."

"My business with Miss Urbane is not up for public discussion or any of your concern for that matter," Cornelius said curtly.

"Yes, I'm sorry, my lord, it's just like I said, my daughter is a friend of with Miss Urbane and you know…girls talk…" he trailed off, unsure of how he wanted to say what was troubling him.

Cornelius stared back, humorlessly. "Is there a point to all of this?"

Mr. Graysan blinked quickly several times. "Yes, my lord. I—I think Tamsin might be in danger."

"What danger do you know of?"

Mr. Graysan had heard the talk flying around the Armillary about Tamsin's abduction and the events surrounding it, and even though he was skeptical of the role Haven played in it, he kept going back to that night when he had overheard Tamsin and Georgiana. Ever since the night of the ball it had been on his mind. "I believe the Ma'diin will come back for her."

Cornelius folded his hands across his lap. "Come back?" he said with indulgent disinterest. "What makes you think so?"

"Because I know the Ma'diin my lord."

This caught his attention. He leaned forward in his chair. "What do you know of the Ma'diin?"

Mr. Graysan took a deep breath, looking at anything but those piercing eyes. He was reticent to tell Cornelius exactly what he knew about Tamsin and what he had learned about her new ability. "Enough. You see, I was with the original expedition to the marshlands with your uncle—."

Cornelius squinted even more, his eyes turning into snake-like slits. "And you've decided to come forward now. After the damage has already been done? Tell me, do you think the death of one of their own will make up for the dozens of my men they killed at the dam?"

This was not going at all like he had imagined. "No, my Lord, I mean I don't think the Ma'diin will see it that way."

After a moment, Cornelius stood up and offered him a chair. "Sit down Mr. Graysan."

Mr. Graysan sat nervously across from Cornelius, wiping his hands on his trousers.

But Cornelius remained standing. "Tell me Mr. Graysan, why are the Watchers the way they are?"

"I'm sorry?"

"Why are they different than the others?"

Mr. Graysan tried to recall the Ma'diin lore he knew, shifting in his seat. The plush chair was unusually uncomfortable. "The Watchers are believed to be a creation of one of their gods, I forget his name, but they came down from the heavens in a time of crisis and helped destroy the very god that created them. They took on human form and have been the Ma'diin's protectors ever since."

"So you're telling me they are what? Angels?"

"If you compare it to the old religion, then yes, *angel* might be the best way to think about them. But they were cursed when they came down to earth."

"Cursed?"

"Yes. They were beings of the night. They were burned by the light of day."

He pondered this for a moment. "So fallen angels then. Abandoned by their own gods."

"The god that made them, he was not a good god, according to the Ma'diin, but the Watchers themselves—they saved the Ma'diin. It was through no fault of their own that they were cursed."

Cornelius looked at him sternly. "Is that the Ma'diin's belief or yours?"

Mr. Graysan swallowed hard. "It is my own. I believe the Ma'diin are superstitious. The Watchers were created by an evil god and therefore possess the same evil. That is what I think they believe."

Cornelius nodded. "Interesting."

Mr. Graysan dabbed his forehead with a handkerchief. He would never have guessed that a Lord would be interested to hear what he had to say about the Ma'diin, but Cornelius continued to ask him questions about them. He seemed mostly interested in the Ma'diin's strength, what their military was like, what weapons they used and so forth, but his questions always came back to the Watchers. He was especially interested in them, how they behaved, what their strengths were…what their weaknesses were.

It was easy to get caught up in talking about it and forget about the immediate reality, but a little seed of doubt started to grow in his mind and Mr. Graysan began to wonder why Lord Saveen was so interested in the Watchers.

He cleared his throat. "Um, Lord Saveen, don't you want to know why I think the Ma'diin will come looking for Tamsin?"

He waved his hand about, as if trying to grasp the answer from the air. "Because of the exchange. The shakpadan or whatever they called it. Don't you worry about that Mr. Graysan. Tamsin is well protected."

Mr. Graysan was about to interject when a man came running into his office, making him jump. The man was out of breath and had a look of urgency about him. He put his hands on the desk for support, not seeming to see Mr. Graysan in the seat next to him.

"What is it Jediah?" Cornelius asked, clearly concerned.

"He is *here*," the man said between ragged breaths.

Cornelius's eyes widened and that superior mask of his momentarily evaporated. Then he motioned towards the door. "Leave us Mr. Graysan."

Mr. Graysan stood up quickly, eager to get away from there, unable to keep his eyes averted from the exhausted looking man and seeing fear in his eyes. He made for the door, but Cornelius called after him.

"I'll be in touch Mr. Graysan," he said. "Soon."

Mr. Graysan nodded and then left, a bad feeling crawling over his skin, like a shadow creeping over the ground.

CHAPTER TWENTY-SIX

In the Cities, a widowed family had thirty-nine days of mourning. There would have been a small ceremony, to mark the first day of mourning, a flag with a six-pointed star nailed to the door and a somber stream of visitors wishing to offer their condolences. On the fortieth day, the flag was removed and quietly brought to the deceased's final resting place by the family, thus ending the time for grieving. Then they would move on.

In Empyria, old customs weren't buried with the dead. Disobeying the Sacramental Bans and the dissolution of the gods was not something that was as severely dealt with as it would have been in the Cities. Though no one spoke of worshipping the banned gods directly, the old habits were still very much in place. The black flag was hung from the Urbane compound and an undertaker came to mark the first day, but among the visitors that stopped by, many brought with them special herbs that they had ground into a fine red powder. They would say a few words of prayer, lift the veil that covered her face, and then mark the middle of Lavinia's lips with it. By the fortieth day her lips had taken on a dark hue and she had heard them so many times that she would say the prayer words along with the other person.

There was another ceremony that day and all those that had travelled from the Cities, Lords and other dignitaries, to offer their condolences gathered at the Armillary. Her mother wore a grey dress. It was the first day she was able to wear something other than black. The undertaker, in his ornate golden robes, led the procession into the great room of the Armillary, followed by the flag bearer and then her mother, and then proceeded to read the Passing Rites, old words that were used to help the deceased find their way to the next world.

Tamsin watched from behind the crowd, her black veil pulled low over her eyes.

The undertaker lifted his staff into the air and then dipped the end that was curved like a small dish into the water basin that had been placed in the middle of the room. He held it horizontally and presented it to her mother, who dipped her fingertips in the tiny pool and then touched the white star in the middle of the flag. The undertaker did the same for the others present, to signify the end of tears and mourning. As he walked through the crowd, some eyes glanced in Tamsin's direction, no doubt curious as to why the daughter of the deceased was holding back, but Tamsin had already told her mother that she would not be partaking in the ceremony.

The dignitaries from the Cities also did not partake, exchanging glances after the undertaker passed them with the water. Tamsin knew they could not be caught participating in such a religious display, but her reasons were much different. Tamsin grieved for two and for her the mourning period was not over. Her father's funeral happened to land on the beginning of the spring solstice, the time of light and warmth and growth. Tamsin faced her own solstice, one of darkness and pain and loneliness.

Eventually, the people returned to watching the undertaker as he continued. Except for one: Cornelius continued to try and catch her eye, though she refused to look at him.

As soon as it had concluded, Tamsin turned around and walked quickly from the room, shadowed by her guards that were never more than a few paces behind. She didn't stop until she got back to the compound and up to the bathing level. Then she collapsed on the floor, grateful that her guards didn't follow her up there as she tried not to vomit. She closed her eyes and cleared her mind of everything but the sound of her breathing, the feel of the stone beneath her palms, and the beat of her heart, tangible things that reminded her she was still here. That she existed in the present world and the memories that barraged her were in the past.

She couldn't remember anything from those first days after it had happened. She had felt like she had fallen into a dark hole, flooded with the awful images of what transpired, reliving them over and over, unable to extricate herself from them.

The first thing she could remember upon awakening was the image of her mother crying by her bedside. It had jarred her. She could remember being confused. Why was her mother crying? It made no sense. But all too soon she found out why.

After that, each day was as sharp as a whip, each passing hour an agonizing reminder of the growing distance between them. It was a long time before she was able to keep any food down without it coming back up. The healer was a regular visitor and how he was able to keep her body from deteriorating into dust was nothing short of a miracle, though even when her body began to regain its strength, she felt a deeper part of her had been lost and could not be recovered. Not all of her had climbed out of that dark hole.

Remembering how to do things, simple things, like walking or breathing, were difficult sometimes. She had to remind herself to pick up her spoon at breakfast or to change clothes before she went to bed. Other times she just sat there, numb, too absorbed with trying to stay together, to breathe, that she was unable to comprehend doing anything else. Just keeping herself from falling apart required all of her energy most days. And then there were the times when she saw someone walk by in a dark cloak or would catch a scent that reminded her of him and it felt as if all the air had been knocked out of her. The first time was the worst. It was the first day she had gone outside. The healer had said it would be good for her to get some fresh air and sun so her mother had taken her out for a small stroll. They had barely made it down the main stairway when a light breeze drifted past and the smell of lilacs and smoke was so strong for a moment that it brought her to her knees. She hyperventilated and was unable to move from the spot; a few of the servants rushed out of the house and had to carry her back inside. She trembled for hours afterwards, curled up in tight ball on her bed. She was terrified to leave the compound after that, but when she finally did, it was after one of the hottest days since they arrived. The night was still warm from the heat of the day and the air was parched of movement. The streets in the city were deserted and she made her way slowly, carefully, across the north bridge to the east side, her feet leading her more than her head, until she came to the street. It looked like a completely normal street, not a grain of sand out of place as if nothing had happened there. She went over to the archway, her heart pounding violently against her chest as the darkness seemed to close in around her until all she could see was a small spot of blood on the ground. Someone found her sometime the next day, huddled on the ground under the arch, and brought her back to the compound. She had no desire to leave the compound after that, but when she did her mother made sure there were at least three guards with her at all times.

She curled her fist against her stomach, counted to ten, and then opened her eyes, taking a moment to recognize where she was. The bathing level. At the compound. She crawled over to the bath square and scooped some lukewarm water in her hands, wetting her face and neck. It had been the first time she had been back to the Armillary and fighting back the ghosts conjured there had left her exhausted. All she wanted to do was crawl back into bed and forget about this day.

Just then, someone cleared their throat behind her and she turned to see one of the servants hesitating in the entryway. "Are you alright, my lady?" he asked.

She nodded. "Yes I'm fine."

Most of the servants kept their distance from her, unsure how to interact with her, but this one made no move to leave.

"What is it? What do you want?" she asked.

He cleared his throat again. "We found the chest my lady. The one your father was asking about when you first arrived. May the gods bring peace to his soul."

Chest? She had to try and work through the fog, to think back before everything got messed up. And then she remembered that first night when she had waited up for him and heard her father asking about a chest, telling him to find it. She wanted to yell at the servant, tell him to leave. Why would she want her father's, her *dead* father's, things? But then she stopped. She was no less devastated by her father's passing, but it was easier to miss him somehow. She thought, maybe, it was because it had happened far away and he had been gone for so long that she could pretend it hadn't happened. She could pretend because she hadn't seen the look on his face, felt the strength leaving his hand, or seen the blood soaking his clothes, expanding across his chest like a...

It took all her effort to stop the images from coming any further. She waved the servant away hastily. "Go," she panted. "Just...take it up to my room. I'll be there...in a minute."

The servant seemed loathe to leave her there, but she turned her back to him so he couldn't see the panic rising in her face and a few moments later she heard his footsteps as he retreated from the bathing room.

She splashed more water on her face, letting it drip back into the rectangular pool. She watched the ripples for a few minutes until the water stilled and she could see her reflection clearly, though the person she saw was not someone she recognized. The face was the same, a little thinner maybe, but the eyes—the eyes were different. She didn't feel like the real person. She felt like she was the reflection: fragile, wavering from only a single drop. She turned away and stood up.

She made her way up to her room and saw the chest in the middle of the room. It wasn't terribly large, with two leather handles on either side so one could easily carry it. There were metal brackets holding the corners together and two wooden pieces running lengthwise across the front side that stuck out slightly from the rest. She brushed away the dust on the lid. There was a word engraved on it, but she didn't know it. It spelled: *I R I N.*

She froze. Her stomach clenched painfully and that familiar feeling of dread washed over her. She did know this word. She had heard it before, but she couldn't remember when or what its meaning was. And it scared her, because somehow the word belonged to *him.*

It was a long time before she could move again. She swallowed the sick feeling that rose in her throat and reminded herself that she was here, that she was still in one piece, that she had not fallen apart.

She eyed the chest warily, like it was a living thing that would attack her again if she got too close. She hated it; she should've told the servant to burn it. She wanted to run, to never look upon it again, but it held her there, entranced under its spell and as soon as she thought it she knew she couldn't leave: *Why did her father want a chest that had a Ma'diin word on it? A word that Haven had spoken?*

She took a deep breath and lifted the iron latch on the front. She removed the lid and propped it to the side. She reached in and took out a thin piece of fabric that was as delicate as a spider's web. It was nearly transparent, shimmering black, folded into a triangle, and had small, silver jewels dangling all around the edges. It seemed to be a scarf of some kind. She took another breath, this one a little easier, and set it carefully aside. She took out a small, velvety pouch. Inside there was a necklace, a bracelet, and a few rings. She slipped one on her finger. It had a simple gold band with a white opal in the center. She rubbed the stone and specks of pink, green, and blue shone in the light. It fit well. She took it off and returned it to the pouch.

Next, she removed a long, dark robe. Her heart began to race as she felt the coarse material. She dropped it, her hands shaking. The hood fell open, revealing a square piece of fabric that was sewn to the side on one of its edges. On one of its corners was a small loop of thick thread. On the other side of the hood was a tiny hook. She looked away and covered her mouth with her hand, squeezing her eyes shut. *It's not his*, she repeated to herself. It was someone else's. There were plenty of cloaks out there like this, she told herself. *None with a n'qab,* another voice whispered in her head. She shoved the cloak away, forcing her trembling hands back into the chest. She pulled out another long piece of clothing. It was a dress. She breathed a sigh. A dress was alright, a dress was safe. She stood up with it and shook out the wrinkles and dust. Time had aged it, but it had been beautiful once, she could tell. It had long sleeves with white ruffles at the ends and a wide train at the bottom. She laid it out on the chair so it looked like a ghost was sitting there.

Then she pulled out a wide, dark piece of lace. There were two holes in it, from age or moths, Tamsin initially thought, but the more she looked at it the more it looked like those holes had been put there on purpose. She held it up to her face; the slits were separated evenly, just wide enough where she could see through them.

She gasped, clutching the fabric so tightly she thought it might tear, but the thought was so sudden and clear that she knew then exactly whose chest this was.

It was her father's Ma'diin woman.

She had completely forgotten all about her with everything that had happened and for a brief, wonderful moment, all she felt was curiosity towards this woman. She had pieces of her life right in front of her, pieces connected to her father. It was from a life he had kept hidden, a part of his past he had never shared with her, kept buried like the items in this chest. Tamsin remembered what Mr. Graysan told her, about the woman's death and the massacre that had followed. She put the lace veil down, sobered, but put her hands back in the chest, hoping to find something that would reveal a little more about her. And maybe something about her father.

There were a few more pieces of clothing, a bottle of some liquid that smelled like it could have been perfume at one time, and a round ceramic jar that had a strange, shimmering blue powder in it. But underneath all of that, at the bottom of the chest, were two things that surprised her. She pulled out a tiny pair of shoes, no bigger than the length of her pinky finger, and a baby blanket. The shoes were made of soft animal skin and hand-sewn together, perfectly preserved as if they had been made yesterday. The baby blanket was in poorer condition. There were holes in it and had the musky smell of wood from being at the bottom of the chest. She rubbed a corner of the blanket between her fingers, realizing that these things were all things that a mother might give to her baby when she was all grown up, heirlooms, to pass down to the next generation. The jeweled scarf, the opal ring, the dress, the baby shoes, the blanket.

She turned the blanket over and noticed something on the corner of it. There was a name embroidered in dark stitching, the baby's name…

Her breath caught in her throat and she stared at the name, scared to comprehend its meaning.

Tamsin

CHAPTER TWENTY-SEVEN

It was dark before Tamsin was able to move, her stiff limbs finally protesting against sitting on the floor for so long. She went over to her dresser and pulled the bottom drawer open. Tucked away in the back was the picture of the Ma'diin woman. She pulled it out and stared at it, her eyes finally open to the truth. This was not just her father's dead lover, but her mother. Her birth mother. She had been born right here, in Empyria, and after she had died her father had taken Tamsin back to the Cities while she was too young to remember any of it.

Tamsin touched the picture of the Ma'diin woman, of a stranger she had never known yet now yearned to know, though that was quite beyond her reach now. She didn't think she had any more room in her to be sad, especially about something she never had, but she still felt the painful sting of loss, of a life that had been robbed from her. A choked laugh bubbled through her lips, remembering when she had wondered what it would have been like to grow up in the marshlands.

Clutching the picture in her hands, she went down the stairs, past the servants who were cleaning up after a dinner nobody had eaten, and up to her mother's quarters, intent on confronting her. Her mother had to have known all along.

Who else had known? She needed time to sift through it all. Mr. Graysan surely knew or else he would never have given her the picture. Had Ysallah known? Was that why she had been so interested in her? Suddenly the sh'pav'danya made sense, why

Ysallah had insisted that it be Tamsin, so she would have the chance to bring her back to her mother's people. And then a terrible thought struck her: had Haven known? She dared not go down that path yet of wondering. She couldn't face those memories, but she could feel the truth. He had known, maybe not right away, but she was sure he had figured it out.

She was dizzy by the time she reached her mother's room, her head spinning with all of the lies that had been fabricated and circulated just so Tamsin wouldn't know who she really was. She looked at her life differently now; every experience was now bent and fractured, as if she was looking at them through a twisted piece of glass. The new light refracted differently on each picture, giving new meaning to every look, every conversation, staining certain things that had been clear before. She wasn't certain of anything anymore, the feeling of betrayal so potent it was like she was choking on it. She wasn't a real person. She *was* that reflection in the pool. Imaginary. Unrecognizable. Unsalvageable.

All of those feelings came to an abrupt halt as she stepped in her mother's room and saw her, fully clothed, asleep on the bed, holding onto one of her father's shirts. Her expression was troubled, her brows scrunched together and there were tear streaks on her cheeks and across her nose. Tamsin went over and grabbed a blanket off the ottoman and laid it over her mother. In her grief she had forgotten that her mother grieved as well. She picked up her father's shirt, held it to her face. His scent still lingered, bringing tears to her eyes. She put it back down and went back to her own room.

That night while she slept, he haunted her. She had built a fortress around herself, to protect her from the pain and grief that had consumed her after he had been taken from her. She avoided everything that reminded her of him, sights, smells, sounds. She did not say his name aloud. She did not look under the bed where his firestone lay. She had shut herself off, because opening herself up to his memory just caused her more pain. But tonight, he bombarded her mercilessly, shrieking and beating down her walls that had kept her intact. At night, in her dreams, she was defenseless.

She saw his lips and the scar that cut across his chiseled chin. The corner of his mouth twitched upwards into one of those rare smiles that he had always tried to hide.

I was wondering when you'd get here. She heard his voice, but his lips never moved.

She trembled. She had missed that voice, as rough as a cat's tongue, but smooth as honey. She wanted to melt into it, to sink into its depths. *I miss you.*

I'm right here. He cocked his head to the side as if she had said some funny joke.

She reached out to touch him, but her fingers slipped through as if he were made of fog. She stared at her hand as if it were not her own. *Why didn't you tell me?*

I did, Irinbaat. You just have to remember.

I'm scared.

He smiled knowingly. *I know. Remember: no fear.* He reached up and unhooked the veil under his hood and revealed…nothing. Where his face should have been there was only blackness.

Tamsin screamed and then blinked. She was in her room. It was dark and she was alone. She hugged her knees to her chest, trying to keep herself whole as it all replayed itself in her mind. The cracks had widened far enough that little moments had slipped in. She remembered holding him in the desert during the storm. She remembered his face the first time he had lowered his hood and the awe she felt at the light in his glowing eyes. The first time she had seen his scars and when she had figured out what it all meant. The look on his face when she had created fire from ashes. When he came back for her, despite everything.

She shook from the effort of holding the sobs back. She wanted him back, she wanted her father back, she wanted to be five years old again, and curled up in her mother's arms during a thunderstorm, listening to her say everything was going to be alright. She wanted so many things that could never be again.

The next day, Lady Allard and Lady Wohlrick came to visit. It was the first time since Lord Urbane and the Commander's funerals, but the ladies made a good effort to lighten the atmosphere and each other's spirits. And it was good to have the other dignitaries' wives there as well to provide fresh topics of conversation.

Sherene walked into the north veranda which had been sectioned off by gauzy curtains, with a tray of tea and sandwiches, and when she went to go back down to the kitchens a minute later she paused and looked at the girl with the stricken face, sitting at the foot of the stairs. She walked over and sat next to her on the steps. It was a long while before Tamsin said anything or even looked at her. She shivered and then turned her head, like she had been somewhere else and was just noticing her now.

She exhaled deeply, as if she had been holding her breath. "Everything is different."

Sherene nodded. "Yes, some things have changed, but others are still the same."

Tamsin looked at her, confused.

"Your mother loves you just as much now, if not more, as the day she met you."

Her eyes flashed. "You knew? How…?"

"I found the chest in your room. I'm sorry Tamsin. I was just doing what your parents asked me to do. I never wanted you to find out like this."

She looked away. "Nobody wanted me to find out. Especially my mother."

"You say that because you are angry, because you were deceived. But she has raised you and loved you like you were her own. You *are* Lavinia's daughter. She took someone else's child and shaped her into the beautiful, kind woman she is today."

"That girl is gone. Even before I knew any of this." She sighed. "I don't know who I am anymore, Sherene. I don't know how to exist in this world I don't recognize, not when I can't even recognize myself."

Sherene looked at Tamsin. She seemed whisper thin, like a cloud, not quite whole, but trapped in a living world all the same. "That can happen when you lose someone you care about. And your father was a big part of your life."

Tamsin made a moaning sound and curled in on herself, like her stomach hurt.

"Tamsin?"

Lavinia appeared by the stairs then and asked what was going on.

"Nothing my Lady," Sherene said, standing up quickly. "I was just taking her to get something to eat."

Lavinia took a step forward and reached out as if she were going to comfort her daughter, but then stopped and her hand recoiled. "Alright. Please make sure she does, Sherene." She walked slowly back to the veranda, worry lingering on her features.

Sherene didn't make it a habit to question her ladyship's decisions, but when they directly affected her daughter, someone

Sherene had spent a good portion of her adult life taking care of, she wished she had the nerve to speak her mind. Tamsin didn't need distance, she needed someone that she could talk to, who would listen to her and *be there* for her. She didn't doubt Lavinia's love for her and she certainly didn't blame her for the circumstances they were in, but she needed to stop giving Tamsin so much time alone. It wasn't good for either of them.

She coaxed Tamsin up. "Come on my dear, come with me," and she led her onto the south veranda, away from the rest of the ladies. She went back into the kitchens and brought back some lemonade and bread wafers. Once they were settled and Tamsin had eaten most of one of the wafers, did Sherene tell her that they were going to sit out there all day until she told her what else was wrong.

Sherene knew what was wrong. She had known it since the night Tamsin came back to the compound over a month ago and had seen her covered in blood, Mr. Haven's blood, for the next day she found out the Ma'diin man had been killed. She knew of Tamsin's affection for him, but had not realized how serious it had been until then. She wasn't going to let this girl slip any further into the cracks. She believed that she wasn't too far gone, that she could be saved yet, but she needed Tamsin to believe it too, otherwise it wouldn't matter what she said.

Tamsin looked out across the lower levels. There was a slight breeze and it brought with it the sound and the coolness of the river. It was a pleasant day out with a cloud-speckled blue sky, but Tamsin's eyes were as dark and brooding as a thunderstorm.

"Tamsin, you are not responsible for anything that happened. To your father, to your birth mother, to Mr. Haven. None of it."

"But I am responsible. He warned me that they would use me to get to him. And he was right. I handed him right to them."

"What are you talking about?"

Tamsin took a few deep breaths to compose herself, but it seemed like she trembled more with every breath. Sherene took her hand, coaxing her to tell her anything she could and after a few minutes she did. She told her what Haven had said to her when he first began teaching her how to use a sword, about the soldiers following him and the ones they had seen leaving the city, and about the night at the Armillary, how it had all been a trap to get him. Cornelius knew Haven would not be far from wherever Tamsin was and he had used that knowledge to bait him. Haven never had a chance of making it out of there alive.

"And he knew," she said, the guilt on her face apparent. "He knew and he came back anyway."

"And this is how you're choosing to repay his sacrifice?" Sherene asked. "By wallowing in grief? I think we taught you better than that Miss Tamsin. Mr. Haven didn't teach you how to use a sword so you could be weak."

"He wanted me to be strong on my own," Tamsin whispered.

"That's right. He wanted you to be able to stand tall by yourself," she said, though she still didn't think sword fighting was an appropriate undertaking for a lady. "If we put all of our bread in other people's baskets we would be left with nothing."

"Then I am nothing."

The deadpanned tone of her voice startled Sherene. "You are not nothing Tamsin. You are a daughter and a friend, beloved by your family and everyone who knows you. You were a strong, smart young woman before all of this and you still are. You may be hurting, but you are not nothing."

Tamsin flinched as if Sherene had physically struck her and Sherene hoped that it meant something had gotten through to her. There were many times when Tamsin was growing up where Sherene had wanted to just shake her out of her stubbornness, but now she was afraid that if she did Tamsin would crumble beneath her fingertips. She needed to give Tamsin something to look forward to, something to live for, but what that thing was she didn't know yet.

She heard footsteps approaching and turned to see a servant from another compound approaching. She had gotten to know most of the men and women who worked the Urbane compound, but this man was unfamiliar.

"May I help you?" she asked brusquely.

He held out a scroll. "My lord has summoned your lording lady to dinner this evening."

Sherene took the scroll. "Summoned?"

The man nodded. "It is not a request." Then he turned on his heel and left.

Sherene could guess by the man's attitude which lord he served and when she read the brief contents on the parchment her suspicion was confirmed. Only Cornelius Saveen's men could be so arrogant. Since his promotion to lordship and Lord Urbane's death, he seemed to think he controlled the whole city, and with the Empyrian army in his back pocket none of the other lords would stand up to him.

She tucked the parchment away and turned back to Tamsin. "The Commander's funeral is tomorrow. Do you feel up to going? I know Madame Corinthia would be grateful if you came." It seemed every other day now there was a funeral for someone who was never coming back from the dam. It was going to be a hard couple of days for the people of Empyria, but maybe if Tamsin went to the other funerals she might be able to talk to those who lost someone as well. Empathy was a strong emotion and if Tamsin could connect to another person, then it would be a start.

"Who is that from?" Tamsin asked, ignoring her question.

Sherene hesitated, but then thought keeping secrets from her was not a good idea at this point. "It is from Cornelius." Nothing more had been said on his and Tamsin's engagement and for that Sherene was grateful considering the state Tamsin was in. But the mourning period was over and now Cornelius could start negotiations with Lavinia again without the risk of looking insensitive. With Lord Urbane's passing, Lavinia was sure to be more eager than ever to settle Tamsin down with someone and a month ago Sherene would have agreed with her, but her attitude towards the new lord had changed, especially after hearing Tamsin's story. No doubt preparations for the wedding would soon be underway, and yes the city could probably use something to celebrate about, but knowing it would make Tamsin's life worse lessened the whole notion of it. And Tamsin had lost the only person who could have stood up for her and prevented the union.

"Well, I suppose I should give this to your mother," Sherene said with a heavy sigh. It was no use putting off the inevitable, but she wasn't going to tell Tamsin her suspicions about what would be discussed at the dinner.

Tamsin looked up suddenly, her eyes still cloudy, but now they held something else, a new kind of storm rolling in. "I'll go," she said.

"I'm perfectly capable of giving this to your mother, there's no need for you to do it," Sherene said, getting up. "Why don't you eat some more and I'll be back in a moment and we can finish talking."

But Tamsin stood up as well. "No. I will go. To the dinner."

Sherene had to take a moment before she responded, the meaning of Tamsin's words not quite making sense. "Why would you go?" she finally asked, realizing that Tamsin had probably guessed what the dinner was about.

"You were just telling me I needed to stand on my own," she said, and Sherene knew that empathy was not going to be Tamsin's path back to normalcy. "I'm going to do just that."

Sherene was wary about letting Tamsin go, especially if she stood up for herself and Cornelius refused her, but defiance was as strong an emotion as any and if this was how Tamsin was going to mend, then it was a good place to start.

Sherene took the parchment and ripped it in half. "Good girl," she told her and Tamsin's lips curved up into a small smile, the first she had seen in weeks.

CHAPTER TWENTY-EIGHT

Tamsin's hands shook as she made her way through the lower part of the compounds and to Cornelius's residence, though it only made her more determined to confront him. It made her sick to think that he wanted to go ahead with the engagement after everything that had occurred for what else could he possibly want to discuss with Lavinia? But despite the growing sense of nausea, she knew that what Sherene had said was right. She needed to stand up for herself and she would rather die than marry Cornelius. And though she still felt the guilt of Haven's death, she knew she wasn't the only one who was responsible for that. Cornelius needed to answer for his end of it.

Once she got to the compound, she made her way up through the working levels, earning herself a few curious looks from the servants, but she ignored them and kept going. She reached the top of the stairs to the third level and nearly went tumbling back down as she collided with someone coming around the wall. Strong hands were around her in a second, lifting her up over the last couple steps and planting her firmly at the top.

Tamsin had to catch her breath a moment and realized there were actually two men: the one she had run into and the one who had grabbed her. The first man was tall, his white hair parted neatly down the center and tied at the nape of his neck. He wore maroon-colored robes with a golden sash tied around his waist. He had a crooked nose on an otherwise elegant face, though his eyes were pure ice under dark brows. But his manservant made any intimidating qualities about him look demure in comparison. His manservant, for that's all this brute of a man could be, was a giant next to the white-haired man. He had a thick black beard, but not a hair on the top of his round head. His tan clothing stood out starkly against his dark skin and he carried several instruments on his belt, one of them a two-sided hammer.

"I'm so sorry," she apologized. "I must pay better attention to where I'm going."

"Not at all," the white-haired man said calmly. There was a strange, snake-like hissing to his voice that sent shivers up her arms. "The blame lies with me. And what is your name, my dear?" he asked, taking her hand with one of his black-gloved ones.

"Tamsin."

"Ah yes, Tamsin Urbane in the flesh," he said, petting the back of her hand affectionately. "I was wondering when I would be meeting you." Then, "What a pretty bracelet," he said, looking at the beads Haven had given her.

"And you are?" Tamsin asked, uncomfortable with his seeming familiarity with her. He must have been one of the dignitaries from the Cities, but she didn't remember seeing him or his giant manservant at her father's funeral.

"I am Alhexander Monstran. Ambassador from Alamorgro," he said with a slight smile. "I am quite familiar with your loved one," he said, turning as Cornelius hurried towards them from across the veranda, two guards flanking him.

Tamsin felt her anger rising at the sight of Cornelius. "He is neither loved nor mine," she said, withdrawing her hand. If this man was a friend of Cornelius's then he was no friend of hers.

"Mr. Monstran, I thought you were going to be…occupied this evening?" Cornelius said as he reached them. Cornelius's collar and wrist cuffs weren't buttoned and his hair was shaggier.

His face wasn't shaved either, sporting several weeks of new growth. She had never seen him with a beard before. He looked haggard and despite her hatred for him she felt a twinge of pity.

She quickly squashed the feeling.

"Yes, I was just on my way. I hope we meet again soon," Mr. Monstran said silkily to Tamsin. He nodded to Cornelius and then walked down the stairs, his manservant following behind.

Cornelius watched until Mr. Monstran had slithered out of sight and then turned to speak with her. Without thinking, Tamsin raised her hand and slapped him across the face.

The guards took a step forward, but he waved them off, flexing his jaw. After his initial shock and anger subsided he said, "I was wondering when that was coming."

"You deserve worse than that," Tamsin spat, balling her fists in case she had the urge to hit him again.

"Tamsin, what are you doing here? Where is your mother?"

"I decided to come on her behalf," she said coldly. "How can you possibly think I would marry you after what you've done?" Her blood boiled and her head pounded, but it wasn't one of her normal headaches that came with being upset. The familiar pressure begged to be released and it startled her how easy it had responded to her and how close she was to letting it go. She reigned it back in, afraid that if she released the fire she wouldn't be able to stop it and would burn the whole compound to the ground.

"Tamsin, can we go somewhere to talk?"

"No." She folded her arms across her chest. She didn't want to take another step into his home if she could help it.

He turned to the guards. "Leave us," he commanded and they obeyed. Once they were out of sight (but Tamsin knew not far away), he rubbed a hand over his beard. "Tamsin, there are things you don't know—reasons why I did what I did."

Her eyes flashed. "How dare you try to talk your way out of the blame! You're a liar and a coward Cornelius! Sending your men to provoke the Ma'diin into attacking. For what? Your men are dead. My *father* is dead! Haven—," her voice cracked when she said his name, "—is dead."

"You don't know what you're talking about."

"I saw your men leave the city that night. I know they weren't going to help. And I know you used me to get to Haven." Her vision blurred from tears, but she was too angry to be embarrassed. "And now you think you can go through my mother to get to me. I would cut your throat before I would share your bed."

His eyes were angry, defensive, but he held whatever excuse he was going to give. Instead, he caught her off guard by saying, "I didn't ask your mother here to talk about marriage. I was going to tell her that the caravan to take the other lords back is leaving for the Cities at the end of the week. Both of you will be going with it."

Tamsin felt her world shift again and she saw Cornelius's lips still moving, but she didn't hear what else he was saying. A caravan going back to the Cities. She and her mother would be going back to the Cities. She would be going… *home.*

"…for your own good," Cornelius was saying. "It won't be safe here for much longer and I want you as far away from here as possible."

"What do you mean, not safe?" Tamsin asked, her head still reeling from the possibility of going back to the Cities. "You think the Ma'diin are going to attack? Good. I hope they do and I hope they find you. You won't be able to hide the blood on your hands from them." Even if Cornelius was actually thinking about someone else's well-being for once, it didn't excuse him from the terrible things he had done. She turned and walked back down the stairs.

She went to bed late that night, and though she was exhausted from the meeting with Cornelius, she couldn't fall asleep. She didn't know how she felt about going back to the Cities. Lavinia had been shocked when Tamsin told her, but she could already see the relief in her face as the idea settled on her. Lavinia would be better for it. She would be back in her home, surrounded by her friends and familiar things. The atmosphere would be good for her. It would be easier to get over her husband's passing there.

But Tamsin knew she wouldn't be able to slip back into her old life as easily as her mother. She was different. Empyria had changed her. She couldn't imagine confiding in her friends there; they wouldn't understand. She could already see herself going to luncheons, but she wouldn't know what to talk about and her friends wouldn't know what to say. Pretty soon she would stop going and they would stop coming over and there would only be stares and whispers cast surreptitiously in her direction. And she was in on the secret now about her heritage, which would only widen the rift between her and the people of her old life. Secrets didn't bring people together; they drove them apart, but how could she tell anyone when she knew it would only alienate them further?

You're not the person you think you are.

Tamsin's eyes snapped open, the old seer's words pulling her back to consciousness. *Mora* had known.

As soon as the thought popped into her head the wheels started spinning and she couldn't stop them. If Tamsin wasn't who she thought she had been, then maybe she could find out who she was supposed to be. Maybe Mora knew. She had known about her past, so maybe she knew about her future. She was supposed to be a seer after all. She could remember some of the things Mora had said, but it was confusing and Tamsin couldn't make any sense of it. She needed more of the pieces. She needed to talk to Mora.

She had three days until the caravan left, but she couldn't wait until morning. She pushed the covers aside and climbed out of bed. She slipped on a robe and some shoes and was about to head down the stairs when she remembered that the last time she had seen Mora was in the catacombs under the Armillary.

She hadn't realized just how much strength she had lost until she tried pushing the stone door open behind the partition. After a few minutes, though, she managed to move it enough so she could slip behind it. Once inside, she took the dark torch out of its hanger on the wall, brushed away the cobwebs, and let the pressure she had felt earlier that day release. Flames jumped up from the end of the torch, throwing light into the dark corners and for a moment she thought it would consume the whole room, but then the flames relaxed and crackled with steady ease.

She hadn't used her ability since before that night. Without Haven, the prospect of using it had been too terrifying to think about. He had been the one to realize what she was capable of, but without him she didn't want it. She had almost fooled herself into thinking she could forget about it. But since getting angry at Cornelius it seemed that the power came naturally, as if it had been building up in the time she had refused to use it, waiting for her to come out of the void and *feel* again.

Doubt spread through her and she almost extinguished the fire. What if Mora couldn't answer her questions? What if she didn't know who Tamsin really was? Or worse, what if she told Tamsin that she was an abomination? A monster?

She shook her head, shaking away the doubt. She wasn't a coward like Cornelius. She would face whatever the old seer had to say.

She made her way down the stairway and through the long hall until she came to the room with the rope. The grate was already moved from last time so all she had to do was make sure the rope was securely fastened and didn't have any tears in it, hang her torch up, and climb down. The rope held fast this time and it reached just enough so she only had to drop a few feet and she was in the catacombs.

The torches were all lit along the hall, illuminating the hollowed out sections carved into the walls. She walked over to the one she remembered Mora being in, but it was empty. Frowning, she walked a little further, looking into each compartment as she went, but each one was just as deserted. Had they released her?

Just then she heard footsteps coming from farther down the hall and saw shadows growing on the wall from around the corner. She ducked into one of the compartments and flattened herself against the wall. Soon the footsteps were almost upon her and she could hear the voices of two people conversing.

She sucked in her breath, recognizing one of the voices. It was silky and a little breathy, as if it was rolling off a forked tongue. It was Mr. Monstran's voice. A few moments later she recognized his maroon robes and white hair as he walked by. His manservant was with him, wiping his hammer with a cloth.

And Cornelius was there. What were they doing down here? Cornelius hated it down here.

"The arrangements have been made. The transport will leave tonight," Cornelius said.

There was a fourth man, but she couldn't get a clear sight of him, for Mr. Monstran's manservant was blocking her view.

"Good. Brunos will stay here and keep an eye on things for me. I've enjoyed our time together Lord Saveen, but I've found the desert to be irritatingly hot," Mr. Monstran said.

Cornelius stopped and after a few paces Mr. Monstran did as well, turning around to face him.

Tamsin shrunk back as far as she could, hoping they wouldn't see her.

"What are you going to do with him?" Cornelius asked.

"Ah, I know you were hoping to keep him for yourself, but he will be much more useful with me. Don't get me wrong, I'm grateful for your efforts, but you did fail to deliver the one my liege wanted. You see Lord Saveen, preparing the body is one thing, but preparing the mind, now that is my specialty and if I can change him, then your failure might be forgiven."

Cornelius looked agitated, but nodded.

"You get your throne, Lord Saveen, but don't forget who's letting you keep it," Mr. Monstran warned. Then he chuckled, patted a tense Cornelius on the back, and continued walking.

She waited until they had disappeared before she crept out back into the hall. She looked behind her to where they had come from, wondering what was down that way and deciding she wanted to find out. Their conversation had an ominous tone to it and it reminded her of when she overheard Lieutenant Riggs in the kitchens. She hadn't understood their conversation then and thought it better to wait, but she knew what waiting got her. She should have acted then and she wasn't going to make the same mistake twice. She moved quickly, glancing around the other compartments, but there was nothing in them. She rounded the corner and saw it extended a little ways more, the walls on both sides solid and ending in a large iron door at the end. There was a stool next to it and a cloak on the ground as if someone had been keeping watch over the door, but no one was around now. This was the only place they could have come from. There were two planks that held the door shut and with some effort, for one was nearly above her head, she was able to lift them from the brackets and set them against the wall. Then she pulled the door open.

A harsh odor struck her and she covered her nose as she stepped inside. It was darker than the eye of a thunderstorm and the ground was even more rough and uneven than in the hall. From what she could tell the room was a little smaller than her bedroom and closer to the river, for she could hear the steady thrumming from the Elglas even through the thick stone walls and when she took a step her foot landed in a small puddle.

She heard the sharp intake of breath that was not her own and froze, wondering what else was in here. Her eyes darted around, still adjusting to the darkness, and came upon a darker form near the far wall, huddled close to the ground.

Man or beast, she did not know, but it was definitely alive. "Hello?" she called out softly.

The figure stirred and she heard the rough clanking of metal chains.

Was this where they had moved the seer? "Mora?" Tamsin called out again, taking another step forward.

The figure moved again and this time rose up and by the time Tamsin realized that the figure was too large, too tall to be the old seer, hands were already around her throat.

CHAPTER TWENTY-NINE

Tamsin gasped for air, seizing up in panic as the hands around her throat tightened. She tried to pull the hands apart, but they were too strong and she could already feel herself getting weaker. She tried kicking and scratching at her attacker but her thoughts were becoming less focused and her movements more sluggish. She could feel herself slipping away. She didn't believe in an afterlife; it was a concept foreign to her, one they only learned about when they studied the old religion, but suddenly it was all she could think about, wondering if she would see her loved ones again. She could almost see glowing eyes staring back at her… "Nooo—feeaarrr," she gurgled out.

The hands let go and the figure staggered back. Tamsin fell to the ground, coughing and clutching her throat. The sudden onrush of air was almost too much and for a few long moments all she could do was lie on the floor and gape, her mouth opening and closing with a horrible gulping sound like a fish out of water. Then her wits started to trickle back and she crawled away, hoping the figure's chains wouldn't let him reach her.

But through the darkness she could see he wasn't making any advancements towards her. He was kneeling on the ground, his chest heaving and the chains rattling as his hands visibly shook. His head was bent forward, his nostrils flared, and his cheeks puffed in and out as if letting go of her had taken a physical toll on him.

Despite just being attacked by the man, she felt sorry for him. Nobody deserved this kind of wretched confinement.

"Tamsin?" a gravelly voice spoke.

Cold ice shot up her spine, making the hairs on her neck stand up.

Then the man looked up and Tamsin felt all the air leave her again as she beheld glowing eyes. His brows knitted together and this time he couldn't help the gasping sob that escaped him as he said her name again.

The anguished sound sent cracks racing through the ice that held her frozen and she lurched forward, trembling so badly she thought she would fall apart.

He held up a hand. "No, no closer—."

But the sight of him held her together, kept moving her closer. She was terrified that it was all just an illusion, that her sanity had finally forsaken her and she was descending into madness. But despite his warning, despite him almost killing her a moment ago, her hand reached up anyways and touched his face and it was like gravity reclaiming her, pulling her back from the grey space she had been drifting through.

"Haven?" she breathed, his name like a whisper from a ghost through her lips. She should have felt relief, but she was horrified. These last two months Haven had been alive. He had been right here below her feet this whole time and she had been too numb to see it. Her hands took in his appearance, quivering over his skin, touching all the things she recognized: the shape of his lips, his hollow cheeks, the scar on his strong jaw, the curve of his collarbone. The silvery pulsing over his heart. They grazed over his bare chest and felt the ridges where his skin had healed. There were three of them. Three scars for three arrows.

Then she broke. She latched onto him, hugging him with such ferocity that nothing would part them again. She cried shamelessly, burying her face into his neck and clinging to him until she was sure her tears would flood the room and drown them both. But his muscles were tight underneath her and she finally pulled away, afraid that she was causing him pain.

They had saved him, for reasons her shaken mind couldn't comprehend, they had saved him. But they had also abused him. She began to see other scars as well. Layers of dirt and sweat and blood hid most of his natural markings from being a Watcher, but there were places where dark lines cut across his skin, severing the glowing marks that managed to show through. They were torturing him.

That thought sent sparks of anger through her and a sense of urgency began to cut through the shock. She felt the chains around his wrists and noticed the shackles around his ankles.

"You not do that," he said, the soft velvet in his voice all but gone. "Not trust me."

"It's okay, Haven," she said, her own voice sounding hoarse. "You won't hurt me. It's going to be okay." The doubt in his voice scared her. She looked around for something, anything that would help her get the chains off him. Then she felt his hands on her face and she went rigid. But they were soft this time, cradling her like she was a fragile bubble, as if she would burst and disappear if he squeezed too hard. Her throat hurt, but not from his hands this time.

"I not think you be real," he said, his eyes searching like he still didn't quite believe she was here in front of him.

She was finding it difficult to do the same. "I thought you were dead," she whispered.

"Dead?" The corners of his eyebrows went up and he started chuckling as if she had said something amusing.

The sound alarmed her even more than his appearance so she took his hands and held them tightly, not knowing what else to do.

His gaze came back to her and his devastating blue eyes were ashamed and etched with confusion, the chuckles turning into gasps. "They—not let—me die."

They had taken him. The strong, beautiful, fearless man he had been had been stripped away. And Tamsin realized then that she wasn't the one on the brink of madness. He was trying to hide it from her, but they had taken his mask too, and she could see clearly the terror on his face.

He hung his head and long locks of hair fell over his eyes as he got his breath back. "I not know why I be alive. I not remember what happen. I not even know where we be Tamsin. How—how long I be here?"

"Too long," she said, swallowing the burning lump in her throat. "Two months, maybe."

He seemed stunned. "It be months?" The chains rattled as he sat back. He rubbed his face in his hands. "I sorry," he said. "I not remember what happen. I not know how I got here. I—." His chest heaved as he took a few shaky breaths and his hand crossed over his chest and touched the spot where one of the arrows had pierced him.

Her throat constricted painfully as she watched him. For so long, all she had wanted was to see his face again, to touch his hand, to have the man she loved back, but this wasn't how it was supposed to be. They had taken him from her—.

But she wasn't going to let them take any more of him.

She almost envied his lack of memory of the events of that night. She had tried so hard to keep those memories away, to lock them up and never think about them again. But now, she realized, she had to remember everything. Everything was important.

"That night, you told me that you had been through worse," she said, taking his hands. "The worst is over, Haven. It's all in the past now. I'm going to get you out of here."

She hadn't seen keys hanging outside and Cornelius wasn't stupid enough to leave them in here. If she could just find something that would break the chains from the wall…or melt them.

Hope leaped inside her and she took a section of chain near his wrist and held it up. She started concentrating and found that feeling of power within her. She focused on the chain and imagined it burning bright orange. It started to get warm in her hands, but it held fast and stayed a cold grey color. She pushed harder, blocking everything else out. The metal got hotter, but she ignored the pain and held on. Time fell away like autumn leaves and it was just her, the chains, and her determination.

And then her head started to pound, like she was under water in the middle of a storm and the waves were pulsing back and forth over her. Her vision started to blur and the ground swayed beneath her as the pounding increased until it was finally too much and she dropped the chain. She could hear Haven calling her name, but his voice was muffled, far away. She could barely feel his hands on her, steadying her, as her whole body was numb compared to the throbbing in her head.

Her hands grappled for the chain despite the hot pain lancing through her burnt palms, but Haven took her wrists, stopping her.

"Tamsin, okay. Okay."

"No. No, it's not. I'm going to get you out of here. I can't give up. I promised I wouldn't give up on you." Her tongue felt swollen as she said the words. "Does Cornelius have the keys?"

He shook his head and his eyes scrunched in concentration. "No…the other one…"

Mr. Monstran. What did he have to do with this? Why was he here? "I'm going to get them from him," she said.

"No! He catch you. He catch you and hurt you. No—not go. Not leave me. Stay."

It took everything she had to keep from weeping, his plea tearing through her heart. She took his face in her hands, touching her forehead to his, and she felt his hands clutching her robes. "Remember what you used to tell me? Do you remember?"

He blinked several times. She knew he was still in there. It wouldn't be enough just to get him out of here. She had to bring him back to himself.

"No fear," he whispered, recognition lighting his face.

She nodded, tears falling down her cheeks. "No fear. Do not be afraid. I am right here," she put her hand over his heart, the silver pulsing in between her fingers, "and I'm not leaving you ever again. But we can't stay here Haven. We have to go home."

A shiver ran through him.

"I will get the keys. I will get you out of here and we will go there, together," she promised. "Do you believe me?"

His gaze hardened and for a brief moment she saw his old strength return. "Yes."

She kissed him then, her lips, salty with passionate tears, colliding with his desperate, blood-stained ones. With that kiss she gave him her love, her promise, and a reason to keep fighting. She knew he was tired, but she needed him to keep going. When their lips finally parted she said, "Then I will return to you."

His glowing eyes met hers and he nodded, letting her go.

She stumbled to the door before she could change her mind. Red spots danced in her vision in the torch light as she staggered against the wall in the hall. She shook her head, trying to clear her sight, but it only made her dizzier. She felt something wet on her upper lip and wiped it with her arm, her sleeve coming away bloody. Her head still pounded as if all of the fire she had tried to summon was now built up behind her eyes.

"Tamsin?"

She looked up at the sound and saw a blurry figure standing in the hallway.

"Tamsin, my dear girl, what are you doing down here?"

She knew that voice and confusion swept through her. "Mr. Graysan?"

Then everything went dark.

CHAPTER THIRTY

Something cool was pressed against her temple. It felt good, soothing away the thrumming around her skull that lingered like a bad dream. Something tugged at her consciousness, telling her she needed to get up, that there was something important she needed to do, but the bed underneath her was so soft and it felt so nice to lie there. The feeling wouldn't go away though, and her heavy eyelids eventually drifted open.

She didn't recognize the room she was in which was simply furnished with a single dresser and the bed she was on. There were three small candles on the dresser that gave a soft glow to the small room, but there were no windows so she didn't know if it was day or night.

Then she felt something cold and slimy touch her palm and she hissed at the stinging sensation it produced, looking over to see someone in a black cloak applying some kind of salve to her burns.

Haven.

She shot straight up, making him jump and the thrumming in her head flare for a moment as the memories of what happened barraged her. She stared at him, trying to remember how they had gotten here and wondering where here was. "Haven? What happened? How…?"

And then he removed his hood and her heart fell. It wasn't Haven.

But glowing eyes stared back at her. It was another Watcher. He called for someone in Ma'diin and a moment later Sherene appeared through the doorway. Relief showered her features and she rushed to Tamsin's bedside, but Tamsin was more confused than ever. "What's going on Sherene? Where's Haven?"

"Lie back down Miss Tamsin, you've had quite a spell," Sherene said. She had dark circles under her eyes and her hair was sticking out from under her head scarf. Then to the Watcher she said, "Have you finished with that yet?"

The Watcher mumbled something in Ma'diin and began applying the salve again to Tamsin's hands.

"Sherene, what's going on?" Tamsin asked again, staying upright. "Who is this?"

"Don't worry yourself right now. He's helping—."

Tamsin shook her head and turned to the Watcher. *"Who are you?"* she asked in Ma'diin, ignoring the look of surprise on Sherene's face.

The Watcher raised an eyebrow at her, wrapping her hand with strips of cloth. He was smaller than Haven and younger too, perhaps even younger than Tamsin. His face was lean and had the look of any teenager whom premature responsibility had been thrust upon them. His eyes smoldered gold, only a few shades brighter than his dusty brown hair. *"I am Samih,"* he said. *"Your hands should heal in a few days. How did you burn yourself?"*

"Trying to save your brother."

Samih looked up sharply. *"You know where Haven is?"*

"He was in the catacombs. Below the city."

His eyes lowered. *"I have looked there. He is not there."*

"How did you know where to look?"

"The gray man."

Mr. Graysan. She remembered seeing him just before she fainted. She looked to Sherene. "Did Mr. Graysan bring me here?"

"Yes, last night."

"Where is he? I need to speak with him," she said, a hint of panic creeping into her voice.

"Settle yourself for a moment my lady. He's around here somewhere, skulking around like a nervous cat. I almost had him flogged for bringing you to me in such a state. Then Mr. Samih showed up and, well…he changed everything."

It was almost with fondness with which she spoke of the Watcher and Tamsin certainly saw gratitude in her eyes, which she didn't understand. Sherene had only ever tolerated the Ma'diin. And were those tears in her eyes?

"Is Samih the only one that came back?" Tamsin asked, wondering if Ysallah and the others had come as well. Had the Kazsera decided to follow through on her threat to take her back to the marshlands?

"No," Sherene said, dabbing the corners of her eyes.

"Who…" she started to ask, but then another figure stepped through the doorway, limping slightly, and at first she thought the candlelight was playing tricks on her, but then her heart swelled and gave a mighty push against her chest as if it wanted to leap out and go straight to the man before her.

Another ghost had been resurrected from the hooks of death.

Before her, unshaven and gaunt, though no less lordly, was her father.

After giving Tamsin and her father some time alone to reunite, Sherene procured some extra chairs and for the next few hours they sat around her bedside while they recounted the last few months. Her father started by briefly describing their journey to the dam. Briefly, Tamsin thought, because he was unaware of her knowledge about her birth mother, something he and Ysallah must have discussed at length. The dam itself, he described, was the biggest piece of architecture he had ever seen, even by the Cities' standards. It spanned the entire width of the river and then several hundred yards on either side up the ridge it was situated between, rising up into the sky (as the Ma'diin so perfectly called it) like a wall. It was nearly complete when they arrived; the only piece yet to be finished was the massive stone door that would slide down through the center that would cut off all water flow to the south. They inspected it thoroughly, but it was quite clear that the design of it wasn't to control the water flow, but to sever it. *The guillotine* the local workers were calling it, men the late Lord Saveen had hired from the Cities. Lord Urbane's initial feelings that the dam could work in a way to help both parties was irrevocably crushed. The dam's location and use would benefit neither the Ma'diin nor the Empyrians. They reached an agreement with the Ma'diin quickly to halt production.

Samih remained quiet throughout and only when her father said that Samih's disappearance had not gone unnoticed by him, did Samih speak. Tamsin translated quietly for Sherene, pretending not to notice the look of surprise and pride that flickered across her father's face. Samih said he had left under Ysallah's insistence; her distrust of the northerners and concern for Haven overruling her precautions for the ripples it might cause. So he had returned and had kept his eyes and ears open until he discovered some of the northern soldiers leaving in their large boats.

He glanced briefly at Tamsin a moment and she remembered that night at the portcullis. She nodded for him to keep going.

He continued, telling them he had found Haven and the plan they had come up with to follow the northerners, how Haven was supposed to meet up with him. He waited as long as he could for Haven, but he knew what Haven would tell him to do so he followed the northerners. And he still almost arrived too late.

Her father took over the story again from that point, telling them how the Empyrian newcomers had pretended to be there to help disassemble the dam after getting word from Captain Saveen, but that night they tried to sneak into the Ma'diin's encampment and take Ysallah. But they forgot the Watchers are nocturnal and they were caught almost immediately. By that point, though, any truce that was in place fell apart, and the camp erupted into chaos. It wasn't just the Empyrians fighting the Ma'diin, however. The newcomers started killing any workers who got in their way. They killed the Commander almost right away and then they came for him, which was how he acquired his limp.

Her father's eyes were sad. "If young Samih here hadn't arrived when he did and gotten me out, I would be dead right now."

Tamsin reached out and squeezed her father's hand and he smiled appreciatively.

"I don't know what happened to Ysallah or the others. Samih hid me in the desert and treated my wounds, but it was a long time before I could walk. Once I was able we returned to the dam, but it was overrun, so I convinced Samih to bring me back here."

"Not much convincing," Samih said. *"I needed to know what happened to my brother."*

"Cornelius has been keeping him prisoner, torturing him. He—he's been made a lord now."

"Mr. Graysan has filled us in on some of the details already," her father said, though his eyes betrayed his ignorance of the last part. "We will have plenty of time to go over things on the way back to the Cities. You should get some rest, though. It is late."

"We're still going? But what about Haven?"

Her father gave her a regretful, but questioning look. "Samih will manage that."

Tamsin had to look away, reminding herself that her father didn't know how she felt about Haven. But the thought of leaving without knowing where Haven was or if he was safe was too hard to think about. "What about Cornelius? He needs to answer for what he's done. He's a traitor and a murderer."

"Cornelius has the whole Empyrian army at his disposal now. It's not safe to stay here. I'm powerless until we get back to the Cities, which is why we must keep my return a secret. Understood?"

"Does Mathri know?" Tamsin asked, wondering for the first time why her mother wasn't here with them.

He shook his head. "I will tell your mother in time, but right now it's best if she still thinks I'm dead. If she's convinced, then everyone else will be too, and it will make it easier to get all of us out of here in one piece."

But Tamsin couldn't think of leaving, not without Haven, and after her father had kissed her goodnight and taken his leave with Sherene, did she ask Samih a favor. *"Can you find the grey man and bring him here?"*

It wasn't long before Samih returned with a rattled looking Mr. Graysan in tow. *"If you want me to I will kill the deceitful cur'zak right now,"* he said.

Tamsin shook her head. *"That won't be necessary, yet."* She almost wished she could take the Ma'diin up on his offer because she had gone over her memories and realized that Mr. Graysan had been the fourth man with Mr. Monstran and Cornelius, else he would not have been down in the tunnels. He had known Haven was down there, that he was alive, and what they were doing to him. She didn't think Mr. Graysan was the kind of man that would torture another, but if he had so much as touched Haven…

"I don't want to make Georgiana an orphan," she told Mr. Graysan, "but if you don't explain to me why you didn't tell me about Haven I'm going to let Samih deal out the justice he thinks you deserve."

Guilt and shame were written all over Mr. Graysan's features, from his sad eyes to his hunched shoulders, but Tamsin wanted to hear his confession from his own mouth. She had no room left in her for pity.

"I'm so sorry, Tamsin," he said, his chin quivering. Samih let go of his collar and Mr. Graysan slumped into a chair. "I had no idea how complicated everything was. When I saw you down there, bloodied and barely conscious, I panicked. I thought my fears had been realized—."

"What fears?"

"When I realized what you were capable of, with your powers to control fire, I—I went to Cornelius because I was afraid the Ma'diin knew who you were and that—that they would try and kidnap you." His eyes darted away.

Tamsin was surprised to hear that Mr. Graysan knew about her abilities; maybe Georgiana had told him, she really didn't care, but she knew what other subject he was skirting around. "I know who my real mother was," she said. "I know she was the woman in your drawing. Keep going."

It took him a moment to get over his surprise. "I, uh, I went to Cornelius and he asked me questions about the Ma'diin, they weren't normal questions, and I didn't want to tell him anything else."

Tamsin remembered how excited he had been to tell her about the Ma'diin that night she went over to the Graysan residence for dinner, acknowledging that he probably hadn't known Cornelius's intentions when he went there and had gotten caught in the excitement of another eager listener.

"But then Mr. Monstran came and they—they forced me to help them."

That's when Tamsin noticed the splints sticking out from under the sleeve on his left arm.

"I wanted to tell you Tamsin, so many times, but I couldn't. They threatened to hurt Georgiana if I told anyone. I helped Haven when I could; I brought him food, medicine, but I swear I never hurt him."

She believed him and she didn't want to blame him anymore, but the feeling of betrayal still simmered. *Betrayed by the guiltless one…*Tamsin shook her head, trying to clear away the echo of Mora's words. "Why are they keeping him alive? Cornelius hates him."

"I know he does. I saw it in his eyes the first time he took me down there. But he's not the one calling the shots. Mr. Monstran is. I don't know what he's holding over Cornelius, but he's the one keeping Haven alive."

"Who is he? Where did he come from?"

"I don't know. He's not from the Cities though."

"And what about Haven? Where is he?"

"When I brought you back here and saw Samih I thought for sure they had come for you, but then your father explained to me what had happened. So I took him back to the tunnels, but Haven was gone."

She barely dared to hope. "Do you think he got out?"

Mr. Graysan shook his head sadly. "I don't think so. If he escaped I think Mr. Monstran would have Cornelius's men scouring the city right now."

Tamsin tried to recall what she had heard them talking about in the tunnels. Mr. Monstran had spoken of a transport leaving that night. If they took Haven, then he was already gone. "Mr. Monstran left. Where did he say he was going?"

"I don't know. They didn't include me in most of their conversations." He shook his head again.

Tamsin tried to remember when she had spoken to Mr. Monstran. What he had told her in that snake-like voice of his. A voice that sounded a lot like Mora's, who was also missing, she realized. "He said he was an ambassador from Alamorgro." The name had sounded familiar somehow, but she hadn't recognized it. "That's not in the Cities."

"I've never heard of it. I'm sorry Tamsin." His expression was truly pained as he knew this information was practically useless.

Tamsin saw Samih's eyes flash briefly at the name Alamorgro, but she ignored it for the moment. "I know you were only trying to protect me, and Georgiana," she said, "so I cannot fault you for that, but you've hidden a lot of things from me Mr. Graysan and that I can't so easily forgive."

His eyes lowered and he nodded.

"If you really want to protect Georgiana, though, you will come with us when the caravan leaves for the Cities. My father is right; it's not safe in Empyria anymore."

"It is a good offer," he said and Tamsin knew then that he wasn't going to take it, "one that I do not deserve, but my home is here."

Tamsin studied him for a moment. "You already made a deal with my father, didn't you?" There was nothing Mr. Graysan loved more than Georgiana, so the only thing that could make him risk her safety by staying here was something that would absolve him of his sins. She suddenly felt horrible for her interrogation and judgment.

"Your father asked me to be his eyes and ears here. He said he couldn't trust anyone else with the task." His voice cracked a little as he spoke.

It was kind of perfect, when she thought about it, since Mr. Graysan was already in Cornelius's circle and he would be able to provide information to her father that Cornelius might keep hidden from the other lords. But it was also dangerous and she didn't want to think about what would happen if he was found out. Cornelius would most certainly brand him a traitor.

"Then do not let him down," she told him, holding his gaze so he would know that she had not written him off completely. That she was counting on him as much as her father was.

He nodded vigorously and stood up. With a nod from Tamsin, Samih moved out of the way so he could leave, but when he got to the door, Mr. Graysan paused. "Mr. Monstran is trying to change him Tamsin. I don't know why, but if you see him again, and I pray to the gods you do, be prepared for that." Then he stepped out.

Sherene came back after he had gone, bringing a fresh change of clothes for Tamsin and after she had left, Samih turned to go as well so she could dress in private, but Tamsin stopped him.

She set the clothes aside. "You can understand me?" she asked in the common tongue.

He paused, his eyebrows furrowing in a way that said he had misjudged her. *"I can understand some things,"* he said in his own language.

"You understood then when I spoke of Alamorgro?"

"Yes."

"You've heard of it before. Where is it Samih?"

He watched her for a moment, as if he were trying to figure something out about her, like how she had so easily ensnared the affections of his brother and caused so much chaos in doing so.

His gaze reminded her of how Haven used to look at her sometimes, like he was trying to figure out a puzzle. It unnerved her a little, but she held his stare. *"I have to save him Samih. I can't give up on him now."*

He seemed to hear the conviction in her voice because he sat down then, his golden eyes boring into her. *"He told me you were special,"* he said. *"Ysallah thinks you are special. Tell me why."*

She could lie to him, feign ignorance, but she wasn't going to do that. Samih seemed to be the only one in her corner whose main goal at this point was to get Haven back. *"Because I'm half Ma'diin,"* she told him. *"My mother was from the marshlands."*

He didn't hide his surprise very well and Tamsin hoped that her confession would satisfy his question. If he hadn't known about that, then she didn't think Haven would've told him about her abilities either, and she did not want to go into that right now, especially since her headache had eased some and she did not wish to give him a demonstration as proof. It had almost killed her, she realized.

"And Haven knew this?" he asked.

She remembered that night she had first made fire, when he had told her the story of the Watchers, of the Q'atorii and…Baat. Baat was the daughter of Mahirii and Bherun. He had told her: *'It means you are special, Irinbaat.'* And then again in the dream she had had a couple weeks ago. In her dream she had asked him why he hadn't told her. She closed her eyes and she could recall the sound of his voice as he said, *'I did, Irinbaat.'* Irin. The same word that was carved on her birth mother's chest. He had told her, she realized. In his own way, he had told her who she was. Irin's *daughter.*

"Yes," she said. *"I believe he knew."*

After a minute he nodded, seeming to accept her answer after he had made the connections between her words and Ysallah and

Haven's. *"The desert is wide. It goes for many hundreds of miles. But it does end eventually."*

"Where?"

"We call it The Ravine of Bones. It is a series of canyons, all connected by one large one called the Backbone. That is where Alamorgro is."

The Ravine of Bones. *"That is where he's taking him."*

Tamsin was completely confident, but Samih's eyes were troubled, haunted even.

"What is it Samih?"

"It is the heart of amon'jii territory."

"But I thought the amon'jii lived in the marshlands?"

"The Ravine of Bones is northeast of the marshlands. The amon'jii live in the caves in the canyons and come to the marshlands to hunt."

"Then that is where we must go," Tamsin said, undaunted.

Samih raised his eyebrow at her use of the word 'we,' but then blew a sharp blast of air through his nose. *"We cannot go there. It would be certain death. Only one person has ever gone there and come back alive."*

She didn't have to ask him who by the look he gave her. Haven.

"If anyone can survive there it's going to be him," he said.

"But you didn't see him Samih," she said, squeezing her eyes shut against the image it produced. *"What they've done to him…We have to try. We owe him that."*

"We do," he said, frustration edging into his voice. *"Me more than anyone. But we wouldn't make it a week in the desert."*

His youth and the weeks of hardship were starting to show and now she was asking him to endure more. *"But you brought my father back. You survived out there for—."*

"We had the river," he said, shaking his head. *"Mr. Monstran has supplies, men,* help. *He might follow the river south for a little while, but he won't go near Ma'diin territory. The gray man was right about that at least.*

We have nothing. Our water would run out in a matter of days. And even if we did manage to get to the canyons somehow, what then? Not without an army of Watchers would we be able to get him out of there." He ran his hands over his head

Tamsin sat up straighter, the back of her mind tingling with an idea. *"Samih,"* she said slowly, hardly breathing as if she did too hard it would blow the frail wisp of hope away. *"If we asked the Ma'diin, would they help?"*

The waning candlelight flickered in his eyes and she knew then that she had found an ally. No more would they be bending to others' plans. It was time to make their own.

CHAPTER THIRTY-ONE

She stared into the desert, into the sun sinking below the mountains that were too far away to see, but were there nonetheless. It seemed a lifetime ago when she had crossed those very mountains, coming east, into the unfamiliar desert and the unknown. So much had changed since then, since she had been that little, naïve girl whose only wish was to have an adventure like her father. To ride into the unknown under white sails, to explore exotic lands, conquer foes, return home to the triumphant cries of her people, and resume her life where the only thing that changed was that she now had a great story to tell. She thought Empyria would be an adventure and she would walk over the coals and be unscathed by it. But adventures have a way of changing people. The sure become uncertain. The steady waver. The invincible are broken. Her eyes were open now and they had seen too much to go back. Now she was going into another unknown, but this time she was wiser to the fact that adventures were not to be placed on a crystal pedestal.

A week ago, their caravan had left Empyria, to go back across the lonely road and the mountains to the Cities, but Tamsin had not been with them. She realized the importance of what her father had to do and she would not jeopardize that, so she had to make everyone believe that she had gone with them. Her father had disguised himself as one of the servants and followed the wheelhouse on foot with the others. As long as he carried his weight, no one would look twice at the haggard servant, though

Tamsin worried about him with his limp. It was a long journey back to the Cities. Once they realized she was not among them they would be well away from Empyria and her father knew his position was too precarious to risk going back for her. They would have no choice but to continue on as if nothing was wrong and by then Samih and herself would be long gone.

The day before, she and Samih had discussed what needed to be done into the early hours of the morning. Tamsin had lost a day recovering and though she was still exhausted they only had one left to put their plan in motion. Her mother had been so busy making arrangements and getting things organized for the move that she had hardly noticed Tamsin was missing, which worked to their advantage. With the servants occupied carrying out Lavinia's orders, it was an easy enough task to procure food from the kitchens without any raised eyebrows. She put their provisions together and that night, followed Samih to the secret tunnel he and her father had used to get back into the city. It was in the servants' level of the Allard compound, hidden underneath a rug in the pantry of the kitchens. It was easier to get Samih out then, than try to do so during the day when the compound was active. She would follow his footsteps later and he would wait for her at the other end of the tunnel.

That same night, on the eve of the caravan's departure, Tamsin had gone to the Regoran compound. She was glad Lady Mary was out, otherwise she probably would have been banned from the premises; Tamsin knew she probably still held contempt for the girl after their last meeting. Lord Regoran was more sympathetic to her case though, still under the impression that Lord Urbane was dead and less prone to the prejudices that influenced his wife's outlook, and let her inside despite the lateness of the hour.

She had thought about what Samih had said, about needing help getting into Alamorgro, and she realized she would need help getting out of the city, especially when the whole compound expected her to be getting in that caravan departing for the Cities.

She was shown to Emilia's room, where she was just getting ready to retire for the evening. She went almost rigid with unease at Tamsin's sudden appearance. And rightly so, had Tamsin been there for any other purpose.

"Look, Tamsin, about what I did…"

But Tamsin didn't have time to rehash what had happened. "I'm not here about that. I have a proposition for you."

Emilia still looked wary, having kept herself out of Tamsin's circles until now, but she seemed resigned knowing that she couldn't avoid her forever. "Leave us," she signaled to her maids and a moment later they were alone. "What kind of proposition?"

Tamsin took a deep breath and explained what needed to be done as quickly as she could and without giving too much away. "Will you help me?" she asked when she had finished.

Emilia looked like she had been slapped. "What you're suggesting—that I pretend to be you—I—it's…"

"It's your chance to get out of here. That's what you've always wanted, isn't it?"

Emilia bit her lip. With trembling hands she pulled open one of the drawers to her nightstand and withdrew a flask, the same one Tamsin had seen her with before. She took a large swallow.

"I wouldn't have come to you if I had any other choice, but more than one life depends on this, and you're my only option." Emilia was her only choice: she was the same height as Tamsin with similar hair color, but more importantly she knew how to lie.

"When are you supposed to leave?"

"Tomorrow."

Emilia sucked in her breath and looked like she wanted to say something, but then held her tongue.

Tamsin knew this wasn't an easy decision for her, but she couldn't help tapping her fingers impatiently against her leg.

Finally, Emilia spoke. "I want to tell you something." She started pacing at the foot of her bed, wringing her hands around the flask. "My mother had an affair with a man who had some business with Lord Regoran when they lived in Fairmoore. My mother went on holiday in the country and nine months later I was born. She left me there with my aunt, afraid what would happen if Lord Regoran found out."

Tamsin sat down in the nearest chair, not taking her eyes off Emilia. She had not expected this. Lord Regoran was not Emilia's father.

"My aunt raised me until I was five. Then, one day, a man I didn't know showed up and took me away. It was Lord Regoran. And we left for Empyria two days later. Apparently my mother couldn't handle the thought of being so far away from the only child she ever had and when Lord Regoran told her about his plans to move here she finally confessed her secret. But it wasn't until I was older that I connected the dots." Her eyes flickered to Tamsin. "When I found out that Lord Urbane was coming to Empyria."

Emilia stopped pacing and closed her eyes for a moment and when she opened them the hardness that Tamsin was accustomed to seeing there had changed.

"My relationships with them have been hard built and I will not go into the complicated details, for I know you still grieve for the loss of your father, and I am sorry for it, whether you believe me or not."

"I believe you."

"Then ask me again, but do not ask me why."

Tamsin leaned forward, resting her elbows on her knees and crossing her arms, the likeness between her and Emilia all too apparent. "Will you do it?"

"Yes."

Tamsin smiled. She had gambled on the allure of the Cities to draw her in, but she hadn't guessed that Emilia had any previous history there. Emilia's story had struck a chord with her, one all too familiar, but Emilia had asked her not to ask and Tamsin didn't want to. Whatever family history Emilia had or whoever her real father had been, Tamsin wanted to remain ignorant. She had to if she was to stay focused on what she needed to do.

"What do I tell my parents?"

"Leave them this." Tamsin took out the note she had already written out that stated Lavinia had invited Emilia to the Cities on extended holiday. "Copy it in your own hand so they don't get suspicious."

Emilia's hands shook as she took it. "What will happen when your mother realizes who I am? Won't she send me back?"

"No. When that happens, you'll need to find my maid, Sherene. Tell her I'm alright and that it's time to tell my mother the truth. She'll know what to do." Tamsin knew Sherene would go to her father and that he would realize what Tamsin had done. He would have to reveal himself to Lavinia and explain everything to her.

Emilia took another drink and then offered Tamsin the flask and this time she took it. The liquid was bittersweet. Just like the choice she had given to Emilia. Just like the unspoken tie that would forever hover between them now.

When Tamsin got back to her own compound that night, she snuck up to her mother's room with the intention of saying a silent goodbye while she slept. She didn't know when she would see her again, but as she passed her father's study she stopped and hid just outside the archway. Her father was sitting at his desk reading a letter by the light of a single dim candle. For a moment, just a moment, Tamsin was transported back to when she was little and this was a common occurrence: stumbling to her father's study because she had been woken by a bad dream in the middle of the night and knowing he would still be up late working. He would carry her to their room, blow out the light, and let her sleep between them. But this time when he blew out the candle, Tamsin slunk back into the shadows to avoid being seen. Her father's comfort and kiss goodnight would not be enough this time to keep the bad dream away. When her father finally snuck out, Tamsin went in and pulled the drawer open where he had put the letter away. She recognized it. It was the one she had seen before here. The one with the Saveen's seal on it. She shoved it in her pocket and took it with her.

The next morning, Emilia came to the compound, under the pretense of saying farewell, and Tamsin gave her a black mourning dress and veil to change into. She had already gone over what Emilia needed to do, though she knew she would still be nervous until the caravan was outside of the city walls.

"It's time," she said.

Emilia nodded and Tamsin could see the grim determination in her face. "I will pretend as long as I can. I won't let you down."

Tamsin nodded. "I know you won't. My mother will keep you secret when she realizes who you are and once you get to the Cities you'll be taken care of." She gave Emilia's shoulder a reassuring squeeze and dropped the dark veil over her face.

A strange feeling settled over her, like she had turned around to look behind her, but everyone was far away and obscured in fog. The path forward was the only thing that was clear now. Resolve, that's what she was feeling she decided. She knew she was making the right choice, even though she was afraid to leave everything and everyone else behind. Her choice was clear, but her future was not. "Don't let them come back for me," she said, the words trembling on her lips. "Go now. Hurry."

Emilia pressed her hand into hers. "Good luck Tamsin. I—I hope you find what you're looking for." And then she left to join the others.

Tamsin watched discreetly from her room, high above the rest of the compound and the carts being loaded at the front entrance that would take them to the wheelhouses in the main square. She could see Lavinia and Sherene climb into one and Emilia, disguised as her, below. As the last of the trunks were being loaded, Tamsin saw a small contingent of soldiers approach, but they were only there to escort their commander: Cornelius. She had hoped he wouldn't make an appearance, but she also knew he was too vainglorious not to. He approached Emilia just before she could step into a cart of her own. Tamsin couldn't hear what he was saying to her and sweat beaded on her back underneath the servants' clothes she was wearing as she prayed that the ruse wasn't over before it had even begun. She saw her father, recognizable from the turban he wore to obscure his face, take a step forward from where he was standing by one of the carts with the other servants, barely indistinguishable from the rest, and for a second she was afraid that his emotions would get the better of him. But then he stopped and seemed to reign in his impulses. It looked like Cornelius was going to lift Emilia's veil up, but then Lavinia said something quick and unintelligible from Tamsin's standpoint, and then Emilia raised her hand, palm down, in front of Cornelius before he could lift it any further. He took her hand, kissed the top of it, and then Emilia climbed into the cart.

Tamsin let out the breath she was holding, allowing herself a small smile for her little victory.

She didn't go to see them join up with the others in the main square by the west gate. She had no time. She had a very short window while everyone was distracted by the caravan's departure to get out of the city. She grabbed the bag that contained some clothes, her cloak and the cloak out of Irin's chest, food, and the letter from her father's study.

As she grabbed it, she saw another bundle. It was Haven's firestone. She hesitated, but then reached for it anyways and stuffed it in the bag with the rest. One more thing to remind her of her purpose wasn't a bad thing, especially since she had lost the bracelet he had given her. It had nearly killed her when she realized it wasn't around her wrist. Somewhere in the tunnels she must have lost it, but if losing it meant gaining Haven's life, then she would gladly exchange it.

She then hid her bag in a basket of bread loaves and went to the Allard compound, dressed in pale blue, and made her way to the kitchens. She was nearly there when she saw Georgiana conversing with another maid. Their eyes touched briefly and she saw a confused look of recognition on Georgiana's face, but then Tamsin ducked down another hallway, walking swiftly to avoid her. It pained her not to say goodbye to the one true friend she had here, but Georgiana and her father were already in Cornelius's target zone and she did not want to give him any more ammunition. Georgiana had tried to see her several times after the ball, but Tamsin had refused everyone then. She had wasted so much time then and now she had none.

She took the long way to the kitchens, nodding politely to other servants on the way, but managed to remain unrecognized. She pretended to be depositing the bread in the walk-in pantry for a minute and then found the presence of the fire in the hearth on the other side of the room. She was nervous, but she had no choice. She felt the flames and then with a little pressure from her mind, the fire erupted into a billowing ball of heat, instantly boiling the soup that had been cooking and sending waves of smoke rolling into the kitchen. There was a chorus of screams from the maids and kitchen workers as some fled and others grabbed pots of water to put it out. Tamsin shoved a corner of the rug aside and pulled the latch that lifted the secret door. She dropped her bag down the dark hole and climbed down after it, releasing the energy of fire before she closed the door again.

Then it was a long, dark walk through the tunnel. She had nothing to burn for light and the endless blackness seemed to stretch on forever. She lost track of distance and time, but she knew Samih was waiting for her so she kept a steady pace and her doubts and fears at bay. Then, after an eternity it seemed, she saw a sliver of light and hurried towards it. She had to climb up a few boulders and when she emerged she realized she was at the Hollow Cliffs. She blinked a few times, her eyes readjusting to the light, and then a dark shape appeared before her.

Samih held out his hand. *"Are you ready?"*

It didn't seem real: that they had been gone a week already, but as Tamsin watched the falling sun, she knew that there was still a long way to go, that there would be a hundred more sunsets before this was over. She clutched the letter in her hand, the one that she had taken from her father's study, the one the late Lord Saveen had written to her father. The one she read every afternoon when she and Samih stopped to sleep. The one whose words had become engrained behind her eyes like ink on skin…

Eleazar,

I know I don't deserve it, and I know by reading this that it won't change how you feel, but if you could find it in yourself to forgive me for just enough time to read this, then maybe you can understand why I did what I did, because gods know the burden I keep is not forgivable. I let you believe that her death was caused by illness because I couldn't face the true horror of what I had done. That terrible night, she came to me. She came to tell me that I had to stop my pursuit of her, to end the chase. She was in love with you and it was you and her child that she held closest to her heart. She told me she never wanted to see me again, that she would never change her mind. Though she had told me before, her words had never struck me with such finality before, but just as she denied me with such ferocity, I felt, more than ever, just as passionately for her. It was not my right, but I loved her. I felt her slipping away from me. I couldn't be without her. In my darkest hour, I let my weakness blindly rule me. And we have all paid the price.

I took her, against her will, into the desert. I thought I could convince her yet, that if she was away from you, away from her child, that she would realize what we could be together. But she wouldn't listen. And then the sun rose like a bloody spear into the sky and she did not have her cloak. I didn't realize the consequences, Eleazar. I didn't know that it would kill her. I brought her back as quickly as I could, but she was already dying.

Now you know the truth. I will spare you any more details of those moments (ones that haunt me every day, sleeping and waking) so as not to cause you any further torment, though I know that my mere confession will bring it in heaps. That is not my intention of writing this. I tell myself that it's because we were friends once and that you deserve to know the truth, but deep in my heart I'm afraid that I'm doing this to ease my own mind and heart, that revealing my greatest sin will diminish the amount of suffering I am sure to endure in the afterlife, because I have not much time left among the living. The blackest pit of fire and smoke that Apollyon and the old gods see fit to fling me into will not be deep enough to bury my regret and sorrow. My soul is already lost to demons, haunted by the faces of the dead. It is only a matter of time until I join them again and they take their vengeance.

This letter is my only redemption, if any is to be given, for my cowardice. I must warn you: the end is upon us all. I have done something even more terrible than the deeds I just described to you. I have made a deal with the devil. He promised me an end to my suffering, so I did as He bid, but it has only caused me more suffering. I built a wall for Him and I foolishly thought the Ma'diin would be too blind to see it. The Ma'diin will start a war, one that they cannot win, but they will seek retribution just the same and when they do they will take her from you. And if they don't, then He will.

Hate me, despise me, spit upon my grave, but heed my words here. Do not bring her back. You were right to flee with her when they came for their revenge. They might have spared our men, but she would not be with you now, nearly a grown woman now I suppose. She must be as beautiful as her mother was. You must protect her, as her mother would have done. Keep her safe.

Saveen

She had read the letter, over and over, until each line was etched in her mind. The letter left her with more questions than answers, like who had told Saveen to build the dam, but it did answer one in particular. Irin had been one of them, one of the Watchers. And she had died because of it. But it explained it, or at least a little of it, why Tamsin was able to do the things she could with fire. The cloak Tamsin now wore, her mother's cloak, was the one thing that had kept Irin alive. Haven had never really explained it to her before, why they were the way they were and he had never led her to believe that any women were Watchers. And ever since she found out what Irin was, a nagging question kept creeping into the back of her mind: Was she going to become like that? It was already in her blood. Haven had found it, he had known. But she was different than the others. She was *Irinbaat*.

A southerly breeze blew a few wisps of hair around her face as Samih pushed the canoe into the river and she was reminded of the present again. She pulled the hood of Irin's cloak up and turned away from the setting sun. She stepped into the canoe, glancing one last time towards the city. Her father, her mother, Georgiana, Sherene…she would picture their faces everyday so as not to forget them, though it was quite possible she would never see them again.

Maybe, if she was lucky, their paths would cross again, but right now, her path lay to the south.

To the marshlands.

To the Ma'diin.

EPILOGUE

The ground beneath his cage had changed. It was no longer soft sand, but hard rock, rough and uneven, jarring his rolling prison violently. He grasped the bars underneath him, feeling the familiar waves of nausea as the drink wore off again. It was the same drink they had given him in his underground cell. It dulled his mind, blurred his senses, making him less able to fight back the painful images, faces, and memories that tormented him. And that voice. That voice that whispered lies and promises to him. Days, weeks, months, he wasn't sure how long it was after that, that they had been moving, but there were moments of clarity when the drink wore off and cut through the haze, though it was like his thoughts were wading through mud. Every time he thought he had grasped an image of something that was true, he would sink even further and the meaning would be lost. He tried to cling to them, to the important questions, like where they were taking him and why, but the longer he remained in his muddled state, the less important they seemed. He was filled with anger during those moments of clarity, knowing he was being robbed of his memories. Of his identity. Of *her*.

He clung to her memory most tightly, repeating her name over and over again when he could remember it.

The rolling prison came to a halt and he could hear voices and see shadows moving about outside. Someone flipped up a corner of the burlap that covered his cage, sending in a flood of light before shoving a cloak through the bars.

Haven grasped the cloak and pulled it over himself, relishing the darkness it offered. *"Why...?"* His voice was harsh, though hardly above a whisper. He barely recognized it.

But *he* heard. He always heard. A moment later Mr. Monstran appeared by the open burlap. "You've asked that question many times Haven," he said, his silvery voice patient and painfully cheerful.

Haven wished he could block it out. He was surrounded by thorns and every word out of Mr. Monstran's voice dripped with poison. Sometimes the oblivion caused by the drink was better than listening to this man.

"Which is it this time? Surely I've answered all of them by now. Why are you here? Why have I kept you alive? Why not just kill you? Why has no one come for you?"

Tamsin's face skittered across the edges of his vision and he turned his head sharply, but she was already gone.

"Ah, it's the last one, isn't it?" Mr. Monstran paced outside the bars, his hands clasped behind his back. "Or rather, why has *she* not come for you?"

Haven balled his fists against the side of his head, trying to remember, but he couldn't and it only made the anger worse. His anger was the only thing that reassured him that his hatred for this man was earned, otherwise he had no way of knowing what Mr. Monstran said was true. *"What have you done with her?"* he growled.

"We let her go. She is alive and well and on her way back to the Cities as we speak."

A lie. He was almost certain of it. He could nearly remember Tamsin there in his dark cell, promising to take him home. They weren't going home though. But he wouldn't let this man manipulate him. *"You lie."*

Mr. Monstran smiled. "That is the one thing I will never do to you Haven. You will realize that soon enough."

"*She would not leave*," he said firmly, feeling a grain of confidence in his words. Tamsin would not have left.

"What you mean to say is: she would not have left *you*."

Haven glared at him, using every muscle he had to radiate defiance. He didn't know who this man was or how he knew about Tamsin, but he was not going to let himself be manipulated. He could feel the drink wearing off; he had to take advantage of it.

"I'm sorry to tell you that she did in fact leave," Mr. Monstran continued, stopping his pacing to watch the Ma'diin curiously, "and I am sorry because I can see that you still have feelings for her, but she is gone."

"*She would not give up.*"

"Give up? No, she didn't give up. She just realized what was best for her…and she chose to leave."

Haven watched him silently, pushing away the sick fear in his stomach.

Mr. Monstran sighed. "I didn't want to show you this," he said, digging around in his pocket for a moment, "but the proof will validate my words to you."

Then he withdrew the beaded bracelet. He held it out so Haven could see clearly.

Haven couldn't forget that bracelet. Not ever. Panic coursed through him, unwelcome, but insistent nonetheless.

Mr. Monstran smiled. "This is important to you isn't it?" He studied the bracelet for a moment, noting its unique qualities. "Something from your homeland. I imagine that's why she didn't want it anymore."

"*Please*," Haven said, his nostrils flaring with emotion. He stretched out his hand.

"This is from your old life Haven." He returned the bracelet to his pocket and it was like he had buried it under a hundred feet of dirt. "You should no longer concern yourself with it."

Haven started hurling curses, anything he could remember, his eyes ablaze with anger.

Mr. Monstran shook his head. "That won't do Haven." He signaled to some of the men, who opened the door to his cage and hauled him out. They beat him with blunt sticks until he was forced to his knees.

"I'm going to tell you something," Mr. Monstran said as the Ma'diin struggled to regain his senses.

There were usually two types of people: those that shied away from the pain and succumbed rather quickly to despair and those that used the pain to fuel their rebellion. No matter what Mr. Monstran did or said, Haven knew he had to fight.

Mr. Monstran knelt in front of him and looked directly into his glowing eyes. "You are going to be my masterpiece."

Then he stepped out of the way and Haven saw where they were: standing on the edge of a giant crevice, as wide as a river and twice as deep, cutting through rock like a crack of lightning. One that connected to dozens of others, too far away for him to see. A steady haze clung to the air and drafts of smoke wafted up from somewhere far below.

He had been here before. He could remember its name. *The Ravine of Bones.* Not that he could remember anything specific about it; flashes of images, of darkness, of fighting, of *killing*, of being utterly alone. Only the feeling of dread and his instincts told him this was not somewhere he was meant to be again.

On the opposite side of the canyon, partially hidden in shadows were stairways and arches, layered into the side of the canyon. The remnants of some abandoned city, masked from a glancing eye by their resemblance to caves. He did not remember these.

Mr. Monstran breathed a sigh next to him. "It's good to be home." Then he turned to the old woman two of the soldiers were holding securely between them, though she was already bound in chains. "Isn't it, Mora?"

The old woman's eyes were wide, terrified. She shrieked and wailed and struggled against her captors, but her time in captivity had weakened her as well and she soon slumped to the ground, raking her hands over her face in despair.

"Come," Mr. Monstran said, looking into the fading sun. "We don't want to be out here when the children awaken."

Haven looked up at the early stars sprinkling the pale eastern horizon. *Tamsin, where are you?*

Here Ends Book One of An Empyrian Odyssey

I would like to thank my incredible tribe of supporters for their years of encouragement (and patience!) while I wrote this story. My husband, who is an unwavering champion for my dreams; my family, who've influenced my love of everything Sci-fi and fantasy; my friends, for making sure I get away from the computer from time to time; my A-team, for showing me how to believe in myself and take ownership of my goals; my awesome beta readers! And finally to God, for He has made all of it possible.

The journey doesn't end here.

Explore the legends, ideas, creativity, and emotions behind the pages with Behind the Quill, a podcast that takes you behind the scenes and deeper into the world of "An Empyrian Odyssey."

Hosted by N. L. Willcome and Mina Witte

Scan the QR code below
or listen wherever you get your podcasts

www.ingramcontent.com/pod-product-compliance
Lightning Source LLC
Chambersburg PA
CBHW010713020826
48980CB00020B/815/J